She shocked him by leaning in and planting a kiss on his cheek.

"What was that for?" Not that he minded, but it wasn't exactly typical Katie behavior.

"I don't know. For everything."

"Seems like all that ought to get me more than a peck on the cheek."

She fiddled with her glass and gave him a sidelong look. "Do you . . . um . . . want more?"

He planted one foot on the floor, hooked the other around the leg of his stool and scooted it next to hers. Their thighs touched. His groin jumped. "I seem to recall a kiss that went way past peck on the cheek."

"You remember that?" The light from the candle made her eyes look huge. They drew him in, closer and closer.

"I remember you tasted like honeysuckle. I remember we almost didn't stop there."

Romances by Jennifer Bernard

THE FIREMAN WHO LOVED ME
HOT FOR FIREMAN

HOT *for* FIREMAN

A BACHELOR FIREMEN NOVEL

Jennifer Bernard

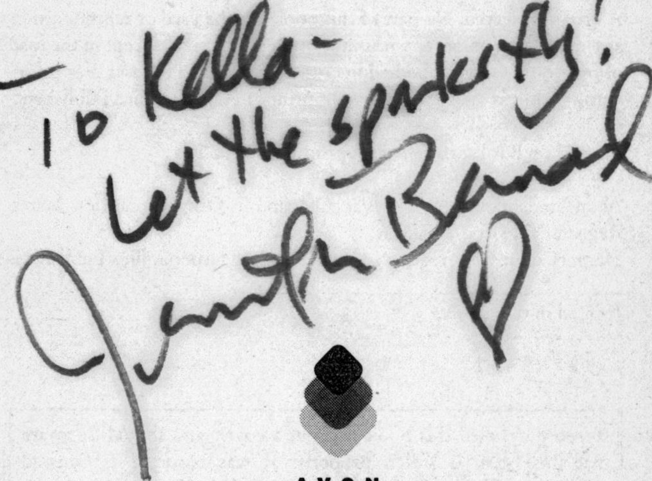

AVON
An Imprint of HarperCollins*Publishers*

This book is a work of fiction. References to real people, events, establishments, organizations, or locales are intended only to provide a sense of authenticity, and are used fictitiously. All other characters, and all incidents and dialogue, are drawn from the author's imagination and are not to be construed as real.

AVON BOOKS
An Imprint of HarperCollins*Publishers*
10 East 53rd Street
New York, New York 10022-5299

ISBN 978-0-06-208897-0
www.avonromance.com

First Avon Books mass market printing: June 2012

Printed in the U.S.A.

10 9 8 7 6 5 4 3 2

For everyone who puts their own life in danger for the sake of others. Thank you.

Acknowledgments

Once again, thanks to Rick A. Godinez, Captain II of the Los Angeles Fire Department, for his technical expertise. Any mistakes are mine, not his. Thanks to Maxine Mansfield for her assistance with my medical questions. This book wouldn't exist without Scott's patient support and Indigo's willingness to entertain herself. Thanks so much to both of you, and to Lizbeth Selvig for her exquisite critiquing and constant friendship. And finally, thanks to Tessa Woodward and the entire brilliant Avon team.

Chapter One

Ryan Blake needed a drink. Preferably somewhere no one would recognize him. Finding such a spot in the sun-blasted town of San Gabriel on a summer afternoon didn't come easy. The town had quaint little crafts shops up the wazoo, but so far he hadn't spotted a single gritty, anonymous hellhole where he could prepare himself for his meeting with Captain Harry Brody.

Right on cue, he passed Fire Station 1, home of the famous Bachelor Firemen of San Gabriel and legendary for the heroics of its captain and crew. Time was, he'd been on the frontlines of those life-saving, death-defying deeds.

He slowed his pickup truck and willed himself to turn into the parking lot, drink or no drink. Lord knew, his Chevy had made the turn so many times it could probably do it without him. But this time, it drove straight past the squat brick building with the cheerful red geraniums planted out front.

Face it, Ryan wasn't ready for his appointment with Captain Brody yet. Wasn't ready to beg for his job back. He needed a goddamn drink first.

A green and white Starbucks sign caught his eye. Several cuties in sundresses gathered around the outdoor tables like hummingbirds around a feeder. In olden days he would have strolled right in and spent the rest of the afternoon flirting with one—or all—of them.

But unless Starbucks had started adding tequila to their iced mocha lattes, the girls would have to get along with him.

He scanned the street ahead with its Spanish-style stucco office buildings and parched palm trees. Too bad he'd never been much of a drinker. He had no idea where to find the kind of drink-yourself-stupid-on-a-Wednesday-afternoon, out-of-the-way, loserville place he needed right now.

And then, as if the word "loserville" had conjured it out of his imagination, the sign for the Hair of the Dog appeared on the left side of the street. Towns in the sunny California suburban desert didn't have dark back alleys. But the Hair of the Dog did its best to inhabit one. Located on a corner, it seemed to cringe away from its only neighbor, a shop called Milt and Myrna's Dry Cleaner's, whose name was spelled out on a marquee along with an inspirational saying, "The bigger the dream, the bigger the reward."

If the Hair of the Dog had a dream, it would probably be to wake up as a medieval tavern. Faced with weathered wood, it had black planks nailed at random angles across its front. Either someone had done a clever job making the Hair of the Dog look decrepit or it was about to collapse. It looked like the kind of place where old geezers spent their Social Security checks, the kind of place frat boys invaded when they felt like slumming, and pretty girls avoided like poison because merely walking in gave them wrinkles. The kind of place guaranteed to be serving alcohol at two in the afternoon.

Perfect.

Ryan pulled over and parked his Chevy as close as legal to a fire hydrant. Silly habit left over from his firefighting days, when he'd always wanted to be close to any potential action.

Time to get blotto.

When he pushed open the door, the dim light stopped him in his tracks. As did the hostile voice addressing him with an unfriendly "What do you want?"

"Tequila," answered Ryan. "The cheap stuff."

"I'm not the bartender, moron. I'm the bouncer."

Ryan's eyes adjusted enough to make out a slouchy, dark-haired guy about his age who looked too skinny to be a bouncer.

"This place needs a bouncer?" He surveyed the interior of the Hair of the Dog. Just as crappy as the outside promised. Everything was painted in shades of black ranging from soot to shoe polish, except for the booths, which seemed to be a formerly hunter-green color. Just as he'd expected, a motley collection of oldsters slumped on the bar stools. He squinted. Was that an oxygen tank? The old man attached to it gave him a snaggletoothed grin. He nodded back.

Yep, this place was perfect.

"My so-called job is to weed out the jerkwads," said the bouncer.

"Yeah? What's your name?"

The friendly question seemed to throw the dude off. "Doug." He added a menacing frown.

"Hey, Doug, nice to meet you. I'm Ryan." He shook the bouncer's hand before the guy knew what was coming. "You're doing a great job, keep up the good work. How 'bout I buy you a shot when you get off?" He breezed past Doug with the confidence of someone who'd been in too many fights to seek one out with someone who wouldn't even provide a satisfying brawling experience. If Ryan wanted a fight, he knew how to find one. Right now, he just wanted a drink.

The bouncer seemed to get the message. Ryan heard no more out of him as he made his way into the darkness up ahead.

Was this a bar or a haunted house? Maybe the men on the bar stools were ghosts still hanging around for a last call that never came. A couple of them certainly looked ghoulish enough, although the intensely unflattering light provided by the overhead fluorescents might be misleading. Maybe they were captains of industry enjoying the tail end of a three-martini lunch. Maybe the atmosphere added thirty years and several age-related illnesses.

A girl rose from behind the scuffed-wood bar, her head clearing it by barely a foot. She fixed snapping black eyes on him, nearly making him take a step back. What had he done? Why did everyone seem irritated that a customer had walked into their bar? The girl had big dark eyes, straight eyebrows like two ink marks, and tumbled hair pushed behind her ears. She would have been pretty if not for that frown. No, scratch that. She was plenty pretty just as she was.

He gave her the smile that had made so many women his eager laundry doers, tax preparers, and back massagers. Not to mention other parts of his anatomy.

She scowled even harder at him. And geez, was that a snarl? Maybe she was some kind of creature of the night, hanging out with the ghosts.

"Well? Are you going to order or just smile for the security camera we don't have?" Her throaty voice, though grouchy, set off a pleasant shiver at the base of his spine.

"Is that why you need a bouncer?"

"What?"

"Because you tell everyone off the street that you don't have a security camera?"

"Would you order? I don't have all day."

"Yes, I can tell this place keeps you busy."

Could her scowl get any deeper? Ryan cocked his head and scanned her face, amazed that he still wanted to look at her anyway. Why, he couldn't say. Stubborn-looking mouth, a nose that turned up at the tip, long eyelashes, flashing dark eyes that took up half her face. Small too, like those kittens who have no idea they're half the size of the dogs they try to beat up. Probably a few years younger than he, maybe mid-twenties.

She shrugged and turned away.

"Shot of tequila," he said quickly. Something told him this girl wouldn't mind blowing him off and refusing to take his order.

With a sidelong look that told him how close he'd cut it, she folded her arms and surveyed the bottles lined up on the wall behind the bar. "We have Patrón Silver and Patrón Gold. The Gold's a little dusty."

All the bottles looked dusty to Ryan.

"What's inside's still good, right?"

"Got me. Any of you guys tried the Patrón?" She flung her question to the geezers at the end of the bar.

"Tried a glass back in '92, Saint Patrick's Day. Thought it said Patrick, not Patrón. Hit the spot."

The first hint of a smile brightened the girl's face. "You're the man, Sid."

"Any time, Katie, my love," crooned Sid.

"He has the memory of an elephant when it comes to his liquor," she told Ryan.

So that was her name. Katie. He liked it. A lot. It made her seem more human. He stared at her, fascinated by the change a whisper of a smile brought to her face. Good thing he caught it, because it disappeared in the next second.

"So? Silver or Gold?"

"Cheap," he said.

"Excellent choice." She gave him a sarcastic look and reached for the bottle of Patrón Silver. Up she stretched, high on her tiptoes, higher and higher. Ryan held his breath as her black top inched its way up, up, until it pulled away from the waistband of her jeans, revealing a sliver of gracefully curving, ghostly white flesh. It bugged him that his mouth watered at the sight, that he wanted to run his tongue from the soft tip of her lower rib along the delicious slope that led to her hipbone. This girl had serious friendliness issues.

But she was kind of hot, in her own particular way.

The view slammed shut as her heels hit the floor and she yanked down her top. She plopped a shot glass onto the bar and sloshed golden liquid into it. "That'll be four dollars."

"Can't I run a tab?"

"No tabs at the Dog." The old man with the oxygen tank cackled. "Case you croak before you finish your drink."

Katie smirked, even though Ryan could tell she was trying hard not to smile. "It's the policy of the Hair of the Dog to request payment with each drink. If you have a problem with that, you're free to go down the street to T.G.I. Friday's. They have that super-fun trivia game there."

She wasn't going to get rid of him that easily. "It's Wednesday," he said, pulling out a fiver along with his smile. "Wouldn't be right."

She snickered. Then looked so annoyed with herself that she turned away and headed for the cluster of men at the other end of the bar. He watched her every step of the way. Each line of her body radiated energy. She didn't walk in the flirty way he was used to. He'd watched many a girl sway her hips back and forth on her way to the ladies' room during a date. He always looked forward to the moment a girl would excuse herself and give him a show, a tempting promise of what was to come later on.

Not this girl. She had a direct and to-the-point stride, and was either unaware of her sexiness or in deliberate denial. Her odd choice of clothing—long-sleeved black top on a hot day—could go either way.

He tossed back his tequila. As the liquor entered his system, the dingy room acquired a lovely, blurry sheen. Just what the doctor ordered. And the doctor would definitely recommend another dose. He tapped the glass on the scuffed wood of the counter. Katie glanced down the length of the bar at him, pinning him with a look of disgust. "You aren't planning to get drunk, are you?"

"Do you interrogate all your customers about their future plans?"

"Only the troublemakers." She graced the geezer brigade with a glowing smile and headed back his way. For one moment, Ryan wished he'd brought his grandfather. Maybe this girl had a thing for older men.

"What makes you think I'm a troublemaker?" He motioned for her to refill his glass. "I'm all about peace and harmony. Kumbaya, my friend, kumbaya."

She looked revolted.

"We have more in common than what keeps us apart," he added wisely, after downing the second shot. He'd always loved a good affirmation, especially with a buzz on.

"You can stop now."

Aha. He'd found a sore spot.

"A hand offered in friendship opens more doors than a fist raised in anger. You catch more flies with sugar than vinegar." Okay, that last one wasn't an affirmation, but he threw it in for free.

"Do you want me to kick you out of here?"

"Make friends with your anger."

"Doug!" she called to the bouncer.

Ryan laughed. "You're cute as a button when you're mad."

"I'm not cute. And I'm not a damn button. Doug!"

But Doug didn't answer. Scuffling sounds came from the front door. Ryan turned on his bar stool, which wobbled a bit. Doug must be outside, because his bouncer stool was empty. Something or someone banged against the front door.

"Uh oh." Katie didn't sound irritated anymore. A quick look in her direction gave him a glimpse of dark eyes round with alarm.

"Sounds like your bouncer's getting a chance to earn his pay."

"Bouncer." She snorted. "Doug doesn't even know how to throw a punch. I gave him the job because he can't tend bar. He's no good with people."

Maybe it was the tequila talking, but Ryan found so many aspects of that statement hilarious that he laughed out loud.

"What's so funny?"

"Oh, I don't know. A bouncer who can't fight? Or the fact that apparently you're the one who's good with people?"

The Glare reappeared. This time Ryan was prepared. It even felt warm and fuzzy to him. Must be the tequila.

"Never fear." He took the bottle, poured himself a shot, downed it, then stood up. "Sir Ryan to the rescue."

"What? No, that's ridiculous. Sit back down. Seriously."

But Ryan was three Patrón shots past listening. Whether she wanted it or not, she was getting a goddamn act of derring-do. Or should that be derring doo-doo, considering where they were?

He chuckled. Yep, definitely the tequila. Not to mention the anticipation of a good knuckle-buster. He'd sworn off fighting as part of his effort to rehabilitate himself and get back on the force, but when circumstances demanded it . . .

He flexed his fists and opened the door. Doug fell into him. Ryan caught him and ducked the hard punch that came next. While the man with the flying fists regained his balance, Ryan propped Doug against the wall, out of the line of fire. When he stood up, two men faced him. Two tough-looking dudes in black leather and black beard stubble.

"Man, am I glad to see you guys," Ryan told them with a big smile.

True, so true. Tequila was nice, but a throw down was even nicer.

He braced himself. The second man, who also happened to be the larger of the two, came after him first. Ryan lowered his head and caught him under the left arm. He lifted him up in the air and spun him around so his legs mowed down man number one, who stumbled to his knees. Ryan dumped the larger man on top of him. Painful groans ensued.

Ryan went into his fighting stance. It wouldn't be fair to kick the men while they were down. He wasn't fighting for survival here. This was strictly recreation. The two men scrambled to their feet. The larger one, who had so recently been twirling through the air, roared and charged him. The next few minutes passed in a blur of vicious punches and ducks and parries and all the tricks Ryan knew from his years as an impulsive hothead.

God, it felt good. Even the punches he took hit the spot. He knew from experience he'd suffer the consequences later. But that's what ice was for. He'd recovered from plenty of brawls, with nothing worse than a slightly off-kilter nose. And, frankly, he was grateful for that one flaw in his looks. Without that, someone might think him nothing but a pretty boy.

"Hey, pretty boy," growled the large man.

That did it. No one called him that without paying the price. Time to stop playing with these guys. Ryan kicked into turbo drive.

A jab to the kidney. An uppercut to the jaw.

When he got serious in a fight, whether against a

man or a fire, he saw things in quick flashes moments before they happened. As if he existed in a time warp a few seconds earlier than the rest of the world.

A head jerked backward. Bloody slobber slung through the air. A man fell to his knees. The other man slumped on top of him. A hand lifted in submission, then dropped limp to the floor.

When Ryan stopped moving and things returned to their regular pace, he stood panting over the two fallen bodies of the intruders. By their movements and the whimpers filling the air, he knew they were fine. Pissed as hell, but fine. He wouldn't want to meet them in a dark alley, but then again, San Gabriel didn't have any dark alleys.

He shook out his shoulders and arms. He had a cut on the middle knuckle of his right hand, and what felt like a massive bruise on the left side of his rib cage. Nothing too serious.

He glanced over at the bouncer, Doug. His eyes were half closed in pain and his arm seemed to be hanging kind of strange. Someone better get the guy some help.

"Call 911," he called to the bar. "I think his arm is broken."

"Already did," said Katie, so close he jumped. Christ, she was right behind him. She must have been with Doug. Then he saw the baseball bat in her hand and took an alarmed step back.

"What was that you were saying?" She stepped toward him with blazing eyes. "Right before you got my bar all bloody?" Another step forward. Was she really going to whack him with a bat? After all he'd done for her?

"Um . . . kumbaya?" he ventured, hands in the air. "My friend. Kumbaya?"

"Yes! That was it." She drew back the bat.

"Now, now, Katie" came a wheezing voice. "Put down the bat."

Never had Ryan been so glad to see an old man with an oxygen tank, especially one who moved that quickly across the floor. He took advantage of Katie's moment of inattention to pluck the bat from her hands.

She stomped her foot with a furious look. "I wasn't going to bonk you, but if I did, you'd deserve it."

He shook a finger at her. "Peace and harmony, my friend. Peace and harmony."

Too late, he realized he should have taken away her left foot along with the bat.

"Ow."

Chapter Two

Why Katie felt the need to kick the most drop-dead gorgeous man she'd ever set eyes on, a man who'd thrown himself into a dangerous brawl to help Doug out, she really couldn't say.

Blame it on the bad mood that had plagued her all day—the past two months, in fact, ever since her family had dumped this place on her. "Dump" being an ironically appropriate choice of word.

"I'm sorry," she grudgingly told the blue-eyed god who looked like he'd stepped off a movie set. Actually, maybe he was an actor traveling through San Gabriel on his way to Los Angeles and his next gig. "My foot slipped."

"Right." The man bent down to check on Doug. That movement had the effect of pulling his tan-colored T-shirt tight against his shoulder muscles. Which, in turn, had the effect of making her stare—

which put her in an even worse mood. "You okay, man?"

"He's fine," said Katie. "Well, mostly fine. The paramedics are on their way."

Doug muttered something. Katie knew he must be totally humiliated. Why had she let him talk her into that stupid bouncer job? The Hair of the Dog needed someone to bring people in, not keep them out.

The stranger stood up, unfurling himself to his full six feet plus of high-octane masculinity. "Look, I'm sorry I butted in if it wasn't what you wanted." The impact of his summer-blue eyes took away any chance of her answering.

Instead, she turned away to face the goggle-eyed "Drinking Crew," as her father called them, who were practically falling off their bar stools. She put her arm under Dr. Burwell's elbow. "Let's get you back to your seat. Can't have you gallivanting all over the bar, it's not good for your health."

Dr. Burwell resisted. "Want to offer the young hero my services. I used to be a doctor, lad. Want me to take a look at anything?"

Katie bit her lip at the deeply uneasy look that spread across Mr. Gorgeous's face. She noticed Dr. Burwell didn't offer to help Doug. The Crew had never taken to him.

"No thanks, sir. This is nothing. I'll shake it off in no time."

"And what's your name, young Galahad?"

Those devastating blue eyes flicked to hers. She felt a flush creep up her cheeks. At least it was too dark in this hellhole for anyone to notice but her.

"Name's Ryan. Thanks for the visit. Can't remember a more enjoyable afternoon." He spoke in a slow drawl that didn't fool her. She'd seen how fast he was with his fists.

Sirens sounded outside.

Ryan cleared his throat. "I should get going now." Interesting. Clearly he wanted to be gone before the paramedics came inside. He lifted a hand in a general wave.

"Come back any time and I'll stand you a drink," called Dr. Burwell.

Katie snorted. "You haven't paid for a drink in five years."

"You're exaggerating, my dear. Why, just the other day . . ."

But she tuned him out so she could focus her attention on Ryan's exit. The rear view was as pulse-tingling as the front. His blue jeans rode just right on his hips, his T-shirt had come untucked in the back. She watched, fascinated, as he dug one hand into his front pocket. That action tightened his jeans against his butt in the most hypnotic way.

She snapped out of it just in time to not be staring at his rear when he turned.

"Forgot to pay for those last two shots," he said, sorting through a handful of bills.

"Oh, forget it." Embarrassed, she waved him off. Did he really think she'd let him pay after she'd kicked him in the shin? "It's on the Hair of the Dog."

"Appreciate it." One slow wink, and he was gone.

"My, my," said Dr. Burwell. "Katie giving away drinks. Never thought I'd see the day."

"What are you talking about? I might as well be running a charity here."

A small gang of paramedics burst through the door. Katie gestured toward Doug. They immediately began tending to him.

"Will he be okay?" she asked after they'd tested his vitals and strapped him onto a gurney. She wasn't too worried about Doug, who was both accident-prone and a hypochondriac. Over the years she'd learned that worrying over him was a waste of energy.

A young paramedic answered, "Looks like a broken arm. He'll be at the Good Samaritan. Do you want to come with us?"

"I'll be fine," said Doug, with a white-lipped, martyred look. "Don't leave on my account."

"I'll come see you later," she promised. She couldn't leave the bar, and even if she could, hovering over Doug would give him the wrong idea—the same wrong idea he'd had ever since she'd broken up with him.

The paramedics whisked Doug off. Katie guided old Dr. Burwell back to his bar stool. It took the full length of that walk for her to get her pulse back to normal. Ryan the Gorgeous was trouble. Bad for her blood pressure. Good thing she'd likely never see him again. She had enough to worry about.

Starting with certain bar tabs.

She walked behind the bar—which she hoped was her power position—and stood facing the four members of the Crew. "Okay, you guys, this is getting serious. None of you has paid up in weeks. You know I instituted that new policy. No more bar tabs."

The old men hung their heads and exchanged sidelong looks with one another. Katie felt as if she were chastising a bunch of third-graders.

"Aw, Katie. You know we would if we could," said Sid.

"You don't get it. They're about to cut off our beer

deliveries. Like, next week, if I don't figure something out. I can't pay the bill. I can't even pay part of the bill."

"Beer is highly overrated," rumbled Archie, a former newspaper columnist for the *San Gabriel Herald*. "A serious drinker will always choose one of the hard liquors. When he decided to drink himself to death, Ian Fleming chose Chartreuse, not Budweiser."

Katie winced. The phrase "drink himself to death" seemed a bad choice given the average age of her customers. "Well, whatever Ian Fleming drank, hopefully he paid for it. And the fact is that the Hair of the Dog is a bar, and a bar without beer is like a . . . a . . ."

"Fish without a bicycle," offered Archie.

"No, that's my whole point—"

Sid chimed in. "A woman without a man?"

Katie rolled her eyes. "Let's not go there. Bars need beer. Beer distributors need money."

"Ergo, you need our money. *Quod erat demonstrandum*." The fourth member of the crew, Mr. Jamieson, a former Latin and French teacher at the local private school, gave a flourish. "Quite easily done." He pulled a rattling pile of coins from his pocket. "The next round is on me."

Katie peered at the coins, none of which looked familiar. "What are these?"

"Part of my collection. One of those coins is actually quite valuable, if you'd care to take it to an antiquarian."

Katie laughed despite herself. She had to admit the Crew had their entertaining moments. "Look, keep your coin collection. But do me a favor. I'm trying something new tonight. A promotion."

"You're promoting someone?"

"But you barely have any employees."

"No, a *promotion*. To bring more people in."

Sid looked horrified. "Do we know them?"

"No. That's the whole point. These are going to be new people. People who might have money."

Dr. Burwell shook his head. "I'm not sure that's wise. Who knows what riffraff might show up?"

"We'll have to take that chance. Tonight, I don't want all the bar stools filled up by you guys. Do you think you could find another place to hang out for one night?"

"Absolutely," said Archie. "Count on us, my dear. We'll remove ourselves to one of the booths."

The men cackled and agreed, looking delighted with one another.

Katie threw up her hands in utter frustration. Maybe she should lock them in a closet during the party tonight. Part of her wished she could cut them off entirely, but her father would throw a fit. He loved the Crew and knew how to handle them, but she was hopeless at it. They walked all over her. They really didn't seem to grasp the dire state of things at the Hair of the Dog. Not even her father seemed to get it.

Unless he did, and her parents had skipped off to Baja with the intention of leaving her permanently in charge. In which case she'd be fully within her rights to lock the door of the Dog for good and get back to her regularly scheduled life. The one in which her peace of mind was rarely—make that never—disturbed by freakishly handsome strangers.

Ryan's gut tightened as he approached the side door of Station 1. It had been a year and a half since he'd left in disgrace. From hotshot to hell in the time it took to answer a doorbell.

The door swung open easily. Captain Brody ran a tight ship and demanded that everything, even the door hinges, be kept in topnotch working condition. Ryan walked into the apparatus bay where the rigs lived. His eyes went immediately to his beloved Engine 1. Tingles shot through him, a physical reaction to the sight of the magnificent piece of equipment that had transported him, provided the wet stuff, and generally backed him up at so many fires he couldn't even count them. Engine 1 had never let him down. The crew had never let him down.

But he'd let them down.

"Back to the scene of the crime, eh?"

Ryan looked up to find Captain Brody, feet spread, arms crossed. He would have looked awe-inspiring without that giveaway twinkle in his gray eyes.

"Captain." Ryan stepped forward to shake Brody's hand, only to find himself pulled into a bear hug.

"Good to see you, Hoagie." Ryan winced. It had been a while since anyone had called him Hoagie—the nickname he'd acquired as a rookie thanks to his favorite sandwich.

"Good to see you too." His chest tightened under Brody's penetrating gaze. That man saw everything. He'd even seen through Ryan's teenage recklessness and spotted a natural-born firefighter. He'd mentored Ryan, taught him, guided him, and been the closest thing to a caring father Ryan had ever had.

Even though Brody had ordered him to take a leave of absence or get fired, Ryan still loved the man. "How's Melissa?"

Brody's face lightened, as mention of his wife

always guaranteed. "Great. You'll have to come over some time, meet Danielle."

"I heard you'd taken in a foster child. She's still with you?"

"We filed papers to adopt her."

Ryan smiled broadly. Brody and Melissa would be great parents to any child, foster, adopted, or otherwise. If anyone deserved a happy family, Brody did. Personally, Ryan had no experience of such a thing. "So . . . uh . . . I was hoping we could talk."

"Sure. Come in the office."

"Anyone around?" He didn't want to see any of his former crew members until he knew where he stood.

Brody seemed to understand. "Business first, then you can catch up." He clapped a hand onto Ryan's shoulder and led him down the corridor that passed through the living quarters of the station. Ryan didn't let his eyes stray to the tiny room where he'd spent two nights a week for so many years. It hurt too much. They passed through the kitchen, where the sound of a TV echoed. Someone was watching the *Iron Chef*. Maybe looking for ideas for that night's dinner.

When they were safely in Brody's office with the door closed, Ryan sank down into a chair. The office looked different, though it took a moment for him to pin it down. It had toys in it, that's what it was. A smiley-face doll lay slumped in a corner, about to get run over by a plastic tricycle. Stan, the firehouse dog, a beagle mutt with a mangled ear and an obsession with Captain Brody, napped among the toys. "I didn't know how tough it was going to be to come back here."

"We've missed you," said Brody as he took his

seat behind his desk. "You've been gone longer than I expected."

"Well, I had a lot of thinking to do."

"Did you?" Brody gave him that see-to-the-bottom-of-his-soul look. "What have you been up to since you left?"

Ryan shifted in his chair. He trusted Brody above all men, but some things were hard to talk about in a testosterone-loaded place like a firehouse. "I went to the desert. Camped out. Looked at the stars. Read a lot."

"Yeah?"

"I've always liked to read, you know." Ryan said this defensively. Fire stations were notorious for their relentless teasing, and he'd always been a favorite target thanks to his looks. He'd learned to keep a lot of stuff private.

"I know."

Of course he did. Brody knew everything.

"Anyway, I ran into this hermit guy who lives out in the desert, and we got to be buddies. He had some damn good cactus . . ." Ryan cleared his throat. "He told me about this monastery. So I went there."

Brody's quick look of surprise told Ryan he'd finally caught his captain off guard.

"You can never tell the guys."

Brody merely lifted one shoulder a fraction of an inch, but that single motion conveyed so much. Ryan relaxed, knowing Brody wouldn't say a word, and that he was eager to hear all about the monastery.

"It was the first time in my life I wasn't moving around all the time, you know? That's what I liked most. They had some talks too, not that I understood everything they were saying. Mostly I liked having a chance to catch my breath. Especially after what happened."

Brody leaned back in his chair. "So you did some contemplating."

"I guess so. Then I ran out of money, so I hitched into Los Angeles and picked up some work there."

"What kind of work?"

"Nothing to do with fires. Landscaping, mostly. Digging, building rock walls." He'd worked harder than he ever had in his life, but every blister-ridden moment had felt good.

"So. You did some thinking at the monastery. Then you sweated it out with some manual labor. Now what?"

"I want to come back, Captain. I think I'm ready."

Brody picked up a paperweight shaped like a volcano and hefted it in his hand.

"It wasn't just the damage you did to the plug-buggy."

"I know."

"That woman nearly died."

"I swear to God, I didn't even know she was there."

"You should have known. We had girls pulling all kinds of crazy stunts after Melissa's report aired."

"I know. Whoever came up with that Bachelor Firemen of San Gabriel crap ought to be shot. Oops." He paled. "It wasn't Melissa, was it?"

"Of course not. Don't try to blame this on her." The fire in Brody's eyes rivaled the lava that would have poured out of that volcano had it not been a paperweight.

"God, no. It was my fault. I should have checked inside the rig."

The girl, Ginny Lee, had hidden herself in the

station's pickup truck, known as the plug-buggy, after she'd seen him return from EMT recertification. She'd hoped to surprise Ryan. Instead she'd gotten a gunshot wound when a fire scene had gone haywire. If Ryan had followed procedure and not rushed out alone, she would have faced nothing worse than a scolding from the captain. When Ryan had tried to visit her at the hospital, she'd refused to see him. Then she'd moved back to Illinois, no forwarding address.

"You were careless and thoughtless and reckless."

"I know." Ryan looked at the floor. Of course he'd been those things. But how could he convince Brody he'd changed?

"It practically killed me to lose you." Brody slapped the paperweight onto the desk with a sharp *crack*. Stan opened an eye halfway, then dropped it shut again. "The best goddamn firefighter I've ever known. You were like a force of nature, Ryan. It was a thing of beauty to watch you fight a fire. Not to mention all the work I put into training you. All that, up in smoke thanks to one moment of stupidity."

Ryan tried to speak, but Brody rolled right over him, growing ever more heated with each word.

"And yet it wasn't one moment. If it had been only one moment, I could have overlooked it. A couple days without pay, end of story. But no. It was a pattern of reckless, daredevil behavior. Every time you risked your own neck, you put the rest of my guys in danger."

Ryan felt sick. In the heat of the moment, he didn't think about the others. He thought about the fire and how he could beat it.

"You were goddamn lucky you never killed anyone. And now you want me to put you back on the job?"

Ryan stared at a spot on the floor, a stain on the scarred linoleum, fighting to not explode into anger. The biting tone in the captain's voice made him want to beat up ten more back-alley guys. He breathed deep. The captain had some good points, harsh as they might be. He'd fucked up. Nearly gotten a girl killed. How dare he ask to come back?

And yet . . . slowly, he got a grip on himself. He lifted his eyes and squarely met the captain's blistering gaze.

"Yes. I want to come back." He was a firefighter, through and through. He ought to be fighting fires.

"What's that cut on your knuckle?"

"Nothing." Ryan had forgotten about it.

"Were you fighting?"

Ryan got to his feet. In the old days, he would have either hidden the truth or lashed out. Now he gave Brody a level look. "I don't fight anymore, not unless I have to. Two guys were beating down a bouncer. I had to step in. I'm not going to say I didn't enjoy it. But I didn't start it." He hoped Brody would believe him, but he wasn't going to beg like a child.

Brody's eyebrows drew together. "Well, I guess that is a change."

Ryan held his gaze, something that had always been a challenge in the past. A long moment passed while they took each other's measure. Brody spoke first.

"I'll have to think about it. Give me a couple of days."

"Thanks, Captain." It was all he could ask. More than he could ask.

"Now go say hello to everyone. Gone over a year and only one postcard? Of a cactus?"

"A Christmas cactus. Didn't you see the twinkle lights?"

"I saw. Very festive. I'll call you soon."

Ryan spent the next hour shaking hands and hearing about all the fires he'd missed while he'd been gone. He gritted his teeth and listened to Double D tell him how he and Vader had put out a fire at a day care center while everyone else was busy with a brushfire in the hills. He heard how Captain Brody had added thirteen more lives to his long list of rescues. It seemed the last year and a half had been filled with exciting acts of heroism, not to mention hilarious practical jokes and a visitation from the cast of *America's Next Top Model*—televised, of course.

"Everyone thought the Bachelor Curse was broken when the captain got married, but not a single one of us has hooked up. I mean, we've hooked up. Some of us. But not, you know, permanently," Fred told him. In the perverse way of firefighters, he was known as Stud thanks to his bad luck with women.

Ryan shrugged. "I always said it wasn't so much a curse as a gift from God." According to firehouse legend, Virgil Rush, a volunteer fireman from the 1850s, had been heartbroken when Constancia B. Sidwell, his mail order bride, had run off with a robber on her way West. The other firemen, always quick to tease, tormented him so much he laid a curse on the town, vowing that the firemen of San Gabriel would have as much trouble finding love as he had. Ever since then, the firehouse had possessed an unusually high number of bachelors. Which worked out just fine from Ryan's perspective. "Keep playing that field, Freddie boy. No need to worry about rings and aisles."

"But I kind of want . . ."

"Sorry, dude. We're cursed. Everyone knows it. You're a Bachelor Fireman of San Gabriel. Might as well relax and enjoy it, like me."

"It's different for you." Fred sulked as Vader, who'd apparently added some new muscles to his fearsome physique in the last year and half, elbowed him aside.

"Hoagie, you hear about how Double D and me saved twenty kids? The mayor gave us an award for being badasses."

"It was called the Hot Shot Award," interjected Two, one of San Gabriel's two female firefighters, shaking out her long brown braid. "And I was there too. No one seems to remember that."

"The mayor sure knew. You should have seen him, Hoagie. Thought he'd come in his pants when he saw Two in a dress."

"Vader . . ." Fury flashed in Two's pretty turquoise eyes, which had inspired many an inappropriate fantasy among her fellow firemen. Vader grinned, awaiting the explosion with a crack of his knuckles. "Don't talk that way in front of Fred."

Two and Vader both cracked up. Ryan rolled his eyes, wondering why the pair of them didn't get a room somewhere.

"Hey!" Fred looked indignantly from one to the other. "I just *look* young. You want to see my driver's license? Again? I ought to just hang it around my neck."

The bittersweet pain of listening to the familiar firehouse jokes and rhythms was pure torture. By the time he made his escape, Ryan desperately needed another drink. Or another brawl, whichever came his way first.

Chapter Three

Katie Dane had spent long stretches of her life blissfully oblivious to the fact that her father had acquired a bar after he'd sold his car dealership. Occasionally she'd dropped by after school. And sometimes she didn't manage to find an excuse to skip the bar's annual mid-August Dog Day Celebration, during which her father grilled hot dogs in the swooning heat and made ice cubes shaped like dog bones.

She'd gone through high school, college, and nearly a year of graduate studies in nineteenth-century French literature without even filling in for an absent waitress. She'd never shown any interest in the restaurant business, marketing, entrepreneurship, or anything involving gatherings of people. In her family, she was known as the bookworm, the antisocial one, especially as compared to her older sister, Bridget, the social butterfly on speed (metaphorically, of course).

So when her father had suffered a stress-induced heart attack, and her mother had begged her to run the Hair of the Dog while she whisked him off to Mexico for his recuperation, she'd known there was only one possible reason.

No one else happened to be available.

Okay, two. Her mother knew she'd do anything for her father.

In the back office of the Dog, she opened the top drawer of her father's desk, toppling a stack of Guy de Maupassant novels left over from her last seminar. She pulled out a package of balloons shaped like dog heads. Since she didn't have a clue about promotion, she'd followed her father's lead and chosen a dog theme. And parties were supposed to have balloons, right? She called it a stroke of luck that Party World actually stocked dog-head balloons.

She sat with one hip on the desk and blew air into a lime-green dog. Kind of goofy, if you asked her. But what did she know about this sort of thing? Bridget would know, but she was unreachable these days. Apparently being her friend's maid of honor demanded single-minded, focused attention every second of every day until the wedding. Which had conveniently put her out of the running when it came to the Dog.

The more air Katie blew into the green dog balloon, the more sickly-looking it became. She stopped and tied a knot at its neck. Kind of cute, she supposed. One ear had less air than the other, so it looked lopsided. And the painted-on smile looked cheerfully demented.

What did it matter? Everyone would be wasted anyway. She tied a string to the balloon and picked up a yellow one.

This was all her fault. Graduate school wasn't far enough away; she should have moved to Argentina or Bhutan, somewhere with intermittent cell service and spotty Internet. She should have acquired a friend who needed a maid of honor. She shouldn't have been such a pushover.

So many things had to have gone wrong for her to find herself blowing up dog balloons.

And it wouldn't be so bad—she'd be happy to do it since she adored her father—but she had absolutely no aptitude for bar management.

The phone rang. Startled, she let go of a yellow balloon and it shot around the room like a rabid, runaway, shrinking golden retriever. After it landed limply on top of one of her brothers' baseball trophies, she answered.

"Hello? Hair of the Dog."

"Don't mind if I do!"

She smiled at the sound of her father's booming voice. She loved her father, even if he had stuck her with this ridiculous job.

"Hey, Daddy. How's the recovery going?"

"Oh, pretty good, pretty good. Walked nearly half a mile this morning. Swam in the ocean. Had myself a virgin margarita. Life's good, Katie girl, every moment's a precious goddamn gift."

"Yeah." Whatever. "So when are you coming back?"

"If your mom has her way, never." Katie felt a moment of blind, stupid panic. "She's got this little condo all picked out right near a golf course. Pretty sweet. But I couldn't leave San Gabriel. How's things going at the Dog? Are you treating the Drinking Crew right? Are ya having fun?"

"Um . . . well . . ." Katie didn't know quite how to

handle that question. She didn't want him to come rushing back on her account. On the other hand, too much longer and she might self-induce a heart attack. And what about all the bills that kept showing up? Should she mention them, or would that be too stressful?

Better play it safe. "I'm doing a promotion tonight. I'm trying to bring in a new crowd."

"Darn, Katie girl, you're a genius! Now that's good thinking! Nothing wrong with the crowd we got, of course."

"No, no, they're great."

"Our bread and butter, that's what they are. But we could stand to shake things up, no question there. So what's the gig?"

"Well, I figured we should play off the name, Hair of the Dog. Like you always did."

"Learning from the old man, I like that."

Katie felt pleased with herself. She loved it when she made her father happy instead of giving him that familiar worried look on his ruddy face. "You know how everyone has a Ladies' Night. Well, we're going to have a Doggies' Night."

Silence followed.

"Hello?"

"Yes, Katie girl. I don't exactly understand. Doggies' Night? Free drinks for dogs?"

"No, no." Nervous now, she picked up a handful of balloons and fussed with them. "It's a two-for-one night. Two drinks for the price of one, if you have a dog."

"Dogs in the bar? Oh Katie, there's all sorts of trouble with that—"

"Not in the bar, Daddy. The health department would go nuts." Her father seriously underestimated her if he believed she hadn't thought of that. "All they have to do is bring a picture of their dog."

"A picture of their dog." Why didn't her father sound more impressed? When she'd come up with this plan, she'd considered it a stroke of genius.

"Yes. Bring a picture of your dog, get two drinks for the price of one."

"What if they have several dogs?"

"Well . . ."

"Is there a time limit on it? Happy Hour's usually an hour or two at the most."

Katie was starting to get a bad feeling about this. "I can play that part by ear."

"I don't know about that. People get overexcited when it comes to free drinks."

Gulp.

"How are they going to prove it's their dog in the picture?"

Her stomach clenched. Had she totally screwed this up? "It doesn't matter! The point is to get a new clientele in here."

More silence. Katie gripped the phone. This wasn't her fault. She was doing the best she could. Why hadn't anyone believed her when she kept saying she wasn't cut out for this job? She was about to launch into a long explanation of how her particular personality was unsuited to anything having to do with people, when her mother's voice took the place of her father's.

"What did you say to him? He's turning red and muttering to himself. I think I heard something about plane tickets."

Katie brightened. "Really?"

"No, no, no, it's too soon. Look what happened after one little phone call! Do you know how hard it is to get that man to slow down?" Katie could picture her mother's anxious, lovely face puckering with displeasure.

"I'm sorry, Mom. I thought he'd be happy with my ideas. And I told you I know nothing about managing a bar, I told you I'd suck at this . . ." She trailed off, realizing she was talking to herself. Her mother was now arguing with her father in the background. She sighed. Her parents always did this. Things like phone calls from other people were temporary interruptions of their own ongoing conversation and easily dropped.

Maybe she should hang up—Lord knew she had enough to do—but the suggestion that they might head back early kept her on the line.

"Well, that crisis is solved." Her mother gave a puff of relief. "He's not going to change our plane tickets and rush back to rescue you from whatever oddball project he's chattering on about."

"Oh." Disappointment. "Hey!" Indignation.

Her mother ignored her. "We'll be back in a couple weeks. No more phone calls until then. I'm sorry, but his heart can't handle it. Neither can my nerves."

Her mother's voice rose again. "What?" she called. A pause. "Something about the insurance bill. He wants to know if you've gotten the insurance bill yet. It should be due soon. And why are you worrying about things like that, when I just put a plate of fresh pineapple in front of you . . ."

This time, Katie hung up. Sooner or later her mother would get around to doing the same on her end.

Insurance bill, insurance bill . . . She rummaged through the piles of paper on the desk. After so many unpleasant conversations with the beer distributor, she'd been avoiding the paperwork that kept arriving with horrifying frequency. Everything looked like a bill, and nothing looked like a big fat check that would pay the bills.

It must be this one, from Fidelity Trust. It was a thick envelope that she hadn't bothered to open because it looked like it came from a solid, respectable company that wouldn't yell at her for being late with a payment. She tore it open and searched through the thick sheaf of paper to find the only piece of information that mattered.

A balloon payment—what was that?—of ten thousand dollars was due in exactly . . . well, it had been due a month ago. Now it was overdue. Why hadn't they sent her another one? She scrabbled through the papers. There it was. Past due notice. Six more weeks and the policy would lapse.

Panic scrambled her brain. Ten thousand dollars wasn't an outrageous amount of money. But on top of the past due beer payment, and the overdue salaries to the staff, and the cleaning service that had stopped coming and the stale Chex Mix that really ought to be thrown out and replaced with peanuts or that delicious Japanese wasabi snack mix she'd been eyeing in the catalogue . . .

It was impossible.

Could they do without insurance? Cars needed insurance. There was a law about that. Was there a law that bars needed insurance? She picked up the policy and looked at it closely. It covered fires but not floods. Not much chance of floods in San Gabriel, where even a light rain induced citywide panic. It didn't cover earthquakes. In Southern California, earthquake insurance would probably double the cost of the policy. Most importantly, it didn't cover lack of money. What use was it?

Her eye strayed back to the part about fire coverage. Kind of ironic. The bar was so close to the San Gabriel Fire Station, it had zero chance of burning down.

"Katie, are you back there?" Mr. Jamieson's voice managed to penetrate the thick fake-Tudor door of the office. *"Où est le vin rouge? Nous sommes prêt pour une autre tournée."* She and Mr. Jamieson liked to keep up their French with each other, even though hers was strictly from language tapes. She'd never actually been to France.

"Un petit moment."

Where the heck was Kent? She checked her watch. Five o'clock. That flaky pothead of a bartender was supposed to be here by now. He ought to be setting up for Doggies' Night. Instead he was probably sneaking weed into the hospital for Doug.

"Sois patient," she called. "I'm sure Kent'll show up soon."

"Some of us might not make it that long," said Mr. Jamieson. But Katie was too busy worrying about the balloons to come up with a smart-aleck response, especially in French. Maybe she should get a helium tank delivered. Or borrow Dr. Burwell's oxygen tank. Would that work on balloons? People might start arriving any second. She had to make the place look like a party not a deathwatch.

Ryan shoved his hands in his pockets and gazed in wonder at the down-and-out pub that had looked so dismal just hours ago. Something big was happening at the Hair of the Dog. Something big and . . . strange. People crammed in the doorway and overflowed onto the street, not only people, but dogs. Lots of dogs. Why had so many people brought their pets? Who brought their dog to a bar?

He hesitated. Maybe he should head to T.G.I. Friday's instead. Or go home and crack open a six-pack. But now he was curious. He had to find out what was happening here.

Besides, the irritating yet intriguing Katie wouldn't be at T.G.I. Friday's.

Mind made up, he strolled toward the crowded entrance. The knot of people milled and chattered and the closer he got, the edgier they sounded. They were all arguing about something. Or complaining. A dog barked. Then another one.

Seriously, why *would* anyone bring their dog to a bar? Maybe he should have brought Stan. Poor dog didn't get out much.

His gaze rose to the banner hung over the front door. "Hair of the Dog Presents Doggies' Night! Two Drinks for the Price of One!"

He still didn't really get it, but obviously someone must have a plan.

He reached the crowd at the front door just in time to catch one dog owner giving another a shove. Someone needed to take charge here. He raised his voice over the din. "Hey, hey, keep it cool. We've got way too many animals with teeth here to start getting emotional."

"Sorry, dude. But this is seriously fucked."

"You said it!"

"It's false advertising," shouted someone. "Bait and switch."

"Says Doggies' Night, and they won't even let dogs in!"

Ryan addressed a large black man who seemed to

have assumed a leadership role. "They can't let dogs in. Health code."

"Then why call it Doggies' Night?"

"No clue. I don't have a dog, so why don't you let me through and I'll find out what the deal is?"

"Better get back here quick."

"You got it. Keep the bloodshed to a minimum until I get back." He clapped the man on the shoulder. The crowd parted to let him through. Inside, something bopped against his head. He swatted it away. A misshapen balloon smiled at him like some kind of beheaded monster. It wasn't the only one; crowds of them dangled from the ceiling. The place stank of spilled beer. The din of drunken chatter rang in his ears. He didn't see Katie anywhere. The only person behind the bar was one of the old men he recognized from earlier.

"Katie?" He called into the madness. "Katie, are you here?"

He took a step forward and heard a yelp. A beagle who reminded him of Stan scampered past, followed by Katie at top speed. He snagged her by the arm as she passed.

"Katie. What the hell is going on here?"

Her dark eyes, big with indignation, swung to his. "You! What are you doing here?"

"I was hoping to get another drink. But this place seems to have turned into Animal Planet."

"Let me go. I have to get that dog out of here."

"I'll take care of the dog. But there's a crowd out front that's about to go postal. I gotta tell them something."

She tried to tug herself free, but he tightened his grip. "I already told them they can't bring their dogs in here. They're supposed to bring a *picture* of their dog. It's all in the ad. If they misunderstood it's their fault, not mine."

"Let me see the ad."

She snatched a flyer off a nearby table. Ryan squinted at the tiny print at the bottom of the ad. "It says 'bong a puncture of logs.'"

"I hate you."

"Hey, I'm trying to rescue you for the second time in one day." Ryan snagged the beagle, which had decided to chase circles around a sinking balloon.

A woman holding a glass of wine tottered after the beagle. "Oh my sweetie-kins, leave the handsome man alone." She winked at Ryan as he handed the dog's leash to her. He turned back to Katie before the woman could start a very badly timed flirtation.

"So why did all these people bring their dogs?"

"I don't know. That's their problem. Look, I have enough to deal with here. Do you know how many pictures of the same cute little puppy I've seen tonight? Don't people have any integrity anymore? My bartender just texted me that he's on his way to Burning Man, which is like months from now, and my bouncer is in the hospital. Oh, and I have a former Latin teacher telling people that 'canines' are 'interdictum' or something."

As she talked, his gaze wandered down her body. She'd changed her clothes, from jeans to a short, flirty skirt that showed off her legs. His eyes scanned her slender ankles, ran along the curve of her calf to the last glimpse of flesh under the hem, then back down again. Then back up, as if riding a half-pipe.

She took advantage of his distraction and yanked her arm free. "Do you mind?"

Another dog, a St. Bernard big enough to sit on, ran past. With his other hand, Ryan grabbed its collar. He bent down and squinted at the name on the dog tag. He stood up and shouted in his fire scene voice, "Would the owner of Vishnu please meet your dog outside? If no one's claimed him in the next five minutes, there's always the pound."

No one answered.

"Come on," he told Katie. He pulled her to the front door, where he explained the concept behind Doggies' Night to the assembled crowd. The presence of the intimidating Vishnu made the announcement go over a bit more easily.

"If you have a picture of a dog with you, come on in and you can have a drink. If you have an actual dog with you, you're going to have to take it home. Or tie it up outside."

He held up his hand to stop the roar of protest.

"To make up for this embarrassing misunderstanding, for which Katie here sincerely apologizes, she's offering a rain check to every one of you."

The crowd's angry edge melted into a few scattered cheers.

She glared up at him and hissed. "It was right there in the ad, bring a picture."

Ryan ignored her. "She says she's really sorry and hopes to see you back here sometime this week. After that, no one will remember there ever was a Doggies' Night."

Katie visibly ground her teeth. "Fine."

Ryan pulled out his phone. "To sweeten the deal, if you guys want, I'll take a picture of your dog for you. But you still have to leave your dogs outside."

The large black man started to argue. Katie pushed forward and went onto tiptoe. Even though she still had to tilt her head way back to meet his gaze, her fierceness had quite an impact. "Look, mister, I'm sorry to inconvenience you, but the health department would shut us down. As you should have known if you gave it two seconds' thought . . ."

Ryan cut her off. "Take your dog home, man, come back, and I'll buy you a drink myself. Make that two. That's two for the price of zero. Can't argue with that."

Slowly the crowd dispersed. Katie pulled the door shut and leaned against it. She let out a deep breath. "Mr. Jamieson, you all right?"

On the bouncer's stool, a gaunt man with wire-rimmed glasses, who Ryan hadn't noticed until now, put his hand over his heart. "Oh, I imagine I'll recover. A glass of Merlot might aid the process." He added something in what sounded like French.

Katie rattled off something that sounded equally French but much sexier. She finished with, "Help yourself. Go tell Archie."

Mr. Jamieson limped gratefully toward the bar. She turned to Ryan. "Um . . . thanks. I had things under control, but still, thanks."

He raised an eyebrow. "I guess you don't need me, then." He turned to go. "And here I was going to offer to tend bar for the night. Or play bouncer. But nah, I see you have it covered." He opened the door and stepped onto the now quiet sidewalk. Would she let him go? Did she want him to go away? Maybe she was still mad about him spilling blood in her bar. Maybe she figured he was trouble. Maybe she didn't like him. Maybe she was immune to the smile that made every other girl melt.

Ryan wasn't used to this kind of self-doubt, at least when it came to women.

"I suppose I could use a hand," she said grudgingly.

He turned, blasting her with a smile, pleased when she blinked.

"But no punching anyone. No more rain checks. And none of that."

"What?"

"That smiling. I don't like it."

As if to prove it, she frowned. Ryan's smile broadened. The world righted itself. Definitely, no doubt about it, he was getting to her.

Chapter Four

Katie knew it was a mistake as soon as the words left her mouth. A whole night working side by side with a man with such devastating good looks, the kind of looks that belonged on a movie screen where they could remain a fantasy, would lead to nothing but trouble. She knew guys like that—they were Bridget's type, not hers. They were players, flirters, daters. She didn't speak their language. As soon as Bridget showed up, he'd flock to her like a homing pigeon.

"I want to get one thing straight," she told Ryan as she led the way through the throng to the bar. "This is one night only. And it's because I'm desperate. It doesn't mean I'm going to start drooling at your feet."

His startled look made her wince. Her bluntness had always been her downfall.

"What I mean is, obviously you're very . . . um . . .

good-looking. I mean, let's get that right out in the open. What are you, an actor or something?"

"No." He looked revolted, a reaction she found dangerously endearing.

"Model?"

"No!"

"Well, whatever, I just want you to know that your smile and your eyes and your . . ."

"What?"

Killer ass. "Uh . . . the rest of you. Anyway, it won't work on me."

He seemed to have stopped listening. They'd reached the bar, and he was frowning at Archie, who held a bottle of wine in each hand. One bottle was positioned perfectly over a glass, the other poured straight onto the floor.

"Archie! What are you doing?"

He jolted around so neither bottle pointed anywhere near a glass. "Katie, my dear, we must do Doggies' Night more often. I say we make it a monthly event. I've met the most marv—"

Ryan deftly removed the bottles from Archie's grasp.

"You've returned." The older man stuck out his hand.

Ryan, hands full of bottles, bowed his head. "Couldn't stay away. I'm hired for one night only. But if you catch me smiling or anything nasty like that, kick me. Why don't you go join your compadres over there in the booth? We got this, Katie and me."

Katie and me. The phrase made her shiver. Crap. Was it already happening? She grabbed one of the bottles of wine.

"Who ordered wine?" She directed a glare the length of the bar.

"I did." A timid-looking man raised his hand. "If that's okay."

"Right. The standard poodle with the purple collar."

She filled the glass Archie had been aiming for, then busied herself fielding orders from the rest of the customers. Ryan did the same at the other end of the bar. Now that she had someone actually helping her, as opposed to conducting long conversations with every single customer while pouring Cabernet onto the floor, she relaxed and began to enjoy the evening. The Hair of the Dog felt like a happening place, for the first time since she'd taken it on.

People were actually having fun. *At the Dog.* Her father would be so proud. Total strangers were striking up conversations with one another. Many showed off their pictures of their dogs. The Drinking Crew was having the time of their lives watching all the action. For once, there were women present, a rare sight at the Dog. The sound of female laughter—light trills, flirtatious giggles—added a nice touch to the evening.

If only she had a laugh like that. Bridget called her laugh a "pig snort." As an insecure teenager she'd practiced a different laugh, but given up in despair.

As she poured ice cubes into a row of glasses for an order of vodka tonics, she noticed something else about the laughter. It all came from the other end of the bar. She looked in Ryan's direction. Sure enough, a cluster of women pressed against the bar. They kept tossing back their hair and laughing at everything Ryan said.

And he was barely smiling at all. She'd seen his real smile in all its knee-weakening power. This qualified as a half smile, with one corner of his mouth tilted up in the sexiest possible way. His blue eyes drooped halfway shut as he poured a beer from the tap.

A clattering noise brought her back to herself. Damn it, she was pouring ice cubes onto the floor. She tossed the scooper back in the ice chest and bent down to pick up the fallen cubes.

"Where's my vodka tonic?" someone yelled. Sounded like that obnoxious guy with the pretentious-looking matched whippets, the one who had demanded four drinks for the price of one.

"It's coming!" she hollered, shoving the ice cubes into a pile. There were too many to pick up with two hands, so she scooped them into her shirt and stood up.

She hit a hard wall of flesh. Ryan. He must have come over to help when the whippet guy started yelling. He smelled good, like clean laundry and sweet grass. Too good. She took a step back. His blue eyes skimmed her from head to toe, with a long, lingering stop at the bare belly revealed by the shirt being used as a bag of ice. Heat flushed across her body. She was surprised the ice cubes didn't melt.

"Ice," she said, as if that explained everything.

"Need a hand?" He reached toward her and she took another step back. No way would she survive feeling his hands that close to her.

"I'm fine. If you could just, pour those vodka tonics, I'll—" Her butt hit the ice chest. Maybe if she fell in, she'd return to her normal, unrattled self. She turned and dumped the ice cubes into the sink.

Great. Now her top, made of some clingy synthetic fabric, stuck to her body. Why had she chosen white? She never wore white. But somehow white top and black skirt had seemed a good combination of manager and server. Wet, the white fabric was practically see-through.

When she turned back, Ryan still hadn't budged. She held her hands over her tummy to block the view. He gazed at her for a long moment.

"You should probably go change your shirt," he finally said. "You've got a bar full of drunk, horny guys."

"I don't have another shirt here."

He put his hands behind his neck and grabbed the back of his shirt, a long-sleeved thermal. Oh God, he was going to take off his shirt.

"No!"

"I've got a T-shirt on underneath."

"I don't care. Stop that, right now."

But he didn't stop. He pulled off his overshirt and, as she had anticipated, the T-shirt rode up along with it, revealing ridges of muscle lurking under tanned skin. A sigh left her mouth. She couldn't pull her eyes away from that hard belly, those golden-brown hairs catching the light, the line of his torso broadening out on the way up to his shoulders. She'd never seen anyone so fit. He must work out all the time, and yet she'd seen his hands. Callused and capable, they didn't look like hands that spent their days in a gym doing reps.

He pulled the bottom of his T-shirt back over his jeans. Not that it made a difference. How would she ever get him out of her mind now? He dangled the thermal in front of her. "Shirt. Put it on. It's Doggies' Night, not Wet T-shirt Night."

"Fine." She took his shirt and pulled it on, grateful to be able to hide her face for a second. The scent of Ryan surrounded her. Clean, warm, like rolling in laundry that had just been taken down from an outdoor clothesline. She took a deep breath, cursing herself for her foolishness. This man was so far out of her league, they didn't even play the same sport. *Get a grip.*

When she popped her head out of the neck of his shirt, she'd gotten control of herself. Hopefully the naked lust had been tucked away, the pointless desire hidden.

"Thank you," she said, with all the dignity she could muster, considering the shirt fell to her knees and the sleeves dangled nearly to the floor.

"Here." Before she could stop him, he lifted one of her arms and rolled the sleeve halfway up her forearm. At his closeness, heat gathered in her lower belly. Little prickles danced across her nerve endings all the way to her fingernails. His expression, part absorbed, part practical, as he tended to her made her want to throw herself at his feet and beg him to make love to her.

Make love to her? Why was she thinking these things?

She hadn't had sex since she and Doug broke up. She hadn't wanted to upset him. Maybe she was sex-starved. If so, she'd never noticed it before.

She shook her head violently, surprising Ryan.

"Did I hurt you?"

"No. Sorry. I just thought of something. Bills. Insurance. That stuff."

Maybe if she thought about Fidelity Trust, she'd get ahold of herself.

"Gotcha. Well, let's get back to work. Maybe after tonight you can pay some of those bills."

One last adjustment of her sleeves, and he picked up the bottle of vodka and got to work filling glasses. Katie ordered her knees to straighten, commanded her feet to step forward, and joined him at the bar. Lots of drinks to be poured, lots of dog photos to be checked.

But first, to find a way to get through the rest of the night. She picked up a clean glass and put it at the end of the line Ryan was filling. Vodka, straight, no ice. That would help. She drained it in one long swallow.

Okay, so there was one benefit to running a bar.

The sight of Katie wearing his shirt did something unexpected to Ryan's insides. She looked so little in it, yet so alive, like a squawking baby bird in a giant shoebox. Of course she would despise that comparison, he knew that much about her already. She would hate anything that made her sound cute or girly or flirty. But despite her best efforts, there was something kind of adorable about her.

All night long, even while a parade of beautiful women fought for his attention, his eyes kept straying to the other end of the bar where Katie would be either moving a mile a minute like a hummingbird, or frowning intently at a photo and interrogating a customer.

All her sexiness seemed to happen without her approval. She didn't dress to emphasize her high breasts or her subtle curves. Another woman with that exact same body would be dressed in belly shirts or halter tops, or something that showed lots of cleavage. Not Katie.

And really, a woman that small shouldn't be putting away the vodka like that. After her third shot, he decided he'd better keep a careful eye on her before she accidentally destroyed the bar. When she upended the bucket of stale Chex Mix, he slid next to her and righted it just in time. When she looked everywhere for the corkscrew she'd left on top of the espresso machine, he knew right where she'd put it. He handed it over without comment, shrugging off her suspicious look. When she tried ten times without success to get the bottle cap off a longneck Corona, he gently took it from her hands and took care of it himself.

"I don't need a babysister," she hissed at him. "Babysittser. Sitter."

"I sure do," purred a blonde who had shifted seats when Ryan had begun focusing on Katie's end of the bar.

"Well, he's taken." Katie slammed both hands on the bar and leaned forward to stare down the blonde. "All night long."

"Another night, then. I'm flexible." The blonde gave that last word all kinds of double meanings.

"He's not available. He's the new bartender at the Hair of the Dog."

He was? Ryan did a double take.

"Guess I know where to find you, then. And vice versa." She flipped a card at him. Ryan caught it and tucked it in his pocket.

"I appreciate that. Thanks for coming in. Spread the word," Ryan told her.

"Oh, I'll do that." She gave him a slow wink and slid sensuously off the bar stool. Ryan watched her go; how could he help it? She'd been teasing and flirting with him all evening.

It occurred to him that he needed something to do while he waited to get back on the force.

"I'm not sure if you were serious, but I could use a job, at least for a few weeks." He looked down at Katie and caught a look of hurt on her face. Had he upset her by taking the blonde's number? Why would she care? She didn't even seem to like him much, going by her unfriendly attitude.

"Good. You're hired." She busied herself with collecting empty shot glasses off the bar.

"Sorry about that." He indicated the departing blonde with a shrug of one shoulder.

"Sorry? Why? You shouldn't be sorry. Why sorry?" She was looking around for something. He moved her glass of vodka out of sight.

"I don't know. She was coming on to me all evening, and I just . . ." Why was he explaining himself?

"You should call her. Really. I think she liiikes you." Katie mimicked the blonde's sexy sashay, moving her hips from side to side and tossing him a come-hither look over her shoulder. He instantly went hard as a fire axe.

Damn.

As soon as Katie turned away, Ryan took a quick swallow of her vodka. This girl rattled his nerves in the strangest way. He didn't like it.

Closing time came three belts of vodka later. He'd lost track of Katie's alcohol consumption somewhere around the second beer chaser. Katie didn't seem too worried about it. In fact, she seemed a lot happier than he'd yet seen her. Not that he'd known her long, but after a crazy night of bartending together, it felt like he'd known her forever.

As soon as everyone had left, she danced around the bar in a kind of manic joy.

"It went great, absolutely, fantabulously, wonderfully great, don't you think? I can't wait to tell Dad what a marketing genie I am. I mean genius. Genius!" She skipped from table to table, picking up bottles and bar napkins. One of the bottles slipped from her grasp. Ryan dashed across the room to rescue it before it smashed to the floor. She blinked up at him. "Where did you come from?"

He took the rest of the bottles from her hands. "This may come as a shock, but I've been here all night." Despite her antipeople attitude, or maybe because of it, Katie was fun to tease.

"I know *that*. You're kinda hard to miss. You're very . . ." She leaned in and growled. "Sexy."

Half of Ryan's blood rushed right to his groin.

"The way your T-shirt pulls against your muscles like that . . ." She touched his arm just below the sleeve of his T-shirt, then ran her finger under it, along his shoulder muscle. Her touch was light, but it packed a punch, arousal-wise.

"And your butt is so so so, *so so*, very nice. I really like your butt. A lot."

"That's—er, thanks, I'll tell it you said so." He fought to keep from bursting out laughing. Just how drunk was she?

"Oh, I almost forgot." In one quick motion, she stripped his shirt off her body. Her white shirt seemed to be dry, but it was still tight and clingy enough to outline her breasts.

He dropped the bottles onto the nearest table, then took the shirt from her and pulled it on like an extra layer of armor. With a woozy look in her big brown eyes, she leaned in to him.

Her nipples poked against his chest. Like the rest of her, they were small and fierce. He clenched his hands into fists because he really, really wanted to feel them against his palms.

"Look, Katie," he told her, "I'm a little drunk, and you're a lot drunk, and you already told me I don't—"

She didn't let him finish. She reached up and pulled his head down to hers, down into a kiss that surprised the hell out of him. In his experience, first kisses were more about performance art than anything else, each person trying to prove how good they were at it. Katie, on the other hand, kissed with her whole being. This kiss felt like diving into a deep, clear pond while holding hands with a wildly sensual mermaid. Almost out of curiosity, he took her head in his hands and dove deeper. Her tongue moved feverishly against his.

He moved his hands down her back, feeling each delicate bone, each shiver of her flesh. It shocked him how much he wanted her. He wanted to feel the texture of her skin, watch how the after-hours lights picked up the amber shadows on her pale flesh. Her body was lithe and warm and pliant to his touch. They could have sex right now on the grungy floor, or a beer-ringed table, he knew without a doubt. Since he was a man, and she was hot, he'd be fine with that.

But it would be wrong.

She didn't seem to know that, though. He felt her push up the back of his T-shirt to reach the bare skin of his back. Her excited, exploring hands seemed to want to feel everything. His shoulders, his spine, his hips, his . . .

Shit, she was going for his ass. If one tip of one finger made it under the waistband of his jeans, it would be a lot harder to put a stop to this.

He put his hands behind his back with the intent of pulling her arms away from his body. She took the opportunity to press her soft breasts with their pointy nipples even closer to him.

"Katie," he groaned. "You'd better stop that."

"Take me, now."

She wrapped one leg around his thigh and fixed wide, dark eyes on him. This close, he saw a ring of black around the outer edge, and deep chocolate brown closer to the iris. When she wasn't frowning, her eyes were beautiful, especially when they were so urgent, so darkened with desire, so under the influence . . .

"Katie, this is not a good—"

"Right here," she went on, rubbing her pelvis against his groin, though she had to be on tiptoe to do so. "Right on the floor. I don't care if it has beer stains and, and, and . . . dog slobber on it. I want to have sex with you, Ryan. Right. This. Second."

Chapter Five

Katie opened her eyes, somehow knowing that her pleasant dream about riding a unicorn would be the last enjoyable thought of the morning. She sat up. Pain zinged around her head like a razor-studded pinball.

Water. She needed water, immediately. First she'd drink a tall glassful. Then she'd drown herself.

She rolled off her bed, fighting her way past the books that always wound up tangled in her blankets, and crawled into the kitchenette portion of her tiny apartment. Man, she really needed to sweep the floor more often. She flicked a Cheerio out of her path. Her favorite pajama pants, the ones with the flaming skulls printed on them, were going to get filthy. But what did it matter, for someone intending to drown herself?

In the kitchenette, she pulled herself to her feet and shoved aside a pile of dirty cereal bowls. Breakfast was the only meal she'd eaten at home since she'd taken over the bar. Every morning she washed exactly one bowl and ate her Cheerios. But right now she couldn't think past a glass of water.

After she downed one glass, her mind cleared enough for her to miss her former fuzziness. *Oh crap.* She'd thrown herself at Ryan like a sex-starved groupie. Worse, like a sex-starved character in a soap opera. *Take me.* She'd actually said, *Take me.* Had her bosom been heaving at the time? Had her thighs been trembling?

God, this was a total, unmitigated disaster.

She rolled the cold glass across her forehead. Aspirin. Aspirin needed to happen. Maybe it wasn't her fault. She was clearly sex-starved, and no wonder. When she'd broken up with Doug, she'd taken it in careful stages. First she'd redefined their relationship, from boyfriend-girlfriend to friends with benefits. He hadn't minded the new arrangement, and neither had she, at first, until it became clear he didn't really get the distinction. Then she'd downgraded them from friends with benefits to friends.

That meant no benefits.

Doug hadn't liked that. They'd been together so long, ever since freshman year in high school, that she couldn't stand to hurt his feelings. Breaking up with him in phases had taken so much energy that she'd written off the possibility of another man. No sex for Katie. Even though something told her Doug wasn't the world's expert in bed, she'd always liked sex. She didn't apologize for that. A normal twenty-five-year-old was supposed to like sex. But she hadn't had any for over a year.

And then the sexiest man she'd ever seen walked through the door.

No wonder she'd jumped him like a tiger in heat.

She scrambled through her purse for her aspirin, and checked the clock. Almost noon. Time to get to the bar. She'd never finished cleaning up last night. Ryan had called her a cab. He'd even given the driver an extra twenty to wait until she was safely inside. Of course he had to be a perfect gentleman on top of everything else. Unless it wasn't about being a gentleman. Maybe he hadn't been attracted enough to her.

Groan.

Although . . . she remembered a certain hard swell against her stomach, when she'd ground herself against him like a nymphomaniac. And he'd kissed her like . . . like he'd wanted her. When he'd cradled her head in his hands and sent his tongue deep into her mouth, had he been humoring her? She'd never experienced a kiss like that. During it she'd lost all sense of time and reality, until she wasn't Katie anymore, head-in-a-book, people-phobic, hopeless-at-running-a-bar Katie, but simply a hot-blooded woman craving a sexually potent man.

A smile stole onto her face. She was pretty sure he'd wanted her. And yet, the fact remained that he'd rejected her. Her smile disappeared. Humiliating.

She took her time getting dressed, letting the aspirin do its work while she downed glass after glass of water. Slowly, her mortification faded. Blame it on the vodka. Blame it on her recent lack of a sex life. Blame it on Ryan's killer smile. She'd made a mistake, but she'd survive. No harm done. With any luck, she'd never see the guy again.

When she put her key into the lock of the Hair of the Dog's front door, she found it already open. When she stepped cautiously inside, she squinted at what had to be a hallucination.

Someone had broken into the bar and . . . and . . . cleaned up the mess from last night. The floor had been swept. All the bottles and glasses and bar napkins and dog-shaped balloons had been whisked away somewhere. The scent of lemon and fresh-brewed espresso almost masked the stale smell of spilled beer. Behind the bar, she caught the clattering of bottles being dumped into the recycle bin.

Had some homeless man stumbled in and been inspired to tidy up? Had the Drinking Crew decided to pay off their tabs with cleaning duties?

"Hello?" she called into the dark interior. "Who's there?"

Ryan's head popped up from behind the bar. "Bartender, reporting for duty."

"What?"

"Don't you remember? You hired me last night." He straightened up and wiped his hands on a dish towel. Katie's head throbbed, or maybe it was some other body part, come to think of it. She wished she had another aspirin, or five. His gorgeousness was too much for a hangover like hers.

"Oh, right." She frowned. That memory had been overshadowed by the bigger event of her shamelessly begging him to have sex with her. But she remembered now. And it made sense. He'd done well last night. She needed a bartender, now that Kent had moved on and Doug was nursing a broken arm. "Well, you don't have to feel obligated. It was kind of a crazy night."

"I don't feel obligated. I told you, I could use a job for a few weeks. I figure your bouncer will be back by then."

"Probably." If she knew Doug, he'd be back long before then, if only to keep an eye on her. "Well." She'd never hired anyone before. Maybe she should do it in a more official way. "Can I ask you some questions?"

He shrugged. "Sure. I fired up the espresso machine. Want a cup?"

God, he was too perfect to bear.

The two of them sat at the bar with cups of espresso. Since Ryan had entered her life, she'd only seen him in the dark. She'd watched from across the room while he punched people out, poured drinks, and flirted. Sure, there had been that kiss, but she hadn't really been looking while she plastered herself against him. Now, she got her first close-up, sit-down, daylight look at his magnificence.

His light brown hair, cut short, had bits of gold winding through it. His nose veered just a bit from pure straight. Laugh lines spread from the corners of his eyes. One eyebrow tilted up higher than the other, giving him a permanent look of playfulness. And most of all, his eyes, the pure blue of a perfect July sky, made her heart sing. Those eyes promised all kinds of summery things—a leisurely float down a slow-moving river, a barbecue on a sunny afternoon, catching fireflies on a twilit lawn, and getting tickled until you begged for mercy and fell into the deepest kiss ever, serenaded by the evening crickets.

She gave herself a shake. Must be the hangover. She realized he'd just asked her something.

"What?"

"How are you feeling today?" he repeated.

"Oh no. No, no, no. None of that."

"None of what?" Ryan stirred his espresso with a little spoon that looked like he could snap it in two with those strong hands of his.

"Friendliness. We're boss and employee now."

He shrugged one shoulder. "All right, boss. What do you want to know?"

"Do you have any prior experience as a bartender?"

"Some. I picked up a shift here and there at a place in Los Angeles. El Coyote."

"Los Angeles." She pounced. "Is that where you're from?"

"No. I'm from outside of Fresno. Little town you've never heard of. But I've been hanging out in LA the last year or so."

"Doing what?" She sipped her espresso. Posing for magazine ads? Working as a gigolo? Male stripper, maybe?

"Landscaping, mostly. Some rock work."

Her eyes flew to his hands, one of which cradled his espresso cup, the other of which rested on the bar. That explained the nicks and scars and calluses. It didn't explain how he'd touched her, with so much knowledge and sensitivity.

"About last night," she said abruptly. "I'm sorry."

He looked up, startled, his eyes gone darker blue. "You don't have to—"

"I said, I'm sorry. It was a mistake. My fault. My bad. And if you're going to work for me, it can't ever happen again. I mean, I know you didn't make it happen, it was all me. But just so you know. It won't."

He started to say something.

"I've always found that it helps to be really clear about defining things."

"Defining things?"

"Yeah. For instance, obviously I . . . um . . . made sexual advances on you last night because you're very attractive and it's been a while since I had sex."

There, she'd said it, in her typical truth-blurting way. It seemed to stun him.

"But I've gotten that out of my system now." God, she hoped so. "I'll be your boss, you'll be my employee, and that's where it ends. I promise not to assault you again."

He stayed quiet for a long moment, looking first at his coffee, then back up at her, then back down. If only she were a mind reader. She'd give anything to know what he was thinking right now. Then again, if it was along the lines of *Thank the Lord I won't have to put up with that again,* maybe she'd rather not know.

Finally he said, "You're the boss. So what shifts do you want me to take?"

They discussed schedules and pay and other details, and when they were done, Katie went into the back office, sat at her father's desk, and clutched her pounding head in her hands.

In the space of twenty-four hours, Ryan had caused her more ups and downs than Doug had over the course of ten years. He'd made her heart skip more beats, made her misbehave, inspired more lust and longing than the boy she'd assumed she'd marry someday.

And now she was going to be seeing him every single day, sexy and unattainable, like a beautiful dress locked behind a glass display window.

Ryan set himself to studying the checklist Kent, the runaway stoner bartender, had left. *Check stock. Notify manager if low on anything. Check ice machine. Unload dishwasher. Consider killing next customer who asks for a Hair of the Dog.*

He did a double take on that one. Apparently Kent had some frustration building up. Wouldn't surprise him. Maybe he'd been attracted to Katie too.

That darn girl confused the hell out of him. He'd figured her behavior last night was the result of some serious vodka consumption. That's why he'd sent her home without falling into bed the way he would have under normal circumstances. He'd behaved himself, and that didn't come easy.

But today, when she'd broken things down so brutally—he looked good to her because she hadn't gotten laid in a while—that hurt. As soon as she'd walked in, with her lovely, cinnamon latte hair loose around her shoulders, her skin reddened as though she'd scrubbed her face clean of last night, her dark eyes shadowed with fatigue, he'd wanted to wrap her in his arms. Maybe see if that kiss had been a fluke.

And then she'd come out with her little speech about her "sexual advances."

Truth to tell, he felt a little used.

The door opened and the first customers of the day walked in. Probably one of the old guys, figured Ryan, scanning the checklist. *Item number twenty-two: the "regulars" shelf. Make sure the old coots' beer mugs are ready for them.*

The sound of a soft giggle made Ryan straighten up in surprise. The arrivals weren't dragging oxygen tanks or walking with canes. Three pretty girls stood in the doorway, peering over their sunglasses.

"Can I help you?" he asked in surprise. "Are you looking for the Gap? It's three doors down."

"Oh, I think we're in the right place," said the tallest girl of the bunch, a redhead, with a wicked wink. They advanced toward the bar and fluttered onto the bar stools like a flock of birds.

He surveyed them, a broad smile spreading across his face. They'd come for him. Maybe it was shallow, but that felt good after Katie's rejection. "Now ladies, you know the Hair of the Dog isn't a spa, right? We serve liquor here. Hard liquor."

"The harder the better," said the redhead.

"Bring it on," her friend chimed in.

Ryan grinned and settled in for some serious flirtation. Nothing soothed the soul like attention from a pretty girl—except attention from three pretty girls. Make that seven, when the next batch of customers walked in a few minutes later. Nine when twin sisters arrived.

When they finally showed up, the old guys nearly left right away, disoriented by the sight of so many skimpy sundresses and shades of lipstick. But they adapted well enough after Ryan located their favorite beer mugs and set them up with their first cold ones of the day. Archie, the newspaper guy, chimed right in with the flirting, even though Ryan had a feeling he was gay.

If he couldn't be fighting fires, flirting with girls might well be the next best thing. The only shadow came when Katie dashed out from the back room and stopped dead in her tracks.

"Who the . . . what the . . ." She wiped her hand over her eyes as if convinced she was hallucinating. "Where'd they come from?" she hissed to Ryan, pulling him aside.

"They live around here. Neighborhood girls. Good kids."

"Are they legal? Cuz I can't be serving alcohol to—"

"Of course they're legal. By the way, why is it that every single girl hates her driver's license photo?"

"I don't know. Take a survey," she snapped.

But just then, a new arrival made him forget all the women at the bar. He hurried to the center of the room, where a smiling woman stood holding the hand of a wide-eyed little girl. He folded Captain Brody's wife into a tight hug.

"Melissa. God, it's good to see you."

She pulled away, her deep green eyes lit with joy. "Right back at you, Hoagie."

"How'd you know I was here?"

"I saw your truck out front. This is Danielle. She's heard a lot about you."

Ryan looked down into the face of an adorable, skinny little imp of a girl. She was dark-skinned, at least part Mexican, he guessed. Probably about four years old. He knelt and reached out his hand to shake hers.

"It's really great to meet you, Danielle."

She hid her face in her mother's sleeve, then peeked at him, then hid again. He made a pretend crying face. She giggled.

"We can't stay because, well, this is a bar," said Melissa. "But I wanted to invite you to a barbecue this weekend."

Ryan straightened up slowly. "The guys will be there?"

"They're invited. Along with others."

He gazed at the floor, kicked at a stray peanut he'd missed during his cleanup. Hanging out with the guys off duty, grilling burgers and kidding around. Sounded like heaven. And hell, until he knew where he stood with Captain Brody.

"Can't do it, Melissa. Maybe later on."

She gave him that level look he remembered from when she first showed up at the fire station with her white-haired grandma and made Brody act like a teenager with a crush. "No problem, Ryan. Some other time. Give us a call whenever you want to come over." She leaned in and kissed him on the cheek, whispering, "Don't break too many hearts, okay?"

He laughed as she led her little girl to the door. At the last second, Danielle turned her head and gave him a shy smile over her shoulder.

"Maybe I can stop by and take Danielle out for an ice cream," he called.

The little girl's face lit up as Melissa shook her head. "I can't believe you said the I word. But maybe."

When Ryan turned back, he faced a row of women who looked like they'd just seen a Hollywood tear-jerker. One girl held her hand over her heart and gazed at him with swimming eyes. Another dashed a tear—an actual tear—from her eye. What the hell was wrong with them all?

"He likes kids," sighed the redhead.

"Have you ever seen anything so sweet?"

"So precious!"

Embarrassed, he looked for Katie, for anyone who hadn't temporarily lost her mind. Sure enough, Katie came through. Like a lifeline, she stood behind the bar, glaring at him as always, fists on hips. "Could you get back to work, please? This is a bar, not a day care center. We gotta set up for Happy Hour." She wheeled around and disappeared into the office.

Maybe he'd better keep his fondness for kids to himself from now on, Ryan thought as he whipped up a new batch of cosmopolitans. He preferred flirtation to adoration. And even flirtation got old when it lacked a certain . . . bite, or edge, or unpredictability. Like what he'd get if he ambled into Katie's office and teased her for a while.

As the afternoon wore on, he felt like he was going through the motions, even though the girls didn't seem to notice.

At the beginning of Happy Hour, his cell phone rang.

"Ryan, Brody here."

"Captain Brody." At the sound of that quiet, commanding voice, he felt his whole body automatically straighten. He took a few steps away from the chatter of voices at the bar. Was Brody about to save him, bring him back on the force?

"I want you back. But I have to be sure you're not going to fall back into the same kind of behavior."

"I won't, you know I won't."

"I need more than that. Here's what I want you to do. I want you to take a proficiency exam."

"No problem." Piece of cake. Everyone knew he was hellaciously proficient.

"Hang on. I want you to study the Manual of Operations all over again. Besides general firefighting knowledge, you need to be up to date on all policy changes, all training bulletins, sexual harassment policies, that sort of thing. And I want you to learn something new. I figure wildland fire procedures make for a good change of pace. Study hard. Take all the time you need, then come in and I'll test you on your knowledge. This isn't an official requirement, obviously. This is between you and me. Sound good?"

It sounded like the equivalent of sticking hot needles in his brain, which was no doubt why Brody had chosen it. "Yes," he managed to say.

"Good. Happy studying."

Chapter Six

For Katie, life at the Hair of the Dog could be neatly divided into the pre-Ryan period and the post-Ryan era. If she wrote a paper about it, she'd have to compare the pre-Ryan time to the Dark Ages, minus the bubonic plague and sketchy bathing habits. In fact, by the time her parents were scheduled to return, Katie could barely remember the pre-Ryan era. Even while she drove to the San Gabriel Valley Airport, when she ought to be planning how to approach her father about the bar's future, thoughts of Ryan got in the way.

The man was a mystery. He had a slow-moving style, a slight drawl like a cowboy, and a way of holding still while he listened to people. And yet she knew how fast he could move when it counted. She'd seen him in that fight the first day she'd met him. And that wasn't the only time he'd punched someone out. One night a drunken jerk was ranting about gay men, and Ryan reached right over the bar and socked him in the nose. The guy had wanted to take the fight outside.

"Tell you what." Ryan scrawled his number on a bar napkin. "You call me tomorrow when you're sober and we'll pick up where we left off."

"You aren't gay, are you?" A bar full of women had waited breathlessly for his answer after he'd escorted the drunk guy outside.

"Nah. You don't have to be gay to stand up for the dudes," he'd said with that easy smile of his.

If only he were gay, then maybe Katie could get him out of her mind.

She pulled up to the curb outside the baggage claim and scanned the crowd for her parents. Her eyes slid past her father, then back, almost not recognizing the sunburned man in the Hawaiian shirt. But sure enough, he was headed for her ancient Datsun, followed by her equally sun-kissed mother. He heaved their suitcases into her trunk—should he be doing that?—then leaned in her window. She gaped at him.

"Daddy?"

"Scoot over, kiddo, I'll drive us back."

Since she knew her father was constitutionally incapable of letting someone else drive, she crawled over the gearshift into the passenger seat. He inserted himself into the driver's seat, filling the car with his tanned bulk and big grin. For the first time in two months, Katie felt the nagging worry ease. Her father was fine. It had all been worth it. "You look great. Both of you do."

"Thanks, dear." Her mother blew her a kiss from the backseat. Nina had been a beauty, the prize Frank Dane had won out of sheer persistent charisma. He adored her, brought her breakfast in bed on Sundays, lavished her with surprise pashminas and porcelain fairy figurines for her collection. He'd always taken care of her. Now, checking her mom out in the rearview mirror, Katie saw lines of worry tightening her face. Becoming the caretaker must have been a shock to her system. "You're looking well, Katie. A bit tired. Have you been working too hard?"

"Yes, I have, and as a matter of fact, we really need to talk about—"

Her mother gave her a meaningful rap on the shoulder. When Katie looked back, her mother shook her head and mouthed, "Not now."

"So what's this I hear about a new bartender?" her father asked, steering into the airport traffic.

"Who told you about that?"

"Got my sources. Hear he's quite a looker. My Katie girl wouldn't be hiring herself a new boyfriend, would she?"

"Dad. Please. That's insulting."

How did her father manage to dump a huge responsibility on her and treat her like a child at the same time?

"Heard he punched out poor Dougie boy to get the job. He must really like you."

"Tell your sources they have their heads up their butts," said Katie hotly. "Ryan saved Doug from getting beaten to a bloody pulp. Is Doug the one who told you that?"

Her father gave her a sidelong, delighted look. "Well, looky here, you see that, Nina? She's all up in arms to defend her boy."

"Leave her alone, Frank. Let's not talk about the bar yet. I'm sure she'd rather hear about Baja."

And that was that. Conversation during the rest of the drive home consisted of snorkeling trips, dolphin sightings, and detailed explanations of the differences between the various cactuses used to make tequila. If her family could be described in one word, it would be "loud." Crammed inside her car, her parents' combined decibel level was overwhelming.

By the time they pulled into the carport of her parents' home, a sprawling, ranch-style slice of suburban blah, Katie had decided that hearing about tequila gave you as bad a headache as drinking it. A few cars, including Bridget's bright yellow Miata, were parked out front.

As soon as they all extracted themselves from her car, her father opened his arms wide.

"I still need my Katie-hug!" She flew into them and buried her face against his burly chest. His familiar smell, bourbon overlaid with minty Nicorette gum, wrapped around her like a favorite quilt. Tears pricked her eyes and a wave of gratitude made her squeeze him tight. Thank God he was okay.

Her mother's hug was more briskly affectionate. Katie had always been a daddy's girl, and everyone knew it.

Her parents hurried inside, while Katie lagged behind dragging their suitcases. A chorus of shrieks and hugs and "Welcome homes" rang from the living room.

"Here, lemme help." Doug greeted her at the door, holding out his nonbandaged arm. She suffered the usual pang of irritated guilt at the sight of his morose expression. He had shoulder-length, tangled hair and a fallen-angel face that used to make her swoon. Now it just made her sad. They'd met when they'd both joined a wannabe rock group that called themselves the Losers. He'd played bass, she'd played drums, and they'd started hanging out every possible moment when not practicing in their friend's garage.

"What are you doing here?" She let him take one of the suitcases.

"You know how Bridget is. Won't take a no."

No sense in wondering why Bridget had interfered. A noninterfering Bridget would be like a fish without gills. Katie made her way into the crowded house, wincing at the din. Not only were the Danes loud, so were most of their friends.

A big hand-drawn banner hung in the living room. "Welcome Back to Los Estados Unidos," it read. With her usual efficiency, Bridget had finished hugging their parents and was passing around a tray of red drinks with paper umbrellas in them.

Katie and Doug dragged the suitcases into her parents' room. She sighed. How many ex-boyfriends felt this comfortable in their ex's parents' home?

"How's the arm?" she asked as they made their way back to the party.

"My dad says I should sue."

"What? Sue who?"

"I don't know. Someone. It happened on the premises of the Hair of the Dog." He gave her a sidelong look past a stray lock of mussed hair.

A shaft of fear tightened her stomach. If Doug's father sued them, they didn't stand a chance. He was a high-powered attorney who lived for revenge.

"So you might want to be nicer to me," continued Doug with a smirk.

"Excuse me?"

But she didn't get a chance to continue. Bridget

appeared before them like a vision of Snow White, all shining blue eyes and glossy black hair. Katie always felt like Grumpy the dwarf in her presence. "Surprised?"

"Kinda, since you said you were too busy to pick them up." She took the drink Bridget offered. Doug wandered away, mumbling something about taking a pill. Katie knew he was probably going out back for a smoke.

"This is why I was busy, crabby. You know they love surprises."

"And *you* know that Doug and I broke up."

"So? He's a friend of the family. It wouldn't be the same without him. Now try for once to enjoy the occasion." Bridget lifted a finger to the corner of Katie's mouth, but Katie dodged it. She hated when Bridget tried to make her smile. "Besides, Gidget, Dougie's doing so much better."

Katie hated her nickname even more than being forced to smile, but Bridget had a point. Three years ago, Doug had been hospitalized for clinical depression—right when she'd finally screwed up her courage to break up with him. The breakup had gone into slow motion after that. What was the correct way to dump someone who might go off his meds? She was still trying to figure that one out. But at least they'd phased into friends-slash-coworkers.

"I will do my utmost not to jeopardize Doug's recovery."

"And enjoy yourself."

"That's pushing it. I don't want to give him false hope."

To Katie's relief, someone in the kitchen yelled for Bridget's attention. She shrugged a shoulder, bare under her blue halter top, and hurried away with her tray of drinks.

For the six thousand and thirty-second time, Katie wondered what it would be like to be that tall and confident. The world must look so different when you could meet it eye to eye instead of constantly craning your neck and standing on tiptoe. Sometimes Katie felt she had to be twice as forceful so people knew she was there. And usually that felt like too much work.

She sat next to her father on his favorite brown leather couch. "Daddy, we really need to find some time to talk about the bar. I'm a little—"

"Katie," interrupted her mother. "Just wait till you see what I got you in Cancun." Where the heck had her mother come from? It was practically supernatural. Her mom leaned over the back of the couch and tugged at her hand. "You're going to love it. Come on, now."

Her father winked at her as she reluctantly got to her feet. "Get used to it, Katie girl. I have. Every time I try to do anything fun, she pops up like a jack-in-the-box." The affectionate look they exchanged took the bite out of his words.

Katie let her mother draw her into the kitchen. Two of Bridget's friends were there, sticking toothpicks through mini hot dogs and placing them on a tray. Bridget always had friends around. She trailed them behind her like perfume.

"Katie, I'm asking you this with complete seriousness. Are you listening?"

"Yes." She looked into her mother's angelic face, which now held the look of someone running an army boot camp.

Her mother lowered her voice. "Your father is not

ready to hear about the bar. Period. Every time it's mentioned, his blood pressure goes up. He gets all excited, his face gets red, he starts waving his arms around."

"But, Mom, I only said I'd take care of the bar while you guys were gone. I don't know anything about running a business. I'm studying nineteenth-century French literature, for cripes' sake."

Her mother tightened her lips, no doubt to restrain herself from the inevitable lecture about Katie's random and inexplicable decisions. Her family treated her choice to go to graduate school with a kind of pat-on-the-head, she'll-get-over-it-soon indulgence. "And I'm sure all the dead French people appreciate your dedication. But your father needs you."

"But I have no experience and some of the bills coming in are freaking me out. We can't pay the beer distributor, and the insurance bill is due, and more come every day."

"What about that event you held, what was it again?"

Katie gritted her teeth. "Doggies' Night." She never wanted to hear those words again.

"We heard it drew quite a crowd."

"Yes, but we lost money on it. We've been getting a few more customers since then"—almost exclusively women, but no need to mention that—"but I still can't pay the beer bill."

Her mother fiddled with her bracelets, a nervous habit Katie had seen many times. "I know it's a lot to ask, Gidget. I'm sure you'll figure something out, dear. You're so smart. This is a chance to direct all that brainpower into something useful, something that will help your daddy."

Her mother knew Katie's soft spot all too well.

"I'll tell you something, Katie, and you must never share this with your father." She leaned in so close Katie could smell the faint, familiar scent of Jean Naté gardenia body powder. "Part of me wishes that bar didn't even exist. Frank has been like a new man since we went away. I thought he'd miss the bar, but he never even mentioned it in Mexico, except for when he spoke to you on the phone. He needed that time away." Her mother's clear blue eyes, so like Bridget's, grew misty. "I know in my heart it saved his life. And it kills me to think of him going back to that dark, unhealthy place and all that stress. I want to put it off as long as I possibly can. For your father's sake."

Katie's heart sank into the bottom of her sneakers. She was stuck like a fly in a spiderweb, like toilet paper on someone's shoe. "Can I at least ask him about the insurance policy?"

"No. Absolutely not. That's exactly the kind of thing that'll get him revved up. Why don't you go check his files in his study? Maybe you'll find something that'll help."

"All right." Katie could barely squeeze the words out of her throat.

"You're a good girl, Katie. Truly. I'm sorry I have to burden you with this. I wish I had another solution."

After her mother left to rejoin her father on the couch, Katie sagged against the refrigerator, ignoring the fruit-shaped magnets digging into her back. *Stuck like a tail on a donkey. Stuck like ants in molasses.*

"Hey, Katie." One of Bridget's friends tossed her a friendly smile. "Everyone's talking about the hottie you hired at your dad's bar. We're thinking of stopping by later on."

"What hours does he work?" Bridget's other friend, Meredith, asked.

Katie stared at her. "Aren't you getting married? Isn't Bridget your maid of honor?"

"I'm asking on behalf of all my single friends. He is single, right?"

"I don't know."

"Have you ever seen him with a girl?" They closed in to interrogate her.

"Only about a hundred." She tried to back up, but she was already flattened against the fridge.

"Someone special."

"I haven't paid attention." A lie if ever there was one.

"Well, I intend to conduct a thorough investigation." Bridget joined the little cluster, with Doug right behind her. From the sullen look in Doug's mud-brown eyes, Katie knew talk of Ryan irritated him.

"That would require actually coming into the Hair of the Dog."

Bridget gave a slight shudder, as she always did when anyone spoke the name of the bar. "He sounds like he's worth it. Is he?"

Katie's eyes strayed to Doug. He stood with shoulders hunched, his standard posture ever since he'd shot up a foot in junior year. "You'll have to ask his groupies. All I know is he shows up on time and doesn't get too many drink orders wrong."

Doug still looked worried.

"And he probably won't be there long. He said he was only looking for a job for a few weeks."

That piece of intel finally drew a smile from Doug.

"That does it. I'm coming in," declared Bridget. "Is it true he beat up four guys who were making fun of a gay kid?"

Katie rolled her eyes. "Yes, and he lifts pickup trucks with one hand, helps little old ladies cross the street, and, oh, did you hear about how much he likes kids?"

As if Ryan knew they were talking about him, her phone flashed an incoming call from the bar phone.

"Katie, we had a little incident," he said as soon as she answered.

"What happened?"

Katie shushed everyone while she listened to Ryan's calm voice. "Archie tried to light a candle and set his napkin on fire. Then he poured whiskey on it, which made it worse. The fire spread to his jacket."

"His *jacket*?"

Her mother, with her perfect knack for picking up on disaster, hurried into the kitchen with an armful of glasses. "What's wrong?"

Ryan continued, "Don't worry, it was on the bar next to him. Mr. Jamieson tore off his shirt and smothered the flames before I even got over there. And a girl threw her club soda on it too. No one was hurt. Wet, but not injured. But we have some new scorch marks on the bar."

"Scorch marks . . ." Katie's heart pounded. The thought of the Drinking Crew—and Dr. Burwell with his oxygen tank—that close to a fire horrified her.

"Scorch marks?" her mother repeated. "Was there a fire?"

Her father bustled into the kitchen. "A fire? Where?"

Katie held up her hand for silence. "So everything's okay now?"

"Yep, under control. But I thought you'd want to know."

"Thanks. I'll call you right back."

"Sure, boss."

She hung up and looked solemnly at her parents. "Don't freak out, but there was a fire at the Hair of the Dog. No one was hurt. No real damage done."

Bridget and her friends gasped and began lobbing questions at her. But her parents merely exchanged a long, odd look.

"So long as no one was injured," said Frank Dane, with what Katie considered a shocking lack of concern.

"Yes, that's all that really matters," agreed her mother. With a rueful shrug, she took her husband's arm and coaxed him back to the living room.

Katie stared after her parents. A fire at the Dog . . . shouldn't they be reacting in their usual over-the-top fashion? Calling the fire department, rushing to the scene, issuing orders to various family members. But their only emotion had seemed to be a sort of . . . disappointment.

Doug was trying to catch her eye. He was always trying to catch her eye. Keeping her distance from Doug had been so much easier at grad school.

She hurried to the bathroom before he could catch up with her. This room had always been her haven back when she'd shared a bedroom with Bridget. She closed the door behind her and dialed the bar.

"Hello, darlin'."

"That's how you answer the phone?"

"Only when it's you, darlin'."

Darlin'. Just kill me now. She plopped onto the toilet seat, with its comfy lavender covering. "So everything's really okay?"

"Everything's groovy. Archie's completely recovered and telling the story to everyone who will listen. Right now he's hitting on the guy from the real estate office."

"What? Archie's *gay*?"

"Course. Why do you think I went after that dickhead the other night? Aside from intolerance bugging the crap out of me. Can't have our steady customers insulted."

Oh God, this phone call was a mistake. She'd trained herself to ignore Ryan at the bar, but his voice, with that playful wink in it, got through her defenses in no time. Her nerves fluttered, her insides melted.

"Well, better get back to the party here. I'll see you later."

"Don't worry about a thing, boss. What kind of bartender would I be if I let the place burn down?"

After she hung up, she stood and looked at herself in the mirror. She looked different. Kind of supercharged and electrified, as if she'd put her hand in a socket. Her eyes looked more sparkly than usual, her face more pink. She pulled her straight black eyebrows together into the classic Katie scowl. That was more like it.

Talking to Doug had never made her face go pink.

Speaking of Doug . . . she opened the door a crack and peered out. No sign of him. She slipped out of the bathroom and headed down the hall to her father's study, as her mother had suggested.

The room was crammed with piles of magazines—*National Geographic, Field and Stream, Saveur, Bartender's Monthly*. Rows of baseball trophies lined a shelf her father had put up for the purpose. Her twin brothers had racked up the trophies all through high school, then gotten snapped up as fresh meat for the minor leagues. Framed family photos filled every inch of available space on the walls. A fine layer of dust covered everything—no one had been in here for a while. It smelled of Scotch and old cigar smoke.

Several black filing cabinets lurked against the back wall. Feeling like a spy, Katie opened each one and rifled through. The label "Sale" caught her eye. The papers inside made her eyes go wide. About a year ago, according to a fax from a real estate agent, her father had tried to sell the Hair of the Dog. But not a single offer had come in. They'd decided to take it off the market until the economy recovered. Katie was starting to understand her father's heart attack.

Finally she located the folder labeled "Insurance for HD." The manila folder contained the complete policy, along with all the various payment options. She read it through carefully. Her father, for some reason, had chosen to insure the bar for a million dollars, far more than it could possibly be worth. Had he been anticipating some kind of disaster? He'd selected one hundred percent coverage with a tiny deductible. That all made sense, she supposed. If there was a catastrophe—a fire, for instance—they wouldn't have to dig into their savings to pay the deductible. They'd make enough money to rebuild with no problems.

The one thing she couldn't understand was why he hadn't spread the payments out over the year, instead of signing up for the balloon payment option. True, the payment plan would have been more expensive over the long run, so maybe it made sense. Or maybe he'd been foolishly optimistic about the bar's finances. Most likely he was hoping the sale would go through before the next gigantic payment was due.

She looked around the office, at the photos, the trophies, the magazines. Not one of those photos showed the bar. And the *Bartender* magazines were still in their plastic wrapping. Had her father lost interest in the Hair of the Dog? He hadn't talked about it in Mexico, according to her mother. He clearly hadn't entered this office in quite some time. She remembered that strange look her parents had shared when she'd told them about the fire. Did her father even care about the bar anymore? Did he want it . . . gone? For good?

Chapter Seven

Ryan squinted at a page in the Rules and Regulations binder. "No firefighter shall leave the station without the permission of the station commander." Right. He knew that. But he'd come back from EMT recert alone and found everyone out on a call. Then the doorbell had rung, and the pretty girl had said her house was on fire, and he'd jumped in the plug-buggy and . . .

He kicked back in his favorite piece of furniture, an old, yellowed leather recliner that had fallen victim to a neighbor's divorce. Ryan had rescued it from the curb before the garbage truck could whisk it away into oblivion. He'd lovingly cleaned it and disinfected it and had enjoyed its relaxing qualities ever since.

The binder, one of six that comprised the Manual of Operations, was spread out on his lap. He stared at it without seeing the words. Studying brought back so many painful school memories. Trying to make sense out of black markings on the page that seemed to change shape right before his eyes. Sounding like a moron in front of the other kids who all picked it up so much faster than he did.

Wishing he could ask his father for help, but knowing that would earn him only a scornful cackle or a kick in the ass.

He hadn't been diagnosed as dyslexic until later in life, by a junior high teacher who had a crush on him. By then most of the psychological trauma had been inflicted. He'd already been categorized as a good-looking jock type who'd be lucky to get a C in anything except shop or PE. Despite all that, he loved to read, when he could take his time and thoroughly enjoy and process the words on the page.

But he still hated to study, unless it involved a pretty girl taking off a piece of clothing every time he got a right answer, the way it had when he'd studied for the firefighter exam. No wonder Brody had given him this assignment. His mentor was making him work for his reinstatement.

He closed the binder with a sharp snap, and coughed at the puff of dust that rose into the air. Brody hadn't given him a time limit. He'd done enough studying for one day.

He clicked on the TV with his remote control. Channel Six's midday newscast, the Sunny Side of the News, was on. Ella Joy's exquisite face appeared next to a graphic of a gas pump. Since when had Ella Joy come back to San Gabriel? Last he'd heard, she'd gone to Los Angeles to become a superstar. He shrugged. Another in the long list of women who'd gone for him because of his looks.

In his mind, Katie's face took the place of Ella

Joy's. He'd like to see Katie read the news. He pictured her, hair shoved behind her ears, eyebrows drawn together.

In other news, this story is a load of crap, she'd say indignantly. *I can't believe they're making me read this. Who writes this stuff?* And she'd fling off her microphone and storm off the set.

He chuckled. For some reason, thinking about Katie always cheered him up. She made him laugh. She was so completely herself, without apology. Hostile, unfriendly, clueless about how to run a bar, yet throwing herself completely into it anyway. He could think about her, off and on, for hours on end without getting bored. He still remembered the feel of her eager mouth on his. Still tasted her sweetness, like honeysuckle with a dash of vodka.

Katie was sticking with her business-only policy, but he had a feeling it was harder than she'd expected. He'd caught her checking out his ass the other day when he'd bent down to pick up a case of rum. And every time he talked to a girl at the bar, he felt Katie get antsy.

Ella Joy reached the part of the news where she talked about random ridiculous things, in this case a water-skiing squirrel caught on tape. That meant the newscast was almost over. His shift started in an hour.

Fuck it. Might as well go in early.

Teasing Katie was guaranteed to be a lot more fun than reading about smoke ejectors and chain of command policies.

Katie drove up to the front curb of the Hair of the Dog, surveying it with new eyes. The squat little ramshackle building looked so out of place in this neighborhood. All the other buildings looked like they were deliberately keeping their distance from the bar. Milt and Myrna's Dry Cleaner's was separated from the Hair of the Dog by the width of two driveways and a cement block wall draped in jasmine vines. An empty lot covered in brown grass and cigarette butts stretched behind the bar. People used it as a parking lot, even though it had never been paved. It doubled as an outdoor smoking room now that smoking was banned in California bars.

If a fire struck the Hair of the Dog, chances were good that no other buildings would be harmed. After all, the fire station was pretty close. A throng of firefighters would probably show up in minutes.

Was she actually considering the idea that had come to her yesterday in her father's study?

She shivered, picturing flames licking up the outside of the Hair of the Dog's wooden façade. The boards looked like they were already torched, even though she knew it was just black paint. Maybe she could save the sign that her father had commissioned, with the silhouette of a Great Dane howling the name of the bar. If she took it down before the fire started, would that be considered suspicious? She didn't know much about these things, but she was pretty sure it had to look like a complete accident.

One thing was certain. She needed to talk to someone first, someone she trusted.

She got out of her Datsun, slung her backpack over one shoulder, and walked toward the bar, her feet dragging. The bar was such a staple of her life. For years it had been there in the background, along with her tormenting older sister and her teasing twin brothers. It was part of the underlying static of irritation that she associated with her family, much as she loved them.

She stepped inside, squinting as always to prepare for the low light. Except this time she had to shield her eyes from the blinking fluorescent glare. Someone had turned on the overhead lights. Maybe the cleaning company hadn't gotten the message that she couldn't afford them anymore.

And what was that smell? Disinfectant? It smelled like strong bleach. And that strange sound? Music. Rolling Stones, as a matter of fact. Someone was blasting the radio and singing along at the top of their lungs.

A male someone. Then she spotted him.

Ryan, wearing his usual worn jeans and T-shirt, an apron wrapped around his middle, was pushing a mop across the floor in time to "Satisfaction."

He sang along, moving his hips and swirling the mop into the far corner. She watched in utter, slack-jawed fascination. He encountered something too sticky for the mop and whipped a tool from his pocket, clicked it so a knife popped out, and bent down to pry the gunk off the floor. As he did so, his T-shirt stretched across his wide shoulders and she caught a vulnerable sliver of untanned skin just under its top edge.

The sticky thing gave up easily, and Ryan stood and flicked it into an empty industrial-size pickle relish container.

"What are you doing?" she shouted over the music.

He jumped and turned to face her. He reached over to an ancient boom box on the nearest table and turned down the music. A smile lit his summer-blue eyes. "Can I carry your books for you, boss?"

God, he was cute. "Very funny. Why are you cleaning the floor?"

"Because it's outright disgusting. You should see some of the things I found." He kicked the relish container toward her.

She shuddered. "I believe you. But why mess with it? No one's giving us the white glove test."

"Where I come from, it's important to keep things orderly. Clean and orderly. A mess can cost lives."

She frowned. "I thought you were from Fresno."

"Yeah. Well, it's what I've learned since then. I've been meaning to do this since I started. Today I got inspired and decided to come in early and knock it out."

"Well, knock it off. It doesn't need to be clean." Not if she was going to burn the place down.

A puzzled look crossed his beautiful face. He leaned on the mop and gazed closely at her. "What's wrong?"

"Nothing." She gripped her backpack and stepped carefully across the floor. The last thing she wanted to do was fall on her ass in front of Ryan.

"Watch your step, floor's still wet in spots. Seriously, what's up?"

"Nothing. Is the coffee started?"

"Yes, boss."

"You can knock that off too." She hopped from one dry spot to the next.

"But what about that boss-employee relationship of ours?"

She shot him a scathing look. She didn't buy his innocent act for a second. The man enjoyed teasing her far too much. "Don't forget the firing aspect of being a boss."

He ducked his head, looking wounded. "You'd

fire me for mopping the floor? I thought you'd like it. I thought it'd be a nice surprise for a Thursday."

She waited for him to break into that playful laugh of his. But his shoulders drooped, his foot scuffed the floor. She'd hurt his feelings. Why did she always have to be so harsh?

"It's a great surprise, Ryan. I really appreciate it. I don't think anyone's mopped the floor in years, not even the cleaners, back when we had them." She took an impulsive step toward him and in the next instant realized two things.

First, he wasn't hurt—he was laughing at her, the jerk. Second, she was now airborne.

The room spun around her head like a fluorescent kaleidoscope. She spotted a couple limp balloons left over from Doggies' Night. And then Ryan's face filled her field of vision. She felt his hand grab her arm with a grip so strong it reversed her course through the air and plopped her on her feet. He didn't let go until she'd stopped swaying and could stand on her own.

Then he still didn't let go. He gazed down at her with worried eyes. "Are you all right?"

Light-headed, for sure. But that might be from standing this close to him again, the way she'd fantasized so many times since that one night.

"I-I don't know. My knee is—" She broke off with a moan.

"Your knee? Hang on."

He picked her up in both arms, cradling her like a baby, and picked his way across the floor. His chest felt so warm and hard against her side. His heartbeat thumped steadily under her ear.

She moaned even louder. "And my ankle's throbbing."

"Oh shit. I'm sorry, Katie. I shouldn't have let you cross that floor until it was dry. This is all my fault. Do you want me to call a doctor? Paramedics? You should get some ice on it right away."

She burst out laughing. "You should see your face right now. You look like you just ran over a kitten."

"You . . ." His mouth dropped open. His eyes darted to meet hers with a blue flash of surprise. "You got me. You got me good."

She giggled up at him. Boy, it felt good to turn the tables on him. He didn't know about the two brothers who had given her a crash course in being teased.

"I ought to drop you in the mop bucket for that. Or . . ."

She caught her breath as his eyes darkened to a deep cobalt. "Or what?"

"I'll think of something." He bent his head down so his mouth hovered over hers. Oh Lord, he was going to kiss her. Good thing he still held her in his arms, because her knees had already gone liquid. Her eyes half closed as the memory of their last kiss shivered through her. It was going to happen again, just as she'd hoped during all the restless nights since then. His lips drew closer. Hers tingled in anticipation. He'd probably start gently, touching his lips lightly against hers until she sighed and opened her mouth. Then he'd—

"Katie? What the fuck is going on?"

Ryan's head jerked up. Katie closed her eyes, wanting to cry. How had she managed to forget that she'd asked Doug to meet her at the bar before it opened?

Ryan put her down. "She slipped and nearly fell. Watch the wet floor if you're coming in."

Doug ignored him and looked at Katie. She sighed. "I'll be right there." Part of her wished she could talk to Ryan about her idea instead of Doug. But could she trust him? She'd known him only a few days. She snagged her backpack off the floor. "If I'm not back by opening time, can you handle things, Ryan?"

"Sure thing." He turned his back on the two of them.

"Nice apron, dude," said Doug, with what sounded like a snicker. Ryan didn't seem to hear. Katie never thought she'd actually dislike her ex-boyfriend, but in that moment, she did.

Nevertheless, Katie took Doug to Starbucks, picked a table in the corner, and told him her idea. She'd decided to tell him because he was a master of the wet blanket. Surely he'd talk her out of it, just as he'd scorned graduate school and the band competitions she'd wanted them to enter.

"Set fire to the Hair of the Dog?"

"I know, it's crazy. You're right."

"Crazy can be good." He gestured with his straw for her to continue, spattering drops of iced tea across the table.

"The thing is, my dad would get a million dollars from the insurance company. He could go buy a condo in Baja and retire. He'd never have to worry about the bar again."

Doug pursed his lip thoughtfully. "Million bucks. Your family would be set for life."

"We're only about ten blocks from the fire station. I figure nothing too bad can happen before the fire truck gets there. But the place is in such bad shape, the insurance company will call it a loss."

"Like a totaled car."

"Exactly. We don't have anything valuable at the bar. Even the computer in the back is ten years old. The cash register is a relic. There's nothing in the place that's worth hanging on to."

"So what's the catch?"

"Well, it's dangerous. Illegal."

"Meh." Doug shrugged. "Not if we do it right."

"We?"

Doug scrawled demon faces on his cast with a black Sharpie. "It would give me something to do while I can't work."

"Yeah," she said dubiously. His position at the Hair of the Dog was completely unnecessary. He didn't know it, but she took his salary out of her own.

"What about that bartender?" Doug clearly couldn't bring himself to say Ryan's name. "He could help."

"I barely know the guy. He might be a . . . an undercover cop for all I know. I can't take that chance. If I even decide to do this."

Doug looked happy with that answer, or as happy as Doug ever looked. "Then we can do it together. It'll be like before."

"Doug. You know we're in a new phase of our relationship now."

"The friend phase," he said sullenly.

"Yes. I'll always be your friend, Doug. You know I care about you."

She wanted to put her hand on his, but she knew it was a slippery slope. She'd had to institute a no-physical-contact policy after the last time she'd hugged him and he'd put his hand on her breast.

"I always thought we'd end up together." His voice dropped further into moroseness.

Katie gritted her teeth. When Doug sulked like this, she used to be terrified that he was relapsing. Now she knew better, knew how he used his moods to get a reaction, and all she wanted to do was get the hell out. Go crank some Rolling Stones or something.

"Who knows where we're going to end up? We're still young. But I know we'll always be friends."

"Let me do it," he said suddenly. "You've always been there for me. I'll do this for you."

"I didn't mean for you to—"

"I want to. It might be hard for you, with all the history there."

Katie was surprised into silence. Moments like this made her remember why they'd been together. Unless . . .

"Um . . . I'm not going to sleep with you," she said cautiously.

He rolled his eyes. "I got that part. We're in a new phase of our relationship. The criminal phase." A spark of humor lit his muddy brown eyes. He almost looked like the cute, gangly-geeky teenager she'd once fallen for.

He lifted his cast and showed her the flames he'd drawn around the demon faces.

She snorted. "Very funny."

He clutched at his arm with a fake look of agony. "It burns, it burns!"

"Stop that. No one's going to get burned." She shivered. That sounded a little too much like famous last words. "You'd have to do it early in the day when no one's around. Like, for miles."

"Exactly what I was thinking. I'll check at the fire station first and make sure the fire engines are there."

"That makes sense." She hadn't even thought of that. Maybe Doug did know what he was doing. Then she shook her head, feeling a little sick. "It's too crazy. Forget it. I don't know what I was thinking."

"You're *over*thinking, Katie. You always do that. No one's going to miss the place. Think about how relaxed your dad would be if he didn't have to worry about it anymore. Your mom told me the bar actually gave him that heart attack."

No wonder her parents hadn't seemed upset about yesterday's fire. Doug was right. What was she so worried about? Katie steeled herself. "As long as no one is hurt, it's a victimless crime, right?"

"Exactly," Doug, the lawyer's son, sounded utterly confident. "Don't worry. Remember the extensive Boy Scout training my father forced me into? I still remember the important stuff. I can start fires and dig a snow cave in the wilderness."

"I feel better already."

Chapter Eight

Once again, Ryan woke up with every intention of studying the San Gabriel Fire Department's Manual of Operations. He even spread it open on his knees while he ate his fried eggs and rye toast. But all he did was get crumbs between the pages. Who could worry about details like the various diameters of hoses when he could look forward to teasing Katie?

He still hadn't gotten a chance to interrogate her about Doug. The guy gave him a bad feeling. The possessive, smirky look on Doug's face when they'd left together rubbed him wrong. He wanted to make sure Katie knew she deserved better, but the bar kept him too busy. Business was picking up and the clientele was improving, at least from his perspective. Not that he didn't enjoy the Drinking Crew. But you wouldn't find him complaining about adding females to the mix.

He abandoned the manual and decided he might

as well head to the bar. He'd gotten into the habit of showing up an hour early. Once Katie had clarified that she wouldn't pay him for the extra time, she didn't seem to object. It gave him a chance to put things into the kind of order he appreciated after his years at the firehouse. If Katie showed up to do paperwork or shoot the shit with him, all the better. He found himself looking forward to that part of his day more than any other.

He chose not to investigate the reason why.

He found Katie banging around in the small kitchen behind the bar. They didn't really use the kitchen anymore—it was left over from the days when the Hair of the Dog used to serve "Great Dane Burgers" and "Golden Retriever Fries." Apparently the menu items had attracted attention from animal rights groups. Instead of renaming them, Katie's father had ranted about the modern-day lack of sense of humor and stopped serving food altogether.

The back door stood open, letting the hot midday air into the kitchen from the vacant lot out back. Katie stood at the long stainless steel counter next to the gas range. She was making a pile of big aluminum pots, stacking one inside the other. He took a moment to take in her appearance. She wore shorts with frayed edges. Her bare legs looked moon-pale, as if they hadn't seen the sun lately. Maybe he ought to chase her around a beach for a while.

But even though the color of her legs would frighten a blind man, he had to admit their shape was just about perfect.

"Top of the morning to you, boss. What are you doing? Are we bringing back the lunch specials?"

She whirled around. "What are you doing here?"

"Do I have to explain it every single time?"

"I mean, this early. I told you to sleep in today. You've been working too hard."

True, she had told him that. But, frankly, he'd rather do just about anything than face that damn manual. "I want to see if I can get that old jukebox going. This place could use some music."

She gave him an exasperated look and plopped a lid on top of her pile of pots. "Why didn't I just hire Mr. Fix-It instead of a bartender?"

"Now you got both. Need a hand with those pots?"

"Nope." She took the lid off the pot, as if forgetting she'd just put it on a moment ago. What the heck was she doing? She sure was acting strange. So distracted. Maybe this wasn't the best time to tease her about Doug the One-Armed Bouncer.

He shrugged and went into the bar to tackle the jukebox. It sat near the front door, to the right, and many a time he'd seen people lean over it, pick out some tunes, then pour quarters into it, only to see them pour right out. He'd finally made Katie tape an "Out of Order" sign on it, but it always seemed to disappear. And in his opinion, a bar needed a soundtrack.

He'd brought his own toolbox with him, since he'd never managed to find one at the Hair of the Dog despite extensive searching. He dragged a table next to the jukebox, put his toolbox on it, and dug around until he found the right kind of screwdriver to remove the side panel of the machine. When he stood up, Katie was right next to him.

"Excuse me," he said politely, reaching past her to tackle the first screw.

"The stupid jukebox can wait. It's waited this long. And, honestly, if we play music people will start dancing. And that could lead to . . . Just leave it alone."

"Why?"

"Because I . . . um . . . I need you to run an errand."

Why did she sound so nervous? "Oh no. I'm a bartender. That means someone who tends the bar. And this jukebox is part of the bar and requires tending. It's been neglected. Like a lot of things around here."

He winked at her, just to see the flush rise in her cheeks. But for once she didn't react.

Instead she fiddled with the end of her ponytail. "Okay, it's not exactly an errand. I was going to see if you wanted to get some coffee with me."

Was that why she was so jittery? Because she wanted to ask him out for coffee? But when he looked at her closely, he saw no hint of flirtation. She wasn't putting the moves on him. Something else was going on.

"I'm already coffee-ed up, thank you."

She paced around in a little circle. Ryan smiled to himself. Whatever she was up to, it was bound to be entertaining. Maybe now was his moment to needle her.

"If you're needing some coffee, or some company, why don't you give your friend Doug a call?"

She jumped about a foot. Ryan congratulated himself; his instincts had been dead on.

"I'm sure he'll come running. Poor dude."

She pressed her lips together in a pink line. Katie was the only girl he knew who never wore so much as a dash of lip gloss. Maybe that's why her lips had tasted so fresh and delicious . . .

"You don't know what you're talking about."

"I'm talking about Doug. And you. Boys and girls. Birds and bees. I know the signs. That boy's into you." He lifted off the jukebox's side panel and peered at the mechanisms inside.

"For your information, not that it's any of your business, we have a platonic relationship. Friends only."

A thrill of satisfaction made him smile into the depths of the jukebox. That's what he'd wanted to know.

"Does he know that? Because I've seen the way he looks at you."

"He knows. Of course he knows. I've told him enough times. Look, this is stupid. End of conversation." She spun around and began straightening chairs around the tables.

Oh no, it wasn't. It was too much fun to end. "So he wants you, but you don't want him. That hurts. No wonder he always has that look in his eyes, like a beaten dog."

"Stop that! Doug is my best friend. He's always been there for me." A strange wave of wistfulness passed through him at those words. "We just don't make a good couple."

Ryan pulled his head from his inspection of the bowels of the jukebox. "That means you used to be a couple?"

Her face turned strawberry-red. "None of your business."

"Doug is your ex-boyfriend? And he works here because . . ." He shook his head. "Poor bastard. He wants back in."

"Shut up. Seriously."

"No wonder he looked like he wanted to shoot me yesterday. I had you in my arms."

"Because I slipped. That's all."

"Well, sure, but he didn't know that. He must

have thought I was coming on to you. Maybe he thought I was going to kiss you."

"That's ridiculous. I wouldn't have let you kiss me." She paused in the middle of moving a chair from one table to another.

Ryan took in her flushed face and furious expression. In his expert opinion, they'd been awfully close to another kiss. Until the ex-boyfriend had walked in. "Why not? You said Doug is your *ex*-boyfriend. I haven't seen any non-ex-boyfriends wandering around. Maybe Doug doesn't let them in the door. I gotta tell you, I'm not sure having an ex-boyfriend as your bouncer is good for your social life."

She raised the chair high. Her eyes shone with dark fury. She wouldn't . . . really, she wouldn't throw a chair at him, would she?

To be safe—and remembering that kick on the shin at their first meeting—he took his hands out of the jukebox and braced himself.

But it wasn't a flying piece of furniture that grabbed his notice. He sniffed, then sniffed again.

Smoke.

Not cigarette smoke, not normal smoke that might float through the air from time to time. This smoke came from a fire, and a close one.

"Did you turn something on in the kitchen?" he asked Katie.

Her expression went from furious to horrified in the space of a second. That was all the answer he needed. He pushed past her and ran across the room. He swung himself over the bar in a move he knew Brody would have yelled at him about. *Too risky, too much chance of injury, take the extra second and run around the bar.* He flung open the swinging door that separated the bar from the kitchen.

Smoke and flames billowed from the gas range. One of the burners had been turned too high, and the flame must have caught the edge of the dish towel that was now a piece of black, nearly incinerated debris. From the dish towel it had managed to find a roll of paper towels, which now burned ferociously. The breeze from the back door fed the flames and sent scraps of burning paper all over the kitchen.

He scanned the kitchen. Not a lot of fuel for the fire to feed on. No more dish towels or paper products nearby. But if there was the tiniest hint of a leak in the gas line that fed the range . . .

He didn't have to look for the fire extinguisher. Out of long habit, he'd located all three of the bar's extinguishers as soon as he'd started working here. Unfortunately the one in the kitchen was mounted next to the back door, on the wall on the other side of the stove. He knew what Brody would say. *Go around. Run out the front door, around to the back door where you can reach the fire extinguisher without getting too close to the fire.*

But in emergency situations, Ryan's brain moved at a speed beyond logic. It performed calculations, measured risks, and decided what to do without much conscious input from him. He knew himself, knew how fast he could move.

Besides, Brody wasn't here. And he was on a leave of absence.

Quickly he pulled his shirt up to protect his mouth and nose, shielded his face with his arm, and dashed across the room. The heat seared his sleeve as he passed the fire. He snatched the fire extinguisher off the wall, aimed it at the flames, and pulled the pin.

Nothing came out.

Goddamn it, didn't they keep their fire extinguishers charged? He couldn't take the time to run back into the bar and find another one. Not even Brody would expect that. He ripped the shirt off his back. Lucky he'd worn a long-sleeved overshirt today. He tossed it on top of the fire. It dampened the flames for a moment, but not enough. In another second, the fire would consider his shirt fuel. He tore off his T-shirt and threw it on top of his shirt.

That slowed the flames enough so he could cross to the sink and turn the faucet on high. He grabbed one of the pots Katie had been piling up and filled it until he saw the flames starting to eat through his T-shirt. Hurrying, he dumped the half-filled pot of water on the flames.

"Katie, come help!" He figured it was safe enough now to get her involved.

"Right here." She appeared at his elbow.

"Keep filling pots of water. As fast as you can."

They worked without talking for the next few frantic moments, Katie filling pots of water and Ryan dumping them on the range, on the counter, everywhere a piece of burning paper had landed. He wanted to make sure every speck of fire had been extinguished. He knew all too well how dangerous kitchen fires could be. He'd seen entire homes destroyed by an initially innocent-looking grease fire.

When they were done, the kitchen was drenched, and so was he. He looked as if he'd just walked through a car wash. Katie stared at the mess, looking all shaken up. He almost felt sorry for her, but not sorry enough to spare her the lecture she had coming.

Katie made herself look at the sodden, blackened kitchen for two good reasons. First, so she couldn't escape the consequences of what she'd set in motion. Second, so she didn't stare too hard at Ryan's bare chest. She knew it was wrong to ogle someone in the midst of a crisis. But good Lord, the way he'd jumped into action, his swiftness, the way he'd stripped his shirt—two shirts—off his body without a second thought . . . well, she'd nearly melted along with the paint on the walls.

"Katie. Katie. Look at me."

She couldn't. She was afraid of what her face would reveal. But then she didn't have a choice, because he was standing right in front of her with both hands on her shoulders. He smelled like smoke. God, that fire had come so close to burning him. She shuddered.

"Did you leave a burner on?" he demanded, in a voice that held not one shred of its usual playfulness.

She bit her tongue. Of course she hadn't left a burner on. But the less she said about the origins of the fire, the better.

"Forget the burner. I'll give you the benefit of the doubt on that one. But Christ, Katie, don't you know you're supposed to keep your fire extinguishers ready? You're supposed to test them every year."

"No one does that."

"You're going to. From now on."

She opened her mouth to ask what made him think he was in charge, and why did he seem to know so much about fire extinguishers, but then she remembered the sight of him running *into* the flames and snapped her mouth shut.

But he still wasn't done. "Do you hear what I'm telling you?"

"Yes," she ground out. "Keep the fire extinguishers up to date."

"And don't leave burners on."

"I won't. I promise."

He gazed down at her with a suspicious expression. His hands felt strong and warm on her shoulders. Tendrils of awareness filtered through her entire body. "Why aren't you arguing?"

"Well." Blunt as she was, it went against the grain to withhold the truth. "I want to argue with you. But whenever I try, I get a picture of you nearly getting burned to death." She ducked her head to hide the tears that suddenly, annoyingly, sprang to her eyes. "I'm sorry, Ryan."

"I didn't nearly burn to death, silly." He squeezed her shoulders. The sternness left his voice, and something husky and tender took its place. "At most, I might have gotten a scorch mark here or there."

"And your clothes . . ." She risked a look at his chest. His naked, muscular, intoxicating chest that was so close she could lick it if she stuck out her tongue.

"You owe me for that. Shirt for a shirt. Come on, hand it over."

What? Did he expect her to . . . ? She jerked her head up to blast him, but right away caught that teasing look that came so easily to him. One blue eye gave her a slow wink.

"Totally inappropriate," she told him, without conviction.

"Hey, I just survived a fiery inferno. Cut me some slack."

"Fiery inferno? A dish towel caught on fire."

"Don't forget the roll of paper towels that made the ultimate sacrifice."

She snorted. With the responsible part of her mind, she knew she ought to clean up this mess before customers showed up. But it felt so good to stand here with his hands on her shoulders. It felt so good to be teased again by Ryan. Ryan, who hadn't burned to death in the fire Doug had set.

As soon as she saw Doug, she was going to tell him to forget the whole thing. Bad, bad idea.

They heard the creaky sound of the front door, followed by a series of light footsteps. Ryan took his hands away and stepped back. "I'd better put that jukebox back together."

"But—"

"And you should clean up back here. And get those fire extinguishers taken care of."

"But—"

He was already pushing open the swinging door. She winced as he disappeared into the bar and waited for the inevitable. And then it came. A cascade of female shrieks of appreciation at the sight of a shirtless Ryan. A "yeah, baby." A "woo-hoo" or two. Lots of breathless laughter and some enthusiastic hooting and hollering.

The door swung open again and Ryan reappeared, red-faced and embarrassed. "Permission to go home and find another shirt, boss."

"And ruin all the fun?"

"My pants got wet too. Can't work in wet pants." He put his hands to the button fly of his jeans.

"Go, go," she squeaked, afraid she'd faint dead away if she saw any more bits of Ryan naked.

"Fire extinguishers," he reminded her as he left through the back door.

Right. Fire extinguishers. Too bad they didn't work on the kind of fire Ryan sparked inside her.

Chapter Nine

His old friend, *fire*. Ryan remembered with perfect clarity the last fire he'd faced. After the blonde girl had rung the station's doorbell and he'd jumped into the plug-buggy, it had turned out the fire had been set by the girl's aunt, who had a mental disturbance and was now defending the blazing house with a rifle. She'd aimed a bullet at the plug-buggy, nearly nailing Ryan. He had no idea Ginny, hiding inside, had been injured until much later. By the time the police arrived, the plug-buggy was destroyed. Ryan figured his career was too.

If it weren't for Brody, it would have been. But Brody had allowed him a second chance.

It had been a year and a half since he'd felt the adrenaline rush that came with the living presence of a fast-growing fire. He loved fires. He respected fires. He didn't fear fires, unless that full-body alertness could be called fear. Around a fire, every one of his senses became totally aware. No bit of information escaped his notice. Everything seemed to slow down into another dimension, one in which he had plenty of time to do what needed to be done.

He'd been told that he moved with unreal speed while fighting fires—or fighting, for that matter—but it didn't feel that way to him. He felt he moved at his normal relaxed pace, but the world slowed down to meet him. Or maybe it was more that time wasn't a factor when he was grappling with a fire.

He loved fire. Fire was like a soul brother to him. He understood fire at a gut level, the suddenness of it, its out-of-control nature, its fierce need to grow and consume. He had that same fire inside him. Sometimes the fire got out of its cage. Then it had to be hunted down and captured.

Putting out a fire always left him with a bittersweet sadness afterward.

In his little bungalow that night, he went from one window to the next until he'd opened them all. A current of cooling air flowed through the place, stirring the fringe on the floor lamp one of his exes had given him in the hopes that if she moved some furniture in, she would be next. He closed his eyes, feeling the evening wind on his face.

Fire. Fighting that fire in the kitchen of the Hair of the Dog, without any equipment, any support, any of the trappings of a fire department, had been like a wake-up slap in the face. He was a firefighter. When he was eye to eye with a fire, things felt right.

The manual lay where he'd left it, on the floor next to his kitchen table. He walked into the kitchen and stood over it. This pile of binders stood between him and his rightful destiny. He nudged them with his toe. Between a fire that could potentially kill him and this hunk of paper, he'd take fire. But he didn't have a choice.

He bent down and picked up a binder.

"*No. Not again.* Ryan nearly got burned."

Doug loped next to Katie as she walked down the street later that night. "I didn't mean for that to happen."

Katie noticed he didn't sound very regretful. "Didn't you know we were in there?"

"I didn't see your car."

"I left it at the oil change place."

"I didn't know that. I yelled into the bar, but no one answered."

"We were up at the front by the jukebox." Completely caught up in their own conversation, she remembered. About kissing.

"I should have checked better. I will next time."

"No next time."

"How're you going to pay the bills then?"

Very good question. Another bill had arrived yesterday. Apparently they owed Southern California Electric for two months of power, and the company wasn't at all happy about it. If the power got shut off, that would be it for the Hair of the Dog. They already kept the lights as low as possible. Any lower and customers would have to bring flashlights.

She could always fork over her grad school money, such as it was. But her entire savings would cover only a couple of weeks of bar expenses. That math felt like a nail in her coffin. She'd found grad school much less thrilling than anticipated, though she'd never confess that to her parents. She'd considered using the money to travel, but maybe instead it would pay for beer and electricity. Not too depressing.

Her cell phone rang.

"Katie, what happened at the bar today?" Her mother. Damn, she should have called before wild rumors started flying.

"Oh, nothing. Little fire. No harm done."

"Oh. The bar's okay." Her mother relayed that fact to someone off the phone. There was that same tone again. Disappointment.

"I should have called you earlier. It took me a while to clean up, and—"

"Honey, it doesn't matter." Her mother cut her off. "I called to make sure you're fine. For a moment I thought we were rid of the place for good. But nothing's that easy, right?"

"Right." There it was. Proof her parents would approve of her plan. Or at least her mother would. "Is Dad upset?"

"No, as long as you're fine. He's been working on that absurd mini golf course in the backyard. Ridiculous, but it keeps him happy. And it keeps his blood pressure down."

"Can't wait to see that."

"It has garden gnomes in it. It's beyond belief. He's calling it Hair of the Gnome to keep it in the family. We'll see you on Sunday."

She hung up and realized they'd nearly passed the shop where she'd left her car that morning. Her Datsun sat forlornly in the back lot. Everyone had left for the night. Hopefully they'd left the keys under the floormat as requested.

"Everything okay?"

Katie glanced up at Doug. The neon light of the

"Mr. Tune-Up" sign created a strange yellow reflection in his eyes. He looked mysterious, different, unlike the boy she'd grown up with. "Yeah, fine. My mom wishes the bar had burned down."

"See? It's a good plan, Katie."

Maybe it was, after all. She barely knew anymore. Ryan's lecture kept ringing in her ears, but if no one was put in danger . . . "I'll set the fire myself."

"Oh, come on, Katie. Give me another chance. I'll do it in the middle of the night. I'll check every single corner of the bar first. I'll put 911 into my speed dial. The fire department will be there in two minutes."

It sounded harmless the way he put it. But still, the sight of those flames licking at the hood over the range had really rattled her. "Why do you care? Are you turning into a firebug?"

"You stood by me when I was in the hospital. I want to make it up to you."

He smiled like the sweet boy she remembered, before all the crap, the hospital, the guilt trips, the manipulations. Despite herself, she swayed toward him. In some ways Doug wasn't so bad. He'd never even flirted with another girl. He was as faithful as a dog. So what if he tried to control her by playing the victim? Maybe it was because he loved her so much.

Her chest bumped against his ribs. No fire raced through her veins, the way it did with Ryan. Doug leaned his head down with puppy dog eagerness. No wave of dizzying excitement transported her into delirium. She saw a gleam of saliva inside his mouth, and noticed a hair follicle on his upper lip that had developed a pimple.

Nausea clutched at her stomach. She stepped back. No way could she kiss Doug. Never again could she kiss him.

"Sorry. I-I'm really tired," she murmured.

"Sure. I get it." Disappointment curled his mouth down at the corners.

"Sorry," she said again.

"It's fine. I'll live."

No thanks to her, his tone implied. She shook off the familiar annoyance and walked to the driver's side door of her car.

"What about the other thing?" he called across the empty lot. At least he was smart enough not to yell the word "fire."

Katie felt under the floor mat and found her car keys. The resignation in her mother's voice came back to her. *Nothing's that easy, right?*

She straightened up and looked back at Doug, who stood hunched under the streetlight where she'd left him. God, how she longed for something new. No more Hair of the Dog hanging around her neck. No more ex-boyfriend hanging around any part of her.

"I don't know, Doug, I think it should be me."

"You don't trust me. I don't blame you." He hung his head. *Crap.* Was she messing with his self-esteem? She couldn't kiss him. But if he really wanted to set the fire, why not let him? Maybe it would give him a confidence boost.

"Okay, you can give it one more try. But you have to make one hundred thousand percent sure no one's around. I mean, seriously. Or I'll never forgive you."

He perked up so quickly, she realized he'd played her. "It'll work. I promise. I have a plan."

She started her car to mask her grumble of annoyance. The urge to scream out of the parking lot and leave Doug in the dust was nearly irresistible. Instead she stopped next to him like a good little girl. "Need a ride home?"

He perked up even more. "Thanks."

One thought pounded through her mind as she drove him home. Would she ever escape?

It was the strangest thing. Ever since that incident in the kitchen, the Hair of the Dog was plagued with one fire after another. Ryan, with his sixth sense when it came to fires, managed to put out every one.

The second fire happened late one night soon after that first one. Ryan hadn't been able to sleep after a long shift at the bar—and a long day of being around Katie. He'd decided to go for a late-night run. He loved running at night because the air wasn't so brutally hot. As if drawn by some magnetic force, he'd modified his course to cruise past the Hair of the Dog.

Automatically he looked for Katie's Datsun. Of course it wasn't there. She was probably in bed by now. Did she sleep curled up in a ball, or did she fling her arms and legs every which way? What did she wear to bed? Anything? His pleasant fantasy broke off when he saw smoke seeping through the edges of the front door.

He knew right away the fire wasn't fully engaged. From the lackadaisical quality of the smoke, it had probably just started. But still, the door would be too hot to touch, and he couldn't risk opening it without his gear on. He ran around the back and kicked open the back door. He grabbed the fire extinguisher off the wall—he'd checked it himself the day after the first fire—and ran through the dark interior toward the flicker of flame beginning to feel its strength.

It took only a few seconds to put it out. He turned the lights on and examined the area. An ancient floor fan lay on its side, a frayed, scorched electrical cord in two severed pieces next to it. He remembered someone complaining about the heat earlier that day. Katie must have set up this fan and forgotten to unplug it at the end of the day. It must have fallen, somehow catching the cord and sparking a fire.

He scolded Katie about that the next day. She merely pressed her lips together and listened stoically. Afterward, she went into the kitchen and banged some stuff around.

That girl did not like to be lectured. He didn't enjoy doing it, but when someone was a magnet for disaster like Katie, and when the thought of that person being harmed, by fire or otherwise, made him unaccountably anxious, a lecture was required.

The next fire happened a couple of days later, very early in the morning. He'd gotten to work early to clean the espresso machine. In his opinion, a functional piece of coffeemaking equipment was essential for a place like the Hair of the Dog. He didn't mind getting people drunk, but he wanted them to leave the place on their own two feet.

Knowing it would take hours to clean it properly, he'd arrived around six in the morning with a thermos of coffee and a bag of mini muffins. His head had been deep in the murky depths of the espresso machine when he heard an unfamiliar noise in the kitchen. It had taken a few minutes to extricate himself, then he'd hurried through the swinging door. A blast of heat stopped him in his tracks. The ancient, greasy old curtain at the kitchen window had caught fire.

And the fire extinguisher was nowhere to be seen.

Didn't matter. He reached back inside the bar for his thermos and doused the flames with a waterfall of black coffee.

What the fuck was going on here?

He cornered Katie later that day, right before Happy Hour. "I think someone's trying to set fire to the Dog."

"Don't be ridiculous."

"Three fires in one week. That's not normal."

"Nothing here is normal." She waved her arm at the motley collection of customers at the bar. Mr. Burwell was talking to his oxygen tank. Archie was writing a poem in tiny letters on a bar napkin. He'd been sulking ever since the real estate guy had hooked up with the office supply guy. Next to him, a sultry brunette checked her lipstick in a heart-shaped pocket mirror.

"I won't argue with that. But you should consider hiring an overnight security guard."

She snorted. "Sure. Right after I redo the floors and put in central air conditioning."

He shook his head at her stubbornness. He knew Katie had a lot to deal with. Her family had dumped the bar on her and no one ever seemed to help her out. The Hair of the Dog took up all her time. She was so smart, she could be doing anything. Instead she was always here, pouring her fierce energy into a lost cause.

That night he decided to play security guard himself. He chose a spot in the shadow of the Dumpster in the vacant lot behind the bar. The nearest streetlight was on the other side of the lot, so he would be invisible to anyone sneaking up to the back door. After kicking aside an old Coke can and some broken glass, he wrapped himself in a blanket and sat down on the grass. He rested his back against the chain-link fence and settled down to wait. He had a good view of the back door, although until the moon rose it would be hard to make out any details. The quiet of the sage-scented San Gabriel night settled around him.

Why would anyone want to burn down the Hair of the Dog? One suspect popped immediately to mind. Doug, the bouncer and ex-boyfriend. He'd gotten a bad feeling about the guy from day one. Something about him didn't sit right with Ryan. But what motive would he have for burning down the Dog? Revenge for getting dumped by Katie?

He'd encountered dumber reasons for starting fires. People got stupid about fire.

If Doug was setting the fires, Ryan would have to beat some sense into him. That part, he looked forward to. Doug rubbed him the wrong way, always hanging around the bar with that annoying mopey look, as if the world owed him something. As if Katie owed him something.

When Doug showed up at the bar, Katie changed. She got quieter, and no matter how much Ryan teased her, her usual snappy spirit didn't return until Doug left. Then she'd get back in the swing of things, answering his jabs with zingers of her own.

Working with Katie was even more fun than a game of beach volleyball. With girls in bikinis. And a cooler of Corona waiting at the sidelines.

His eyes drifted shut as he floated into a lovely dream in which Katie dove for the sand and landed in his lap, where she snuggled and tried to tickle him. Every time she touched his ribs, she made a tapping sound. Or maybe it was a glugging sound. *Tap-tap-glug-glug.*

Suddenly he came wide awake. Someone knelt by the back door. He couldn't make out details, all he saw was a black shape. The sharp, chemical scent of lighter fluid filled his nostrils. The *glug-glug* sound came from a bottle being emptied along the base of the wall.

Sheer insanity. What did this guy intend to do? Step back and toss a match? Then again, with this level of cluelessness, who knew what he'd try to do. Or when. Any minute now the idiot arsonist would light a match and get a face full of flames.

Even if the jerk deserved it, Ryan couldn't let it happen.

He scrambled to his feet, untangling himself from the blanket that had apparently been doubling as Katie in his dream. He launched himself at the black shape crouching outside the door. He heard an alarmed squeak as he hit the body and rolled with it over and over, pulling them both away from the trail of lighter fluid. In the back of his mind, he realized the body belonged to a small person, not a tall one like Doug.

"Are you insane? Are you trying to kill yourself? There's a lot better ways than that," he growled as they kept rolling.

When they stopped a safe distance from the bar, Ryan had the fire starter squashed under him like a bug. That's when he noticed that the person was really quite small. Was it a boy playing a prank? Did Doug have a younger brother he'd roped into this crime?

"Who are you?"

Another squeak made him realize he was probably cutting off the kid's air supply. He eased off a few inches.

The boy spoke in a strangled voice that didn't sound like a boy's at all. "You're smothering me, you big jerk! Get off me!"

Only one person talked to him like that.

Chapter Ten

Ryan rolled Katie over so he could see her face. The dim light from the corner streetlight revealed an indignant scowl. What right did she have to be angry?

"Would you stop crushing me?"

Oh. Right. He sat back, releasing her shoulders but keeping her legs in lockdown.

"What the hell were you doing, Katie?"

She stuck out her chin. "I forgot something in the bar. So I came back to get it."

He had to admire her bravado.

"Well, that explains everything. Especially the lighter fluid."

She blinked, looking disconcerted. "How'd you . . . Hey." She sat up and tried to free her legs. Nothing doing. He wasn't letting her go until he got some answers. "What are you doing here so late at night?"

"Security guard duty. Don't worry, I'll only charge you half my going rate. No overtime."

"Half . . . charge . . ." she spluttered. With a sudden twist of her tiny body, she managed to slide one leg out from under him. A foot, wearing a black Converse, planted itself in the center of his chest. "Let me go."

"Okay." He lifted his weight off her other leg. She sprang to her feet. At which point he picked her up by the back of her black sweatshirt and began hauling her toward the Hair of the Dog.

She kicked and squirmed the whole way. But Ryan didn't care how many bruises he got. He'd given up a perfectly good night's sleep, hung out next to a Dumpster, and he hadn't even gotten to beat up Doug. Explanations were required.

Katie didn't know why she bothered to struggle. Ryan was much stronger than she was, plus he had right on his side. But she didn't like feeling like a naughty child being hauled into the principal's office, so she fought him. When they reached the back door, Ryan finally let her feet touch the ground. He kicked dirt over the trail of lighter fluid.

"Help me," he ordered her.

Gritting her teeth, she followed his lead. Neither of them spoke until they were done.

"Key," he said, putting out his hand.

"Ryan, what is the point of this? You caught me. You can go home now. Let's all go to bed and forget about this."

Unfortunate phrasing. The darkness of the night, the presence of Ryan next to her, and the word "bed" combined to send a shiver up her spine.

"We can go to bed, but we're not going to forget about this. Key, please. Unless you want me to kick the door in."

Not another repair bill. She dug in her pocket and

came up with her key ring, which she childishly slammed into the palm of his hand.

"Ow," he said, very deliberately. "You really don't want to make me lose my temper here. I guarantee, it ain't a pretty sight."

"Fine. I apologize. Let's go inside, shall we, kind sir?"

She knew she was being ridiculous, but she couldn't seem to stop. A toxic mixture of relief and mortification made her want to pummel someone.

He opened the door and pulled her through into the kitchen. He threw the switch, flooding the kitchen with bright light that made them both blink.

"You know how in the movies they interrogate suspects with those floodlights in their faces?" Katie nodded warily. "Pretend we're in one of those."

"Okay." She squared off with him, legs apart, hands on fists. "What the hell are you doing skulking outside my bar without my permission after midnight?"

He laughed, but it wasn't his usual playful, teasing chuckle. It sounded more like the unamused bark of an army colonel.

"Cute. But get it straight, missy. I'm the cop in this movie. You're the suspect who's one joke away from getting reported to the police."

Katie paled. Would he do that? One look at his set, serious face told her he would. She'd never seen Ryan like this before.

"I don't want to call them in, but I will. When it comes to fire, I don't mess around. Are you the one who's been setting all the fires around here?"

Katie considered her options. Pretty simple, they came down to the truth or a lie. Or something in between. "Yes. I've been setting the fires."

"You're lying," he said instantly. "We were both here for that first one. Don't bother to lie. You're not good at it, Katie. Your neck is turning pink"—touching the side of her neck—"and you can't meet my eyes."

She tried to prove him wrong, but damn it, he was right. Her eyes kept sliding away from his and settling on the scorch marks on the yellowed plaster wall.

"I'm going to need the truth, here, Katie."

"Fine." Truthfully, getting caught was a relief. "This is the first fire I've tried to set. Doug did the others. But you kept putting them out. So I told him I'd take over. Is that it?"

She turned toward the back door. She really wanted a bath to get the smell of lighter fluid off her body. Disgusting stuff.

His strong hand clamped onto her shoulder and spun her around. A kind of savage glee shone in his eyes. "I knew it was Doug! Damn, I wish I'd caught him in the act instead of you."

"Why?"

"I've been wanting to kick his ass for a while."

"Don't you dare. He's very . . . um . . ."

"Whiny?"

"Fragile."

"Fragile?"

She had to laugh at the look on his face, as if he'd never heard that word applied to a man before.

"Don't distract me. Why are you and Doug trying to burn down the Hair of the Dog?"

His blue eyes, which didn't look summery anymore, but implacable as stone, drilled into hers. She hated how disapproving he looked. As if she'd suddenly forfeited every bit of good opinion he had about her.

"I have to," she said fiercely. "I can't pay the bills, the business is going under, and no one cares. Not even my dad. My father took out an insurance policy that says we get a million dollars if the place burns down."

"A million *dollars*?" He drew back in shock.

"Can you believe it? The Hair of the Dog is worth far more as a pile of ashes. So I decided that was the only thing that made sense."

"Made sense? So far I'm not hearing anything that makes sense. You're supposed to be afraid of fire. Does Smokey the Bear mean nothing to you?"

"It was scary at first. That time in the kitchen . . ." She shuddered. "After that, Doug promised to make sure no one was here. Except you kept showing up and putting out the fires. Why do you keep doing that?" Her voice rose. "You're messing everything up!"

"You know the phrase 'playing with fire,' right?" Ryan's eyes were now steel-blue.

"I'm not playing—"

"Fire is a dangerous motherfucker. You don't mess with fire." He punctuated each word with a poke at her chest.

"I wasn't messing—"

"That lighter fluid could have blown up in your face if it caught a spark from a cigarette butt. You know people go back there to smoke. If there's a leak in the gas line, the building could have exploded. You could easily be dead right now. Along with any homeless people who might be sacked out in the front doorway. And what about someone who happened to be walking their dog at that moment? Or teenagers making out in a car out front? What about them? What about the neighborhood? Does Milt and Myrna's deserve to burn down because you can't pay your bills?"

Katie flinched away from him. "That wouldn't happen. The fire station's really close. I was going to call 911 right away."

"Not if you're dead, you can't. And even if you did make the call, what if they're already working a fire somewhere else? They only have one engine and one truck. If they're both on the other side of town, it could take up to seven minutes to get a crew here from Camino Ranch. And those guys, believe me, you don't want them at your fire."

He snapped his mouth shut. She gaped at him in utter astonishment.

"How do you know all that stuff?"

"That's not the point."

"Oh my God. Are you a"—she dropped her voice in horror—"*fireman*?"

He snatched his hands off her shoulders, a deeply uneasy look darkening his handsome face. "I'm a bartender now."

"What about before you started here? Come on, I told you the truth."

"All right. I *was* a fireman."

She let out a spurt of giggles, then couldn't make it stop. They kept spewing out, giggle after hysterical giggle. "This could only happen at the Hair of the Dog. Try to burn the place down and it turns out the bartender has a secret identity as some super-dedicated fireman. I swear, this place has like nine hundred lives. My luck is incredible."

"Yes, it is." He speared her with more blue-eyed

fire. "Take it from a firefighter, burning down your bar is the worst possible idea. You should thank your guardian fairy angel godmother I happened to walk in here that day."

She gnawed at her lip. Easy for him to say, when he didn't have ten million bills to pay and a father to save from another heart attack. She let out a long breath and looked around the dingy, slightly charred kitchen. So the Hair of the Dog would live another day. "You want a drink?"

"Hell, yeah."

They sat together at the bar, with one candlelit red globe lantern between them. Katie opened a bottle of Glenfiddich and poured each of them a small glass.

"So when did you stop being a fireman?"

He sipped the scorching, golden liquid, which inspired images of rolling green hills and the Loch Ness monster. The scent of aged liquor blended with leftover eau de lighter fluid. "A year and a half ago. I took a leave of absence. Well, Brody told me to take it. And he was right to."

"Why? I bet you were pretty good."

"I was a wunderkind."

She looked at him with wide eyes.

"You surprised I know that word?"

One straight eyebrow lifted. "Why would I be surprised?"

"People don't usually give me credit for much of a vocabulary."

"I'm just surprised to hear it applied to fighting fires. You were some kind of precocious boy genius?"

"Yeah. I became a firefighter at the age of nineteen. Youngest ever in our department. I'm what they call a natural." He let out a deep breath. Confessing his true nature took a load off his mind—a load he hadn't even known he carried. He liked telling Katie who he really was. And hopefully impressing her.

"So then why'd you leave?" She examined him over the edge of her glass. Her eyes gleamed in the candlelight. He noticed a smudge of dirt on her jaw, which made him remember the feel of her small body fighting him like a wildcat.

He took a slug of the Scotch. "I made a stupid mistake. I used to be a jump-in-with-both-feet, figure-out-if-it-was-a-good-idea-later kind of guy. Turned out it wasn't a good idea."

"Where was that?"

"Here. San Gabriel. I've been a San Gabriel firefighter since the beginning." He couldn't keep the pride out of his voice.

"Seems like I would have seen you around. The firehouse is right nearby. Oh my God!"

He braced himself for the inevitable.

"You're one of the Bachelor Firemen! The ones they did all the stories about. I remember the camera crews coming and all the girls."

"We're not all bachelors. Captain Brody got married. Double D was married all along. And girls always like firemen. We're heroes." He winked at her, hoping to divert the conversation. "Especially when we put out fires all by ourselves, with our bare hands and no gear."

"Right. My hero." But the upturned corner of her lip counteracted her sarcasm.

"You know what they say. Firefighting—one of the few professions left that still makes house calls.

Or bar calls, in your case." He tipped his glass at her and took a long swallow.

She laughed, her face glowing in a way that made him twice as tingly as the Scotch. "Okay, so you took a leave of absence a year and a half ago, now you're back, and you only wanted a job here for a few weeks, so that means . . . you're going back to being a fireman?"

"Trying to. Have to jump through some hoops first. Captain Brody's a tough bastard."

"Should be no trouble for a wunderkind."

"Yeah."

Maybe it was the Scotch, and the rolling green hills, but it felt so good to sit here and talk to Katie about his life. She listened to him with her whole self, in that Katie way of hers, her black-clad body turned toward him, her eyes fastened on his face. He finished his Scotch and poured himself another finger.

"I don't get it," he mused.

"Get what?"

"You've got all this energy, all those brains packed into that adorable head of yours. Why do a bonehead thing like commit arson? Insurance companies have experts who know about things like lighter fluid."

Her face turned as red as the lantern and she shoved her hands in the pockets of her hoodie. "But unless they figure out I did it, we'd still be covered. At least, the way I read the policy."

"Those policies always have loopholes. And a million dollars is a lot of motivation to find one."

She worried at her bottom lip with her teeth, the way he'd seen her do in moments of stress. He put his hand to her mouth. She froze.

"Why do you want to chew those lips up, pretty as they are?"

She frowned. "Pretty?" He felt the soft movement of her mouth against his hand.

"Yes." He took his hand away so he could trace the line of her upper lip with his finger. "I like this curve right here, like a ski slope. I like how the bottom lip swells out. Like a cherry. Your lips are very, very pretty. Even when you're frowning at me." He let his hand drop.

She put her hand to her forehead as if to wipe away the frown. "You should see my sister."

"I've seen your sister. What about her?"

"Bridget came here?"

"Sure. Said she had to make sure you hadn't hired a psycho killer."

The frown came back, two little lines between her eyebrows. "And?"

"She was with another girl and they kept talking about a wedding."

"She's Meredith's maid of honor. It's basically the only thing she talks about anymore."

"They were discussing the bachelorette party, I believe." He felt quite proud of himself that he remembered so much detail. But Katie didn't seem satisfied.

"So what did you think? She's gorgeous, isn't she?"

He tried to remember. He'd been busy that day, and Bridget had hung around for a while wanting to chat. Really, he'd wanted to ask her to step behind the bar and help him out, but something about the way she refused to touch any of the bar stools and the wary glances she aimed at the Drinking Crew stopped him. "Black hair?"

"Yes."

"Eyes?"

A little smile tugged at her lips, which seemed to grow more enticing the more he looked at them. "She has eyes, yes. But they're not black."

He thought hard. Try as he might, he couldn't bring up a picture of Katie's sister. He gave up. "It was Happy Hour. You know how it gets then."

She shocked him by leaning in and planting a kiss on his cheek.

"What was that for?" Not that he minded, but it wasn't exactly typical Katie behavior.

"I don't know. For everything. Stopping that crazy-ass arsonist from burning us down."

"Promise you won't try that again."

She continued as if he hadn't spoken. "For doubling our clientele in the space of two weeks. Never mind that they're all women and mostly they drink club soda."

He eyed her suspiciously. Something told him she was thanking him for something else entirely, but what? He couldn't identify the gleam in her eyes. "Seems like all that ought to get me more than a peck on the cheek."

She fiddled with her glass and gave him a sidelong look. "Do you . . . um . . . want more?"

He planted one foot on the floor, hooked the other around the leg of his stool and scooted it next to hers. Their thighs touched. His groin jumped. "I seem to recall a kiss that went way past peck on the cheek."

"You remember that?" The light from the candle made her eyes look huge. They drew him in, closer and closer.

"I remember you tasted like honeysuckle. I remember we almost didn't stop there."

She swallowed. A shadow moved across her throat. He curved his hand around her warm neck. She tilted her head toward his hand, nestling it between her jaw and her shoulder. Did she want him to stop? He moved his fingers among the strands of satiny hair that had come loose from her ponytail. Her skin felt so delicate. Who would have guessed that scowling Katie would be so soft to the touch?

Maybe she used her frown to keep people from finding out.

Her lips opened on a sigh. Her eyes closed halfway and grew dreamy as he massaged the back of her neck.

"Sweet, delicious Katie, always hiding behind that frown."

Her scent—like wildflowers in sunshine, with a dash of lighter fluid—embraced him. He wanted to bury his face in her hair. He wanted to taste the tender skin of her neck, run his tongue across her collarbone. He wanted to feel her breasts under his hands. His palms still held the memory of those aroused points.

And then his hands were there, on her chest. Even through her sweatshirt and whatever she wore underneath, he felt her nipples rise. His groin tightened, hard. His breath came rough. He wanted her, not as a cute, tipsy stranger this time. He wanted her as Katie, the girl who kept popping into his mind at the oddest times. When he was studying . . . when he was topping off a mug of beer . . . when he was fielding phone numbers from ten beautiful women clustered at the bar.

It was true. Even when the former Miss Vidalia Onion Queen was scrawling her number on his hand in red lipstick, he'd thought of Katie and how she never wore stuff on her lips. Katie's lips didn't taste like some artificial, sickly-sweet, chemical concoction. They tasted real and fresh. Like flower petals warmed by sunshine.

He hovered over her parted lips, letting the anticipation build, craving the taste of wildflowers on his tongue. Then his mouth was on hers, her soft flesh eagerly parting under his invasion as he drank her in. The kiss went right to his head, more intoxicating than any liquor in the bar, any nectar on the planet. She tasted like no other woman in the world. She scrambled his brains, fired his blood, sizzled his senses.

And then it came to him.

He took his hands off her chest and sat back onto his stool. Katie's eyes snapped open and she let out a surprised little whimper of protest.

"What's wrong?"

He tried to answer, but she rushed right over him.

"Is it that whole boss-employee thing? Forget about that. We're off the clock right now. Besides, you're a hero, remember?" She grabbed him by the front of his shirt and tried to pull him in.

But now that he'd had his stroke of genius, he couldn't think of anything else. "I've got it, Katie. I figured out a surefire, guaranteed, can't-go-wrong way to bring some money into the bar. You won't have to break any laws or put a single homeless guy in danger."

Chapter Eleven

Bridget prowled before thirty sweaty women and two men arranged in rows and dressed in spandex. "Grapevine," she shouted. "Pick it up back there, Cindy." She checked her watch. The class was almost over. By the redness of her students' faces, she ought to slow things down anyway. She phased from her dominatrix voice to her Zen voice.

"Okay, people, good job, you're all rock stars. Let's start the cool down."

Thirty pairs of eyes rolled with relief. She checked her front-row regulars. Good, even they were breathing hard. When Lula Blue had gotten a good workout, Bridget knew she'd done her job. Porn stars took their exercise very seriously.

She was about to compliment Lula on her form when she realized the woman wasn't even paying attention to her anymore. Neither was anyone else. How strange. During step class, she was usually the object of the entire class's undivided focus. As if she were some combination of kindergarten teacher and prison torturer.

She turned to see what everyone was looking at and saw, of all people, her sister Katie standing just outside the glass door. Right next to that unbelievable hottie, Ryan, who worked at the bar.

Someone fell off a step stool.

"Focus, people. You know how important the cool down is. Take your time, let your heart rate return to normal, and I'll be back in a moment for our final stretches."

This better be good. Bridget walked toward Katie and the hunk, who aimed a sweet smile her way. She stubbed her toe on the gym floor, trying to identify what was off in that smile. Men came on to her all the time, but this guy didn't have that flirtatious look in his eye. And come to think of it, he was standing awfully close to Katie.

Had hell frozen over? Had the moon turned blue? She gave Katie a quick once-over. No, she hadn't suddenly started dressing to show off her petite figure, per Bridget's advice. She wore jeans rolled up at the ankles, black Converses, and a green and black boat-necked striped top. Granted, the green and black stripes set off the porcelain skin Bridget had always envied. But not to worry, Katie hadn't suddenly turned into a fashion queen. She was staring at the class, looking appalled.

"Stop making faces at my students, you're freaking them out," Bridget hissed at her.

"Sorry." Katie blinked. "Are they okay? Some of them look a little red in the face."

"It's called cardiovascular exercise. It's good for you. Builds your strength and stamina, right?" Bridget turned to Ryan with her best sexy smile.

He gave her a slow, blue wink that nearly stopped her heart. "You're the expert. Looks like you run a helluva class there. You'd have half my buddies in a puddle on the floor by now."

Bridget preened. "People think it's easy to teach exercise classes, but it's not. You've got people at all different levels, from superfit to"—she gave Katie a glance—"allergic to anything that's good for them."

"Hey," protested Katie.

Bridget kept her attention on Ryan. "I try to get her to take my class and eat healthy, I even got her a juicer, but she never, ever listens to me. Ever."

Katie stuck out her chin with that stubborn look that everyone in the family knew so well. "I don't like juice. I like milk shakes."

"Someday those milk shakes are going to start showing up on your thighs, and when they do, I'll have a front-row spot for you in my class."

Ryan cleared his throat. "We'd like to talk to you about something. Do you have some time after your class?"

Indulging in a moment of pure feminine appreciation, she let her eyes travel up his strong brown throat, to the clean line of his jawbone and the playful set of his mouth. Everything about him screamed good times. He'd be fun to flirt with, fun to hang around, fun in bed, fun every which way you cut it.

So why was Katie looking so grumpy?

"Fine, as long as Katie wipes that frown off her face."

"Katie?" Ryan nudged her.

Katie pasted a smile on her face. So her sister actually did what Ryan said. Interesting.

As Katie had warned, Bridget didn't react well to Ryan's idea.

"The Hair of the Dog? Meredith's bachelorette party? You have got to be kidding."

"I knew this was a stupid idea." Katie tried to jump off her bar stool, but Ryan snagged her by the belt loop and made her stay put. He kept his hand at her back to make sure she didn't bolt again—and to enjoy the feel of the silky sliver of skin between her jeans and her shirt.

"Hear me out." Ryan offered Bridget another paper cup full of wheatgrass. Toned, the gym where Bridget worked, had a glass-topped juice bar and insanely overpriced drinks. He'd planted himself between the two sisters and ordered wild berry smoothies with bee pollen for all, with a wheatgrass chaser for Bridget. If this took too long, he'd be broke before he got Bridget's okay.

"Forget about the Hair of the Dog for a second. Focus on what I'm offering. Firemen serving drinks to your guests. Real firemen. Even better, real Bachelor Firemen of San Gabriel. The best-looking ones I can round up. What could be better than the Bachelor Firemen at a *bachelorette* party?"

"They'd do that?"

"I'll have to talk them into it. But enough of them owe me so it shouldn't be a problem." Most likely, they'd be fighting over a chance to ply a bunch of cute girls with Melon Balls or whatever they drank. But he had to make it sound like a challenge. "They'll do it to help me out."

"But why the Hair of the Dog?" Bridget wailed. She slicked back a single hair that had escaped from her ruthless ponytail. Not a speck of mascara had slid from her eyelashes to her cheeks. Ryan had her number. This was a woman who knew exactly how things were supposed to be and didn't tolerate anything less than perfection.

Katie butted in, even though he'd told her he'd do the talking. The two sisters obviously had some issues. "Because it's our family business, because it's about to go under unless we do something—"

"Because they're going to love it," interrupted Ryan. "That's what bachelorette parties are for. One last chance to walk on the wild side before heading down the aisle. I guarantee this'll be a party no one will forget. We'll decorate it up good, right Katie?"

"Right," she said through gritted teeth.

He patted Katie's knee, then leaned to whisper in Bridget's ear, "How about I sweeten the deal?"

Katie watched Bridget's eyes go wide with that fired-up look that meant nothing would get in her way.

"Okay," announced Bridget. "We'll hold the bachelorette party at the Hair of the Dog this Saturday night."

Ryan shot Katie a smug smile. What the heck had he said to Bridget? All kinds of naughty things flitted through her mind. Did he ask her out? Did he tell her how gorgeous she was, much more so than her dorky little sister?

He got up from the chrome suede-topped stool and tucked the back of his shirt into his jeans. "Got a boys' room here, or should I water a plant?"

"Please don't do that. They're plastic." Bridget pointed out the men's room, and Ryan headed that way with his slow-hipped stride. Katie watched female heads swivel as he passed. She bit back a sigh.

"Got a little crush, huh?" Bridget glanced down at her like Venus surveying a toad.

"No. No way."

"Oh, relax. What's the big deal? Any normal red-blooded woman would have a crush on him. I'm sure you're one of hundreds. Thousands."

That didn't make Katie feel one single bit better. "What did he say to you just now?"

"He made me an offer I couldn't refuse."

"What offer?"

"A secret offer. Don't worry, Katie, you'll like it too. Especially since you have a crush on him."

Murderous rage percolated through Katie's bloodstream. She clenched her fists onto the edge of the chrome stool to keep from hurling herself at her smirking sister. Good thing she had long practice with controlling the fury only her sister managed to inspire. When Katie died, she intended to have the words "She Didn't Kill Her Sister" carved on her headstone.

Assuming she hadn't killed her by then, of course.

Bridget lowered her voice. "FYI, since you like him, I consider Ryan strictly hands-off. But no one else at the party will. Just thought you might want to know you'll have some competition."

Katie's tension went up ten more notches. She pressed her lips together. If she lost her temper, Bridget might change her mind.

"I'm trying to give you a heads-up." Bridget offered her a smile that brought to mind the phrase "kill with kindness." "A guy like Ryan is going to have girls throwing themselves at him every time he walks into a room."

"Yeah, I've noticed that. So?"

"So maybe you want to get a crush on someone else. Someone more . . ."

More her league. More her type, more ordinary, more . . . Katie could finish that sentence for her, but refused to give her the satisfaction.

"I don't have a crush on Ryan. I'm not even sure I like him half the time."

She saw Bridget's sapphire-blue eyes lift, and felt a warm hand settle on her shoulder.

"That's a shame. If you did, I might have to take advantage of you."

She jerked her head around to meet Ryan's gaze. Summery blue amusement swam on the surface, but underneath she saw something else. Had she hurt his feelings?

"Well, you should." Bridget said with her typical bossiness. "Someone should. Unless she's going to get back together with Doug, as I have frequently recommended."

Katie hopped off the stool. No way was she going to stick around for a conversation about Doug with Ryan right there. "Better get to work," she said in the most chipper voice she possessed. "I think you're thirty seconds late for your class."

Bridget, she knew, couldn't stand being late. Her sister dashed off toward the glass-walled room where a new rainbow gathering of workout wear milled around.

"I didn't mean that," Katie quickly told Ryan, as he put some bills on the glass counter. "That part about not liking you half the time. That wasn't true. I do like you half the time. My sister makes me crazy. I'm not responsible for my actions around her."

"Did you just admit you like me half the time?" Ryan gave her a half smile, which she supposed was all she deserved.

"At least half. Maybe more."

"More than half? You're scaring me now. Let me know when I'm up to sixty-one percent and I'll tone it down."

She giggled, shocking herself. Katherine Maureen Dane was not the giggling sort.

"Let's get out of here before they make us do laps around the juice bar," Ryan said.

They left the air-conditioned cocoon of fitness and hit the sweltering sidewalk outside Toned. If she was totally honest, Katie liked Ryan much more than sixty-one percent of the time. In fact, she liked him almost all the time. Which added up to more than she liked anyone else.

As for that crush concept? Forget it. She couldn't handle that amount of honesty right now.

Ryan finally took Melissa up on her open invitation to dinner. He figured it was time. He missed Brody and Melissa, and besides, he wanted the captain's permission to recruit guys for the bachelorette party.

The last time he'd seen their house, Brody had still been building it. Ryan had contributed his share of framing and sheetrocking, all part of the San Gabriel firefighters' mission to help Brody recover from his divorce. But now that he'd married the woman of his dreams and adopted a child, the house looked like a gracious, well-lived-in family home.

Brody grilled burgers on their umbrella-shaded patio while Danielle splashed around in a kiddie pool decorated with seahorses. By unspoken agreement, no one talked about the firehouse. Instead Melissa handed him a Dos Equis and caught him up on the events of Danielle's young life. They'd had a scare about six months ago, and were still coming to grips with it.

"Ironic, isn't it, that a fireman's daughter might have asthma? It was the scariest thing I ever saw, Ryan. She kept screaming she couldn't breathe and to open the door. She kept saying, 'Oxygen, oxygen' . . . I didn't even know she knew the word."

"Man, that's tough. Wonder if it's all the smog around here?"

"Who knows? They say it's usually genetic. But we don't have that much information on her birth parents. It could be environmental. I'm pitching a three-part series about it to Channel Six."

"When she grows up, Danielle is going to have major issues about how many news pieces she inspired." Brody shook his dark head and flipped a burger. "The adoption itself was a ten-parter."

"I had a lot of ground to cover." Melissa twinkled at him with an adoration that would have made Ryan gag if he didn't love them both so much. "I'm one of the first to explore the effect of adoption on the grandparents. I actually interviewed my father. He's fairly photogenic, it turns out. He got some fan mail after that."

"Is he good with Danielle?"

"He seems to be trying to make up for my lousy childhood by spoiling Danielle rotten. Amazing how people can change."

Ryan didn't answer that. It would take a lot more than an adorable granddaughter to make his old man change. He'd long ago given up hope of that.

At the sound of her name, Danielle hopped out of the kiddie pool and scampered over to the patio table, leaving little wet footprints across the cement. She made a beeline for Ryan and climbed into his lap.

Ryan wrapped his arms around the ball of wet

little girl. "That's not a shiver, is it? It's a hundred degrees out here."

Danielle grinned at him and cuddled closer. "That water is *too* cold. It's colder than anything, even an ice cube!"

Brody turned from the grill with an indignant scowl. "Now that's unfair. Even the little ones pick you."

"Not all of them." Ryan muttered, thinking of Katie. Not that he expected her to have a crush on him, but did she have to announce her lack of one so loudly? It had hurt. He had no idea why, but it had.

Melissa pounced. "Ooh, is someone giving you a hard time? Playing hard to get?"

Ryan snorted. "Katie doesn't know how to play that game. Or any game. She doesn't go for that stuff."

"Katie." Melissa tapped a finger against her bottom lip. "Katie Dane? The daughter of the bar owner?"

"You know Katie?"

Brody put a burger onto a grilled bun and flipped the whole thing onto a paper plate. "Melissa knows all kinds of people in this town. Curse of being in the news biz." He brought the plate to Ryan and smoothed Danielle's hair.

"I think she's nodding off," he whispered.

Ryan looked down at the little girl's drooping eyes. "Wore herself out in the colder than anything water, huh?"

Brody gazed at his daughter with a tenderness that made Ryan's heart ache. "She plays until she drops. Little kids know how to live."

After he'd given the doting parents enough time, Ryan circled back to the only subject that seemed to interest him at the moment.

"What do you know about Katie?" he asked Melissa.

"Well, let's see. She's smart. Got all kinds of A's in college. Went off to graduate school at Redlands. I'm kind of surprised to hear she's back. Her father thinks the world of her. That's about all I know. I interviewed him once for a story and all he talked about was his kids. Athletic family, I think. Two sons in the minor leagues."

Ryan chuckled, nearly waking Danielle. "She does have a knack with a baseball bat."

"Hey, you should get her to help you study." Brody brought two more burgers over to the table and sat down. "I remember last time you had that girl . . . what was her name . . ."

"I don't need help studying." Not a topic he wanted to talk about. Ryan bit into his burger, leaning forward so as not to spill ketchup on Danielle. They all chewed their burgers. The shadows of the lemon tree and the bougainvillea-covered wall lengthened across the backyard. The grip of the day's heat loosened, and a breath of evening air stirred Danielle's hair. A low murmur of crickets arose.

"Besides," he said when he finished his bite. "She's got enough to do. She's trying to keep that hovel of a bar from closing. Thought I'd give her a hand with that."

He explained his idea about the firemen and the bachelorette party. "We're starting to do well with the female crowd, so why not take advantage of that? I figure it'll put the Hair of the Dog on the map. And where the girls go, the guys will follow."

"Don't you mean, where Ryan Blake goes, the girls will follow?" Melissa asked dryly.

He shrugged one shoulder. "Just trying to help Katie out, poor kid."

"Noble," said Brody, with a glitter of something deep in his charcoal eyes.

"Stupid," said Melissa.

Ryan's head jerked up from his burger.

"If you want Katie to like you, this is the worst possible idea." She gave him a poke on the shoulder.

"Hang on, no one said anything about getting anyone to *like* anyone else." Lord knew, he'd never had any problems with that.

Well, except for Katie.

"If you go prancing around with your fireman's helmet and whatever else you're planning to wear—or not wear—she's going to think you're shallow. Nothing but a pretty—"

"Don't say it."

Melissa barely blinked. "A pretty shallow guy who relies on his looks. There's a lot more to you than that, Ryan. Why don't you let her see the other side of you?"

"Which side? The one that flies off the handle and fu—"—he glanced down at Danielle—"messes up expensive fire trucks?"

Brody raised an eyebrow. Damn, why'd he have to bring that up?

"No, the side that thinks about things."

"I am thinking about things. I thought of this."

"Hm, I sense a story developing here," Melissa teased. "I think one of the Bachelor Firemen of San Gabriel might be following in his captain's footsteps."

"You know how I feel about all that." Ryan winked, aiming to prove she wasn't getting to him. "It's a blessing, not a curse. See all the girls you want, never have to get serious, because you're *cursed*. Genius."

"Oh really?" Melissa waved her burger. "What about—"

"The bachelorette party is fine with me," interrupted Brody, before things got too heated. "As long as they do it when they're off the clock."

"Thanks, boss."

"And as long as no one embarrasses himself or the department. I don't want anything showing up on the morning news."

Ryan decided not to mention the secret part of his plan. It could certainly fall into the category of potentially embarrassing. But without it, Bridget never would have said yes.

"But I have to warn you, Ryan, you can't go wrong listening to Melissa." He covered her hand with his. Her ready-to-rumble expression softened into a sappy smile.

When had his tough, enigmatic captain turned into such a mush ball? Ryan dipped his last bite of burger in the puddle of ketchup on his plate. Not everyone was lucky enough to find what Brody and Melissa had. Some people were better off living in the moment with whatever woman happened to be willing.

As soon as he finished helping Katie with the bar, he'd get back to doing exactly that.

Chapter Twelve

Vader's muscles bulged like mountain ridges off his shoulders. One could practically rock-climb his pecs. When he flexed his biceps, which he did whenever possible, he looked like Arnold Schwarzenegger back in the good old days.

Vader was the first to say yes. "Fuck yeah" being his exact words.

Even though Double D was now following a special wheat-free diet and had lost an inch off his belly, the remaining inches disqualified him, in Ryan's opinion. Besides, Double D, one of their very few married guys, had a wife who might not be happy with a moonlighting gig at a bachelorette party.

Stud also signed up right away. Ryan thought the girls would appreciate his eager-beaver attitude and long-lashed brown eyes. He had a Ferris Bueller quality that seemed to attract older women. Kind of like adopting a puppy.

For the last two members of the crew, Ryan went outside San Gabriel. Camino Ranch might be sloppy compared to San Gabriel's fire department, but he had to admit they had some good-looking guys over there. Carlos brought a Latin flair, and Joe the Toe almost put Vader to shame with his ripped physique.

At the Camino Ranch station, Joe the Toe had crossed his arms over his massive chest and glowered at Ryan, who had to look up about a foot to meet his eyes. "Just because I'm black doesn't mean I can dance. I'm from England. I have a degree from Oxford."

"All we're doing is serving drinks to the girls. No one has to dance if they don't want to."

"I'm not saying I can't dance, mind you."

"I'm sure you can."

"Why are you sure?"

"Okay, I'm not sure. Maybe you can, maybe you can't. That's your business. You in or out?"

"A plethora of hotties letting their hair down for one final bacchanalian night of freedom? Brilliant. But do not stereotype me again."

"Scout's honor." Ryan held out his hand for a bone-crunching handshake. "So is it true English people can't dance?"

He winked just in time to turn Joe the Toe's offended scowl into a belly laugh. From then on, they'd been on the same page and Joe had even signed up for Ryan's special surprise.

On Saturday they all met at the bar before the start of the party. They wore the T-shirts of their respective fire departments and black chinos, which seemed close enough to regulation firefighter wear without actually wearing their uniforms. None of the guys had been to the Hair of the Dog before. Ryan didn't bother explaining that it didn't usually look like this.

"What kind of bar has pink balloons everywhere?" Vader demanded.

"Reminds me of my kid sister's bat mitzvah," said Stud.

"Katie decorated according to her sister's request." "Requirement" would be a better word, thought Ryan. Bridget didn't *request* anything, and she had very high standards. She'd probably already readjusted the positioning of every single pink, heart-shaped balloon.

The red globe lanterns on the tables had been replaced with pink candles in flowery centerpieces. Pink streamers dangled everywhere. He had to admit it worked, in a demented way. The Hair of the Dog looked like an old drag queen in pink lipstick. He wondered if the Drinking Crew would be allowed to hang out tonight for some local color.

As if Bridget would allow that.

He was setting the guys up with tequila shots at the bar when the front door opened. A womanly shape, backlit by the glaring sunshine outside, stepped in. One of the girls must be early. He eyed the sensual curves of the stranger. If the bachelorettes all looked like this, a fun night lay ahead. Slender legs set off by high heels, a skintight dress that revealed the subtle movements of the girl's hipbones as she made her way across the floor. Tiny waist cinched by a skinny, shiny belt. And above the waist . . . But before he could truly investigate the rest of her intriguing body, the girl wobbled a bit on her three-inch heels.

Suddenly suspicious, he skipped up to her face.

He squinted, blinked, squinted again. The woman's hair was pinned on top of her head, with some strands flying free. She had something on her eyes that made them look even bigger and much more come-hither. She looked . . . unbelievable. A complete knockout.

He opened his mouth but nothing came out.

"If you laugh at me, I'll knock your teeth out with my bat," Katie said.

The spell broke.

"No one's laughing," he assured her. "I just didn't know you had it in you."

She came closer, still wobbly on her stilettos. Her finely curved ankles looked like they might snap.

"Did your sister pick that outfit for you?"

Katie looked disgusted. "What do you think? Happiest day of her life. So are these your fireman friends?"

Ryan realized he wasn't the only one staring. The four other firefighters looked equally as fixated on Katie. Vader sported his Elvis lip curl, the one he was convinced girls couldn't resist. Carlos murmured something about "mamacita."

Ryan discovered he didn't like that one bit. He rapped on the bar to get everyone's attention. "Guys, this is Katie Dane, she runs the bar. For tonight, she's your boss, and don't you forget it. She's *very* strict when it comes to boss-employee relations."

Carlos got to his feet and took Katie's hand. "It's a pleasure to meet you. Nice bar you got here."

Ryan braced himself. Would Katie scowl, snatch her hand away, or launch into a rant about what a godforsaken pit the Hair of the Dog was? She did none of the above.

Instead she gave Carlos a pretty smile and said,

"That's very nice of you. I appreciate it." She tilted her head and scattered more smiles, as if they were flower petals, to the rest of the guys. "We're so grateful you're willing to help us out tonight. I just know everyone's going to be thrilled. Real firemen. Oh my!"

Was that a mocking hint of Scarlett O'Hara he heard in her voice? Ryan narrowed his eyes at her in warning. But she paid no attention, continuing with her Miss America routine until he wanted to shake the lipstick off her pretty mouth.

The guys said things like, "Our pleasure," "Happy to be here," and "Firemen to the rescue," as they introduced themselves to her.

"Why are you called Joe the Toe?" she asked Joe, in her usual blunt way.

"I happen to be lacking one of those particular appendages," explained Joe.

"Firemen like nicknames," said Ryan.

"I bet I can guess yours. Hero? Knight in Shining Armor?"

Ryan nearly choked on his tequila. Katie smiled innocently and moved behind the bar. As she passed, Ryan hissed, "Overdoing it a bit, don't you think?"

"Don't know what you're talking about." She swept past him and through the swinging doors. "I've got to go check on the hors d'oeuvres."

He followed her in. "Are you crazy, dressing like that on a night like this?"

"What are you talking about?" In the brighter light of the kitchen, she looked even better. Her dress was a rose-pink color that made her look like candy. He fought to keep his eyes above her neckline. If he looked at her chest, he might have a problem.

"It's asking for trouble."

"What trouble? This is a bachelorette party. All girls. Are you picturing some kind of female prison sex scene?"

Was she trying to kill him? One more second and he wouldn't be responsible for the consequences. He wheeled around and returned to the bar.

"Nice!" Vader said to him with a low whistle. "She single?"

Ryan grabbed him by the neck of his T-shirt. "Consider her taken."

Vader raised his hands. "Nuff said."

Ryan released him. He ought to clarify that he hadn't said Katie actually *was* taken. But he didn't feel like it right now. Besides, she wouldn't want all that extra attention from the guys. She'd thank him for sparing her a lot of aggravation.

Joe the Toe caught his eye and raised one eyebrow meaningfully. Damn Camino Ranch guy might be missing a toe, but he didn't miss a trick.

In the kitchen. Katie took deep gulps of air and randomly rearranged crab cakes on the trays. She wasn't used to being the sole object of attention of five studly men. Bridget probably saw that look all the time, but men didn't usually spend much time checking Katie out. Five hot, ripped guys had looked her up and down the entire time she'd walked across the room. They'd looked at her with appreciation and admiration and lust, yes, definitely lust.

But that was nothing compared to how Ryan's expression had affected her. She still felt the impact. He'd looked . . . stunned, at first. Shocked, even. As if his pet lizard had transformed into a fire-breathing dragon. Before he'd recognized her, he'd looked at her as if she were a stranger. A beautiful, sexy stranger.

It was a miracle she hadn't fainted into a puddle at his feet.

She had to get a grip. Tonight was all about business. It was about saving the Hair of the Dog. It was about helping her dad—so she could hand the bar back to him and move on with her life.

"Oh my gawwwwwd!" A piercing shriek carried from the bar through the swinging door into the kitchen. She recognized Meredith's voice. "Who are you handsome hunks?"

She heard the rumble of Ryan's playful voice.

"So awesommme!! Bridget, you rock!! This is so cool!"

Katie heaved a sigh. Better go say hi.

Meredith's excitement even extended to Katie, who found herself wrapped in a Calvin Klein–scented hug. "Katie, you look amazing. Bridget, are you responsible for this?"

Bridget, who looked especially stunning in a silver minidress, nodded modestly. "I always told her she'd clean up nice, if she ever took the trouble."

"You should listen to your sister more often." Meredith put Katie aside, sat on a bar stool, and crossed her long, bare legs. "Now who wants to bring me a Sex on the Beach?"

The firemen sprang into action. Katie watched in amazement as they formed a kind of bucket brigade. Stud whipped out a bar recipe book and called out the ingredients to Carlos, who located the peach schnapps and vodka bottles and whirled them onto the bar. Joe the Toe filled a glass of ice cubes, added cranberry and orange juice, and handed it to Vader, who mixed the drink, put a pink umbrella in it, and plopped it on a tray. Ryan delivered the tray to Meredith with a bow, one hand behind his back.

"Sex on the Beach in thirty seconds flat," he said with a wink. "Of course we guarantee the real thing would take a lot longer."

Meredith flipped her long strawberry-blonde hair and let out a sexy trill of laughter. "I would hope so."

"Ryan," Katie interrupted. "You know there's going to be fifty girls here. How many firemen does it take to make one drink?"

"When it's Sex on the Beach, the more the merrier," he answered without missing a beat.

"Ha ha."

But Bridget and Meredith both laughed until they cried.

"Not to worry," Ryan told Katie under his breath. "We have a different system worked out for multiple, simultaneous drinks."

Katie gulped. Did he have to make everything sound dirty?

Dirty, it turned out, was the name of the game at Meredith's bachelorette party. The girls came swarming in, wearing outfits straight out of a strip club, and went right for the hunky firemen and their drinks. Katie knew some of them, and they knew her. She got a lot of "Look at Bridget's little sister!"

Meredith's brother, who worked at a consumer electronics store, had loaned them a pair of top-of-the-line speakers for the night. Bridget plugged in her iPod, and the sound of Lady Gaga shook sprinkles of plaster off the wall of the old Hair of the Dog.

Instant party. *Ro-ro-ro-ro-rom . . .* Meredith grabbed Bridget and they began swiveling and thrusting to the beat. In a few moments, the bar had turned into a sea of sexy moves and the walls shook with the combined voices of fifty girls singing along to "Bad Romance." So this was what Katie been missing all those years she'd been hanging out playing Guitar Hero with Doug. She had to admit, it looked like fun.

Katie quickly figured out she wouldn't last long in the high-heeled shoes Bridget had made her wear. She kicked them off and padded around the bar in her sparkly tights, delivering crab cakes and platters of hummus and pita.

Once the party was in full swing, the firemen were too busy to pay any attention to Katie. They all got busy pouring drinks and dazzling the girls with their smiles, not to mention their physiques. They sure were efficient when it came to drink deliveries. As the evening blurred into drunken revelry, Katie felt like a fly on the wall of a million flirtations.

"I'll have a G-Spot, straight up," a redhead in a tube top asked Vader. "Do you know what that is?"

"Honey, I invented the G-Spot." Vader leered.

"Seriously? The drink or the, you know . . . ?"

"Both. At the same time. With one hand tied to a bedpost."

"You're so cute! Oh my God, isn't he adorable?"

"I think this one's adorable," her friend purred at Stud.

Fred turned red and stuck his head in the bartender manual. "A G-Spot is raspberry liqueur, orange juice, and Southern Comfort."

"No coming on to the guests," hissed Ryan after the girls had left with their drinks.

"Are you fucking kidding me? A girl asks me for a G-Spot, what am I supposed to say?"

"Just . . . don't get crazy."

"*Crazy*? Have you seen these girls? It's like Bridesmaids Gone Wild in here. And check out the bride!"

Meredith and another girl were now dancing on a table, batting around balloons.

"Bridget, are you trying to tell me something? Should I be insulted?" Meredith shouted down to the crowd.

Bridget wasn't drunk enough to tolerate a lapse from perfection. "What's the matter? Whatever it is, I'll fix it."

"There's a balloon with a dog face up here! I think it's barking at me! Ruff, ruff!"

Meredith grabbed the dangling string of a big balloon that looked like Clifford the Big Red Dog.

Bridget aimed a sapphire glare at Katie. "What is that?"

"Sorry!"

" 'T's okay," called Meredith. "I always wanted a dog. Don't have to feed this one."

"No, you just have to blow it!" someone shouted. Meredith nearly fell off the table from laughing. Ryan stationed himself beneath her, moving as she moved, ready to catch her. When she saw that, she launched herself into the air. Everyone screamed as she swan dived into his arms.

Even though he instantly put her on her feet, she clung to him, feeling his arms and shoulders. Katie held tight to her serving tray. It wouldn't do to hurl shrimp cocktail at the guest of honor.

Someone turned the music up. The partying went into turbo drive. One girl twirled a pair of red pantyhose overhead and let it fly. It landed on Joe the Toe, who tossed it to Stud, who turned bright red and handed it off the Vader. Vader tied it around his head like a bandanna.

Katie had to admit that muscleman Vader was

the hit of the party. Carlos came in a close second. Ryan, for some reason, was lying low. As the energy in the room skyrocketed, he looked more and more nervous.

"I don't know if we should go through with it," she overheard him tell Bridget.

"You'd better." She jabbed him with her forefinger. "A deal's a deal."

"But look at these girls. I'm not sure it's safe. I don't want my guys hurt."

Katie couldn't help butting in. "What are you guys talking about?"

"You're about to see," said Bridget. "Right, Ryan? You can't back out now. I promised Meredith the best surprise of her life."

Ryan sighed, then signaled to the other firemen. In a flash, they abandoned the bottles of vodka and jiggers of Kahlua and disappeared into the kitchen.

"What's going on?" Katie tried to follow Ryan, but Bridget dragged her in the other direction, toward the gyrating girls.

"Come on, let's get a front-row seat."

"For what?"

"Listen up, girls!" Bridget turned down the music to get their attention. "The Bachelor Firemen of San Gabriel are about to give us a verrrry special performance in honor of our bride-to-be, Meredith. So hold on to your panties. Make yourselves comfortable. Oh, and you might want to grab some dollar bills."

A shriek of excitement swept across the room. Everyone seemed to know what was about to happen except Katie. Dollar bills? Were they getting a nice tip together for the guys?

Bridget selected a song on her iPod, then turned

the stereo to rock-out level. A familiar bass line throbbed through the bar. Then the guitar joined in, and the Talking Heads sang out, something about getting what you're after.

The door from the kitchen swung open and Vader strutted through it, followed by the other firemen dancing in a conga line behind him. They wore their firemen's helmets and big, goofy grins. The women screamed at the top of their lungs. Katie felt a sound coming from her own mouth. She was shrieking like the others, through a huge smile she couldn't control. They were so damn cute, all of them, cute and muscular and sexy, and God, she wanted to eat them up.

The men danced—fumbled might be more accurate—their way to the end of the bar. But instead of coming around front, they jumped on top of it, one by one, until all five stood gyrating their hips to the sounds of "Burning Down the House."

"Oh my gawwwd," Katie heard herself yell, as if possessed. Bridget rushed the bar and stuck a wad of bills in Vader's waistband. His lip curled up in a hound dog kind of way. On cue, all five men jumped a hundred and eighty degrees so their backsides faced the girls. They swung their hips from side to side, not perfectly synchronized, but close enough so Katie realized with the nonfrenzied part of her brain that they must have practiced this routine.

Which made her love it even more.

What were they doing now?

They did a slow, sexy twist to face frontward again. "Look out below!" Vader yelled.

Oh my God, they were handing off their helmets to the closest girls, who scrambled to grab them. Katie was too mesmerized to move. Then the men put their hands to the bottom edge of their T-shirts and lifted up, up, up in time to the beat of the music. Ryan's broad, tanned chest was unveiled, inch by tantalizing inch. She couldn't seem to drag her eyes away from Ryan to check out the other guys.

They did another hundred-and-eighty-degree turn so their backs faced the girls. She stared, hypnotized, at the rippling muscles under Ryan's taut skin. God, he was absolutely chiseled. Her heart hopped into her throat.

Once again they turned to face their screaming audience. The men crooked their fingers at the girls who held their helmets. A pretty blonde had Ryan's helmet. With sheer magnetism and a playful smile, he drew her toward him, looking deep into her eyes.

"Warned you," said Bridget in her ear. Then . . . "Now for the fun part."

Chapter Thirteen

Ryan took his helmet from the curly-haired girl, who couldn't seem to stop hyperventilating. Maybe this wasn't such a good idea. He put his helmet back on his head and shot a sidelong glance at Joe the Toe next to him. Joe, who most definitely could dance, had lifted a buxom blonde onto the bar next to him. He ground his crotch into hers.

The music shifted to "Bringing the Sexy Back." He caught Joe's eye, and gave the nod. Joe lowered the girl to the floor and put his hands to his zipper.

The sound level went up another ten decibels as all five men eased down their black chinos.

Trying his best to synchronize with the others, Ryan scooted his pants down to below his knees, then kicked them out into the crowd. Five pairs of pants went flying through the air and fifty screaming women scrambled after him. Make that forty-nine. Katie looked too shell-shocked to scramble.

She seemed to be the only one actually looking at him at the moment. More accurately, looking at his crotch.

She peered at his boxers, an incredulous look spreading across her face. He didn't blame her. How often did you see five grown men dancing on a bar wearing pink boxer shorts? With words printed on them? She stepped closer, obviously trying to read the writing.

Uh oh, her scrutiny was making him hard. The last thing he wanted was a major boner at eye level to fifty excited women. To distract himself, he looked over at the guys. Stud's face looked as pink as his boxers, but since he had three women jumping around in front of him, the embarrassment seemed worth it.

Vader kept flexing his biceps and roaring like Tarzan. He did some trick with his stomach muscles that kept the girls riveted. Carlos, surprisingly, kept things low-key. Until he turned around and wiggled his butt, pointing at the writing on his ass. The girls shrieked and crowded around the bar so they could read what it said.

Oops, he'd missed the cue. He spun around so his rear was to the girls. He wiggled in time with Joe the Toe.

"'Meredith plus John,' that's what it says," he heard someone yell. Cheers rose up from the crowd. He smiled. Exactly how they were supposed to react. "What about the front?"

"Turn around, turn around!"

"No, take it off, take it off!"

The chant filled the room. "Take it off, take it off!"

He looked at the other guys. They'd decided to wait until the last minute to determine if they would go all the way. He hadn't promised Bridget anything more than a fun striptease.

"I'll kick in an extra thousand dollars if you take it all off," she'd said. "Just like in the movie."

He'd seen *The Full Monty*, and he'd put his firemen up against those guys any day. But he'd told Bridget to keep her money. If they went all the way, it would be for the fun of it and if it felt right when the moment came.

Now the moment was here. He cocked his head at the other men. Joe was the first to nod. All down the line, nothing but nods.

He gave a shrug. Full Monty, coming up. He moved to the beat, waiting for the line that was their cue. Something about burning up . . . there it was.

With his left hand, he plucked his helmet off his head and covered his crotch with it. With his right, he pulled down one side of the boxers to reveal one butt cheek.

Shrieks of excitement nearly deafened him.

He switched hands and pulled the other side of his boxers down. He looked down the line to see how the other guys were doing. They were all fighting to keep a straight face as they waggled their bare asses around.

He gave a nod. They all jumped around again, helmets held tight over their dicks, and shimmied like a row of ducks shaking off water. Ryan felt his boxers slide down his legs. When the cloth reached his feet, he extracted one foot, then used the other to lift the boxers into the air and kick them into the crowd.

A sea of hands clawed for the pink underwear. The curly-haired girl, who also happened to be half a head taller than the others, snagged them easily. "I got 'em, I got 'em!"

But no one was paying attention. How could they, when five naked men were dancing to the beat wearing nothing but firemen's helmets? The girls went crazy, clutching at each other and jumping up and down. In the middle of the crowd, Meredith was laughing so hard, tears were streaming down her cheeks.

Time to wrap things up.

At the line about watching your back, they spun around one more time, bare asses toward the girls. Vader's helmet tumbled to the bar and bounced off into the crowd. By his smirk, Ryan knew he'd done it on purpose. Ryan kept a tight grip on his own helmet, hoping it covered everything.

As one, the firemen jumped off the bar into the bartender's domain. Stud led the way through the swinging door into the kitchen.

"Hot damn!" Vader leaned against the stainless steel counter, letting it all hang out. Nothing Ryan hadn't seen before. Firehouses didn't keep a lot of secrets.

Still panting from the striptease, Ryan shushed him so he could hear the reaction from the bar. The buzz of shrieks and the last beats of the Justin Timberlake song were punctuated by the sound of girls yelling out the words from the boxers.

"It says 'Too Hot to Handle'? Oh my God, too cute!"

"Mine says 'Fire Me Up.' "

"Ohh, I want that one! Gimme that one! I get to choose, I'm the bride."

Stud looked at Ryan. "They're all different?"

"I couldn't decide. Yours was 'Light My Fire.' "

"Really?" Stud looked pleased. "Cool. I wish I could keep mine. I bet chicks would dig it."

Joe the Toe snorted. "I, on the other hand, have no intention of ever again donning a pair of pink underwear featuring the words, 'Stand Next to My Fire.' And Meredith and John can keep their names off my big black ass."

"I thought it was a nice touch," said Carlos, rummaging through his duffel bag for his other clothes. "My fiancée would have gone nuts over it. I may have to hire you chicos for another performance."

"Count me in," said Vader instantly.

"Don't you want to know what your boxers said?" Ryan asked him. Vader showed no signs of wanting to get dressed. The guy was a freaking exhibitionist.

" 'Too Hot to Handle,' of course." He clenched his abdominal muscles so they quivered.

"Nope. I made a special one for you. It said 'Burn Genitals Burn.' " Ryan tried to keep a straight face, but Vader's horrified expression didn't make it easy.

Vader grabbed his duffel bag and covered his crotch with it. "Damn it, Hoagie, you know I tested negative. I posted the results on Facebook."

As the other firemen cracked up, Ryan finally winked. "Don't get your nonexistent panties in a wad. Yours said 'Feel the Heat.' "

" 'Feel the Heat.' I dig it." Repeating it under his breath, Vader finally started getting dressed. "I might make that my new motto. 'Vader Brown. Feel the Heat.' Might be a waste of time to put clothes on. They're going to rip them off as soon as I get back out there."

Carlos buttoned his shirt. "I gotta go home, Hoagie, or my girl will kill me."

"You don't have to stay. We're done here. What happens from here on out is your business." Ryan held up a hand. "Don't ask, don't tell. And thanks to you all for a job well done. Best damn strip show in town."

The men, some still only partly dressed, slapped hands. It was almost, in a weird way, like the shared satisfaction of putting out a fire.

Carlos heaved his duffel over his shoulder and headed for the back door. "Don't get into too much trouble, dudes. If you do, don't tell me about it. Don't want to know. Just don't want to know." The door slammed shut.

"I'll stay for a while, if anyone else is. You guys staying?" Stud looked around anxiously.

"What do you think, squirt? I got two blondes and a redhead with my name on them." Vader put an arm on Stud's shoulder and dragged him, still zipping his pants, out the door.

Joe the Toe buttoned his shirt. "If you want that girl, you'd better do some quick talking."

"What girl? What do you mean?"

"Oxford, remember?" Joe tapped his head. "Besides, I'm a black man in a white man's world. I see things. You like her."

Ryan shrugged on his shirt. "There's fifty knockouts out there. Why waste time with the one who doesn't want me?"

"Despite my subsequent dismissal of my initial impression, maybe you are as dumb as you look."

Ryan gave Joe the Toe a hard look. "That's a lot of big words to hide a half-assed insult in."

"My apologies. Next time I'll aim for the entire ass."

Ryan snorted. "Thanks for the warning."

"You're welcome. Here's another one. That girl wants you so badly she doesn't know what to do with herself. And you're right there with her. Why would you go through all these shenanigans if you didn't feel something for her?"

"Dude. It was a good deed. I wanted to help her out."

"You're all heart." Joe the Toe rapped him on the head. "And perhaps some brains, all evidence to the contrary. Party time."

Joe dove through the swinging door. The sound of music and laughter came in waves as the door swung back and forth in his wake.

Ryan slowly finished dressing. So Katie liked him, according to Joe. A lot. And according to Joe, he liked her. Of course, he'd already known that. He liked hanging out with her. He wanted to help her out. And on top of all that, he wanted her. In bed.

So what was the problem? Why did all this make him panicky?

Maybe it was the combination. It was one thing to like Katie, to like her a lot. Another to want to sleep with her. Both things together sounded like big trouble.

He'd better clear this up as soon as possible.

With a deep breath, he pushed through the swinging door. A woman hurtled from the top of the bar and flung herself into his arms. He caught her and held her warm softness tight against him. Her legs wrapped around his waist. She licked his neck and ground her sex against his pelvis.

Right away, he got hard. An armful of nice-smelling womanly flesh tended to do that to a guy.

"Hey, I gotta find someone," he choked, as the woman lifted herself up to rub her breasts in his face. She shook out her long, curly hair, forming a peach liqueur–scented shield around the two of them.

"You just did." The woman purred in his ear. "Someone hot and willing. My name's Logan and I've been watching you all night long."

He put his hands under her ass and pulled her tighter against his arousal. Maybe a feminine distraction was the answer to his panicked confusion over Katie. A night with a sexy woman would keep him from overthinking things or getting too involved. Later, he'd explain everything to Katie. With a sense of relief, he nuzzled her neck.

"Nice to meet you, Logan."

"Sorry, Gidget."

"Don't call me that." Katie whirled away from the sight of Ryan mauling Logan Marquez. She couldn't bear the way his hands massaged her rear, the way he tilted his head back so she could kiss him. At least Katie assumed it was a kiss. With all that hair in the way, who knew?

"Okay, I take it back. Sorry, I shouldn't have said anything."

Katie looked Bridget straight in the eyes, ready to commit a felony if she saw any mockery there.

She saw something even worse. Pity.

"I already told you, I don't care what Ryan does."

"Of course you don't."

"We're coworkers, that's all."

"Sure." Bridget's eyes shone with maddening sympathy. "I'm glad you can see that."

"Why do you care?"

"I don't want my little sister getting her feelings hurt. After all, it was beyond nice of him to get his friends in here to help you out. I want to make sure you don't think it means anything."

"What do you mean, anything?" Katie heard her voice falter, and hated it.

"Anything beyond friendship." Bridget touched her on the shoulder. "But Katie, you do look hot tonight. That kid they call Stud was checking you out. He might be more your speed."

Katie shoved her hand away. "I'm not looking for a hookup. Mind your own sex life."

"I think I will. Think I can lure that big guy away from Sophie?" Bridget adjusted the fit of her silver dress over her slim hips. Before she got lost in the throng, she turned back to Katie. "You did good tonight, Katie. I'll make sure Daddy knows what an outstanding job you're doing with the bar."

Katie battled an insane urge to go on a pink candle–throwing, pink balloon–popping rampage. She wanted to rip the speakers out of the wall, throw Bridget's iPod at her head, and make a bonfire out of every hot-pink pair of boxers she could lay her hands on.

Oooh, bonfire. That would clear this place out quick enough. Of course, with all those firemen on the scene, it would be out in two seconds flat.

The sound of the swinging door caught her attention. She got a glimpse of long curly hair and Ryan's hands under the girl's dress before the two of them disappeared into the kitchen.

She caught the knowing glance of the big black guy known as Joe the Toe. He had the same look in his eyes she'd seen in Bridget's. Why did everyone think she needed their pity?

She raised her chin and spun on her heel. Screw them all. She had a lot of work to do before the night was over. First on the agenda, make sure no orgies broke out at the Hair of the Dog.

She found the light switch and flicked the overheads on and off several times. No girl wanted to get caught under fluorescent lights, no matter how drunk she was. She yanked the cable from Bridget's iPod. The sound of speaker static took the place of Lady Gaga's "Poker Face."

"The bachelorette party is officially over," she shouted over the girls' protests. "Big thanks to San Gabriel's finest for their special performance. And best wishes to Meredith and John!"

The girls cheered.

"If you want to keep partying, there's a T.G.I. Friday's right down the street. And I'm sure Bridget knows all the other good clubs in town."

"But Katie, we booked the place for the whole night." Bridget bustled toward her.

"I don't care. We're out of bartenders. I still have to clean up. And it's after midnight."

"Really?"

Katie had to admit, the night had gone fast.

"Fine, we'll go tear up the town. We need some fresh meat anyway. Follow me, party people!" Bridget waved a pair of boxers over her head like a hot pink flag.

It didn't take long for the parade of girls to dance out the front door of the Hair of the Dog in a conga line. The last few firemen went with them. Katie plastered a smile on her face as they passed by, then slammed the door shut behind them.

Peace and quiet, at last.

Peace, quiet, and torture. As soon as she was alone, the image of Ryan's hands on Logan's butt flashed before her eyes. She stomped across the room, kicking aside balled-up napkins and a stray dollar bill or two. What about the way she'd rubbed her boobs in his face? If Katie had done that, he would have felt mostly bone.

She picked up a used toothpick and jabbed viciously at a balloon.

The *pop* didn't distract her from the memory of how he'd leaned his head back for the girl's kiss. Just how deep was his tongue in her throat? It was disgusting, how Logan had thrown herself at him. Not that Ryan had minded. The opposite, actually. Ryan had been all over her, like pink on a balloon.

Katie felt a stab in her chest, a physical pain that made her gasp. *Oh crap.* Knees suddenly weak, she felt for a chair and slumped into it. How stupid. How utterly futile. She'd fallen for Ryan. Hard. So hard, she was in new territory.

Chapter Fourteen

Meredith's bachelorette party brought in enough cash to pay the beer distributor, but not enough to make a dent in the insurance bill. The deadline loomed over Katie's head as she poured wine for the Drinking Crew on Tuesday. The bar closed on Sundays and Mondays, and she'd spent the days off mooning around her apartment, rereading her papers from college and wondering where her life had gone wrong.

"A tip-top Tuesday to you, Katie girl," said Archie, hoisting his glass.

Katie grumbled a response.

"Rumors are flying," Sid rasped. He sipped the wine, rolling it around in his mouth. He claimed it improved the effects of his emphysema. "Seems there was a strip show here this weekend."

"Yes, I'm thinking of turning this place into a strip club. But I might have to change the name. I don't think Hair of the Dog will cut it."

The men exchanged looks of alarm. "Katie, are things really that desperate? You should have told us."

"I did tell you, over and over again." She wiped a trail of wine droplets off the counter.

"But your father never said anything."

"And don't tell him!" She realized her mistake and shook a finger at the men. "He's coming in today, but you can't say a word. Promise me. He doesn't need the stress. Everything's going to be fine. I've already gotten two more calls for private parties."

"But we don't like the private parties," complained Sid. "We had to spend our Saturday night on a bench outside the San Gabriel Retirement Home. We've been discussing it, and we have a proposal for you. We think you should consider a grandfather clause."

Katie snorted. "What kind of grandfather clause?"

"If the only way you can stay solvent is to hold private parties here, *ita sit*. So be it. We can live with that," said Mr. Jamieson.

"Well, as long as we can live at all," added Sid.

"Groups are welcome to their parties, as long as the Drinking Crew remains undisturbed. There's no reason we can't share space with a hen party. Live and let live, I always say." Archie raised his wineglass in a toast.

Dr. Burwell nodded sagely. "In the wise words of Rodney King, can't we all just get along?"

"A quelque chose malheur est bon," added Mr. Jamieson. That meant something about silver linings, Katie was pretty sure.

She hated to throw cold water on the men when they looked so delighted with themselves. But if the Drinking Crew had been present for Saturday night's debauchery, there might have been serious medical consequences. "I'll consider it," she said. "But you might want to find a backup bar. In case someone isn't willing to accept the grandfather clause," she added hastily when she saw their hurt looks.

She escaped to the other end of the bar to cut up lemons and limes. After the bachelorette party, the idea of burning down the bar had returned, full force. Sure, the party had been successful, but the bar still owed so much money. It would take fifty bachelorette parties to pay the insurance.

Besides, Ryan was the one who'd talked her out of the fire plan. And why should she listen to him, when she hadn't even seen him since he'd left with Logan? He was probably still in bed with her now.

That annoying stab of pain jabbed her in the stomach again. Katie always tried to be honest with herself. She'd spent every hour since the party facing the facts about Ryan. Fact number one: He was the most physically attractive man she'd ever seen. She'd already known that. Now she had more facts. Fact number two: He was a fireman. A really, really good fireman who would very soon get his job back and be gone from her life forever. Fact number three: Ryan was a good guy. He wanted to help her out, so much so that he'd danced nearly naked on a bar. And recruited his friends to do the same.

She'd wanted him with every fiber of her being that night, not for his total, absolute hotness, but for his willingness to come to her rescue.

Fact number four: Ryan could have any woman he crooked his finger at. Why would he ever want her? She kept returning to the image of Logan wrapped around his body. Maybe if she kept that picture in her head, she could make herself fall out of love with Ryan Blake.

"Top of the morning to ye fine fellows. And lovely lady."

At the sound of Ryan's deep, playful voice, Katie's knife slipped on the lime and nearly chopped her finger off. Who was she kidding? Every second in Ryan's company, until he quit the Hair of the Dog, would be torture.

The Drinking Crew hailed Ryan with toasts and a rendition of "Hail the Conquering Hero."

Katie stole a look at him as he breezed past her. His blue eyes looked clear as sea glass. He looked fresh and rested and disgustingly good. He dropped a kiss on her hair as he grabbed a bar apron.

"Sorry I missed the cleanup. I owe you, darlin'."

Katie could barely choke out her answer. "Forget it. You did enough. More than enough."

"You liked it, huh? It was a little rough. We only practiced twice."

"You'd never know."

"Vader stole the show, I gotta say. Maybe there's something to those energy drinks of his. I heard they partied until five the next morning. I'm getting too old for that. I was asleep by two."

Wild hope filled her heart. Asleep by two? He'd left around midnight. Of course, that left two hours for . . .

She shoved the thought aside. Math was not her friend at the moment. "Bridget told me to tell you thanks, and she has your bonus."

"*Your* bonus." Ryan checked the supply of maraschino cherries, then opened a new jar. "Hope it helps."

"Ryan, you can't . . . I can't . . . that's not right. You guys earned that money."

"And it was a real ordeal, let me tell you. I've got guys calling me from every firehouse in Southern California volunteering for the next gig. No, Katie, it's for you." He gave her a serious look that nearly brought her to her knees. "But don't spend it on . . ."

He gave a significant look toward the back door.

Lighter fluid. Of course. That's why he'd done the bachelorette party. Not so much to help her out, as to stop her from setting any more fires. Still a noble act, but more of a generalized good deed, not specific to her.

She turned back to her limes. The tears pricking her eyes turned them into blurry green lumps.

"Katie. Katie!"

She jumped, nicking her index finger. Doug leaned on the bar, elbows splayed out as if holding up his body took too much energy. "Geez, Doug. You scared me."

"What's the matter?"

"Nothing. Lime juice spurted in my eye."

"Oh." He moved on. For such a sensitive guy, he'd never had much interest in Katie's feelings. "I came up with something. Can we talk?"

"Go ahead."

"Not here." He cast a wary glance at the Drinking Crew, followed by a hostile one at Ryan. "Maybe after work? Your dad told me he's coming into the bar later on to give you a break."

How did Doug always know what her family was up to? She sighed. "He is, but I need to . . . um . . ."

God, she hated lying. But she didn't have the energy to deal with Doug. She wanted to cry on someone's shoulder about her doomed crush. Doug would be the last person she'd choose for that.

"Need to what?"

"Well, I promised Bridget I'd . . . um . . ." She didn't even have the energy to think up a good lie. With a sigh, she resigned herself and opened her mouth to say yes.

"Katie, I can't believe you forgot." Ryan stepped next to her, wiping his hands on his apron with an offended look. "You're coming to my house for dinner."

"I'm *what*?" Katie dropped her knife with a clatter.

"You're telling me you forgot? I knew I should have cut you off after three Brazilian Orgasms."

Katie nearly choked at the sight of Doug's bulging eyes.

"Vodka, Malibu coconut rum, and peach schnapps, mostly," Ryan told him. "Chick drink."

"I wasn't . . ." She looked from one man to the other, from Doug's sullen face to Ryan's slow smile. "It was a crazy night. It must have slipped my mind."

"Isn't that just like a woman?" Ryan winked at Doug. "You offer to make them dinner with your own two hands, and they forget all about it. You're not getting off that easy, boss. Six o'clock sharp. Or whenever your dad shows up."

She managed a smile. "I'll be there." Ryan moved away, although his body language made it clear he'd be available for further rescuing if necessary.

"But I really need to talk to you," Doug hissed.

"Tomorrow," Katie promised. "I'll give you a call before work."

"Don't forget. You always say you're going to call and then forget."

Katie gritted her teeth. "How about you call me before work."

"But you never answer when I call."

So he'd figured that out. "I promise I'll answer."

"You should. You're definitely going to want to know about this. You're going to thank me. For once." Doug got to his feet and loped to the door with something suspiciously like a strut.

Tuesdays were always slow at the Dog, so Ryan had no trouble skipping out a bit early to start cooking. He left directions for Katie and quickly drove home. His specialty, Thai chicken curry, didn't take long to make, but he had to pick up a few ingredients first.

The dinner invite had been an on-the-spot inspiration. He still wanted to clarify things with Katie. Had to. Because Saturday night the worst had happened. He didn't understand how or why, but he'd turned down a blatant invitation for sex from a hot girl. He'd assumed that a night in the sack with Logan would chase away all his mixed-up thoughts about Katie. But things had gotten hot and heavy with Logan, and then . . . nothing. He couldn't go through with it. He'd taken her home. And been relieved to see the last of her.

But afterward, he'd freaked out. He'd roamed his apartment, skimmed through the manual, put on some Smashing Pumpkins, but nothing helped. Finally he tried some meditation techniques he'd learned at the monastery. When the image of Katie kept popping up, he'd figured out the problem. Until he cleared things up with Katie and made sure he wasn't hurting her somehow, he couldn't sleep with anyone else.

Then something else started bothering him.

What if he'd ruined Katie's opinion of him by doing the striptease, as Melissa had warned? What if she'd lost every speck of respect for him? What if he never got a chance to show his "other side"?

And why the hell did he care?

When he'd seen Doug pulling his poor-me act on Katie at the bar, he'd nearly socked him for the pure adrenaline of it. That's when he'd had his stroke of genius. What better way to prove to Katie he had another side than bring her to his house and cook for her? They could converse in a mature, settle-everything manner at the same time.

Not everyone knew that most firefighters could cook. They rotated kitchen duties at the firehouse, and Ryan always looked forward to his turn. He liked pushing the envelope with exotic dishes like lamb biryani and moo shu pork. Some guys brought McDonald's on Ryan's day to cook, but that was their loss.

Everyone liked his Thai chicken curry. He bet it would win major points with Katie. He parked in front of the Asian store where he liked to buy his lemongrass and coconut milk.

Inside, as he scanned the different brands of green curry paste, he wondered why he cared if his curry impressed Katie. He shrugged off the question. Why overanalyze it? He liked Katie. He had fun with her. He liked her way of getting right to the heart of things. Plus, she'd looked incredible in that little dress with the sparkly stockings.

Maybe she'd wear it to dinner, and he'd get to peel the dress off her ever so slowly. And then roll the stockings off her slim, pale legs, then—

"Ryan!"

Melissa waved a hand in front of his face. "I've been saying your name for the last two minutes."

"Hey there, Melissa." She held Danielle in her arms and looked frazzled, her chocolate-brown hair straggling out of its ponytail. "What's up?"

"I was driving past and saw your truck. Actually, I was rushing past. I have to get across town for an interview and Brody got called into a meeting with the PR people and can't take Danielle. Do you think you could . . . would you mind . . . it would only be an hour . . . Danielle would absolutely love to hang out with you, right, Dani?"

Danielle, thumb in mouth, considered the issue, then gave a definite nod yes.

"I would, I swear, Melissa, but I got Katie coming over for dinner, and—"

"Perfect." Melissa plopped Danielle into his arms. "It'll give Katie a chance to see another side of you. Appreciate it, owe you, love you, call my cell if you need me . . ." And she was out the door.

Danielle grabbed the lemongrass and sniffed it. "Yucky."

"I sure hope you're the last female to say that tonight."

"What's a female?"

"Someone impossible to understand." He headed to the cash register as Danielle grabbed at every mysterious package of Chinese candy they passed.

When Ryan opened the door of the sweet little Spanish-style, stuccoed bungalow with the red terracotta tiles, Katie experienced a disorienting moment of shock. He held a little girl who clung to his neck like a monkey.

"Um . . . hi."

"Come on in, Katie. Oh, this is Danielle. Friend of mine's kid. Actually, my boss's kid." He directed a blue-eyed frown at the impish little girl. "Which doesn't mean you can boss me around."

"Hi Danielle. My name's Katie."

Danielle shrank back against Ryan's neck. Katie didn't take it personally. That's how she usually felt when she met someone new.

Ryan peeled her arms off his neck. "Could you chase her around the house while I finish the curry? It's hard to cook when you have a forty-pound weight hanging off your neck." He placed the girl's feet on the ground, though she still clung to his legs.

Katie's heart sank to the pit of her stomach. In case she'd had any crazy hopes that this was some kind of date, they were now smashed on the floor under the scampering feet of a four-year-old. Might as well accept it. Ryan wanted to be her friend, nothing more. A friend who helped him babysit.

She forced a smile. "Sure thing." Crouching down to Danielle's level, she made lion's paws out of her hands. She clawed at the air. "I'm gonna get you."

Danielle shrieked and took off through the living room. Katie chased after her. She wondered if Ryan would have asked Logan Marquez to play with his boss's kid. Of course not. Girls like that got the date-night, tiramisu, seduction treatment. She got to run in circles with Danielle.

Which, if she was totally honest, she'd pick over tiramisu any day. She loved kids. When they grew into adults, that's when the problems started. Besides, she got a whirlwind, fast-forward tour of Ryan's house this way. His place didn't feel like a hottie bachelor pad. It had comfortable old thrift-shop furniture, more books than she would have guessed, an avocado growing in an old salsa container.

Before long, she and Danielle had formed an unbreakable bond over their desire to bring chaos into Ryan's orderly home. By the time Ryan called, "Dinner's ready," every couch cushion had been thrown onto the floor and a pile of books had been knocked over during a ticklefest.

"I think our job is done." Katie winked at Danielle and hauled her to her feet.

The evening didn't quite qualify as a disaster. But it came close, in Ryan's opinion. Katie paid more attention to Danielle than she did to him. Ryan had never been jealous of a four-year-old before. But Katie didn't scowl at Dani once. And her face kept lighting up in that adorable way, like when he found the two of them giggling hysterically on the floor, surrounded by his binders.

"You two going to clean up that mess?"

"Nope. We're doing you a favor." Katie helped Danielle up and gave Ryan a playful poke on the chest. "You're too tidy. It's not healthy. Right, Danielle?"

"Too tidy!" Danielle bounced around like a bunny. "Too tidy!"

"Firemen like order. We're trained that way."

"That's why we're here to mess you up. You can thank us later." She winked at him. He still felt the imprint of her finger on his chest.

"I'll consider it. You hungry?"

"Nothing gets me hungrier than a tickle fight," said Katie.

"Me too! I'm really really hungry too. I like fish sticks. Or tuna. But you have to cut off the bread crust. I like candy too."

Ryan checked his watch. Melissa ought to be here by now. He couldn't really get down to some serious discussions with Katie until Danielle left. "Let's wait a few more minutes."

"Good. Then you can tell me what all these books are for. They looked interesting as I was tripping over them." Katie bent down and picked up the Rules and Regulations binder.

"That book—known as the Manual of Operations—is my ticket back onto the force. Brody, hard . . . um . . . captain that he is"—he'd come awfully close to saying "hard-ass"—"wants me to study up before I come back."

"Wow." Katie flipped through some pages. "This looks as hard as my grad school exams."

"I used to know it inside out. Still do, but some of the details are fuzzy. Things I know how to do in my sleep look different on paper."

She looked up, an eager light in her eye. "I've always loved studying."

"You love studying?"

"Yes. That's why I was in grad school until my dad had the heart attack. I was studying French literature."

"French literature?" Ryan knew he sounded dumb, repeating everything she said. He didn't think he was dumb, but damn, graduate school . . . French literature. All he knew about French literature was . . . well, it probably came from France.

"If you need any quizzing or anything, you should let me help. In college I was the one everyone begged to help them before a test."

Ryan pictured Katie curled up on his couch, tossing him questions about burn ratios and pump pressure requirements. He opened his mouth to jump on her offer, then remembered Melissa's words. *Why don't you let her see the other side of you?*

Let Katie see the side of him that read at the speed of an eighth-grader? The side that sometimes had to sound out words to make sure he'd gotten them right? She'd lose all respect for him.

"No, thanks. I got it."

A stricken look flashed across Katie's face. Or maybe it was hunger, because in the next instant she bent down to lift Danielle into her arms. "Dani and I are starving. We tried to eat a pillow but it wasn't filling enough. Right, cutie?"

She carried the giggling child into the dining room while Ryan trailed behind.

"What's that yummy smell?"

He must have imagined that hurt look. He didn't want to cause Katie pain—that was the whole point of this dinner. But how could they get all this figured out with Danielle here?

"I made Thai food. Hey Danielle, you ever tried coconut milk? Can you believe they make milk from a tree?"

At dinner, Katie helped convince Danielle to try the curry, and said all the right things about his cooking. But she seemed distracted. Distant.

As soon as they'd finished, Katie said she had to get back to the bar to check on her father. When she left, all the fun went too, and Danielle pouted. He knew exactly how she felt. It took a round of who-can-make-the-funniest-face to cheer her up. When Melissa finally arrived, full of apologies, Ryan felt lower than he had in a long time.

"Where's Katie?"

"She left."

"Oh Ryan." Melissa's comforting hand on his arm made him feel ten times worse. Where had he gone wrong? He still didn't have things straightened out with Katie. She'd practically sprinted out the door. Which might have been a good thing—at least she wasn't pining over him. Except it didn't satisfy him. Not one bit.

Chapter Fifteen

On her way back to the bar, Katie got a text message from her mother. *We're at the hospital. Your father had a relapse.* She turned her car around and raced to the San Gabriel Good Samaritan Hospital, guilt coursing through her.

This was all her fault. Why had she let her father come back to the bar? Why hadn't she stayed to watch over him? Was dinner at Ryan's house more important than her dad's health? Her dad's *life*?

She found her family clustered around a hospital bed on the second floor.

"I'm fine!" her dad was yelling. He looked red in the face and irritated. "Bunch of damn fuss about nothing."

"Is he really fine?" Katie slid next to Bridget and whispered in her ear.

"It wasn't another heart attack. But I guess his blood pressure went super high and he fainted."

"Fainted?"

"Yep, I keeled over right there behind the bar. Usually it's the customers who do that." Her father let loose his familiar belly laugh.

Katie dropped to his side and snuggled her face against his shoulder. She inhaled the comforting smell of him, now overlaid with hospital disinfectant. "I'm so sorry. I never should have left you alone at the bar."

"Bull crap. It was fine. The Drinking Crew knew exactly what to do. Sid pressed his Life Alert button, and Dr. Burwell was all set to give me CPR."

Her father winked at her. They shared a confidential snicker. Katie realized no one else knew the people they were talking about. She hadn't had a secret with her father since they day she turned thirteen and he took her to a Green Day concert. She let out a shuddering sigh of gratitude.

Nina Dane, puffy-faced from crying, stroked Katie's hair. "Don't blame yourself, Gidget. If he wants to be a stubborn ass, what can the rest of us do?"

"Now, now," said Frank peaceably. "Be nice to the guy on the gurney."

"You have to promise. No more Hair of the Dog."

"I promise. At least for the time being. Anyway, my Katie girl's got it handled. Right, honey?" He chucked Katie under the chin in a way that made her feel about twelve.

"Right. No worries at all." She forced her smile to look confident and reassuring.

Her father spent the night in the hospital, but the doctors discharged him the next day with strict instructions to rest and avoid stress of all kinds.

The utter relief of knowing her father was okay—and that she hadn't helped give him another heart attack—kept Katie's spirits up until she got another envelope from Fidelity Trust.

"Final Notice," it said in big red letters, the kind meant to make you drop everything and scurry to your checkbook.

She called the phone number on the notice. Three transfers and two requests to speak to a supervisor later, nothing had changed except two more hours had ticked away to cutoff time.

A little less than two weeks, and the Hair of the Dog would have no more insurance.

She couldn't call her father, of course, but maybe her mother would know what to do. But her mother was "unavailable at the moment, please leave a message."

Katie set up for the day with a sense of helpless doom. It didn't matter how early she got to work. It didn't matter how many drinks she poured, how many private parties she booked, how many long hours she worked. The only break she'd had since her father's heart attack was that disastrous dinner at Ryan's.

Even though the thought of Ryan made her heart ache, she had a lot to thank him for. Business had definitely picked up since Meredith's bachelorette party. Actually, it had picked up ever since Ryan had appeared. But what would happen when he left? As soon as he passed his test, he'd be gone. She'd probably only see him whizzing by in a fire truck.

Would they stay friends? Of course not. He didn't even want her help with his studying. He probably didn't want to spend that much time alone with her. Or maybe someone else was helping him study. Logan Marquez, for instance.

She was drying water glasses when the swinging

door to the kitchen opened. Her whole body went on high alert. It had to be Ryan. He always came in through the kitchen. She heard his low whistle and caught his fresh laundry scent. Without turning around, she knew when he slapped hands with the Drinking Crew, when he tied on his apron, when he poured himself a cup of coffee. She knew exactly when he stepped next to her, and exactly how far away he was. When it came to Ryan, she seemed to have second sight.

"How's your father?"

"He's better. But he's banned from the Hair of the Dog. If you see him, send him home."

"Gotcha. Hey, thanks for playing with Danielle last night. Melissa says you're her new second favorite person."

She made herself look up from the glass in her hands. "Oh yeah? Who's the first favorite?"

He winked. "Me, of course."

That figured. She went back to polishing the water glass. "Hm. Kids are usually smarter than that."

"Hello there, hot stuff." A purr from the other side of the bar made them both look up. Logan Marquez. She looked like a movie star, her thick curly hair piled on top of her head with a pair of white-rimmed sunglasses holding it in place. She wore a red halter top that pushed her cleavage up past her armpits.

"Hi, Logan." Katie leaned to one side to catch Logan's eye, but the girl was too busy ogling Ryan. She didn't even answer.

Katie picked up the rack of glasses and headed for the other end of the bar. Let Ryan and Logan have their alone time.

The Drinking Crew had no such scruples. Sid

scrambled for his bifocals. When he put them on, his eyes got magnified to alien invasion proportions. "My oh my," he sighed. "That one's a throwback to my day. Women used to advertise their curves instead of starving them away."

Katie looked down at her own chest. She'd never starved herself in her life. But it would take an operation to make her look like Logan. "You're disgusting, Sid. She could be your granddaughter. Probably your great-granddaughter."

He didn't answer.

Was everyone planning to ignore her today?

"Katie!" Ryan beckoned to her. "Good news. Logan wants to hold her birthday party here. Do you have anything booked for this Saturday?"

"Actually, we do." Katie pulled her notepad out of her back pocket. Skeletons danced across its cover in honor of the Day of the Dead. Morbid, but it fit in her pocket. She flipped it open and looked through her notes. "April Chin wants to have her nursing school graduation party here. Sorry, Logan."

Logan still didn't spare a glance for her. Instead she itsy-bitsy-spidered her fingers up Ryan's chest. "No problemo. I'm sure we can find another place for my party. Maybe one not quite so . . . public."

Katie shoved her notepad back in her pocket.

Ryan took Logan's hand off his chest. Katie couldn't see every detail, but it looked like he caressed her palm with his thumb before returning her hand to her. "I'm sure we'll figure something out. What can I get you, darlin'?"

Darlin'. That did it. Katie took off her apron. She couldn't spend one more minute in this place, not with Ryan practically making out with Logan right in front of her.

"I have to run some errands," she announced to the whole bar, a little too loudly. "Ryan, can you take over for half an hour?"

He leaned one hip against the bar and gave her a long look that sent heat through every vein in her body. "You all right, darlin'?"

"Yes, *darling*, I'm perfectly fine. I have some things to do, things that need doing during regular working hours. Since I'm usually working those hours, I never have a chance. So do you mind?"

"I don't mind. But you look tense." He reached out one lazy arm and snagged her on her way past. "How about a wee little neck rub?"

"No!" She skittered past him, knowing the feel of his hands on her skin would make her come undone.

Outside, she gulped a deep breath of the oppressive July air before heading to her car. Her cell phone rang. When she saw her mother's number, she flipped it open, her heart in her mouth.

"Is he okay?"

"Oh sure, he's fine. Sparkly clean from the sponge bath I just gave him. When I got married, no one mentioned I'd be sponging off a crabby, overweight bossypants who doesn't take care of himself no matter how much I pester him—" Her mother broke off in a sob.

Katie gulped. She'd never heard her mother sound so upset. "Mom, it'll be okay. He's fine. The doctors said so."

"But he won't be if he doesn't rest, and the man has no patience. You know what I've had to do? Do you know?"

"Um . . ."

But her mother didn't really need an answer. "I've set up a mini golf course on our bedroom floor, that's what. All the garden gnomes are inside now, and he keeps moving them around on the carpet from one corner to the other. What do garden gnomes have to do with golf? What? What, I ask you?"

"Mom, I don't know."

"And now he's talking about using my fairy collection too! I'm at the end of my rope, I swear I am. Maybe I should check myself into the hospital, see how he likes it."

"Do you want me to come look after Daddy for a while? We're not too busy today at the bar."

"No. No no no. You wouldn't last for a minute, you don't have the patience." Her mother's voice softened. "Really, Katie, you're doing enough already. It's such a load off Frank's mind knowing the bar's in good hands and he doesn't have to worry about it. You don't know what it means to us. Hold on, your sister's calling."

Katie reached her car. She leaned against it, then jumped back with a yelp. The midday sun made the Datsun too hot to touch. When her mother came back on, she sounded considerably more cheerful. "Bridget booked me a spa day. She's going to stay with Frank while I go get pampered. My husband may drive me insane, but I got lucky with my daughters."

Spa day. She never would have thought of that. Bridget always knew how to make their mom happy. Katie had always been the daddy's girl in the family. And right now all she could do for her father was keep the bar going.

And withhold the fact that it was exactly twelve days from disaster.

She drove to the Wells Fargo branch where her education fund lived. She walked to the ATM and slid her card into the slot. "Check Account Balance."

Twelve thousand, five hundred and six dollars. And thirty-two cents.

She could walk into the bank right now and close out the account. Give all the money she'd been saving to Fidelity Trust. Solve the immediate crisis, and deal with the next ones as they came up. Maybe the private parties would be enough to pay the bills. Maybe business would keep growing.

Maybe she'd start to like working in a bar.

She swallowed hard. That money represented freedom. The freedom to go back to school if she wanted. Or travel around the world. But what mattered more, freedom or her family? She'd never felt so alone in her life.

She ejected her ATM card and headed for the glass doors of the bank. A shout from the direction of the street caught her attention. Doug leaned out the window of his father's Saab. "Katie! I need to talk to you. You never called me."

It felt like a million years since she'd promised to call Doug, or at least answer his call. So much had happened since then.

Well, what did it matter if she waited a few more minutes before liquidating her future? She walked toward Doug with the enthusiasm of someone on her way to the guillotine.

"Sorry, Doug. I've got a lot on my mind. What's up?" The cool air conditioning billowed from his window.

"Get in."

"No, I don't have time to go anywhere—"

"Would you please get in?" Doug's sudden forcefulness made her start. He didn't usually do forceful, passive-aggressive being more his style. "I figured it out, Katie. Figured out how to solve your problem."

Katie hesitated. "Can you just tell me right now? I have to get back to the bar."

"I will tell you. After you get in. It's okay, Katie. I'm not going to cross your boundaries."

So he'd been talking to his shrink. She liked the effects of his therapy sessions marginally better than the effects of a joint. But only marginally.

"Fine." She got in. He rolled up the tinted windows. She settled into the leather seats and felt the cool air surround her. "What's your big idea?"

"I'll tell you when we get there."

"Get where?"

"You'll see."

"Doug, I swear to God—"

"Relax. It's not far."

He looked absurdly pleased with himself all the way to the Sports Junction Grill. She maintained a resentful silence until they'd seated themselves in a blue vinyl booth and ordered Cokes. The restaurant's twelve TVs were all tuned to sports events.

"This better be good," she told Doug.

"It is. You remember my uncle, who used to be my dad's partner?"

"Sure. The one who went on trial for accepting bribes."

"It wasn't bribes so much as lap dances. And he got acquitted."

Katie remembered well enough. The Atwell family had been in the news for weeks. Doug's father had considered it free publicity. "What about him?"

"I remembered about the guy he hired during the case. I called him up. I figured we should talk to a professional."

"A professional what?" A terrible suspicion filled

her. "Are you talking about . . ." Katie stared at her ex as if he'd just turned into a dog balloon. "You're talking about . . . what . . . *hiring* a . . . what . . . a professional *arsonist*? Doug, what the hell have you been smoking?"

"Don't get all crazy, Katie. You had a good idea, but we didn't know what we were doing. A real professional would know how to do it right. It's safer this way."

"Safer?" Ryan's lectures on fires were still burned into her mind. "Wait, did you tell your uncle about this?"

"No. No way. I wouldn't do that. I told him I wanted to hire a professional killer."

"What?" Katie's hand flew to her throat. Was she about to follow in her father's footsteps and have a heart attack?

"Relax. I'm joking. I said I had an issue with the guys at the bar who broke my arm. Uncle Jay said this guy would know what to do. He said he's completely trustworthy and reliable. Think of him as a friend of the family."

Katie tried to calm her whirling thoughts. Had she stepped into a lost episode of *The Sopranos*? "This sounds like a horrible idea."

"Why? We tried to do it ourselves. What's the difference if we hire someone to do it right?"

Katie shook her head helplessly. It had to be different. It felt different.

"I already gave him a down payment."

"What?"

"Yeah, so the least you can do is listen to him. Here he is." Doug gestured at a pudgy, beaming man making his way toward their booth, mug of Guinness in hand.

"Good to see you again, Doug. And this must be Katie Dane."

Katie blinked up at him. He didn't look anything like her image of an arsonist. He put his mug on the table and held out his hand.

"Carson Smith, nice to meet you."

She shook it automatically, then watched him maneuver himself into the booth next to Doug. With his rumpled tie and round, balding head, he reminded Katie of the pediatrician she'd gone to as a child, the one who always offered her lollipops. "Is Carson Smith your real name?"

"Within a syllable or two." He gestured at one of the TV sets. "Mets are ahead by two, bottom of the seventh. You kids like baseball?"

"No," said Katie quickly, thinking of her brothers. She didn't want him knowing about them.

"Too bad. I have two extra tickets to tonight's Dodgers-Giants game. Good ones, right down front."

Doug shot Katie a quick look, but she shook her head violently. "No, thanks." The thought of the long drive to Los Angeles with Doug, followed by a long baseball game, topped off with a long drive back home . . . She shuddered.

"Let's not waste time, kids. You got me here, now tell me what you need."

Doug started to speak, but Katie stopped him. "What are you? Who are you?"

Smith chuckled. "You get right to the point. I like that. If I had a job title, it would be problem solver. Professional problem solver. People—good people—come to me with their problems and I take care of them."

That didn't sound too terrible. "What sort of problems?"

"The kind you can't find someone in the Yellow Pages to fix. But there's a catch."

"What?"

"I only take jobs I can feel good about. I help innocent people who have gotten in over their heads or who have run up against the wrong sort of element, that type of thing. I only take jobs that make sense, that won't put anyone—including me—in danger. I only work with the good guys, put it that way."

Katie liked the sound of that. She was pretty sure she'd fall into the category of "good guy."

"Doug here told me a bit, but I understand you're the real client. You want to fill me in?"

Katie took a deep breath. What harm could there be in telling him? He might not even want the job. Even if he did, she didn't have to hire him. Besides, maybe he'd have a better idea than burning down the Hair of the Dog.

The man listened closely as she explained the situation with the bar, taking care not to tell him the name. He sipped now and then from his Guinness. It occurred to her that two months ago, she wouldn't have been able to tell a Guinness from a Bud Light. And wouldn't have cared. Somehow, the Hair of the Dog had taken over her life.

As she told him about the insurance bill, her father's heart attack, the bachelorette party, a feeling of lightness came over her. Telling this "problem solver" all about it gave her an enormous feeling of relief. Maybe it was the way he listened, so sympathetically, without judgment. He looked capable. Soothing. Like he'd take care of everything. He looked like a nice old uncle who didn't mind covering for you if you stayed out too late. Or a therapist who would ask questions like, "How does that make you feel?"

When she finished, she felt a hundred times better.

"I think I know the bar you're referring to. Nice place, back in its day."

"Yes." She bit her lip. So much for holding back the name.

He deliberated, rolling a coaster back and forth. "It sounds like you're on the right track. But it's a good thing you came to me. The insurance company won't pay if you start the fire, cause someone else to start the fire, or even if they can make a good faith allegation of either. So it has to be done with absolutely no trace. This is no job for an amateur."

Katie swallowed hard, the full extent of her naiveté hitting home. Ryan had warned her about this. Her Coke curdled in her stomach.

"If I did this, I'd have to make sure no one got hurt. I'm not in the business of causing harm."

She let out a whistling breath of relief. Now she felt a hundred *and fifty* times better. "That's just it, we don't want anyone to get hurt. That's the main thing."

The man mused for a while. "A Viking funeral. That's how I'd see it."

"A what?" Doug looked confused, but Katie knew exactly what the man meant. She'd learned about them in her Norse saga class in college. A smile spread over her face and her eyes got misty.

"The Vikings burned their dead on ships. That's how they sent their warriors to Valhalla. In this case, the building itself is the warrior. It's a fine and honorable way to leave the world."

"You think so?" Katie leaned toward him eagerly.

She'd never thought of her plan in that light, but maybe he was right.

"I do indeed. What better way to pass on than in a blaze of glory, with the additional honor of being able to provide for those who cared for you? I believe the Hair of the Dog would be proud of such an end. It deserves a proper funeral pyre."

A funeral pyre. Yes, that's what the Dog needed. The words fired her imagination. The image of a magnificent, noble, heroic bonfire blotted out words like "arson" and "dangerous." "So this sounds like the sort of job you'd take on?"

"Let's talk financials."

"Well." She hesitated. She had no idea how to negotiate such a thing. "Is there any way I could pay you after it's done? With the insurance money?"

Carson Smith smiled gently. "Normally, no. But Jay Atwell sent you. And you seem like a sweet kid. I'd hate to see you taken advantage of by someone more unscrupulous. But I warn you, if something goes wrong and the insurance money doesn't come through, I'll still require payment."

She swallowed, thinking of her fund. She could always fall back on that. At least her family wouldn't pay the price if this got screwed up. "I understand."

"Well." He drained his Guinness. "Then we have an arrangement. But no time to waste if we want to beat the insurance deadline. I'll get back to you with a plan after I've scoped the place out. We can take it from there."

The sheer relief of handing her dilemma to such a capable person blotted out the last nagging questions in Katie's mind.

Chapter Sixteen

The man nursing a Guinness at the other end of the bar looked vaguely familiar, but Ryan couldn't put his finger on where he'd seen him before. He looked like a friendly enough guy, maybe fifty or so. He wore a light gray business suit, the jacket open over a pudgy belly. He looked completely harmless, like an accountant or a dentist.

So why did he give Ryan the creeps?

For one thing, Ryan didn't like the way the guy kept scoping out the place. He had alert, pale gray eyes behind old-school aviator glasses. He wasn't girl-watching. His gaze scanned right past a gorgeous girl in micro shorts two stools down from him. He eyed the bar in a cold, assessing way that didn't sit right with Ryan.

He finished making a club soda with cranberry juice and strolled toward the man.

"How about those Dodgers," he said. "Helluva game last night."

The man flicked an uninterested look his way. Then his gaze stopped, arrested by something in Ryan's face. A moment later, he shrugged and went back to sipping his Guinness.

"Not much of a baseball fan."

"Do I know you?" Ryan frowned at him. He could have sworn the man recognized him. That meant he ought to recognize the man.

"You tell me."

"Seems to me I've seen you before. Is this your first time in here?"

"No."

Not much of a talker.

A group of college-age guys came in and commandeered the stools at the other end of the bar.

"Be right back," Ryan told the man.

The man didn't respond. He had the personality of a dust bunny. Ryan poured out three Buds from the tap, then ambled back to Aviator-Glasses Man. It bugged him that he couldn't place the dude. Especially because of that creepy feeling.

"My name's Ryan Blake," he said, holding out his hand. "Ring any bells?"

"Can't say that it does. I'm Carson Smith."

The name meant nothing to Ryan. "What kind of work do you do, sir?"

Carson Smith flicked him another dismissive, pale-gray look. "Financial consultant."

Ryan frowned. He couldn't imagine a scenario in which he would have come into contact with a financial consultant. Even though Mr. Smith clearly preferred to be left alone, he risked one more question.

"You from around here?"

But he'd pushed it too far. The man deliberately

lifted his mug, ignoring Ryan's question completely.

"I'll let you drink in peace, then. Let me know when you're ready for another."

Mr. Smith nodded from behind his mug. Something about the way his face was hidden set off a warning bell in Ryan's memory.

He made sure no one at the bar needed anything then went back into the office. Katie hunched over a calculator, glaring at it as if it were a deadly snake.

"Katie, there's someone here I don't like the looks of."

She didn't look up. "You mean they don't have boobs?"

Ryan decided to let that one go. Ever since that fiasco of a dinner with her and Danielle, she'd been acting strange around him. Maybe "distant" was the right word. And she seemed jittery.

"I can't put my finger on it, but I have a bad feeling about him. I think I've seen him before, but I don't know where. Maybe at a fire."

Finally she looked up. Her eyes looked shadowed and a straight up-and-down line dented the space between her eyebrows. His heart went out to her. If only he could whisk her away and give her some playtime.

"Where is he?"

"At the bar. Come here, I'll show you."

She came next to him and peered under his arm. The delicious wildflower scent of her hair tickled his nostrils. He looked down at her dark head and noticed how the lights picked out little glints of amber in her hair. Something tugged at his insides. He felt himself harden. He wasn't worried about that. The bigger mystery was this strange inner softness he experienced when he got around Katie.

"He looks fine to me." She wheeled around and went back to the desk. "Quiet, well-behaved. He's not hitting on anyone. What do you want me to do?"

"My gut says kick him out."

She fixed him with wide brown eyes. "Why?"

"We don't need a reason. My instincts say he's trouble. He told me his name's Carson Smith, but I know it isn't. I know him from somewhere, and that wasn't his name."

"He's fine. Leave him alone." She returned to glaring at her calculator. "Believe me, as long as he's drinking, he's my new best friend."

Ryan stood for a moment, puzzling over their exchange. She'd seemed tight, nervous. There was something she wasn't telling him. He didn't like it. And they still hadn't had That Conversation—the one that had felt so essential, for reasons he didn't quite remember.

"Katie . . ."

She pecked at the keys. "Hm?"

But the moment wasn't right. His little speech seemed superfluous. Obviously Katie didn't have a thing for him. He could hardly drag her attention away from the calculator. Logan would have had him up against the wall as soon as he walked in. And yet he'd turned her down.

None of this made sense. He threw up his hands and left the office. He knew one thing for sure—he planned to watch Carson Smith like a hawk.

But when he got back to the counter, Carson Smith was gone. He'd left a twenty-dollar bill on the bar, enough to cover his Guinness and then some.

Ryan still didn't like him. And then he remembered who he'd seen the man with. His father.

Carson Smith called Katie's cell phone about an hour later.

"We might have a problem."

Uh oh. Had Smith figured out she had a fireman working at the bar? "It won't be—"

He cut her off. "Your bartender, Ryan Blake. I knew him when he was a kid."

"What?"

"He's a no-good, run-amok troublemaker. You shouldn't have someone like that working for you. I hope you keep the key to your cash drawer in a safe place."

Katie's mouth dropped open in shock. She glanced at the open door of her office to make sure Ryan couldn't overhear. "Hang on."

She got up and closed the door. "Okay, tell me more."

"That's about it," he answered impatiently. "He was a bad kid. I'm surprised he isn't in jail, quite frankly. His father always said he'd end up there."

Katie couldn't stand hearing him talk about Ryan that way. "Well, he didn't," she said hotly. "As a matter of fact, he's a fireman."

"What?"

"I mean, he *was* a fireman. Right now he's a bartender."

"Why?"

"What does it matter?"

"I need all the facts, Miss Dane. That's the only way I can do my job."

Katie felt terrible telling this stranger anything about Ryan, but the man had a point. She had to trust him, the way she had to tell her childhood pediatrician how often she brushed her teeth. She cupped her hand over the receiver so Ryan couldn't possibly overhear, even through the closed office door.

"He took a leave of absence. Now he's trying to get his job back. He's been working here in the meantime, and he's been a model employee."

A significant silence followed. "Leave of absence, eh?"

"It wasn't like that!" She didn't actually know what it was like, but she hated that note of contempt in Carson's voice.

"Sure. Well, this changes things. It's more dangerous now. I can't do what you ask with a fireman on the premises."

"You're backing out?" For a moment, Katie went dizzy with relief. The bar wouldn't burn down. The Hair of the Dog would live. Too bad it would drag her family under and ruin her father's retirement.

"Of course not." He sounded mightily offended. "When I take on a job, I pursue it to the end."

"Okay, sorry," she muttered. She wondered if the man had some kind of personality disorder. It was hard to predict how he'd react to anything.

"But you have to make absolutely sure the Blake kid isn't nearby."

"Well, of course."

"You're not understanding me. I'll need visual confirmation of his whereabouts."

Katie stared blankly at the calculator, whose yellow digital readout still showed the amount of yesterday's take, which was fifty dollars short of where it needed to be to break even for the week. "You want me to follow him?"

"Whatever it takes. I'll try again on Saturday

night. I'll need to know where he is before I set foot on the premises."

She didn't like the way he kept using the word "premises." It sounded so impersonal. "I'll put LoJack on him, how's that?"

"I'm not joking. That boy's got a temper like a rocket. And a punch like a jackhammer. It was the only thing his father liked about him, as I recall."

"I'll make sure he's not here."

"Not anywhere nearby."

"I'll make sure he's nowhere within a two-mile radius."

Carson Smith still didn't sound entirely happy. "And of course my fee will go up. You should have told me you had a fireman working for you." He ended the call.

Katie threw her phone onto the desk and paced around the office, shaking herself to get rid of the icky feeling the conversation had provoked. The things he'd said about Ryan . . . blech. But she'd seen Ryan fight. He did have a punch like a hammer, at least to an outside observer.

So maybe he had been a troublemaker in his youth. But he'd changed, hadn't he? She hadn't seen him lose his temper once since he'd been working at the Hair of the Dog.

Not that it mattered. It's not like they were dating or anything. Or ever would. If it turned out she'd hired a dangerous brawler to be her bartender, it would be one more in a string of bad decisions she'd made as manager. And even that wouldn't matter, since the place was about to get burned down.

To that end, she had to figure out a way to keep an eye on Ryan Saturday night. She'd have to secretly follow him and maybe stake out his house. After she got April Chin's party set up, she could skip out. If she got really lucky, she'd have a front-row seat for the Ryan and Logan show.

Katie borrowed Doug's father's Saab on Saturday. She felt ridiculous following Ryan home from work. But also ridiculously relieved. Because he actually went home. Alone.

At least she could stop imagining the horror of following him to Logan's house and sitting outside in a car while Ryan had sex inside. Her other fear remained. What if he spotted her following him? She'd have to pretend she was stalking him instead of spying on him on behalf of an arsonist.

Ryan parked his truck out front, sauntered up his front path, stretched, yawned, and disappeared inside. She parked across the street. The Saab had tinted windows, so she hadn't bothered with any kind of disguise. She waited for a while, in case he planned to change his clothes and head out barhopping or something.

Then she called Carson Smith.

"The swallow has returned to the nest."

"This is not a joke."

"I know. Sorry. He's safe at home. Can I go now?"

"Call me in an hour. I want to make sure."

Katie sat in the Saab for another hour. If only she'd brought something to read. She didn't dare turn on the radio, in case that might draw attention. She scrunched down on the leather seat and tried not to fall asleep. It had been a long day, longer than usual. On most days, the pleasure of having Ryan around kept things moving. Today, after that phone call from Carson, she'd felt uncomfortable around him.

After all, how well did she really know Ryan Blake?

By one in the morning, all his lights were off except the one in the kitchen. She called Carson Smith. "All quiet on the Western front."

"We're a go, then. Go home and stay tuned. Make a call from your home phone to confirm you're there."

Good thing he'd thought of that, since she certainly hadn't. She started up the Saab. What would happen now? Would she hear sirens? Get a panicked call from her parents? This entire thing was surreal. A heavy feeling weighed on her. She had a sudden, unruly longing for one last look at the Hair of the Dog before it got torched. She'd been in such a hurry to follow Ryan home that she'd barely given it a glance before skipping out the back.

The old place deserved better than that. Feeling worse than she ever had in her life, she drove toward home.

At the Hair of the Dog, Ryan sat on a bar stool and stared at the manual. He hadn't been able to ignore the bad feeling tugging at him ever since he'd laid eyes on "Carson Smith." Especially once he'd figured out the dude was a friend of his father.

His father's friends tended to be armchair revolutionary types who wanted to overthrow society, even if all that meant was harassing the occasional census taker. But some of them had acquired various criminal skills—and records—and something told him this man fell into that category.

He wished he could call his father. But the man didn't have a phone. Zeke Blake didn't want anyone to be able to find him—kind of like the Unabomber, except he lived near the suburbs and spent his time ranting rather than actually bombing anything.

Tomorrow was Sunday, and the Hair of the Dog would be closed. Maybe he'd drive out to see his dad. Christ in heaven. He couldn't believe he was actually considering a visit to his father.

The things he did for Miss Katie Dane.

In the meantime, he'd hang around the Dog to make sure nothing bad happened. He could study here just as well as in his kitchen, after all. And the coffee was better.

The sound of a marimba band woke Katie up from a sweaty, restless sleep. Her cell phone rang again, as everything came rushing back. The Hair of the Dog. Carson Smith. Ryan. Fire. She nearly threw up in her anxiety as she clicked on the phone.

"Damn it, I told you to make sure he was gone." Carson Smith. She clutched the phone with sweaty hands.

"I did!"

"He's sitting in the bar right now. I can't do a thorough inspection while he's there."

"Shit."

"Were you watching his door every single second?"

"No-o. I mean, mostly." She wasn't some professional spy, for God's sake.

"Today, you make sure you're with him. All day long. All night long. It's our last chance."

"I don't know . . ."

"Well, make up your mind. But I'll expect some kind of payment either way."

And he was gone. Katie buried her head in the pillows. What had she gotten herself into? He didn't sound like her lollipop-bearing pediatrician anymore. What the hell should she do now? And why was Ryan at the bar this late at night?

Most of all, thank God he hadn't gotten hurt.

Ryan was tossing his fishing rod and cooler in the back of his truck when Katie pulled up in her deathtrap of a Datsun. If possible, she looked even more tense than she had yesterday.

She hopped out of the car and came toward him. He blinked, then blinked again. Katie, in a short, yellow skirt with bright flowers on it? Katie, in a tank top that showed off her slim physique? He lifted his eyes to her face. No, no mistake, it was Katie, and despite her colorful outfit, she looked like hell. Sexy. But tired.

"What are you doing here? It's our day off. And not to be rude, but you could use your beauty sleep."

His jab brought a little of her usual flair back to life.

"Beauty sleep, is that what you do all night with the lucky ladies?"

He gave her an A for effort, F for execution. Something was bothering her if she couldn't come up with a better line than that.

"It's too early, and I'm too excited about my day off to get into a verbal melee."

Now she did smile, a genuine grin that brightened her face and snagged at his gut. "I love it when you use those big fancy words."

"Melee? It's two syllables. About my usual length."

"French counts for at least four."

"Touché."

They grinned at each other. Then Ryan, feeling oddly nervous, turned away and strung a bungee cord over his cooler to strap it in. "What are you doing here, for real? I've got something to do today, so if the bar needs me, it's going to have to wait."

"Really? Where are you going?"

He eyed her suspiciously. "Why are you interested?"

"No real reason. We're friends, right? Can't a friend ask a friendly question?"

"Friends, huh?" He wasn't sure he liked the sound of that. "Is that a promotion? Last I heard, I was the employee and you were the boss."

She smiled at him with an innocence he didn't buy for a second. "Yeah, but I'm a friendly boss. And you're a very friendly employee. After all, I've seen your butt." Something flashed behind her long lashes—something teasing and hot.

He liked that. But still he had to tease her back. "Didn't realize you were paying attention."

"Well, I was dividing my attention between five outstanding rear ends. But yours was on the list. So where are you going, really?"

"Couple hours out of town."

Really, that was all she had to know. This was his personal, off-hours business. But when she kept looking at him with those big dark eyes, he caved in. "I'm going to visit my dad."

"Oh." She looked away, as if trying to figure something out. She looked back, hesitated, started to say something, then stopped.

"Spit it out. Something's bugging that overactive mind of yours."

"Well . . ." She bit her lip. He hated when she

did that. His hands itched to stop her. "Can I come along? I need to get out of this town. Seriously. I need a break."

He looked at her in utter disbelief, as if she'd said she wanted to go to Timbuktu with him.

"You want to visit my father?"

"I'll be nice to your dad, I promise. I won't be, you know, myself." She gave him a self-mocking half smile.

He let out a snort of laughter. Katie in her wildest dreams couldn't come close to the nastiness his father dished out on a daily basis. "I'm not worried about that."

"Then . . ." She cocked her head wistfully, pushing her lips into a delicious pout.

Ryan considered. His purpose in visiting his father was to get to the bottom of the "Carson Smith" mystery. Maybe it would help for Katie to come with him. Hear the truth from the horse's mouth. Or the horse's ass, in this case.

"Hop in," he told her. "No backseat driving, no complaining about the tunes, no bathroom stops."

"No *bathroom stops*?"

He laughed, suddenly looking forward to the trip. Hours of nonstop teasing of Katie Dane lay ahead. And man, did she look good in that little skirt.

Chapter Seventeen

Katie strapped herself into the passenger seat of Ryan's big black pickup. His truck was an old model with a deep front seat that didn't even have an armrest in the middle. That meant only the gearshift separated her and Ryan. At least she was following instructions and staying close to him.

Carson Smith had told her he'd go ahead with the job if the opportunity arose. So by the time they got back from the Fresno area, the Hair of the Dog would most likely be burned to a crisp.

She shoved aside the horrible feeling that thought gave her, and repeated Carson's words to herself. *Blaze of glory. Viking funeral. Noble passing.* In many ways, the Hair of the Dog was already dead. Dead bar walking. Now it was time for the cremation.

Ryan punched buttons on the radio. The little hairs on his arm glinted in the morning sunshine. The muscles of his forearm moved smoothly under his browned skin. She noticed a still-healing scar on his knuckle and had the urge to run her fingers across it.

"Don't you have an iPod or something?"

"Nope. I'm old school. I like to see what the radio gods pick out for me."

"The radio gods?" She cocked a raised-eyebrow look at him, which had the unintended consequence of flooding her senses with his blue-eyed gorgeousness. His profile was perfect, except for the slight bend in his nose. His lips dented at the corner in a half smile. The breeze from the open window tousled his hair around his ears and the back of his neck. She wanted to lick that place just under his ear, run her tongue across the vulnerable skin of his neck.

"Sure. Don't you like to turn the radio on and see what song's playing? If you stick with the songs you already have on your iPod, you never hear anything new."

"Hm." She considered that, grateful for something to focus on besides her lust for him. "What if it's something you'd rather not hear?"

"Don't tell me you're a music snob."

"No. But I was in a band for a while."

"Seriously?" He turned to look her full in the face. "Please tell me you were a backup singer wearing one of those sexy little dresses."

"I was a drummer. I wore all black and moussed my hair into a big pouf ball."

He let out a burst of laughter that sounded like sunshine might. "Damn, I wish I knew you then. I can just picture you, like a big-haired Wednesday. *Addams Family.*"

"Yes, I know," Katie answered gloomily. It wasn't

the first time someone had compared her to Wednesday.

"I always had a crush on her, you know. Christina Ricci is hot. But you know . . ." He shot her a speculative, full-body glance that took her breath away. "You're cuter."

Katie felt her heart melt like a marshmallow at a campfire. She should have known a road trip with Ryan would be trouble. "It's better than Gidget, I guess."

"Gidget? Big brown eyes? Cute as a button?"

She made a face. "My sister wanted us to be Bridget and Gidget. She wanted me to be her mini-me and follow her around everywhere. I did it too, until she turned into a teenager and didn't want me to catch her making out with anyone."

"You're pretty close to your family," he said in a neutral manner, his attention back on the road.

She shrugged. She'd hired an arsonist for her family's sake. Did that qualify as close?

"There's something I've been wondering about," he continued. "Now that I have you trapped here in my truck, I'm going for it. I already figured out that running the Hair of the Dog isn't your top choice of activities."

"I'm only doing it for my father."

His jaw muscle twitched at the word "father." "So what do you really want to do? French literature professor? Drummer? Drill sergeant? Dominatrix?"

She shot him a glare.

He shrugged. "Make that scowl work for you. Might be a turn-on for some."

"Really. Not you, though?"

"Didn't say that."

Okay, dangerous territory. Time to change the

subject. "I don't know what I'll do next. I like school. I love school. But . . ."

"But what?" He seemed genuinely interested, his head cocked her direction, the wind ruffling his hair.

"I'm not even sure why I picked French literature. It seemed glamorous and exotic and different from everything else my family does. Mostly I wanted to get away. But I don't know about being a professor. Don't tell my family, but . . ."

"What?"

She couldn't believe she was telling him something she hadn't confessed to anyone. "I didn't like graduate school. It's a lot of debating. This theory versus that theory. It's like you're supposed to pick a team. Freudian or Jungian? And why? There's a lot of politics too, like who's going to be chair of the department next. Two of my professors hadn't spoken to each other in fifteen years and they were always plotting against each other. I don't know what I was expecting, but not that. I just like to read."

"I do too," he said, surprising her. "Maybe you could give me a reading list sometime so I know what you're talking about."

She gave him a doubtful glance. "You want to learn about French literature?"

"Sure, why not? Don't want to debate it, but I wouldn't mind reading it. Hey, isn't *The Little Prince* a French book?"

"Yes. Saint-Exupéry."

"I read that book about a hundred times when I was a kid. In English, obviously."

"You did?" Katie blinked in astonishment.

"Yeah. I always felt like I lived on my own personal planet. And the fox. 'You become responsible, forever, for what you have tamed.' I loved that fox."

Katie was struck speechless.

"You're surprised?" He glanced at her, a challenging glint in his eyes. "Do I seem that dumb?"

"That's so unfair," she said hotly. "I've never thought that."

"Well, I used to think I was dumb, but it turned out I was dyslexic." He turned back to the road to focus on passing a slow-moving van. She had the feeling the topic made him uncomfortable. "*The Little Prince* had easy words. But every time I read it I picked up something new."

Would Ryan never cease to surprise her? She gazed out the window at the brown hills sliding past, the telephone poles flickering in a regular pulse. Grad school sure hadn't helped her when it came to judging people. Or misjudging them, in this case.

She looked at his strong hands, one steering, one resting on his thigh, and imagined a little boy poring over *The Little Prince.* She hadn't thought Ryan could get more attractive, but he'd pulled it off. She swallowed hard.

"As long as we're confessing stuff, why'd you become a firefighter?"

"Long story. Short version, I set a fire on purpose. Got arrested. I was underage, first offense, so I got sentenced to community service at a firehouse. I got lucky. Captain Brody was filling in for the captain there, who was on paternity leave. Cap liked me, no clue why. I got a serious case of hero worship after that. He took a no-good kid and made him into a fireman."

Katie got a chill from the tone of his voice, the deep respect and gratitude she heard there. "Sounds like an amazing person."

"Best man I know. He's the father I never had. That includes the one you're about to meet."

"What's your father like?"

"Hard to explain." Ryan shut down then. His jaw tightened, and he looked as stony as Mount Rushmore. Confession time had ended.

Ryan's plan to tease Katie had taken a left turn along the way. He couldn't recall telling any of his many girlfriends much about Captain Brody and how much he owed him. For sure, he'd never revealed his dyslexia. She now knew more about him than any woman ever had. Then again, Katie wasn't a girlfriend. She was a . . . something different. He didn't quite have a word for it. How did you define someone you really liked being with, had the hots for, and wanted to help, even if it meant shaking your ass on a bar or, a thousand times worse, visiting your father?

He puzzled over that as the sounds of "Redneck Girl" poured out of the radio. Katie started swinging her head up and down to the rhythm. Her hair, which looked somewhere between cinnamon and mahogany in the sun, came loose from her ponytail. She gave him a teasing smile as she yelled out the "hell yeah" the singer asked for. His black mood, brought on by talk of his father, lifted.

Katie was trying to cheer him up. The girl with so many worries and pressures, the girl famous for her scowl, was playing the fool to bring a smile to his face. He wanted to kiss her. Hug her. Lay her on the backseat and lick her up and down . . .

He snapped out of it. His father's place was only a few turns away. Pretty soon Katie would see where he came from, the lunacy-infested gene pool that had created Ryan Blake. She'd probably call a cab to flee back to San Gabriel.

For now, he watched her rock out, and enjoyed every moment.

At the end of a long dirt road, he pulled up outside a ratty old trailer with a broken lawn chair out front. His father despised trailer parks, preferring to squat on a piece of land belonging to a drug dealer whose dirty secrets he knew.

"This is it. You can stay in the truck if you want."

Ryan didn't look at Katie, not wanting to see her disgust. He got out of the Chevy. When he knocked on the door of the trailer, he was almost surprised to find Katie right behind him.

Then again, he should have figured she wouldn't be scared off by a trailer. The man inside, now . . .

"Get the hell off my property or I'll shoot you right between the eyes," came his father's voice.

Ryan sighed. "Zeke, it's me."

A long pause. "I'm lowering the rifle."

"I got a friend with me. Don't shoot her either."

"Not unless she pisses me off."

"Got that?" He gave Katie a sidelong look. She nodded, looking somewhere between rattled and entertained. "He's only shot a few of my friends, and they usually deserved it."

She raised her straight eyebrows, her dark eyes clinging to his. "That's good to know, but maybe you should go first."

"Good call." He stepped inside, into the familiar rank smell of propane, sewage from the toilet that always backed up, and his father's favorite dinner—fried eggs in a cast-iron pan. A swamp of emotions assaulted him. Fear of his father's fists, fear for his father's sanity, rage, despair . . .

Zeke Blake lurked at the battered table like a white-haired spider.

"Zeke, this is Katie. She's my boss."

"Guess that means you have a job. Working for the man. Or the girl." He took in Katie. "Little thing, aren'cha?"

"Five feet, two and a half inches." Katie didn't look cowed by his father at all. With her yellow skirt and bright eyes, she lit up the trailer like a firecracker.

"You don't fool me. The corporate empire uses girls like you to disguise their money-grubbing greed."

"Zeke is a little down on civilization," explained Ryan. "He's a fan of anarchy, except when it comes to getting his propane refilled."

Zeke's veiny cheeks turned redder. Ryan's fists twitched, his reflexes kicking into gear. *Fight or flight*. From an early age, he'd picked *fight*.

Katie met his father scowl for scowl. "You shouldn't jump to conclusions. A corporation tried to buy us out once. My father kicked the guy out. He said he'd rot in hell before letting the bar become a Foot Locker."

Zeke's jaw worked, then he threw back his head and let out a guffaw.

"So why are you here, Ryan?" Zeke asked. He got up and hulked over to the tiny, cluttered sink. At six foot five, he had to stoop inside his trailer, a habit that had transformed his posture over the years.

"Someone came into the . . . place where we work." He felt Katie's sharp, surprised glance. He hadn't told her the purpose of this visit. "I thought I knew him. But I can't put a name to the face. Or a rap sheet to the face, more like."

Zeke cackled as he poured himself a glass of water from the tap. Ryan had set up the water system himself at the age of fourteen. "He must be a friend of mine, is that it?"

"I remember him coming here. About fifty, on the chunky side, wears aviator glasses, balding."

"Not much of a description."

"I think the glasses are the same. They rang a bell. He drinks Guinness."

"And why should I rat him out to you?"

Zeke came back to the table, holding on to each piece of furniture he passed. Years ago, he'd gotten an infection in his leg, and had refused to get any medical help for it. Stubborn old man was paying the price now. Ryan reached a hand to help him.

Zeke swatted it away as if it were a fly.

The rage of a million such swats rushed through Ryan. His body clenched. Blood sang in his ears. Every nerve pulsed with the need to strike out. Fast. Hard. Now.

But something tugging at his arm wouldn't let him. He turned on whatever was holding him back.

Katie flinched from the blind fury in Ryan's eyes but refused to let go of his arm. He couldn't hit his father, he just couldn't. The force of his rage felt like a hurricane in the rickety trailer. She screwed up her face, squeezed her eyes shut, and held on to his arm for dear life.

Nothing. When she opened her eyes to peer at Ryan, he looked appalled. Horrified. He grabbed her other hand and swung her toward the door.

"Call me if you remember," he told his father through clenched teeth.

"Bye, Zeke," Katie tossed over her shoulder. The man was scary, but she'd told Ryan she'd be nice. "I'll watch out for those evil corporations."

"Don't talk to him," hissed Ryan. "We're outta here."

Katie stopped talking while Ryan whisked her outside. He stalked to the truck, dragging her after him. She tried to pull her hand out of his grasp. "Let go, would you?"

Instantly, he dropped her hand. "Sorry. I'm sorry. I'll be in the truck. Take your time."

She stood on the trash-strewn crabgrass while Ryan strode to the truck. She needed a minute. He probably needed a minute too. It was a lot to take in. How had someone like Ryan come from a place like this, from a father like that? She'd seen the demons surface when he wheeled on her, and it made her look at him in a whole new light.

Not as a gorgeous dreamboat out of her league. But as a man with struggles of his own. Serious struggles.

Slowly, she got into the truck. Ryan already had the key in the ignition and a hand on the steering wheel. "I want you to know," he said without looking at her, "that I've never hit a woman. I never would. Since the age of sixteen, I've never hit anyone when it wasn't a fair fight. Maybe it looked like I was going to, but I wouldn't have."

She nodded. "I didn't think you were going to."

"You didn't?"

"Of course not. I didn't want you to hit *him*."

"I wouldn't have done that either." He glanced at her sideways, with a kind of wonder. "I can't believe you put yourself between me and my father. He's bloodied grown men for doing that."

She wasn't sure what to say to that. The lost, pained look in his eyes made her want to wrap her arms around him. But he was still vibrating with tension, so she didn't quite dare.

"I'm sorry," he muttered, looking away from her. "Sorry you saw that." He turned the key in the ignition and backed out of Zeke's front yard, which was little more than a bare patch of ground.

She wasn't sorry. But she didn't know quite how to tell him that. "It's not your fault your father's kind of . . . harsh."

He hunched a shoulder. "Didn't say it was. I always figured I took after my mother. But she left early on and I don't remember her."

Katie's heart ached for him. Her own complaints about her family seemed so trivial suddenly.

In silence, they drove down the dirt road to the highway. When they'd reached the town limits, the tension in the truck finally seemed to ease. Katie glanced over at Ryan.

"You hungry?" she asked. "I could use some pancakes."

"Pancakes?"

"Or waffles. I skipped breakfast. Now my blood sugar's getting low. And there's a good chance I'll be crabby if it gets much lower."

He slanted a funny kind of smile at her. "You want to eat pancakes with me? Even though . . ."

She frowned, puzzled. "Even though what?"

His eyes stayed on her, direct and bluer than the smoggy sky outside.

"Hey," she warned him, indicating the road.

"Right. Hang on." He spun the wheel to the side and the Chevy hurtled toward the shoulder. It stopped in a roostertail of gravel. Dusty greenish-brown fields spread out from either side of the highway. Cars whizzed past in a hypnotic whir. Katie looked into Ryan's eyes, grave, blue, questioning. She had the sense she'd never really seen him before.

"I figured something out," he said.

She made a question with her face, since her voice had decided to make itself scarce.

He leaned toward her, easing himself around the gearshift. "I figured out . . ."

She caught her breath at his nearness. Her eyes dropped to his strong throat. Mesmerized, she watched his Adam's apple move.

". . . that you do something to me. Something good. I like it."

She made a little face. For some reason, that word "like" didn't make her feel good. "We're friends, after all. Kind of."

"Maybe we are. But that's not what I'm talking about." He lifted her chin so she couldn't avoid his look. "I think about you a lot, you know."

Vibrations shot from her scalp to her toes. "You do?"

"Oh yeah. And I don't mean in the what-crazy-thing-is-she-going-to-do-to-the-bar-now kind of way. I mean in the I-want-you way. The under-my-skin way."

The movement of his lips, so close to hers, drove her crazy. His sweet breath drifted over her face. His eyes were so blue, so clear, so beckoning. If she didn't do something soon, she'd die. But the first time they'd kissed, she'd thrown herself at him. This time she stayed still, letting him decide what to do.

He brushed his lips against hers.

She sighed. Her lips opened of their own accord. His tongue flicked them open further, lighting little sparks around the circle of her mouth. He took her lower lip between his teeth and nibbled.

Fire erupted in her veins. She tossed aside her determined stillness and pulled him toward her. He met her with equal force, gripping her with an intensity that shook her to the bone. His kiss, deep and long and burning, rattled her even more. He tasted so good, like heat and hope and sun. She melted against him. When he pulled away, she nearly whimpered.

"What's wrong?"

"I have to make sure," he said in a harsh whisper. "You still want me, after what you saw? Where I come from?"

Her eyes snapped open, in utter shock. "Is that a serious question?"

He didn't answer, but he looked pretty serious, even though his hair stood up and his breathing came ragged.

She frowned at him in a scolding way. "I'm going to let it slide this one time. But if you ever imply, ever again, that I give a crap where you come from, I'll have to go for my baseball bat, and you know how that—"

She couldn't finish, because he crushed her against him in a grip of iron. It might have hurt, except it got her closer to him, which was all she wanted in this world. They dove together into another world-shattering kiss. Then she felt his warm hand on her breast.

"But . . . Logan . . ."

"What about her?" His hand stilled.

"Aren't you and her, you know . . ."

"Never happened." His hoarse voice sent a mass of shivers across her skin. "All I could think about was you. I think you cursed me worse than old Virgil with the Bachelor Curse."

Her last scrap of inhibition fled into the ether. She pushed herself against his hand, wanting more of his touch. It felt even better than she'd fantasized all those nights. He ran his fingers across her collarbones and slid her spaghetti straps down her shoulders.

Oh my God, were they actually doing this? Katie's head swam. It felt like a dream. But if it was a dream, would his muscular arms feel so solid under her hands? Would the ridges on his back make her feel so safe and yet so wild? Would the bulge in his pants harden under her fingers, so she felt drunk with possibility?

She moaned as he slid her top all the way down, baring her breasts. She knew how hard her nipples were, how they ached for him. He skimmed his palms across them. The thrill shot straight to her sex. She squirmed, trying to press against his crotch.

"Wait," he panted. "We can't do this here. Where can we go?"

"What's wrong with here?" Her desire made her sound cranky. "What are you waiting for, a hotel to magically appear? A random phone booth?"

"Oh Katie." He wrenched himself away, pulled up her top, and started the truck. "Hang on." She held on to her seat, vibrating like a wind-up doll. A frantic rhythm pounded through her.

He drove on the shoulder until the first turnoff, a deserted-looking farm road. At the first grove of trees, he pulled over. White blossoms drifted through the air from the trees overhead. Cicadas murmured. He turned to her, eyes blue as heaven. "This okay?"

Chapter Eighteen

"Perfect," Katie breathed. She swung her legs up on the seat, ripped off her seat belt, and dove into his arms. For a long moment he simply held her, drinking in the scent of her hair, the soft, vibrant warmth of her body against his. He could have stayed that way for a long time, except an urgent beat drummed in his veins—the need to see more, feel more. He flicked the straps back off her shoulders and drew down her top.

He sucked in a deep breath at the sight of her beautifully small, high breasts. Her nipples had so much personality. They rose up to meet his touch with the same direct feistiness Katie had. He hadn't gotten a good view the first time. Now he looked his fill while she sat, trembling.

He couldn't keep his hands off her tender flesh another second. He cupped her breasts, their skin as soft as feathery down. Her nipples swelled to a dark rose color that drew his mouth as if she were sweet candy. He helped himself, drawing those pert points into his mouth, rolling them with his tongue until she moaned.

"Katie," he whispered as he ran his palms across the pale flesh of her belly. The lower edge of her skirt rode up on her thighs, and the glimpse of skin made him see stars. "I want you. So bad, you have no idea."

"Oh yes, I do," she said in a fervent voice. "I want you just as bad. More." She reached for his zipper. "It's been on my mind, if you want to know."

He laughed, a sound made ragged by the way her little hands took charge of the front of his jeans. When she'd gotten them down his thighs, he kicked them off the rest of the way. "Now we've got to get rid of that skirt that's been driving me crazy."

"Is that thing still on?"

"Yep, and it's cramping my style."

He put his hands on the small of her back and flipped her so she lay on her back on the seat. He braced himself over her, one leg on the seat, the other jammed in between the floorboards and the door. Her surprised gasp only lasted a second, then she put her hands to the back of her waist, raising her butt off the seat. This had the effect of pressing her pelvis against his arousal, which threatened to tear his boxers in two. He let out a heartfelt groan.

"You're killing me, just so you know."

"Don't die yet. Hang on a little longer." Her eyes danced as she smiled up at him and unzipped her skirt.

"With so much to live for, how could I not?"

She shimmied her skirt down her legs. He circled her hips with his hands and drank in the sight of her. Everything about her was exquisite, her glowing skin, her fine-boned build, her graceful curves. Even her underwear was perfect. Black cotton undies with a white imprint of a one-eyed pirate.

He snorted.

She glared at him. "Do you mind? This is not the right moment to make fun of me."

"I was laughing at your pirate underwear," he said indignantly. "Do you really think I would laugh at you? Even if you weren't the sexiest thing in an eye patch I ever saw."

Her mouth twitched. She pressed her lips together, as if determined not to laugh, then gave in to it, her eyes going all sparkly.

"For the record, I think you're beautiful. I thought you were cute all along, then it grew and grew and now, well . . . Can we skip to the part where I make you come so hard you forget your name?"

Her cheeks went pink and she let out a raggedy sigh. "Oh, all right." And she took his cock in her hands.

His body went rigid from sheer pleasure. With her eager hands on his shaft, he knew it wouldn't take long for him to lose his grip.

He pulled down her panties. The sight of the black silk nestled at the juncture of her thighs was like a shot of tequila to his senses. He wanted to lick the fresh pink lips that peeked through. Maybe another time, when they could roll around on an actual bed.

And there would be another time. There better be another time. Because one encounter in the front seat of a truck on the side of the road wasn't nearly enough for all the things he wanted to do to her.

Instead he touched her gently, reverently. A spasm went through her body. Wet and silky, she must be as close as he was. He fingered the tiny bundle of flesh that made her body vibrate and her breath come in pants.

"Oh Ryan, oh my God, oh please . . ."

"Katie, begging. That's what I want to hear," he growled, then bent his lips to her nipples and licked them until her moans grew to panting gasps. Her dark eyes, cloudy with passion, pleaded with him.

"Hang on," he choked, and pushed the latch on his glove compartment. It fell open, nearly bonking her on the head. "Sorry."

"I'm fine. Doesn't hurt. Just hurry."

"I am, I am." He scrabbled for a condom. When he found one, he yanked his boxers down so his raging erection sprang free. Katie touched it with hot hands. He thought he might die from pleasure before he ever got the condom on. He tore open the package in record time. She pulled her hands away to let him sheath himself.

"Ready?" His chest felt so tight, he thought it might burst. And a pounding pressure at the base of his spine said, *Now, now, now.*

She nodded. It looked like she held her breath. He felt her wetness with one hand—so sweet—and guided his cock to the heat that called to him. Her gaze clung to his, her dark eyes gone dreamy with desire. He paused a moment, soaking in every detail of this moment. Her head thrown back on the seat cover, cinnamon hair mussed against the blue cloth. Her graceful torso arched up to meet him, a sweet white stretch of flesh punctuated by two wild cherry nipples. She looked so free, so immersed in her pleasure.

"You're wonderful," he said, awe tinting his voice.

"Please," she begged.

Slowly, inch by inch, he sheathed himself in her wet silkiness. Her body drew him in with a hot, welcoming embrace. His vision went wonky. He took a deep breath, fighting for control. Her inner walls clutched at him.

Holy fuck, he was about to come just from entering her. Quickly he drew out again, then couldn't stand the feeling of being outside her body, and thrust forward again.

"Aahhhh!" A cry of joy burst from her lips. He thrust again, unable to stop himself, unable to slow down the hurtling train of his need. She wrapped her legs around him and lifted her hips to meet his grinding cock. He loved the feeling of her soft flesh all around him, the silky skin of her thighs gripping him tight, the velvet of her channel pulling at him.

Making love to Katie felt like every thrill rolled into one. Like riding a roller coaster. Like holding a lightning bolt in his arms. Like catching a firefly and watching it glow in your hands. Like diving into the heart of a fire.

Wild spasms shook her body. With fierce satisfaction, he heard her cries of completion. And then all conscious thought dissolved into a primal dance, more, more, more, until everything shimmered and his release exploded the world into a million dancing stars.

After, it took some time to gather the strength to lift his body off her. "Holy Mother of God," he muttered. He craned his neck to look at her. Her eyes were closed. The crescents of her eyelashes and her straight black eyebrows looked like calligraphy against her flushed skin. She was beautiful.

A sweet hazy feeling filtered through his body. He'd never felt so complete after sex before. It felt right, bone-deep right, to be close to Katie like this, even though it wasn't the most comfortable place to cuddle. Bracing himself over her, he heard her quick little breaths and knew her heart was still racing, just the way his was. A breeze from the open window fanned her hair, damp against her forehead. They'd come together like two firecrackers, fast and spectacular. What would it be like if they could stretch out and take their time?

He ran a thumb tenderly across her cheekbone.

Her eyes shot open. "I have to tell you something. I just have to. I wasn't going to, but now I have to."

He went rigid. He hated when women said things like that. It always meant trouble. They'd never had That Conversation. And now they'd slept together. Sex changed everything. She'd probably start talking about their relationship, and where things stood, and . . .

She took a long breath. "You know that man? The one you asked your dad about?"

He went dead still. "Yeah?"

"He's supposed to be torching the bar today."

The pickup raced down the highway at ninety miles an hour. Katie held on tight to her seat belt.

"Hand me my cell phone," barked Ryan. "Or yours. I think mine fell out while we were screwing."

She winced at that phrasing. And at the memory of what had just happened. Sex with Ryan had reordered her entire world. And now she didn't even have time to sort it out.

She dug out her cell phone and handed it to him. He punched in a number with one hand.

"Brody. You mind checking out the Hair of the Dog? Someone might be trying to burn it down. Yes, might be. I know how it sounds. I'll explain when I get there. I'm twenty minutes out. Thanks, Cap."

He tossed her the phone. He looked completely furious. And she supposed she couldn't blame him, even though it was her bar. Her business.

"He said he'd do it safely," she ventured. "He's a professional."

"Don't talk to me right now."

"Okay." She bit her lip, cursing the impulse that had made her tell him. But after the intimacy of their lovemaking, so many confused feelings had burst through her. The secret that had been eating at her all day had come spilling out.

At least it wasn't the other secret, the deeper, more disastrous one. She could handle the bar burning down. She couldn't handle Ryan knowing how completely, thoroughly in love with him she was.

Especially now that he must detest her.

"If you could only understand . . ."

He held up a hand to stop her. "Not now. I have to drive. Don't upset me."

Amazingly, not a single police cruiser pulled them over before they reached town. Ryan whizzed through traffic as if the other cars were computer-generated images in a video game. As they closed in on the bar, Katie listened for sirens, but didn't hear any.

"It's okay! He hasn't done it yet."

Ryan ignored her. And then the Hair of the Dog came into view. Smoke poured from the back door.

Thick, dark smoke, with flames darting through it.

The truck hadn't even come to a complete stop when Ryan dashed out the driver's side door.

"Call 911," he yelled to Katie.

"On their way." A deep male voice called from

the back of the bar. Ryan ran to the back, Katie following after him.

A dark-haired, commanding sort of man, who must be the famous Captain Brody, stood calmly near the fire, as if it were a campfire and he was roasting marshmallows. But instead of a long stick he held a hose. Katie recognized it as the garden hose they used to wash out the garbage cans.

Ryan ran to stand next to him. "Need a break, Brody?"

"Sure. I'll go look out for the guys." He handed the hose to Ryan, who held it with casual confidence. An air of complete alertness came over him.

So this was how a wunderkind fireman did his thing.

"For this little thing? Looked a lot worse from the road."

"I got here just in time. You get some kind of psychic message about it?"

Ryan looked grim. "Not exactly."

Captain Brody's dark gray eyes flicked to Katie, who knew she had guilt written all over her face.

"Sounds like an interesting story."

Katie's stomach clenched. Captain Brody was a fire chief. He wouldn't be too crazy about people setting fires on purpose. If he knew the truth, would he report her to the police? Or, maybe worse, to the insurance company?

She held her breath. Would Ryan tell him? Why wouldn't he? He idolized his captain, and he wasn't too fond of arson.

"I had a hunch," said Ryan, the muscles in his jaw tensing. "You know how I am about fires. Besides, we've had a couple scares lately."

Captain Brody's penetrating look felt like a

thousand-pound weight on Katie's soul. She pulled her glance away, back to the flames. Ryan was definitely getting the upper hand. She saw less orange and more smoke. The fire made a hissing sound that made her think of the Wicked Witch of the West melting. "I think the fire's going out. You got it!"

A bright spark leaped from the fire, flew through the air, and landed on Ryan's left leg.

"Son of a bitch!" He swatted at his jeans. Katie saw a black hole appear in the fabric.

"Oh my God! Do something! He's hurt!" She wheeled on Captain Brody, who didn't move a single muscle other than what it took to raise an eyebrow.

"You might be right, but I'm not worried about the fire," he said cryptically. He cocked his head, and in the next instant Katie heard sirens. "I'll be right back."

"Ryan, are you okay?" Katie stepped as close to him as she could, until heat fanned against her face. A blast of smoke made her eyes water. "Want me to hold the hose while you see if you got burned?"

"Good God, woman! Stay back, would you?" He shoved her behind him. A stream of blistering curse words made her wince. "You think this is a game?"

"Of course I don't!"

"I ought to turn you in, Katie. Swear to God I ought to. Maybe you'd learn that way. This is not cool. Not cool. And my leg stings like a mother . . ." He trailed off, glowering at the fire.

She took a step back, then another, until she was far enough away so Ryan wouldn't notice the tears that sprang to her eyes, stubborn tears that had nothing to do with the smoke.

Disaster. That sweet moment they'd shared, that wild sexual madness—torched right along with the Hair of the Dog.

Chapter Nineteen

By the time Engine 1 arrived, the fire was virtually out. The guys on shift surrounded Ryan with the familiar ribbing.

"Way to put the wet stuff on the red stuff, Hoagie," said Double D, clapping him on the back. "Don't know why you called us in, though. You interrupted a Jenga marathon for that? But we're sure glad to have you back on the job. Maybe the girls will start coming around again."

"I'm not back," he tried to explain, but Two interrupted.

"It's a firehouse, not a *Blind Date* episode." She took off her helmet so her long brown braid fell down her back.

"All I ask is a friendly female for a change."

Ryan stepped in before any blood got spilled. Double D wasn't exactly good at changing with the times, and Two had no patience for his old-school ways. "I'm not back yet. I've been moonlighting here until the captain makes the call. Drinks on me tomorrow night, if we can open after this."

Double D surveyed the ramshackle bar with a skeptical air. "You get many girls in here?"

Two shook her head in disgust and headed back to Engine 1.

"We get our fair share. And why do you care? Having trouble with Mrs. Double D? Is the curse striking again?"

"Don't know why that curse works on everyone except me. What'd I do wrong?"

Ryan coiled up the hose and took it to the rusty hose reel mounted to the side of the house. For some reason, Double D's caustic humor didn't sit well with him right now. He wished he hadn't called Brody, wished Brody hadn't called the guys and made it official. When it came to fires, no one could fool Captain Brody. The man knew damn well something wasn't right with this scenario. Question was, how far would he push it? Would he question Katie about the fire?

Damn it, Ryan wanted to be the one to let Katie have it. He wanted to ream her up one side and down the other, until the stubborn girl never wanted to so much as light another match. When she truly understood her crime, they'd have spectacular makeup sex. In a bed, where he could explore her responsive little body to his heart's content.

Speaking of Katie . . .

He finished stowing the hose and looked around for her. When he didn't see her right away, a horrible thought struck him. Would she be crazy enough to go inside and start cleaning up? That's probably exactly what she would do, determined to get the bar open for business by tomorrow.

He dashed around to the back, where smoke still wafted from the charred doorway. "Katie! Katie, are you in there?"

The stench of wet, burnt wood and plaster drifted toward him, but no Katie.

"Shit," he muttered, and moved closer, preparing himself for a plunge into the unknown. He didn't even have any gear on. If the fire decided to flare back to life, he'd be fresh meat. But Katie would be even more vulnerable. She knew nothing about fires.

"Ryan!" Brody shouted. "What the hell are you doing?"

"I gotta get Katie out."

"She left."

"Left?"

Ryan frowned. Katie had left before he could yell at her? What the fuck? She'd left while he was rescuing her from her own foolishness. While he was performing another act of derring-do for the Hair of the Dog. She'd left after all they'd shared that day. Just walked away.

He saw Brody watch him narrowly. Diving into dangerous situations without proper forethought was the habit that had nearly gotten him fired. He ground his teeth. Way to make a good impression on the boss.

Another thing he could pin on Katie.

By the time the scene had been cleared and Brody and the crew of Engine 1 had left, Ryan was boiling mad. He called Katie's cell phone, but got her voice mail.

"You've reached Katie Dane. Please leave a message, because people who don't leave messages bug me."

He punched the end button. The hell if he'd

leave a message if she put it that way. He felt steam coming out of his ears. If he didn't talk to Katie soon he'd explode. But he had no idea where she lived.

Ten minutes later, he strode into Toned feeling like the Terminator on a mission. He found Bridget in the same large glass-walled room as before, yelling out commands to rows of pretty girls in colorful workout outfits. Not in the mood for manners, he barged right in. The smell of sweat assaulted him.

Bridget was shouting something about "walk it around, up and down."

"Bridget," he said, tapping her on the shoulder.

She jumped about a foot, then shot him a glare that reminded him right away of Katie.

Which made him even more determined to find her and have his say. "I'm looking for Katie. Where does she live?"

"Why do you want to know? And how dare you interrupt my class?"

"Ryan?" One of the girls in the class called out to him. He glanced her way. Oh right, Alison something. He'd dated her a couple years ago. She looked different. Skinnier.

"Hey Alison. You're looking great."

She blinked, a huge smile lighting up her face.

"Are you messing with my sister?" Bridget hissed at him. "Don't you dare hurt her."

"What?" For a moment, he forgot his anger at Katie. "I thought you two didn't get along."

"So what? She's still my sister. Just because she doesn't know how to dress and refuses to do anything the normal way doesn't mean she isn't a fantastic person. So don't play your games with her. She's not that type."

Bridget put her hands on her hips like some kind

of avenging spandex-clad angel. For the first time, Ryan saw her appeal. But he still preferred Katie. "I need to talk to her. There was a fire at the Hair of the Dog."

"Really? Did it burn down?"

Was that hope he saw on her face? What was wrong with this family? "No, it didn't burn down. We caught it in time."

"Oh. Well." She glanced at the women, some of whom were hopping in place, others sitting on the little step stools, panting. "Get up, get moving!" she barked at the class. "Keep that heart rate going!" The women leaped to their feet.

"Slackers," she muttered. "Katie lives on El Contento Drive." She gave him the full address. "But if anything bad comes of this, I'll hurt you."

He had no doubt she could. And would. Bridget Dane was an intimidating woman. It almost made him sorry he'd yelled at Katie—and that he intended to do more yelling as soon as he saw her.

Almost.

Katie lived in the worst neighborhood in town. The building looked like a place that rented out rooms by the night. Or the kind of place a homeless man might sleep off a bender. Iron bars protected the windows, which made him feel better about Katie's personal security, but not about the neighborhood.

Katie shouldn't be living in a place like this. Every time she left home she put herself at risk from druggies and crazies. And when she came back at night after work . . . His annoyance with her mushroomed as he considered the possibilities. By the time she opened the door he was just as mad as before.

"What the hell kind of place is this?" he exploded, without even saying hello.

She tried to close the door in his face. He slammed out a hand to prop it open.

"This isn't safe. You have to find someplace else." She spun around and escaped inside. He followed. "I can't believe your family allows you to live here. What are they thinking?"

She whirled around to face him, planting her bare feet on the hardwood floor as if ready for a throw down. "When exactly did I invite you here to insult my place, and what the hell makes you think my family has any say in where I live? Not to mention you!"

"Mention me?" He saw now that she'd been crying. The skin around her eyes looked puffy. Katie, crying. The sight worked like a dagger to his heart. "What's the matter?" He aimed for gentle but didn't quite make it.

"Oh no, don't you dare go acting all nice now. I have a memory, you know. Two seconds ago you were yelling at me."

"Actually, I think two seconds ago it was you yelling at me. I finished at least ten seconds ago."

She lifted her eyes to the ceiling as if asking for help from the acoustic tiles above. "So you're finished yelling? I assume that means you can go now?"

"Nope." He folded his arms and looked around for a chair. He had to admit her apartment looked a lot nicer inside. The hardwood floors gave it a cheerful ambience. Bookshelves overflowed with an amazing number of books, which spilled onto piles on the floor. He spotted a cherry-red futon in the corner next to a bright yellow beanbag chair. It looked a bit like kindergarten.

"Danielle would love your place," he said.

"Kids always do. In general, I get along with kids a lot better than adults."

"Which explains why you work at a bar."

"So now you're going after my job too? What's left? My clothes? Hair?"

"I love your hair. I could do without the clothes."

Her eyes flew to his with a wounded look. Oh shit. That had come out all wrong.

"You know, because I like you better naked," he said quickly. Images of their time together in the truck flashed through his mind. His cock responded with a twitch. He reminded himself he'd come here to yell at her, damn it.

"Stop changing the subject," he told her sternly. "I have some things to get off my chest."

She bit her lip, but not in her usual worrying way. More in a trying-not-to-laugh kind of way. "Fine. Why don't you sit down? Would you like anything to drink?"

"No."

He wasn't about to fall for that trick. Trying to soften him up. He lowered himself onto the beanbag chair. "Don't think I've ever actually sat in one of these."

"Comfy, isn't it?"

More than comfy. Almost womblike. He felt like he'd reverted to preschool years. And when he tried to resume his planned tirade, it felt ridiculous. Like trying to yell at someone while carrying a balloon and licking a clown-shaped lollipop.

"Brody could have gotten hurt," he began.

"You can skip the lecture. I already decided I'm

going to call the whole thing off." She sat on the edge of the futon. "I realize it was insanely stupid. If the bar goes under, it goes under. We'll manage. Besides, I have another plan."

"What?"

"Well . . ." She plucked at her skirt. The same skirt he'd pushed up her thighs not long ago. "I don't want to say."

"You owe me." Between the lulling coziness of the beanbag chair and the hypnotic movement of her fingers, he couldn't drum up much conviction. Those bare legs of hers ought to be wrapped around his waist. Those fingers ought to be doing clever things to his cock.

She didn't seem to realize all that. "I promise, cross my heart and hope to die, it has nothing to do with fire. That was wrong and stupid. When I saw that cinder hit your leg . . ."

She refused to meet his eyes, but he heard the catch in her voice.

"Bet you felt horrible."

She nodded.

"Bet you felt really sorry for me, like you wanted to take care of me and kiss me all over."

Now she met his eyes, dark sparks of indignation shooting his way. "Ryan! That's what you're thinking about, while I'm racked with guilt over my evil deed?"

"It wasn't evil. You had your reasons. It was . . . misguided." He couldn't stand it another moment. He had to touch her. "Come here."

She looked suspicious, but gamely stepped to his side. He took her hand and pulled her off balance so she toppled into his lap with a squeak. He shifted his body so she cuddled on top of him, her hips nicely cupping his growing erection. He saw desire flash in her eyes, but she kept her arms stiff so her chest didn't touch his.

"I thought you were mad at me."

He tried to remember all the things she'd done. She smelled so sweet, her own honeysuckle scent mixed with smoke. "You said the fire thing was history."

"It is."

"Then I'm good. Can we kiss now?"

Her lips twitched. He traced them with his index finger. He loved the contrast between her two lips, the stubborn look of the upper one and the rounded, sensual look of the lower. Both were so sensitive. As he caressed the soft lines of her mouth, her breathing picked up, little puffs of air warming his finger.

Then she dropped onto his chest and he gathered her against him. What bliss to have her back in his arms. So warm, so alive, so . . . real. She kissed his neck. "Ryan," she whispered.

"Hmmm."

"When you get your job back, please don't ever get burned."

The distress in her voice reached inside him, deep inside to a place he wasn't sure had ever been touched before. He shied away, adopting a flippant tone.

"Me? Burned? Nah."

After that, he lost himself in the fine texture of her skin and the variations of her scent—different in the crook of her elbow than in the curve of her jaw. He shoved her clothes aside, piece by piece. The delicacy of her bones required his attention, as did the sweet, sweet flesh of her nipples. He gorged himself on her with tongue and hands and nose and mouth. He listened to her heart beating crazy rhythms in time with his caresses. He hummed along with her sighs and moans.

And when she couldn't bear it anymore, and lifted herself onto him, he felt like he was floating through pink sunset clouds along a river of gold.

That was Katie. A heart of gold. The phrase didn't leave his head as he moved inside her, feeling every nuance of her inner walls responding to him. God, she was tight, so tight and hot. She moved over him, completely naked now, her dark pink nipples taunting him, just out of reach of his mouth. He gathered them in his hands instead and watched her throw her head back in pleasure.

He thrust up, hard, wrenching a hot moan from her. And then her body arched and twisted. He felt her orgasm all the way to the base of his spine. He delayed his so he could watch her face go pink with ecstasy.

He'd never get tired of watching Katie come.

And then he let himself go, let his orgasm rip through him. It felt like stepping off a tall, tall building and floating through the air. Katie caught him in her slim arms and they drifted through the new land of joy they'd discovered together.

Holy crap.

He lay blinking at his own flight of imagination. He never got all poetic after sex. Never. He looked at Katie to see if she was feeling it too.

Oh yes, she felt it too, if her glazed eyes and parted lips were any indication. Ryan sighed happily. Sex in a yellow beanbag chair ought to be followed by sex on a red futon, and he hadn't even seen the bedroom furniture yet. But those pleasant visions fled when Katie extricated herself from his lap with a suddenly businesslike look.

"Did you . . . are you . . ." He didn't even know what to ask, that's how discombobulated he was.

"I have to go see Carson Smith," she said briskly. "About the fire."

He sat up too. "I'll come with you."

"What, don't you trust me?"

"I trust *you*, but that type of guy's slippery like a snake. You can't deal with them like normal people."

"I'm not going to deal with him. I'm just going to tell him the whole thing's canceled." She disappeared into a dark room that must be her bedroom. "I could call him, but I want to explain in person."

Ryan fought with his pants, which didn't want to slide back onto a body in a beanbag chair. He rolled off the chair and landed on his side on the floor. He looked up to find Katie staring down at him. She'd switched from the skirt to black jeans and T-shirt. "I think I should go instead," he told her from his awkward position. "It's the kind of thing that's better coming from another man."

He knew how ridiculous he must look, but she didn't laugh. "I know you're trying to help me. But I need to do this by myself. I started it. Actually, Doug kind of started the Carson Smith part, but it was my fault for letting him. From now on, the buck stops here. It's my mess to clean up."

She started for the door, as Ryan struggled to get his jeans to cooperate. "The door locks automatically. Thanks for stopping by. It was a great"—tossing him a wicked look over her shoulder—"lecture."

He limped after her, one leg still out of his jeans, only to watch her hop into her Datsun and zoom off.

No other woman had ever skedaddled that quickly after sex before. It was enough to make a guy worry. Not that Ryan Blake, the heartbreaker of

Fire Station 1, ever worried about such things.

Until now.

This cannot keep happening, Katie lectured herself as she drove to the Sports Junction where Carson Smith was waiting. *No more sex with Ryan. Your heart can't take it. Might as well chop it up into little bits and throw it into a frying pan. Got it? Good.*

If only hearts did what they were told.

He was so sweet, wanting to deal with Carson Smith for her. She wouldn't have minded. She'd had enough of that man for one lifetime. But she couldn't let Ryan come because she knew he wouldn't go along with her plan to pay Smith off with her graduate school fund.

But she didn't have a choice. Carson Smith had made that clear on the phone. Sure, he'd back off. But she still owed him money for his time and trouble. If she didn't fork over nine thousand dollars, he'd make an anonymous tip to the insurance company and the fire department.

After she handed him her savings, the countdown to catastrophe would really begin. The Hair of the Dog's insurance policy was due to lapse in one week unless she paid *them* ten thousand dollars. Which would be hard to do once she'd given all her money to Carson Smith.

Ironic. In a week, instead of wishing for the bar to burn down, she'd be doing everything possible to prevent a fire since they had no insurance.

At least Ryan would be proud of her.

Chapter Twenty

Channel Six's Ella Joy stood in front of the Hair of the Dog, surrounded by a TV crew. A light shone on her hair, picking up bits of bronze among the caramel strands. Katie had seen her on TV over the years, but never in person. In person she was almost unnervingly perfect.

"I'm here at one of San Gabriel's most historic drinking establishments, the Hair of the Dog, although some are now saying it ought to be called the Hair of the Phoenix." She paused to give everyone a chance to appreciate her cleverness. The small knot of onlookers exchanged puzzled frowns, perhaps trying to picture hair on a phoenix.

"The Hair of the Dog has nearly burned down at least five times over the past two weeks, and yet, as you see behind me, it's still standing, and still serving drinks to thirsty San Gabrielenos. With me is Katie Dane, who manages this family-run business."

Katie attempted a frozen smile that probably looked more like a Tourette's syndrome twitch. She'd known this would be trouble as soon as Ella Joy had contacted her. But if it drew people to the bar, she'd do a headstand on live TV.

"Katie, how do you account for the Hair of the Dog's remarkable resilience?" The anchor held out the microphone for Katie.

"Well." She cleared her throat. "One thing is, we're really close to the fire station."

Ella Joy waited, but Katie didn't see much more to add to that. "You must be very grateful to the heroic men and women of Station 1. Aren't you doing something special . . . ?" she prompted.

"Oh. Right. In thanks to all the firemen and firewomen . . ." Uh oh, that didn't sound right. "Firepeople." That sounded worse, like something supernatural. She tried again. Time to dredge up some clichés. "In thanks to anyone who puts their lives on the line to protect our life, property, liberty, and the pursuit of happiness . . ."

Where had that come from? God, she was totally babbling. She caught a smirk from the man behind the camera.

She soldiered on. "We're offering a special drink all this week. It's called a Hair on Fire. You know, because we're the Hair of the Dog and we've had a few fires. It's got spiced rum . . ."

Ella flicked the microphone back to herself. "We don't need the details." She gave the camera a stern look. "The Sunny Side of the News does not promote alcohol use. Always drink responsibly, and select a designated driver."

Katie gave the camera an embarrassed smile and leaned across Ella to speak into the microphone.

"We also have something for any kids who'd like to stop by. It's called Dogs on Fire. Grilled hot dogs. No actual dogs will be harmed."

"Well," said Ella Joy brightly. "Hair on Fire, Dogs on Fire. It sounds like everything's on fire at the Hair of the Dog. Except the bar itself, we hope. Thank you, Katie. And now, Jeff, back to you in the studio."

She waited until the red light went off, then fluffed her hair. "Whew. I think that went well. Did you like my phoenix reference?"

"Well . . . um . . ."

"Slow day at the Sunny Side of the News?" The sound of Ryan's teasing voice made them both turn.

"Ryan Blake, City Hall hero, interview ruiner." Ella Joy pouted her cotton candy–colored lips at him. "I still haven't forgiven you."

He bent to kiss her cheek. "Should I beg?"

"Begging never hurts."

"I'll consider it. Nice job, Katie. I'm glad you slipped the word 'rum' in there. It's the only hard liquor we have left."

Katie glanced from Ella Joy to Ryan. She sensed history. "You two know each other?"

Ella sniffed. "I know a lot of people. Better people than him." She held his glance. Katie suddenly felt like a party crasher.

"I'll let you two catch up then." She backed away. Was there anyone in this town who didn't "know" Ryan Blake? Oh God, had he slept with Ella Joy?

But Ryan quickly said good-bye to Ella and caught up with Katie. "In case you're wondering, yes, we had a thing; no, it meant nothing. City Hall caught on fire just in time. I saw her true colors."

"What makes you think I was wondering?"

He opened the front door of the Hair of the Dog. The smoky smell still lingered, but in a pleasant, barbecue kind of way instead of a disaster zone way. Katie's entire family had spent all night scrubbing and reconstructing. Even her brothers had flown in. Todd was on the disabled list with tendonitis in his elbow, and Jake, with that eerie twin timing, had gotten suspended for several games. The Dane family planned to make the most of their whirlwind visit, with a combined "Welcome Home-Goodbye" party after the cleanup.

Ryan took her elbow. "Katie, I got a call from my father. He remembered who Carson Smith is. His real name is John Springer and he's got a long criminal record and several fraud convictions. He used to be a plain old anarchist like Zeke, then he got greedy."

Katie didn't want to hear anything more about Carson Smith, no matter what his real name was. "It's already dealt with. I saw him yesterday and it's over."

"What did you tell him? You didn't give him any money, did you?"

Katie shook him off and hurried to the bar. If her TV appearance on the Sunny Side of the News noon show had any effect at all, she had to be ready. "I don't want to talk about it. Ever again." She slipped under the hinged pass-through on the counter.

"Katie."

"Look." She turned to face him, steeling herself for the impact of his blue eyes. "I really appreciate you not turning me in to Captain Brody. In return, I vow never to try to burn anything down, ever again. Which means that this place has to start making money. Lots of money. Right away. Why else would I go on TV? I hate TV. Now I want to get to work. If you still work here, I could use some help."

Ryan's spidey sense told him something was wrong. Or maybe it was his Katie sense. He knew his Katie. Knew how she hated lying, or fudging the truth in any way. From the tension in the slim lines of her body and the way she attacked the counter with a rag, he knew something was bugging her.

He blamed John Springer.

The day passed quickly, their busiest day yet at the Hair of the Dog. They served massive numbers of Hair on Fire drinks. And not only to girls. Men came in too, and not just elderly men. Businessmen, college students, firefighters. Many, many firefighters. Word spread fast from firehouse to firehouse.

Katie's brothers, Todd and Jake, pitched in, twin laughing-eyed baseball players who kept picking Katie up and hugging her like a pet panda. Every time, she spluttered and kicked.

"Big party coming up," one brother told Ryan. "The Dane Family Posedown. You gotta come."

"No, he doesn't." Katie sounded mortified.

"Wouldn't miss it," said Ryan promptly.

"I might have to kill myself first," Katie hissed at him as she emptied a bottle of rum.

"And ruin the Posedown? What is it, anyway?"

"You really don't want to know." She winged the glass down the bar to a fireman from LA County.

"Are you busy later?"

Her face turned pink. He loved that. "Maybe."

"Well, come by if you want. I'll set your hair on

fire." He waggled an eyebrow suggestively, then stopped when one of the twins gave him a Katie-style glare.

He skipped out early and went to find John Springer, who preferred long-term hotel rentals to houses, apparently. He'd booked a room at the Days Inn, according to his father.

Why his father had suddenly decided to help him out, he didn't know. Maybe he thought years of neglect could be wiped away by one phone call.

Carson Smith, aka John Springer, opened the door little more than a crack. His pale gray eyes gleamed behind his aviator glasses. "I had a feeling I hadn't seen the last of you."

"Can I come in?"

"Do you need a problem solved?"

"Yes." In a manner of speaking, he did.

Springer shrugged and allowed him inside. His suite contained a double bed, a huge TV in a console, a desk, and an armchair in the far corner. He went to the desk, where a bucket of ice sat next to a liquor bottle.

"Like a drink? I recently purchased a bottle of Johnnie Walker Blue Label. Most expensive Scotch you can buy in this town. I was about to pour myself a finger or two."

Ryan's hackles rose. Had he bought that bottle with Katie's money? Guys like Springer didn't back off, or do anything, unless there was a financial incentive. "No, thanks."

Springer poured himself a glass. The warm amber liquid splashed gently over the ice. It smelled heathery and expensive. He sat down on the chair and crossed one ankle over the opposite knee. His belly pushed against his shirt buttons, so Ryan saw the white undershirt underneath. "Well?"

"I want to know what happened with Katie Dane."

"That's confidential." The lenses of his aviator glasses caught the light, so Ryan couldn't see his eyes.

"I never heard of a criminal confidentiality law."

"I have to protect my clients."

"But she's not your client. She told you to ditch the job."

Springer took a hit of Scotch and smacked his lips. "Ditched it is. It goes against the grain to leave a mission without completing it. But she's the boss. Cutest little boss I ever had."

"So you . . . dropped it? No play, no pay?"

Springer answered with a smug smile that told Ryan all he needed to know.

"She paid you to walk away, you lowdown scum."

"Confidential, my boy, confidential."

"She doesn't have any money."

"What makes you think you know everything about Katie Dane? You appear to be misinformed on that point. Her desire to keep the bar intact, and to keep authorities from pursuing the matter, seemed to be worth quite a bit to her."

Ryan felt the carpeted floor do a slow roll underfoot. Rage flooded his system like poison. The edges of his vision went hazy. "Give it back to her."

Springer rolled Scotch in his mouth for a long moment, followed by a very deliberate "Fuck off."

Ryan scrambled to remember some of his anger management techniques. Deep breaths. Count to ten. "Find someone else to rip off. She can't afford it. She doesn't deserve it. She works her ass off for that place."

"You fucked her, huh?"

The room went fire engine–red. Ryan lunged at him. So much for anger management. Springer didn't deserve the effort. He slammed a vicious uppercut blow into the lowlife's jaw. Springer's head jerked back. Something hit Ryan's stomach. He knew it was a fist, but didn't care. The man's smug, greedy face needed another punch, fast. This time he went for the nose. His fist came away with blood on it. And now the man was scrabbling in the top drawer of the desk.

A gun. With shaky hands, he aimed the gun at Ryan. "Quite a punch you have there, son."

"Don't fucking call me 'son.'"

"I take it back." Springer's voice held a placating note. Clearly he didn't want bloodshed in his hotel room.

Ryan fought for control. More than anything, he wanted to smash this guy to pieces, send him back to the slimy underground world, along with Zeke and all his horrible childhood memories.

But he wasn't stupid. Beating up John Springer would create more problems, not solve any. He dropped his fists to his sides, panting.

"Why didn't you ever go into the ring?" Springer looked genuinely curious. "Good way to channel your anger. We could have made a fortune off you."

"Why didn't you go into the weaselly criminal business?"

Springer held the gun steady. "As you can see, I did. I'm not ashamed. And I have no intention of giving anyone their money back. The capitalist system is growing on me."

"You're not going to shoot me, jackass. The last thing you want is the police investigating a shooting in your hotel room."

"Maybe, maybe not. I don't want to shoot you. But

I don't want any more whacks to the face either." He wiped away a trickle of blood. To Ryan's expert eye, it could have been worse. He'd inflicted some pain, but hadn't even broken the man's nose. "Your gallantry is endearing, if you aren't on my end of it, but may I suggest to you that Ms. Katie Dane is a grown woman making her own decisions. It's the twenty-first century, my boy. Women can vote, run for office, and even hire criminals if they so choose. Does she know you're here?"

Ryan stared at him. He despised the man, hated how he'd popped up from the past like a jack-in-the-box in aviator glasses. Hated how he sounded so educated, how he'd learned certain skills and decided to create mayhem with them. And yet, he had a damn good point. Katie wouldn't want him here. She'd specifically told him to stay out of it.

Now that the adrenaline of rage was fading, he cursed himself for losing it like that. He'd better go before the man said anything else to piss him off.

"I'm leaving now, but if I see you anywhere near Katie again, or the bar, I will get violent. And I won't hold back."

He waited until John Springer acknowledged that statement, then left.

Instead of taking the elevator, he jogged down the stairs from the fifth floor, using the time to chill down. What a pointless fucking thing. He'd made Springer's nose bleed, but he hadn't gotten Katie's money back. He might have even made matters worse by barging into the middle of Katie's business. Guys like Springer—like his father—could be vengeful.

Should he tell Katie what he'd done? Warn her that Springer might try to pull something else? She'd be furious with him. But at least she'd be on guard.

He reached the side door of the Days Inn and burst out into the sunshine. In the last few days, he'd withheld information about an act of arson from Captain Brody. He'd nearly run into a still burning building. And he'd punched out a criminal.

Had he learned nothing in his year and a half off? Did he even deserve to get his job back?

"Why'd you pay him to stop? Doesn't seem right." Doug slouched over the counter and fixed his reddened eyes on Katie. Reddened as in stoned. She knew the signs. Just what she needed, Doug smoking weed again. When he smoked, he went off his mood stabilizers. Perfect.

"Because I wanted him to stop. It's too dangerous. It's too stupid. Pick an adjective, it'll work."

Bleary-eyed from the long, busy day, she wiped the counter down. Todd and Jake had already left. Ryan had taken off before the end of his shift. She really wanted to go home, draw herself a hot bath, and watch mindless TV. *Fear Factor* reruns or something cheerful like that.

Or maybe Ryan would be there, winking up at her from the depths of the beanbag chair. Naked. Aroused. Wanting her.

Doug was still talking. "But what about the insurance?"

"I don't know. I'll figure something out."

"Did you tell your father?"

"No. And don't you dare say a word."

Doug shrugged. "All he talks about is his gnomes anyway." He gave a squeaky giggle. "Little dudes creep me out. It's like they're watching you."

Katie loaded the last glasses into the dishwasher. She went into the kitchen to lock the brand-new back door. Her brothers had installed it yesterday, when it turned out simply nailing up a board wouldn't satisfy the fire department. They needed a working back door in case of fire.

Fire. It always came down to fire.

She took a moment to enjoy the silence of the empty, ravaged kitchen. For an antisocial person, she'd spent a lot of time in the company of other people today. Maybe when she went back out front, Doug would be gone.

No such luck. He drummed his fingers on the bar, suddenly much more alert. "It's because of that dude. The bartender," he accused as she walked through the swinging door.

"What is?"

"Calling off the professional. You did it because of him."

"What makes you think he has anything to do with it?"

"I don't know. Sometimes when I get stoned I see shit I missed before. We stopped setting the fires ourselves after he caught you."

"Well, he's a fireman. He said it was dangerous. He was right."

"He's a *fireman*?"

She bit her lip. She hadn't intended to tell Doug about that. It was Ryan's business, not hers. But her brain was too exhausted to keep everything straight. Things like who knew what about whom.

"Why didn't you tell me?"

"Why do you care?"

"You're into him, aren't you?"

Damn, maybe he did see more stoned. "Let it go, Doug."

"I have a right to know." He pounded his fist on

the bar like a drunken politician. "I have rights. Exes have rights. There oughta be a law. Maybe there is. If there isn't a law, I'm going to make one. Ex's rights. Ignore us at your p-p-peril. My dad could sue."

Oh for Pete's sake. She stomped into the office to grab her backpack. She didn't want to fight with Doug. Really, she didn't.

"Do you have a crush on him? Are you hoping he'll notice you if you do what he says? Cuz that's just pathetic, Katie. I'm sort of embarrassed for you."

She slung her backpack over her shoulder and kicked up the pass-through. It slapped open with a satisfying clank. "For your information, Ryan and I have had sex. Great sex. More than once. So I think he's 'noticed' me."

Doug's disbelieving look did nothing for her ego.

"In fact, he's waiting for me right now. So if you want to call that 'pathetic,' go right ahead. I call it fun. And I deserve some fun. Yes, I do. Ignore *that* at your peril."

It would have been a grand exit, except for the fact that she had to hold the door open for him to leave. He skulked out, giving her sullen, uncomprehending looks as though she'd suddenly turned into a skunk.

"Good night, Doug." And good-bye, she thought as she headed away from the bar. Surely Doug would finally, finally get the message. She'd pay *him* ten thousand dollars to go away, if she still had any money.

She started up her car. But strangely enough, it didn't drive toward her bathtub and TV. All on its own, it headed for Ryan's house. She was too tired to object.

Chapter Twenty-One

A sleepy-eyed Ryan enfolded her in his strong arms, cushioned her against his bare chest, and carried her into his bedroom. They toppled onto the bed and into a deep sleep. Katie's last thought before blessed darkness enclosed her was that heaven contained mussed bedcovers and a naked Ryan.

Who knew?

In the middle of the night, she came vaguely awake to feel his hands moving across her body. He stroked the curve of her waist, the little hidden nook under her hipbone, and tangled his fingers in the nest of hair below. She opened to him like a sleepy flower under the touch of the sun.

"Ryan," she whispered.

"Mmm." His answer came from the middle of her body, just before his warm tongue flicked at the sensitive knot of flesh.

"Oh!" She started, fully awake now. She caught

her lower lip between her teeth, shocked by the sensations vaulting through her nervous system. Opening her mouth to tell him to stop, she surprised herself with a moan. She didn't like this sort of thing. It felt uncomfortable and embarrassing.

But whatever Ryan was doing with his mouth definitely didn't feel uncomfortable. She pushed her hips toward him. Would he laugh at her obvious demonstration of want? She felt so vulnerable like this, her thighs trembling, legs falling open, hands clutching at his hair. But he didn't seem to mind. He gripped her ass with his strong hands and lifted her closer to his mouth. And then something hot and hard was entering into her—oh my God, his finger, delving inside and finding just the right spot, a spot she didn't know existed. White waves of heat scorched across her vision.

"Ryan." She shrieked the word. "I can't, I can't . . ." And then whatever it was she couldn't do—she was doing, flying like a rocket ship through an endless universe. She knew her body rocked and bucked against his mouth. But what happened to her body was out of her hands. Ryan was in charge.

And Ryan knew just what to do. While the spasms still fluttered through her, he lifted himself up and plunged deep inside her. She groaned at the sensation of being filled and spread open, shattered and remade. She moved against him, meeting each stroke with hot urgency. In the shadowed room, he was a dark figure, each tense line of his body screaming his desire for her.

God, she loved that. Loved that he wanted her. Loved how he touched her. It made her crazy. A strong bolt of emotion crashed through her, and she threw herself into the rhythm they were creating together, the thrust and withdrawal, stroke and parry, until another shattering orgasm rocked through her. She held tight to his sweaty back, feeling his muscles clench and tense. He gave a deep, gut-level groan, then went still. She wrapped her legs around his hips as he pumped into her. A sense of glory filled her. Nothing in her life had ever felt like this.

Ryan collapsed next to her, breathing as heavily as if he'd just run a marathon. "Holy crap," he rasped.

She gave an exhausted giggle. "You can say that again."

"Seriously." He raised himself on one elbow and peered at her in the darkness. "That's not normal. Sex doesn't usually feel like that. Does it?"

"Um . . . I'm the wrong person to ask," she said. "I don't have much experience." The truth was the truth, embarrassing though it might be. She stroked the sweat-soaked hair on his chest. "All I know is . . ." She searched for the right words to compliment his lovemaking. "I've never felt like this before."

She winced at her heartfelt tone. Now he'd probably guess at her feelings for him, her hopeless, juvenile crush.

"I can't remember feeling like this either," he said in an odd tone. "Strange."

She scrutinized his face, which looked mysterious and unreadable in the darkness. "Is something wrong?"

"I don't know," he said after a moment. He gave her a puzzled look, then shook it off. "Better get some sleep. You were dead on your feet when you got here."

He nestled her back under the covers.

As if she'd be able to sleep, after that mind-blowing experience. But a delicious drowsiness stole the thought away.

Ryan waited until Katie was fast asleep once again, then cuddled the blankets around her and got out of bed. He had to clear his head. Get a grip on what had happened. He'd had lots of sex in his time. He'd started at the age of fourteen, in the bed of the local pizza shop waitress. He'd never looked back. He loved sex. Loved women. But never had sex touched him as deeply as it had with Katie. Never had it sent energy soaring through him like this. He felt like Superman. Like Tarzan. Like he could rule the world.

What the fuck?

He stood in the kitchen in his boxers, scratching his stomach. He thought of Katie curled up in his bed, a slim lump under his sheets, and a sense of well-being flooded him. It felt good to know Katie was close by. Near enough so he could ravage her again if he felt the urge. Or tickle her until she woke up and glared at him. Or tease her until she turned pink and started shooting insults back at him.

The thing about Katie was, she didn't hide anything. You never had to worry about hidden agendas. Katie was Katie, down to her bones, to the tips of her toes. And she was loyal. Look at how she tried to do her best for her family. Even if she had some sketchy ideas about what was "best."

He chuckled. Katie had a way of making him laugh more than any girl he'd ever known. He had more fun hanging around her than he did with his firehouse buddies. And that was saying a lot. With Katie he didn't have to hide anything. She didn't, so why should he?

Maybe that's why sex with her felt different than with anyone else. Because they were such good friends.

Yes, that must be it.

Relieved by that conclusion, he decided to make himself a snack. Maybe a grilled cheese sandwich or some nachos. Then he spotted his study manual on the table. Why not channel some of this late night energy into something useful? His exam was scheduled for later the next day, after all. He bounded toward the book and settled down to study.

Around seven in the morning, Katie stumbled into the kitchen. She blinked at him in the bright morning light, her dark eyes still blurred from sleep, her yesterday's clothes rumpled. Her shirt was buttoned wrong. His heart gave an unnerving little jump.

"What are you doing?"

"Cramming. I got my test today."

"Oh." A shadow fell over her face. "I'd better go."

"What about breakfast?"

"I'll eat at my parents. We have that, you know, that welcome home/goodbye party for my brothers today. They're leaving soon. I should help get ready." She turned to go.

Ryan felt something close to panic. "But wait. Where is it? The party?"

"You don't have to go," she tossed over her shoulder. "It's stupid. Really. And you have your test today. In fact, you should take the day off from work too."

He stared after her. He didn't like this habit of hers, the way she kept walking off after sex. "Wait!" He jumped up and ran after her, catching her just inside the front door. "Is something wrong? Why the cold shoulder?"

"Nothing's wrong. It's not a cold shoulder." Her eyes met his briefly, enough so he saw that something was definitely wrong. "I have to go. They're having the party early so I can still open the bar. I need to help out."

"Then I'll come with you. I'll bring my manual. I can study there too. Your brothers invited me. Both of them, twice. How can I turn down four invitations?"

She studied him for a long moment. "I don't think you should come." And she fled down the front path.

His jaw dropped. Katie was blowing him off after a wild night of sexual bliss. She'd come as hard as he had. He knew it. She'd been just as affected as he had. So why was she treating him like this now?

She hopped in her car and drove off without a single look back.

Fine.

He closed the door with a satisfying slam and went back to the manual. He should focus on his exam anyway. Getting back on the force mattered more than anything else. But for some reason his concentration was shot. The words on the page blurred before his eyes. The more he thought about Katie's behavior, the angrier he got. He'd been nothing but sweet and respectful to her, and that wasn't even counting the orgasms he'd given her. How dare she walk out on him?

He slammed the manual shut and strode into his bedroom to get dressed. Her brothers had invited him to the party, and he was damn well going to show up, no matter what Katie said.

Katie spread the yellow-checkered picnic cloth over the patio table. Disaster. Catastrophe. Just as she'd expected. Stupid girl, she'd fallen hopelessly, irrevocably in love with the unattainable Ryan Blake.

Maybe the sight of him studying had been the last straw. That little crease between his eyebrows made the bottom of her stomach drop out. Or maybe it had happened the moment he'd first walked into the Hair of the Dog. All she knew was that when he'd looked up from his manual, she'd seen nothing but open, warm friendliness in his eyes.

If a cliff had been nearby, she would have been sorely tempted to walk off it. To make matters worse, her father had cornered her as soon as she'd arrived at the house.

"I've got an offer for you, Katie girl. An offer you can't refuse."

She still hadn't processed it.

At the grill, Jake ripped open a package of hot dogs and tossed them on the flames. "Your boyfriend coming?"

"He's not . . ." Oh, why bother. "No."

"Damn. We need some new blood for the Posedown."

"You need a new game instead of that stupid Posedown."

"Posedown is not a game." Jake brandished the spatula at her.

"Yeah, yeah. First rule of Posedown, you don't talk about Posedown. Second rule of Posedown, we girls have to admire all the big muscles." Her bad mood spilled over. "Ryan's not coming because he thinks the whole thing is ridiculous."

"What's ridiculous?"

She looked up sharply. Ryan, hands in pockets, strolled through the back gate onto the patio. Grinning, Jake slapped him on the back.

"Knew you wouldn't pass up a chance to show off your muscles."

Ryan's summer-blue gaze lingered on Katie. The dangerous look in his eyes sent little tendrils of excitement through her. Todd appeared with a plate of burgers.

"Ryan, glad you showed. Ready for Posedown?"

Ryan shrugged. "Someone's going to have to explain it to me."

"Not much to it." Jake winked and tossed the spatula onto the table. He stripped off his T-shirt and flexed his arms over his head until his biceps jumped. "That's about it. You pose until your blood vessels are about to pop."

Katie felt herself turning red. "My family's . . . um . . . a little competitive."

Todd handed Katie the plate of hamburgers and stripped off his shirt. He bent over like a gorilla and clenched his chest muscles. A ridge of sinew stood out along his neck.

"Nothing wrong with competition," grunted Jake, his face turning red. "Who's winning, Gidge?"

Katie wanted to sink into the ground. Her brothers were like oversize kids. Why couldn't they act like normal people for once and keep their shirts on?

"Ryan, join in any time." Todd squeezed the words through white, clenched lips. "Gidget, hurry. My veins are popping. And my elbow's not too happy."

Ryan met her eyes. She shook her head in a horrified no. An unpleasant smile touched his lips. In slow motion, he reached for the bottom of his T-shirt. He was pulling his shirt over his head when Bridget and their mother appeared with platters of sliced tomatoes, cheese, and hamburger buns.

"Oh my," said Nina. "That's not Doug, is it?"

"Doug never did Posedown," said Bridget. "That's Ryan."

"Frank, get out here! Looks like the boys will have some competition!"

Katie's father had holed himself up with his gnomes, sulking because the doctor had banned him from Posedown. But now he came barreling out.

"Goddamn!" he bellowed at the sight of the three bare-chested men. "Kills me not to do Posedown. Kills me!"

"Don't you dare, Frank," warned his wife, clutching at his arm. "Let the boys duke it out."

"I could take 'em. I swear I could."

Bridget hadn't taken her eyes off Ryan. He'd thrown himself into the goofy spirit of the event. He'd adopted a kind of Egyptian pose, one arm curled over his head, biceps bulging, while the other twisted behind his back. He bared his teeth in a mock snarl. Sunshine bounced off the golden hairs on his skin. "I don't know, Dad. You might get Mom's vote, but Ryan's got the girl bloc sewn up."

Katie gritted her teeth. The sight of shirtless Ryan was torture enough. But Ryan hanging out as if he were part of the family? As if they were really together? Not fair. Her heart couldn't take it. She tossed the platter of burgers on the picnic table and marched to Ryan's side. She grabbed his wrist, where the taut tendons stretched the skin, and yanked him out of his pose.

"Ryan forfeits," she informed her family over her shoulder.

She headed for the gate, nearly tripping over a stray garden gnome.

"I think I could have won. Damn, Vader would love this event. We'll have to do one at the firehouse."

"Would you please put your shirt on?" she hissed.

"Nope. Not until you explain why you keep walking out on me."

"What?"

"You heard me. You come to my house, we make love, then you run for the hills at the first chance. I'm tired of it."

"You're *tired* of it?" Anger flashed through her. What was tired compared to heartbroken? "Is that why you came here, to get revenge?"

"Revenge?" He scowled at her. They'd reached the front yard now, and she saw his big black Chevy. The truck where they'd first made love. His bare chest drew her attention, the sun gleaming on his skin. She blinked and tried to look away.

"Katie, give me an honest answer. You're the girl who doesn't lie, remember? Are you upset with me? Didn't I please you last night?"

The touch of vulnerability in his voice undid her. "Of course you pleased me."

"Good." He grabbed her hand. A shock of lust traveled all the way to the soles of her feet. His voice thickened. "Come with me. I want you again. Already. I don't know what it is you do to me, but I can't get enough."

Numb, she let him drag her toward the truck. The sight of his muscles moving under the bare skin of his back hypnotized her. Being with Ryan was like falling down a rabbit hole. If she went too much farther, she'd never come back.

She dug in her heels. "No. I can't."

He spun around and planted his hands on her shoulders. "Why not? What's going on?"

"Why aren't you studying? Your exam's this afternoon, isn't it?"

"Is that it? You're worried about me getting my job back?"

Sure. That sounded good. "It's not easy finding a good bartender."

But he wasn't falling for it. He narrowed his eyes at her. "What does that matter? You're not going to stay there forever anyway. You hate it."

She stuck out her chin and forced the words out of her mouth. "As a matter of fact, my father just offered to sign the business over to me. I guess he thinks I'm doing a good job."

Suddenly still, he studied her. Awareness of his hands on her shoulders burned through her. "Is that what you want?"

What she wanted? This wasn't about what she wanted. She wanted Ryan more than anything, but she couldn't tell him that. "No, it's not what I want. It's the last thing I want. I'd even rather go back to grad school. But I don't have a choice anymore."

"Why not?"

"Why do you think?" she practically yelled at him.

She could see the wheels turning. If she'd ever thought Ryan wasn't smart, she knew better now. In no time, he'd put it together. "Because you gave all your money to John Springer. Fuck. I told you not to give him anything. How much?"

Dumbly, she shook her head.

"How much did you give him?"

"Nine thousand dollars."

He went white. "Come on. We're going inside. You have to tell your parents. It's not right that you should sacrifice your future to some asshole criminal."

"No. No." She fought against his relentless tug toward the house as if her life depended on it. "I'll deny it. I swear to God, I will. I'll never forgive you."

He finally stopped, but didn't let go of her arm. He stared down at her, all playfulness gone. "This isn't right, Katie. You're going to spend your life in that bar, hating every second?"

"I don't hate every second." She liked the seconds when he was around, but he'd be gone the instant he passed his exam. "I only hate every third second or so. The other two are just fine."

His lips quirked. Then his Adam's apple moved. He snorted. A wide smile spread across his face. He laughed, and that beloved, playful sound, along with the summery light in his eyes and the goddamn groove in his cheek, flooded her being.

He brushed his thumb across her cheek. "You know I get a kick out of you."

Lead, sick and heavy, settled in the bottom of her stomach. "You get a *kick* out of me?"

"Yes. A big kick."

"Well, stop." She brushed his hand away from her face. No touching. Not now. Not while he was breaking her heart. "No more kicks."

"What are you talking about?" He loomed over her, frowning with blue-eyed confusion.

"I want you to leave me alone." She turned blindly, desperate to get away before she started crying.

But he stopped her again, all trace of that easygoing Ryan charm gone. "No. What's going on, Katie?"

"Let me go!"

"Not a chance. Something's wrong and I want to know what. I'm your friend, you can tell me."

At that, Katie lost it completely. She wanted to rip that concerned look off his face with her bare hands, but his grip on her kept her pinned to the ground. "*That's* what's wrong, you idiot!"

"What?"

"I'm in love with you! And to you, I'm a friend. And you get a kick out of me. A *kick*!" She emphasized the point with an actual kick at the air between them.

His grip loosened, his arm fell away from her shoulder. Every part of his body went slack, including his jaw. Even his bare chest looked shocked. And she couldn't bring herself to look at his face. What would she see there? Pity? Alarm? Joy? But no . . . if he wanted her to love him, he would have said something by now. Instead the silence dragged on, and on, and on. She wanted to die right there on the spot.

She ducked under his arm and ran for her car.

"Wait," he called, but his voice sounded weak and confused, as if he knew he ought to say something but couldn't think what.

"No. Forget about it, Ryan. Forget any of this ever happened."

When she finally dared a look at his face, it was in the rearview mirror as she pulled away from the curb. He stood, bare-chested and gorgeous, hands fisted in his pockets, staring down at her parents' lawn.

Chapter Twenty-Two

Forget about it? Not likely, although Ryan almost wished he could. Katie *loved* him? She was *in love* with him? It felt like a new vocabulary word he had to learn. Zeke hadn't ever used it. His former girlfriends had used it in a casual way, a love-ya kind of way. Come to think of it, had he ever in his life told someone he loved her, or him?

Nothing came to mind. He loved the guys at the firehouse. He loved Brody. But he hadn't ever told them so. The very thought made him choke.

When she'd said—well, yelled—the words, a strange feeling had come over him. A warm, tender, itchy, unfamiliar feeling that made him want to find a fire to blast a hose at.

He checked his watch. Almost time for his exam. Brody was probably already waiting for him at the station. He jammed his foot on the accelerator. He didn't have time to work this out right now. He had a job to win back.

In Captain Brody's quiet office, he sat down facing the implacable charcoal eyes of his mentor. The six binders of the Manual of Operations sat on the desk in front of him. As if to emphasize the seriousness of the occasion, Stan had been banished from the office.

"Are you ready for this, Ryan?"

"Yes, sir." He didn't usually call the captain "sir," but the situation seemed to call for it.

"You've been studying?"

"I know that manual inside and out."

Brody nodded thoughtfully. "Did Katie Dane help you?"

"No. Not at all," he answered, more forcefully than he intended. "The opposite."

Brody raised an eyebrow. "How so?"

"Got a little distracted."

Brody looked at him steadily. Something about that calm attitude of his drew the words right out of Ryan's mouth.

"When I should have been studying, I was shaking my ass at a bachelorette party, thanks to her. Then I had to go see my father to check out some . . . lowlife she got hooked up with. Not to mention—" Just in time, he stopped himself from telling the whole story of Katie's nefarious deeds. "Well, I had to keep an eye out for fire. Place has bad luck when it comes to fires."

"Sounds like you've been busy," said Brody.

"Damn right. I haven't had time for anything else besides watching over Katie. And studying."

Brody nodded, considering him. "Well, let's give this a whirl, shall we?" He opened the manual. "We'll start with wildland fire procedures."

But Ryan's mind was still wrapped up in Katie. "It

doesn't seem right that a smart girl like her would get stuck doing something that doesn't suit her. She hates running the bar. And she's gotten bored with graduate school. She doesn't like people much, is the problem. Except kids. Loves kids. They love her too. You should have seen her with Danielle. And now her father wants to sign the Hair of the Dog over to her. It's not fair. It's not right. She deserves to choose what she wants. She could do anything. Well, anything that doesn't involve a lot of people. People are not her thing."

Brody closed the manual, holding his place with his thumb. "She seems to like you pretty well."

"She says she lo—" He stopped himself before he said the whole word.

Brody cocked his head. Ryan snapped his mouth shut and pressed his lips together. He wasn't ready to talk about this.

Brody flipped open a binder. "Well, then—"

"The thing is," burst out Ryan. "I don't know why I can't stop thinking about her. I worry about her when I'm not there. She has a way of getting into trouble, even though she means well. And she has this loser ex-boyfriend who won't leave her alone. And her family calls her whenever they need something. Ride to the airport. Make burgers for a barbecue. Pick up a gnome at the hardware store. *Run the bar.* And she does it. She has a big heart, that's the thing. She loves her family. She'll do anything for them. But that's not always a good thing." He shook his head at Brody when the captain seemed about to speak. "Sometimes she goes too far. It's like she doesn't think she has a right to a life of her own. Her brothers get to go off and play baseball. Did I mention their whole family is athletic? Bridget teaches step class. She's supposedly the beauty of the family, although to me, Katie has her beat by a mile."

Brody snapped the manual shut. "Did I mention this exam is about the procedures and policies of the San Gabriel Fire Department, not the life of Katie Dane?"

"Oh. Of course, Cap. Sorry." Ryan collected himself. Katie's declaration of love had completely thrown him. "I'm ready. Let's do this."

"You sure?"

"Yes. Absolutely."

Brody opened the manual and read. "'All responding fire companies shall utilize and establish LCES.' Walk me through it, step by step."

"LCES. It means you select Lookouts, establish Communications, identify Escape routes, and select Safety zones." As Ryan concentrated on answering the questions Brody threw at him, the image of Katie danced at the edge of his mind the entire time. When Brody finally stopped firing questions, he couldn't remember a single one of them.

"Thanks for coming in, Ryan. I'll let you know what I decide."

"Thanks, Cap." He hauled himself to his feet, feeling wrung out.

"Before you go, one thing." The gleam in Brody's eye made Ryan distinctly nervous.

"Yeah?"

"Have you considered the possibility that you might be in love with Katie?"

Ryan stared at his captain. Was some kind of crazy love virus going around that made everyone harp on that particular word? "Are you nuts?"

"Have you ever been in love before?"

Ryan wanted to say something easy like, *Not since my first dirt bike,* but the question seemed to call for a more serious approach. He considered it the way Brody would, carefully, thoughtfully.

"I don't know," he finally said. "I haven't had many examples of . . . love . . . in my life. Except you and Melissa."

"Do you remember how crazy Melissa drove me when we first met?"

"I remember." The whole station had noticed. They'd been worried. Until they'd all taken Melissa into their hearts.

"Love can do that. Love can do all kinds of things."

Maybe that's what he was afraid of. Ryan dragged himself out to his truck, sure he'd failed the exam. Sure he'd ruined everything with Katie. Sure he'd never been more mixed up in his life.

Doug Atwell knew the exact moment his life had gone to shit. When he'd allowed that freakin' Ryan dude into the Hair of the Dog. Before then, he'd felt one hundred percent sure Katie would come back to him. He knew her. When it came to soft hearts, no one beat Katie Dane.

But Ryan had messed everything up. Now when Katie looked at him Doug saw something new in her eyes. Boredom. Katie was bored with him. He needed to do something spectacular to chase that look away. Nothing he'd tried so far—setting fires, finding Carson Smith—had worked. Because of freakin' Ryan.

Good thing he knew where Carson Smith was

staying. He knocked on the man's door at the Days Inn. When he answered, the sight of a purpling bruise on his cheek and his swollen nose made Doug take a step back.

"What the hell do you want?"

"I . . . um . . ." Doug stammered. Over Smith's shoulder, he saw a packed suitcase ready for departure. He'd caught him just in time. "I want to hire you." He put his hand in his pocket and brought out the wad of cash he'd withdrawn from the bank. The sight seemed to soften Smith. Behind his aviator glasses, his eyes slid to the cash, then back to Doug.

"I'm heading out. What did you need?"

"Can I come in?"

"Make it swift."

Doug followed him into the hotel room. The sound of the door clicking shut gave him an unpleasant start.

"State your business." Smith didn't even sit down. In his tan windbreaker and chinos, he faced Doug like a baseball coach deciding whether to bring in a new pitcher.

"There's someone I want to get rid of. Not kill," he added hastily. "Just chase away. He's a bartender at the Hair of the Dog, and he's trouble."

Carson Smith's gaze sharpened. For the first time, he focused seriously on Doug, who felt vaguely pleased by that.

"Ryan Blake."

"Oh, you know him?"

"I make it a point to know everyone involved in a job."

"That's it. I don't *want* him involved. I want him to leave. I don't want him near Katie anymore."

"Is Katie your girl? I thought you were just friends."

The nasty gleam in the man's gray eyes made Doug's spine stiffen. "We're way more than friends. Way more. From way back."

"So you want your girl back. And Ryan's getting in the way. I can see how he would. Good-looking fellow."

Doug ground his teeth. He didn't like this man knowing his private business. He didn't like the patronizing looks he kept tossing at him. Carson Smith was treating him like a child. For a fleeting moment, he wondered if Smith would treat Ryan Blake like this. The thought made him madder than ever. "So will you do something?"

"Hell no."

"What?"

"I don't get involved in domestic issues. Now get out of here." He waved his hand as if Doug were nothing more than a mosquito.

Dismissed. Doug hung his head and turned to go. His gaze snagged on a desk drawer that stood slightly open. Something black gleamed within. It looked like a gun.

Operating on sheer impulse, he dove toward the drawer and grabbed the black thing. He bobbled it in his hands, shocked to find it actually was a gun. Good thing he'd had a hit of weed before he came here. He always thought better slightly stoned.

He held the gun in both hands and aimed it at Carson Smith, who held his pudgy hands in a calming gesture.

"Like to rephrase that?" Doug put on a nasty tough-guy sneer. Wasn't that a line from a Clint

Eastwood movie? Or one of the *Die Hards*? It worked perfectly, in any case.

"I really don't," said Carson Smith, mildly. "Do you actually think you can shoot me at a Days Inn in the middle of the day? Come now, son, I know you're upset. Put down the gun. It isn't even loaded."

"Oh." Doug tossed the gun onto the desk.

Smith ambled over to the desk and idly picked up the gun. "Did I say it wasn't loaded? Oops." He clicked the safety off and aimed it at Doug, who turned white. "You're dumber than I thought, boy."

"But . . . Days Inn . . . middle of the day . . . all that stuff you said," stammered Doug.

"I'm not going to shoot you, jerkoff." He lowered the gun. "Actually, you've touched my heart with your sad tale of thwarted love. But some things a man has to do for himself. Like get his woman back."

Doug nodded frantically. He would have agreed with anything the dude said right now.

"But I have to admire your tenacity. And you are Jay's nephew, so I suppose I can help you out. For instance, I could tell you about a perfectly obvious solution staring you in the face." Smith caressed the gun, put the safety back on, then bent down to stow it away in a holster strapped to his shin. He pulled his chinos over it. Doug watched every movement with a kind of sick fascination. Was he supposed to be guessing at the brilliant solution right in front of him? His solution had been to come here. So far it hadn't exactly been a raging success.

"Mr. Blake is a fireman, correct? Firemen know a lot about fires. They probably know how to set fires better than anyone. Not only that, they keep highly flammable substances on the premises. They buy a certain brand of varnish in bulk. They use it on their ladders. Do you know what kind?"

Doug shook his head.

"That might be a convenient piece of information to possess. In fact, I happen to have a can of it in my car, but I'll probably drop it by the Dumpster on my way out. If a fire broke out at the Hair of the Dog, and it appeared to be set by a professional fireman, and there happened to be such a person working on the premises, why . . ."

Doug squinted, trying to follow the logic. "They'd blame it on Ryan?"

"Indeed. Arson is a serious crime for a fireman. For anyone, but especially a fireman. He'd be shunned by his own kind."

"But . . . Katie wants the bar to burn down. She might like him more than ever."

"Ah, but my understanding is that the insurance policy runs out in a very, very few days. A little patience goes a long way, son."

"That's, that's . . . evil," whispered Doug. "They'd lose everything."

"Well, yes. She'd probably be quite upset. And she'd certainly never forgive the man who set the fire. Now. Unless you're planning to help me carry my bags to my car, perhaps you can find some other lucky problem solver to pester."

Doug started. "Right. Sorry. Thanks. I'll . . . uh . . . think it over."

Carson pushed his glasses higher on his nose and shouldered his duffel bag. "Do what you want. But don't ever come my way again. I don't usually let young idiots like you point a gun at me and live."

He shoved past Doug on his way into the hall. Doug caught a close-up look at the damage to his face as he passed. Whoever had stood up to Smith like that, Doug would like to shake his hand.

After his exam, a restless, aimless energy consumed Ryan. Normally he would head to work, where the twin distractions of serving drinks and teasing Katie would take his mind off things. But he couldn't go there, not while things with Katie were so up in the air.

Before he saw her, he had to figure this whole thing out. Unfortunately, he didn't have a clue how to approach such a problem. So when Vader called to see how the test had gone, he jumped at the distraction.

"Spread the word. Party at my house. I'll grab some beer and chips."

"How about the Hair of the Dog? That's where the chicks are nowadays."

"It's my day off. You feel like putting out fires on your day off?"

"Yeah."

"Just come to my place."

When Vader, Double D, and Joe the Toe showed up about an hour later, Ryan was pulling a pan of nachos out of the oven.

"You'll make some lucky girl a fine wife someday," said Joe the Toe, settling himself onto the couch. Between him, Vader, and Double D's belly, Ryan's living room suddenly looked tiny.

"Don't you got nothin' low-fat?" Double D complained. "Trying to slim down here."

"Lowest fat thing I got is a Bud Light."

"Give it here."

They all cracked open a beer. "To Hoagie getting back on the force," said Double D.

"Amen to that," said Vader. "We've missed your chicken curry, hotshot."

Ryan gave a modest nod. "First thing I'll make when I get back."

They all downed their first beer within a matter of seconds. The first twelve-pack disappeared in about ten minutes. Gradually, Ryan relaxed. A pleasant buzz took the place of his thoughts about Katie. Male topics of conversation took over. Vader and Double D told the story of a fire at a Korean restaurant that had nearly taken down an entire strip mall. The firehouse had been offered a lifetime supply of kimchi as a reward. Then Vader described his new truck, a baby-blue Ford 250 with crew cab, six-speaker sound system, and a hydraulic lift. The comfort of masculine companionship lulled Ryan off his guard.

Until Joe the Toe ruined the whole thing.

"How's our favorite little bar manager?"

Ryan started. "Katie? Why?"

"Merely inquiring. I worry about that girl. She works much too hard."

"Yes, she does. I keep telling her that, but she doesn't care what I say. Anyway, I'm staying away from her right now. Brody says I might . . ." Sober, he would have stopped there. But five Bud Lights apparently wanted to tell all his secrets. "Brody says I might be in love with her."

"Love? You?" Double D guffawed until his belly shook. "Serves you right." He took another beer from the twelve-pack.

Vader shook his head morosely. "What's the point of having you back if you're going to be in love? So much for chicks hanging around the station."

"Sorry to let you down," muttered Ryan. He

grabbed a handful of chips and dug around for some cheese. "He's probably full of it anyway."

"The captain?" Vader shook his head, joined by the others in a mass rejection of that possibility. "The captain knows shit. Lots of shit. If the captain says it, it's prob'ly true."

Joe the Toe, his huge feet propped on Ryan's coffee table, fixed him with a perplexed look. "I don't quite understand. You say you're avoiding Katie because your captain says you might be in love with her."

Ryan winced. Every time he heard those words, they scared him more. "Right."

"That doesn't follow. Usually when people are in love, they want to be with each other."

"Did you lose half your brain along with your toe?" Vader said. "Katie probably hates him."

"You're the one who shrunk your brain to a polka dot with all those steroids."

"That doesn't make any sense. Polka dots could be big or small. See, I'm smarter than you. I'm smarter than you . . ." Vader segued into a whiny chant.

Ryan frowned at them both. "Why would Katie hate me?" Confused he might be, but he knew for damn sure he didn't want that.

"Have you ever told her how you feel?"

"How could I do that? I don't even know myself. I still think Brody's got it wrong."

"Well, there you are, then."

"Where am I?" Ryan rubbed his forehead and frowned at the pile of beer cans that had robbed him of his reasoning ability.

"Have you slept with her?"

"Yes," he admitted.

"It doesn't take an Oxford degree to know sex changes everything."

Ryan groaned. "I know that." With a sympathetic, poor-bastard nod, Vader tossed him another beer.

Joe the Toe crossed his arms over his massive chest. "Vader, who must be a sort of steroid-induced idiot savant, has put his finger on the problem. Katie hates you because she loves you, but doesn't realize you are very likely—according to the captain—in love with her. You're breaking her heart."

Chapter Twenty-Three

The hangover encased Ryan's head in a ball of nasty fiberglass insulation. Clouds of fluff filled his brain—fluff spun from shards of glass. Every time he blinked, slivers of glass seemed to slice through his eyes. Damn. How much had he and the guys drunk last night?

Ryan rolled off his bed and landed on a body. On the floor next to his bed, Vader was splayed out like a frog about to get dissected. He groaned feebly. Ryan quickly rolled onto the floor. Vader went back to sleep.

Ryan picked his way through the snoring, wheezing bodies littering his house. Double D was slumped against the couch. Joe the Toe, who had rolled a Turkish rug around his bulk, blocked the entrance to the kitchen.

Bracing himself, Ryan jumped over the enormous lump of rug-covered black guy. As he feared, the impact of his landing sent spikes of vengeful pain through his brain. He whimpered and crept to the sink, where he downed two tall glasses of water in quick succession. He found some aspirin in the cupboard and took four of those. Coffee seemed debatable. But the guys might want some when they surfaced. So he pulled his can of Yuban coffee out of the freezer and gently poured some in the filter. Soft and slow, that was the ticket. Nothing sudden. Nothing harsh.

He limped to the kitchen table and put his head in his hands.

Worst hangover ever? Maybe. His memories hid behind a veil of fiberglass. It took too much energy to track them down. Instead he sat dully at the table and waited for the aspirin to kick in.

Bit by bit, scraps of conversation from last night floated to the surface. Vader's truck. The ragging he'd received on account of its being baby blue.

"Blue means boy," he'd said, furious.

"Guess that makes you a baby boy then."

"Chicks dig it."

"That's because chicks dig babies."

Sometime after that had come Joe the Toe's rant about Britney Spears. "She's part of America's nefarious attempt to corrupt the taste and aesthetics of the rest of us, until we can no longer distinguish good from bad, in fact the words have no more meaning."

"Hey," Ryan had protested. "Doesn't Lady Gaga make up for Britney Spears?"

Joe the Toe had turned as purple as a black man could.

One memory kept circling around his bruised and battered consciousness. It had to do with Katie. They'd talked about Katie. His stomach tightened at the thought. It had been upsetting. It had led him to drink many, many more Bud Lights and to dig into his stash of tequila. It had to do with . . .

And then it all came back to him. Katie loved him, and he was breaking her heart. Breaking Katie's heart? The thought of causing her pain hurt more than his hangover. He stood up in the empty kitchen. He needed to go to her this minute and tell her she should stop it, right now. Stop loving him. Stop breaking her heart. He'd go to her apartment and knock on her door. She'd open it, maybe in her pirate undies, maybe with her hair all tumbled around her face, maybe with her big dark eyes all heavy with sleep, her face pink, with marks on her cheek from lying on a book. She'd frown at him and push her hair behind her ears. *What are you doing here?* she'd ask.

And he'd take her in his arms and kiss her all over her sleepy little head . . .

Oh shit.

Electric knowledge shafted through him. He *was* in love with Katie, like the captain said. He loved being with her—he felt better when he was with her, more alive, more himself. He wanted to protect her and take care of her and never leave her. She'd snuck her way into his heart, made a place for herself, and stubbornly dug in her heels, as only Katie could do.

He took a step toward the door, still blocked by the snoring Joe the Toe. The movement sent a needle of queasiness through his head, but nothing he couldn't handle. He checked the clock on the kitchen stove. Eleven o'clock. Katie was probably getting ready to head to the Hair of the Dog.

Which reminded him. The "hair of the dog" was a stupid concept. Did anyone really believe more alcohol was the solution to this misery? Maybe they should change the name of the bar to something more sensible. Like Never Drink Again. Or Alcohol Is Poison. He'd discuss that issue with Katie after he told her he loved her and they figured out what ought to happen next.

Realizing he still wore his clothes from last night, and that they smelled like the Dumpster at the Hair of the Dog, he stumbled over Joe and went back to his bedroom to change. You couldn't declare your love smelling like a homeless man. Then again, Katie liked the offbeat and the unusual. She probably wouldn't mind. Warmth filled him at the thought of her, with her graceful body hidden under her tomboy clothes, and her frown disguising the biggest heart he'd ever known.

Life with Katie would be one fun-filled roller-coaster ride.

He pulled a clean San Gabriel FD T-shirt from his drawer. Surprisingly, the thought of life with one woman didn't freak him out. It made him feel relaxed. Safe.

Strange.

Pulling on the T-shirt, he almost didn't hear his cell phone ring. When his head came free, the phone was winging through the air toward him.

"Goddamn freaking loud-ass cell phone," grumbled Vader.

"All right, all right. Go back to sleep." Ryan clicked on the phone.

"Ryan, it's Melissa. I've got an emergency and I need you to take Danielle for an hour. Can you? Please?"

Ryan groaned. "I'm busy, Melissa. I'm about to do something important. Really important."

"An errand? No problem. Take her with you. I'll owe you, Ryan. Please, please, please . . ."

"Fine." He could talk to Katie with Danielle around. Put the kid in the corner with some crayons or something. "Bring her over."

"She's here. We're at the door."

Ten minutes later, Ryan and Danielle were in his Chevy, driving toward the Hair of the Dog. Thank God he'd taken four aspirin, because her excited chatter alone would have required two. She'd just gotten an inhaler and couldn't wait to tell him all about it.

"It's only for 'mergencies. Like this." She made herself wheeze until her face turned red.

"Yikes. That's pretty scary."

"Uh huh. *Weally* scary. Scarier than a ghost or a . . . a vampire."

"What do you know about vampires?"

"They have giant fangs like this!" She clenched her little hands into claws at her mouth. Bloodthirsty little thing.

Ryan drew the conversation back to more important matters. "Danielle, when we get to where we're going, I need to talk to Katie about something kind of private. Do you think you can be quiet and play by yourself for a little bit?"

"What is it?"

"It's a grown-up thing. I'll tell you when you're older, I promise."

Danielle sulked and stuck her thumb in her mouth. Ryan eyed her warily. Kids were so unpredictable. Would she throw a tantrum and ruin his moment with Katie? Should he wait until after Danielle was gone? But he couldn't. He had to share his feelings with Katie. He could hardly wait.

When they reached the Hair of the Dog, he whisked Danielle into his arms and carried her across the sidewalk with long strides. Katie liked the offbeat, he reminded himself. She liked Danielle. She wouldn't mind if the little girl tagged along while he told her how much he loved her.

Chicks dug babies, after all, according to Double D.

The door was still locked. Damn. No Katie yet.

"Should we wait in the truck?" he asked aloud. Then he remembered the romantic red globe lanterns. "No. I can light some candles. It'll be even better. Come on, Danielle."

He unlocked the door and, hoisting Danielle further up on his hip, stepped into the darkness.

"Do vampires live here?" Danielle asked in a wavering voice.

"Nah. Vampires never come to San Gabriel, it's too sunny." He switched on a fluorescent light, which added illumination if not cheerfulness to the gloomy interior of the Hair of the Dog.

Danielle shielded her eyes. "Ow."

"You know something, darlin'? You're right." He turned the light off. "Ambience. We need ambience. Let's light some candles."

He swung her down to the floor. She held tightly to the leg of his jeans, trotting behind him, as he went to the bar and found a box of matches. He lit one lantern and set it on the scuffed mahogany. A small pool of light lit up her wide-eyed face. The whiff of candle wax drifted into the air. He swung her up onto a bar stool.

"Don't touch the lantern, okay, doll? They get hot."

"I won't," she promised eagerly.

"And let's be very quiet so Katie doesn't know we're here. We can surprise her."

"Yeah! A surprise!" Danielle whispered. He smiled down at her little monkey face. What a cutie-pie. Two years ago, he'd never imagined the enigmatic Brody with such an adorable kid. It proved how quickly your life could change.

"You know, Danielle, your dad would probably kick my . . . patootie if he knew you were in here. As soon as Katie gets here, we'll leave."

"I don't want to leave!" She stuck out her lower lip and crossed her arms over her chest.

"Did Katie teach you that trick?"

"What?"

"Never mind. Okay, more lanterns. What else? Maybe some incense. Hang on, sweetie pie. I gotta hunt down some incense. And remember, shhh."

He put his finger to his lips, then bent down to rummage through the bins under the counter where they kept odds and ends of things that might be useful. A strange bang caught his attention. He straightened up. "Danielle, is that you?"

She blinked at him innocently. He peered over the bar and saw her little foot swinging against the metal legs of the bar stool.

That must have been it. He crouched down again. With his head stuck in the bin, he ignored the sound when he heard it again. Finally he found a long brown stick that must be either incense or a sparkler, though Lord knew how long it had been hanging out here in this bin. He sniffed it. A faint sweet smell still clung to it. And another smell too.

He sniffed again. This time it didn't smell sweet at all. The other smell had taken over completely. A smoky scent, but the incense wasn't even lit, so how could it smell smoky?

Oh my God. Smoke.

He surged to his feet. *Danielle.*

She was sniffing and scrunching up her face. "What's that smell?"

The smoke seemed to be coming from the kitchen. In one swift move, he vaulted over the bar. "We have to get out of here, now." He scooped her off the stool and dashed across the floor. A roaring sound caught his attention. He knew what that sound meant. This fire meant business. Someone must have used a highly flammable accelerant.

Goddamn it. Hadn't Katie promised to make this insanity stop?

A rim of flickering red outlined the front door. Damn. He might be able to break through, but he couldn't take a chance with Danielle in his arms. Maybe the kitchen would be better. He whirled around and headed that direction. Danielle was crying now, frightened shrieks that made his gut tighten.

"I'll get us out, Danielle. Don't cry. Stay calm, try to stay calm." From his EMT training, he knew he had to keep her calm to avoid an asthma attack. She clung to him like a monkey, her body trembling.

"Nine-one-one," he said out loud, yanking his cell phone from his pocket. "Gotta call 911." He punched the numbers into his phone, but before he could complete the call, Danielle flung out her hand and knocked it to the floor. It went skittering into the dark corner somewhere.

Horrified, he looked down at her little face, lit only by the growing light of the flames at the door. Her screams sounded different now. Short, wheezing, frantic. She looked like she was choking. Her breath came in fast little pants, and seemed to squeeze out of her throat as though she were breathing out of a straw. Her eyes went wild with terror.

The smoke was triggering an attack. Shit. He had to stop it before it got worse. Keep her calm. He ran her to the bar and sat her down on a bar stool.

"Danielle," he said, with all the reassuring firmness he could manage. "Everything will be all right. Take deep, slow breaths. That's good, sweetie. Now where is your inhaler? Your inhaler," he repeated, when she looked at him wildly. "Your Albuterol. The puffer. Where is it?"

But she was too panicked to answer. He patted her pockets, but felt nothing. If he left Danielle to look for it, she might freak out even more. And it would be precious moments lost. What the hell had she done with her inhaler?

"I need you to do something for me, Dani," he said in his calmest voice. "Take a nice, deep breath, that's right, nice and slow. Perfect, just like that. Keep breathing, in, out, in out . . . I'm going to get us out of here, don't worry."

He cast a desperate glance around the bar. Which was the greater danger, her asthma attack or the fire? The globe lanterns caught his eye. He'd lit four, but he'd left the others alone. And Dani had been playing with them . . .

He jumped up and plunged his hand into each globe until he found a white plastic object. *Thank God.*

"Here, sweetie. Breathe into this. You know how to do it." He put the inhaler up to her mouth. She scrabbled for it and latched her lips to the mouthpiece. He waited what seemed like forever as she took a puff. He took it away, then gave her another puff. After four puffs the wild, panicked look in her eyes had gone. The Albuterol had bought them some time. He stuck the inhaler in his pocket and gave her a kiss on her cheek.

But in the meantime, the roar of the fire had gotten even more intense. They had to get out. No time to look for his cell phone.

He bent down and took Dani's head in both his hands. He fixed her with his calmest, most commanding look. "Danielle, we're going to get out of here. All you have to do is keep breathing and stay calm. Okay? No matter what, keep breathing. Just relax now and don't worry about a thing. I'm going to take care of it. Ready?"

Finally her eyes seemed to focus on him and she nodded. He gave her a quick hug and lifted her back into his arms.

The kitchen. The only other exit was the kitchen. He yanked off his T-shirt and wrapped it around Danielle's head to keep the smoke away. Then he ran to the other side of the bar. One look inside the swinging door had him backing quickly away. Another fierce line of flames was attacking the rear of the building. Multiple points of origin. This firebug meant business.

Neither exit was usable. He had to get Danielle out. Desperately he scanned the interior. The Hair of the Dog wasn't big on windows. The only one he knew of was a little dormer window hidden behind a black curtain on the wall facing the side street. He ran to the wall and felt the plaster. Warm, but not hot the way it would be if the fire was running the walls.

Thank God.

The window was placed high on the wall, a few feet over his head. "Danielle, I have to put you down for a second."

Her arms tightened around his neck. "It'll just take a second, honey." He peeled her arms off and set her down near him. "This is going to be so much fun, Dani. I'm going to kick a hole through the plasterboard and we can crawl out like it's a tunnel. What do you think of that?"

She clapped her hands together and nodded eagerly.

"Okay, here goes." He swiveled and aimed a hard kick at the wall. The plasterboard dented. Another kick made the hole deeper, deep enough to see that the wall was unexpectedly thick. This was going to take a little longer than he'd hoped.

He glanced at Dani and knew with sudden finality that they didn't have any more time. Her face had turned pale except for the black soot around her nostrils and mouth. *Smoke inhalation.* On top of her asthma. If he didn't get her out, now, she would die.

They'd have to go out the window.

He ran to a table and dragged it under the window. "Okay, Dani, change of plans. I'm going to give you a piggyback ride instead. How does that sound? I'm going to slide you around to my back. All you have to do is hold tight to my shoulders. Not my neck, my shoulders. Got it?"

She managed a nod. "Good girl." He gave her his biggest smile, the one that made women of all ages swoon. "Your dad and your mom would be really proud of you right now. Really proud. Here we go now."

He shifted her to his back and felt her arms come

around him. He heard her frantic little breaths in his ear. The sound scared the crap out of him. *Just keep breathing, keep breathing.*

With the little girl clinging to his back, he climbed onto the table. He pulled aside the black curtain. Dim and coated with grease, the window had no obvious latch.

"Duck your head behind my back, sweetie!" he shouted. When he felt her snuggle her head against his back, he wrapped the black fabric around his fist and slammed it against the window. It shattered in a shower of glass. One shard landed in his forearm. He brushed it away, then knocked out the remaining pieces of glass still lodged in the window frame.

He stuck his head out the window. The street was empty. He looked right, then left. Fire licked around both corners of the building. He didn't have much time. It was roughly a ten-foot drop to the ground. A slight down slope led away from the building. He could squeeze Danielle out the window, but he couldn't just toss her onto the ground. He needed someone to catch her.

"Help!" he shouted, but his voice came out hoarse and weak from the smoke. "Got a little girl here!" he tried again.

Nothing. Where were the rubberneckers, the civilians who loved to watch fires? People must be keeping their distance. Or maybe they were all gathered out front.

Only one option. He spoke over his shoulder. "Here's what we're going to do, Danielle. You need to be super brave, okay? I'm going to pull you up so you're sitting on this window frame. I want you to hold tight to the frame the whole time. Don't let go, no matter what. Then I'm going to pull myself up,

I'm going to give you a big hug, and we're going to fly to the ground. After that, we're going to run for help. All you have to do is hug me tight. Got it?"

Tears streamed from her reddened eyes. Damn smoke. He didn't wait for a yes, just hoisted her up and clamped her shaking hands onto the window frame. He pinned her with his gaze while he pulled himself up, willing her to stay put. Pieces of glass dug into his palms. At least they'd gotten him, not her. When he was sitting on the frame, he pulled her into his lap then lifted his legs to squeeze them through the window so he faced the street.

He hugged her close and felt her cling tightly to him. If only he had his padded firefighter's coat, he could have wrapped her in it and cushioned her fall. But he didn't. All he had was himself. *Please God, let it be enough.* "That's good, darlin'. Squeeze me tight, like your favorite teddy bear. Or do you like those Uglydolls? They're pretty cute, if you ask me . . ." And he launched himself into nothingness. He had one goal. Keep his body beneath hers. Let her land on top of him.

And she did. Right after his back slammed into the ground and the world went as black as the inside of the Hair of the Dog.

Chapter Twenty-Four

Even unconscious, Ryan was the best-looking man in the intensive care unit. It didn't bother Katie that all the nurses kept making excuses to come in and change his pillow or adjust his bed. Some of them had treated him before. Apparently he was no stranger to the Good Samaritan. As long as they let her sit next to him, holding his hand and sobbing into his blanket when no one was looking, she didn't care what they did.

Anyway, they all thought she was his sister. For once, a lie had been absolutely mandatory.

"Ryan," she whispered as soon as the busty blonde nurse had left. "I need to tell you something again. Maybe you can't hear me. Or maybe you can. Doctors don't know everything. Just in case you can, Ryan." She cleared her throat. This was hard, even if he was in a coma. "I love you."

His eyelids didn't so much as flicker.

"This is all my fault, and when you wake up you're probably going to hate me. But I'll still love you. Forever."

The tall nurse with the French twist pulled aside the curtain separating Ryan's bed from the neighboring one. She wore pretty sapphire earrings. Had she been wearing them earlier? It suddenly occurred to Katie that if all the nurses were trying to look good for Ryan, that must mean they believed he'd come out of the coma. Katie gave her a huge, relieved smile.

"How's he doing?" the nurse asked, picking up the chart at the foot of his bed.

"Seems about the same."

"Hm." She checked his pulse. "He's hanging in there. Dr. Kinder says he's in good health, especially considering his history. He's been in here a few times before. That leg should heal quickly. His ribs too."

Katie winced. His fall from the window had broken four of Ryan's ribs and his right tibia. He'd also suffered a small fracture on the back of his skull, since he'd landed backward to cushion Dani's fall. The resulting small bleed in his brain had the doctors worried. They'd put him into a chemically induced coma so they could evaluate him and fix his tibia. They kept mentioning things like ICP and potential damage to his optic nerve. When they talked that way, Katie wanted to scream.

"Quite a hero, your brother. That little girl didn't get a single scratch."

"Yes." Katie managed a smile.

"Ella Joy from Channel Six keeps calling the hospital to see if she can interview your brother. What should I tell her?"

"That it might be kind of boring to interview a guy in a coma."

The nurse smiled at that. "Can I get you anything?"

Katie shook her head. She suspected the nurse's kindness stemmed from a desire to ingratiate herself with Ryan's "sister," but she appreciated it nonetheless. "I just want him to be okay."

"We're doing everything we can. He's in great physical shape, which should help. Is anyone else . . . um . . . planning to visit him?"

"I don't know," Katie said absently. Would his father come? He'd never mentioned any other family members. It made her sad. If she were in a hospital bed, her entire family would be shuttling in and out, day and night.

The nurse gave a satisfied smile and put the chart back. "He's in good hands, don't worry."

"Thanks."

"Sorry about the Hair of the Dog," the nurse said as she slipped through the opening in the curtain. "I went there with my dad once, a long time ago."

"Thanks."

Alone again with Ryan, Katie rested her cheek on the firm muscle of his upper arm. Warmth radiated from his skin. She touched his bandaged hand. The doctors had taken out dozens of slivers of glass. The thought of his hands, so tender, so knowledgeable, shredded by glass made her want to rip her own skin off.

"I should have been there," she whispered to his silent form. "It should have been me. All of this is because of me."

The sight of his still, damaged body had shocked her into a state of crystal-clear comprehension. Not about the fact that she loved him. That was old news, even though it had taken her a while to admit it. But she suddenly understood that her failure to do something very basic, very normal, and very necessary had put Ryan in the hospital.

She'd been doing things all wrong.

The Dane family gathered at the smoking, blackened wreckage of what had been the Hair of the Dog. It stank. Katie covered her nose to shield it from the stale smoke and strange chemical scents that floated from the debris. Jake and Todd kicked at the edges of the Dog's remains, as if the crime scene tape were a personal challenge. Some things had survived, like the nonfunctioning jukebox and a few bar stools.

The office was a total loss, as was the kitchen. The fire had consumed the back part of the building as though it were the devil's candy.

Frank Dane seemed mesmerized. "Never woulda thought it. The Dog, gone."

"I'm sorry, Daddy." Her father's face, when he'd first seen the disaster, had been the hardest moment for Katie.

"It's not your fault, Gidget."

Katie looked away. She didn't know how the fire had started, but one thing she knew. It certainly was her fault.

"I should never have put you in charge. Big responsibility."

Katie gritted her teeth, but before she could answer, Bridget stepped in.

"Dad," said Bridget sharply. "Katie did a great job with the bar. You know she did."

The idea that Bridget would champion her rendered Katie momentarily mute. Nina Dane, her arm locked with her husband's, nodded in agreement, gazing on the charred wreckage with a look of satisfaction. "We owe Katie our thanks, Frank. The Lord works in mysterious ways. After all, the place is insured."

Frank started. "Is it? What's the date? July 28. Yes. Policy runs out end of the month. We're fine." A broad smile wreathed his face.

Katie did a double take. "You remember about the insurance, Daddy?"

"Of course. Important stuff."

"Then why didn't you help me with it? You let me worry about it all by myself."

Her father looked at her as if she'd spoken in a foreign language.

"Figured you had it handled. You would have come to me if you needed anything."

"Mom wouldn't let me."

Nina bristled under the weight of her husband's red-faced frown. "How could I? You needed rest. No stress, remember? You needed your gnomes."

"What do gnomes have to do with it? Don't blame the gnomes," Frank roared.

"I'm not blaming the gnomes," Nina roared back. "I'm not blaming anyone. But your health—"

"I'm not an old man, for Chrissakes."

"Look at you, just talking about this is sending your blood pressure up."

"Stop!" Katie burst out. "Listen to me!"

Everyone went silent. For the first time she could remember, Katie was the sole focus of her family's astonished attention. "I never wanted to run the bar. I never should have done it."

"But you did it so well." Her mother launched into a protest.

Katie held up her hand for silence, which, astonishingly, worked. "I never. Wanted it. But I was afraid to walk away. I didn't want to let you down. I didn't do a very good job with it. The only thing I did right was hire Ryan. He tried to help me. No one else did. And now look where he is."

Suddenly tears dribbled down her face.

"Honey!" Her mother left her father's side and pulled her into a hug. "It's not your fault. You can't blame yourself."

Huge sobs shook Katie's entire body. All the pent-up worry and pressure came pouring out. "But . . . but . . ."

Her father put his arms around the two of them. "You should have told me you didn't want the bar. I figured it would be more fun than some stuffy university."

"But . . ."

"How could she, when she knew your health was at stake? For shame, Frank."

"It's okay . . ." Katie fought to squeeze out some words between the sobs. She didn't want her parents to blame themselves. That wasn't the point at all. She had something important to say, and instead of spitting it out, she was crying in her parents' arms.

"I thought she enjoyed the Drinking Crew and all the crazy high jinks at the old place." Her father's voice rumbled over her head. The entire conversation seemed to be taking place over her head.

"I . . . I did . . ." she squeaked.

"Having a handsome young barkeep didn't hurt either."

"Oh please, Dad, that probably made it worse." Bridget chimed in. "It's obvious she has a crush on him."

That did it. Katie tore herself away from the group hug and confronted her family. "I can speak for myself. Dad, I like the Drinking Crew." Hiccup. She gripped her fists tightly, determined to say what she had to say. "Working at the bar wasn't all bad. But it's not what I want to do with my life. Yes, I should have said so from the beginning. It's true I didn't like grad school that much. But that's not the point. You shouldn't have dumped the whole thing on me without offering any help at all."

Her parents looked thunderstruck. Frank slowly nodded. "You're right there, Katie girl. As a matter of fact, you're making some very good points."

"And Bridget." She whirled on her sister, who stood with one hand on her hip, watching the whole scene with openmouthed amazement.

"I don't have a 'crush' on Ryan. I'm not twelve. I love him." She put every ounce of her heart into that statement. She saw Bridget register her seriousness, as if she'd put on lipstick for the first time, or something equally grown-up. "He's probably going to hate me now that he's in a coma, I mean, when he wakes up from his coma. But that doesn't change anything. I'll still love him."

She saw pity flash across Bridget's beautiful face, which enraged her.

"And just so you know, we've slept together."

Her mother gasped. She didn't dare look in her parents' direction. "Like I said, I'm not twelve. I'm a grown woman and for some reason, Ryan is the only one who seems to recognize that." She gave a sweeping gesture toward the Hair of the Dog. "Everything that happened here is my responsibility. I'm not a particularly good bar manager, but the point is, *I'm not a child.*"

"Well." Her parents looked at each other. Nina Dane shrugged daintily. "I suppose it's a good thing this happened before the insurance ran out then. How much is the policy for?"

Frank Dane puffed up his chest. Katie gestured for him to take center stage. "One. Million. Dollars. Can't say I wasn't thinking ahead."

Bridget and Nina gasped. Nina stepped back, her hand fluttering to her throat. "A million dollars? We could buy that condo in Baja."

"I could make a gnome convention center."

"I could open my own gym," Bridget chimed in. She let out a spurt of delighted laughter.

Frank whirled Nina into a quick waltz. "Didn't I always say I'd take care of you? That the bar wasn't a big waste of time?"

"I take it all back, my dear," laughed Nina. "Every bad thing I ever said about the Hair of the Dog."

Bridget already had her cell phone out, ready to call her friends. "Katie," she said, barely glancing up from it. "I take back everything I ever said about the bar. And you."

Scowling, Katie weighed whether or not to take offense at that. Best to move on, she decided. Why get stuck in the quarrels of the past? She was a new woman, with a new approach to her life. "Woman" being the operative word. "Thank you, Bridget. I appreciate that."

Bridget graced her with a glowing smile and began talking into her phone.

"Jake and Todd, ya hear this?" Frank bellowed toward the twins.

"Hang on, Dad," Jake shouted from the spot where the front door had once been. "There's a dude here asking a bunch of questions."

Katie turned sharply. Her brothers had stopped kicking at scorched chair legs and fallen fake timbers, and stood with a man in a gray business suit. For a dizzy moment, Katie thought it was Carson Smith. Maybe he'd decided to do the job after all, since she'd given him the money. And then hung around to boast about it.

But this man was thinner, slightly hunched, mostly bald. He was taking notes in a very official-looking notebook.

As if moving in slow motion, Katie headed toward the three of them. The smell of the burning debris got even stronger the closer she came. She sneezed. Jake shot her a queasy smile.

"Here's the one you want to talk to," he said to the man. "This is my sister Katie. She's been running the bar for my dad while he recovered from a heart attack. Katie, this guy's from . . . where are you from?"

The man held out a scrawny hand. "Fidelity Trust. I'm a claims adjustor. Bill Feldman."

Katie shook his hand, knowing hers was ice cold. "Thanks for coming by. We're still in shock over the fire."

"Fires are a bad business. Very bad. I'm sorry for your family's loss. You aren't Francis Q. Dane, I take it."

"No. That's my father. But could we, I mean, the bar's my responsibility. He's supposed to be avoiding stress. I can answer any questions you might have."

He assessed her over the top of his rimless glasses. He had surprisingly nice eyes, she noticed. A pleasant amber color. "Very well then. Are you familiar with all the employees?"

She relaxed. Questions about employees posed no challenge. "Yes. We only have two."

"Do you have anyone on staff with expertise in fires? Say, a volunteer fireman of some sort?"

The world seemed to stop turning. She felt the bright sun beat down on her head, caught a glimpse of a boy riding past on a Razor scooter, craning his neck at the wreckage. "Why do you ask?"

"The question is part of my investigation." Now his amber eyes no longer looked nice. They looked reptilian. "I suggest you answer."

Todd piped up. "Ryan used to be a fireman, didn't he? At the San Gabriel firehouse."

"Ryan?" The claims adjustor jotted it down with a blue ballpoint pen. "Last name?"

"Blake," said Katie, mechanically. "He was injured in the fire. He's in the hospital right now."

"So he was here when the fire broke out?" Another note in his book.

"Yes, he was here. He had a little girl with him. He dove out the side window to save her. He nearly died."

"Interesting." More jotting.

Katie was starting to hate ballpoint pens. Not to mention claims adjustors. Was the man trying to imply something about Ryan? "Yes, it's an interesting story. So interesting Channel Six wants to interview him because he's such a hero."

"God save us from heroes," muttered the man, scribbling more notes.

"Excuse me?"

He looked up from his notepad. "Everyone wants to be a hero. It's astonishing how far some people will go to be one. Would Ryan Blake have any motivation for wanting to appear as a hero?"

Appear? Motivation? The words ricocheted around Katie's head. She longed to rip the man's glasses off his face and stomp them into the scorched sidewalk. But she held on to her temper.

"He wouldn't do that. He didn't have to. He already was a hero. He put out tons of fires when he was on the force."

"When he *was* on the force?"

Oh Lord. Katie suddenly saw how things might look to a cynical insurance guy who didn't know Ryan. He'd probably think Ryan had staged the rescue so he could get his job back.

"It's ridiculous. Why would he put Danielle's life in danger? He'd never ever do that."

"Danielle. The little girl? Who is she?"

Katie squeezed her eyes shut. This couldn't be happening. "Captain Brody's daughter," she whispered. "Ryan's fire chief."

"So he managed to rescue the fire chief's daughter. Heroic and convenient."

"You don't know Ryan," she said, desperate. "He would never start a fire. He was terribly injured and could have died."

"Someone started this fire who knows about fires. We found a can of the same varnish they use at Station 1 on the ladders. There were multiple points of origin. I believe the arsonist's hope was that the fire would burn hot enough to destroy all traces of the accelerant. Slight miscalculation there."

"Arsonist?"

"Yes." The adjustor closed his book and gave her a formal smile. "I'm afraid at this juncture I cannot approve your claim, pending determination of the fire's origin. If arson is involved, it's in the hands of the legal system. The fact that your employee, an experienced firefighter, happened to be here when the fire broke out, and happened to rescue the child of his former fire captain in a dramatically heroic fashion, certainly bears serious investigation. And, of course, we'll have to look into his connection to you, the beneficiary. We will inform you of the results in due course. Good day, Ms. Dane."

Chapter Twenty-Five

"Ryan." Did his eyelids flicker, just a tiny bit? Katie tried again. "Ryan."

Katie sighed. She'd been sitting at his side for the past two hours, holding his hand. She needed someone to talk to, and Ryan seemed to be the only one who would do. Even when he was unconscious, she'd rather talk to him than anyone else.

"Your CAT scans are looking good. The doctors are going to cut off the phenobarbital to wake you up soon. Great news, huh?"

Not that he had much to look forward to when he woke up. *Congratulations on waking up from your coma, Ryan, now you get to face an arson charge!* The thought made her ill. How could she make them understand that the last person on earth who would commit arson was Ryan?

She traced her hand along Ryan's muscled forearm. He'd done so much to help her. Sure, he'd been kind of bossy in the process, but always with the best intentions. If she told the investigator about all the fires he'd tried to stop, would he believe that Ryan must be innocent? Or would he still claim Ryan was trying to be a hero? Should she tell Bill Feldman about Carson Smith? At least that would lead him away from investigating Ryan. On the other hand, that would mean the end of any chance of her dad getting the insurance money.

She sat up, jostling Ryan's arm in the process. He made a little sound, a breathy squeak.

"Ryan?" She held her breath. But, still deep in his trance, he made no other sound or movement. "I'm going to start my own investigation," she told him, whether he could hear her or not. "The only way that claims adjustor will believe you didn't set that fire is if I find out who did." She bent to kiss him on his stubble-covered cheek. "I love you."

Funny how those words were becoming so easy to say.

Outside the hospital, the warm evening enveloped her in a smoggy embrace. Not even a whisper of a breeze moved the eucalyptus trees in the small courtyard. She walked to her car, digging her cell phone out of her purse. So much for her determination never to speak to Carson Smith again.

She started to dial his number, then changed her mind. Maybe it would be better to speak to him in person. She dialed Doug instead.

"Hey, Doug."

"Hi, Katie."

"What's the matter?"

"What do you mean?"

"You sound funny. Are you high?" But she knew it wasn't that. When Doug was stoned, he got spacey. Right now he sounded nervous.

"No."

Now he sounded defensive. Oh well. She didn't have time to decipher his moods. "Do you know where I can find Carson Smith?"

"Why?"

"What is with you? I want to talk to him."

"I don't know where he is. You should stay away from him anyway."

Katie reached her car and fumbled for the keys. "Thanks for the advice, but I really need to talk to him. Never mind. I'll just call him."

"Wait! Don't call him. Where are you?"

"At the hospital."

A brief moment of silence followed. No doubt Doug didn't like hearing that, picturing her at Ryan's bedside.

"Fine. I'll go see Smith with you. Meet me at Starbucks, we'll go together."

Katie hung up slowly and got into her car. She drummed her fingers on the steering wheel. Something was off with Doug. He didn't sound like either his normal morose self or his stoned, slightly happier self. Something tugged at the edge of her memory. She'd seen him like this before, nervous and guilt-ridden. When was it?

The calculus test, in their junior year of high school. He'd cheated in order to avoid getting a D. No one had known, or even suspected, not even Katie. But he'd acted exactly like this for three weeks, jumpy and defensive. It had eaten at him so much that finally he'd turned himself in to the school principal. Doug had a lot of problems, but he couldn't handle a guilty conscience.

Guilty conscience.

Good God, had Doug set the fire? It made sense,

in a way. He might have done it to please her, since Carson Smith had been such a bust.

But how would Doug know about the varnish? And why, for God's sake, would he set the fire when Ryan and Danielle were inside the building?

Her anger mounting, she pulled out of the parking lot and headed for downtown San Gabriel.

When she walked in, she spotted Doug at their favorite corner table. He slouched over a tall cup and picked at a chocolate chip scone. His cast looked filthy and raggedy, with bits of thread coming undone.

Doubt flooded her. Could Doug have set the fire with his arm in a cast? Then she steeled herself. This was an investigation. No letting Doug off the hook.

She sat down across from him and waited for him to meet her eyes. It took him a while, and then it lasted only a microsecond. Exactly how he'd acted after that chemistry test.

"Doug. What the fuck?"

"What?"

"You set that fire."

"Are you crazy?" He looked around the café and lowered his voice. "Are you trying to get me in trouble?"

"I'm trying to find out what happened."

"Well, I'm sorry about the bar. The rumor going around is that your bartender set it. Trying to be all heroic." He ended with a sneer.

"You know that's ridiculous."

"Makes sense to me." He broke off a bit of scone and popped it into his mouth. Katie thought of Ryan lying in a hospital bed hooked up to a ventilator, and wanted to wipe the smug look off Doug's face.

"Look, Doug, I know you don't like Ryan. But accusing him of something he didn't do is unforgivable."

He ducked his head sullenly. A strand of black, wavy hair stuck to his cheek. At his best, Doug had the look of a dark fallen angel. In high school she'd thought of him as a beautiful, damaged boy. She'd wanted to heal him, keep him from hurting himself. And yet—it had never worked. He'd still done every brain-dead thing most teenagers did. Drugs, pot, cigarettes, blackout drinking. The only thing he hadn't done was sleep around. He'd always been loyal to her.

"What is it with you and that dude?" he asked suddenly. "You really like him?"

Katie wished she'd gotten a drink to hide behind. Taking a gulp of latte might give her a moment to figure out how to handle that question. Might as well go for the truth. "It's more than that. I love him."

" 'Cause he's good-looking."

"No. It's not that. I'm sorry, Doug. But that's the way it is."

"What about him?" His lip curled. "He's got girls all over him."

"I think he likes me. But you'd have to ask him, and right now . . . Oh my God, Doug."

He started. "What?"

"Did you . . . Were you trying to . . . kill Ryan?"

"No! Jesus, Katie. I already said I didn't do it."

"Well, I don't believe you."

"Fuck. You're so sure your pretty boy is so perfect? It's like everyone's saying. He started it to be the big hero. Those guys are like that. I looked it up on the Internet. Firemen are addicted to adrenaline.

They like the rush of being the hotshot. That's how they get their kicks. I can't believe you fell for someone like that. It's not like you need a lot of brains to put out fires."

Katie sat back in her seat and bit her lip to keep from screaming at him. Had he always been this petty?

"Did you know firemen never wear wedding rings? I got that off the Internet too. They say it's because the metal would burn their fingers, but that's not the real reason. It's because they cheat. Everyone knows it."

"Stop it, Doug!"

But he didn't stop. Katie had the childish urge to stick her fingers in her ears and chant "la-la-la" until he'd finished. But it was high time she made herself see Doug, the real, grown-up Doug, for who he was. So she shut her mouth tight and listened to him rant.

"They have girls after them all the time, like basketball players. You really think Ryan would stick by you like I did? Get real, Katie. I mean, you're cute, but you're no Logan Marquez. He went home with her, you know. She told me so."

She crossed her arms and let his poisonous words flow around her.

"He's going to dump you in a hurry as soon as the next gorgeous girl comes along. You've seen the girls hanging on him. You think you can compete with that?"

"Gee, thanks for the vote of confidence."

"Come on, Gidget, I've always been there for you. When are you going to wake up and see this Ryan dude is no good for you?"

She stared at him, light dawning. "That fire was you, trying to wake me up? Make me think Ryan's an arsonist burning down the bar so my family loses everything, even the insurance money?"

"No." Doug jerked his head up, his eyes scuttling from side to side. "The fire happened before the insurance policy ran out."

A shiver of shock bolted Katie to her chair. She'd suspected, she'd accused, but to hear him virtually admit it . . . "So you planned it for yesterday on purpose. So the insurance would still cover us."

"No!" Doug crumbled bits of scone between his fingers, littering the table in front of him. "I didn't say that. You're twisting everything around. I'm just saying it's better than after the insurance runs out, right?"

"What's the difference? Like Carson Smith said, if they can make a good faith allegation that he set the fire, and did it on our behalf, the insurance company won't pay. There's all these suspicious-looking things they can twist around. Even if you tell the truth, they probably won't pay because of our relationship."

His mouth opened and closed. He looked like a fish flopping on a beach. "I . . . uh . . . I'll be right back." He slid back his chair and slouched toward the bathroom. Katie shook her head in disbelief. Typical Doug, off for a quick hit so he could finish the conversation. When things get tough, get stoned. That was his motto.

She shuddered. Thank God she'd never been tempted to join him in his pot habit. In fact, he'd been the biggest factor in her decision not to. He was a walking advertisement against weed. How many of his boneheaded decisions had been made under the influence? Had this one?

The thought of him getting high, then endangering the lives of two people, one of them a child, made her want to rip his head off.

He plopped back onto his chair, red-eyed but much more relaxed.

"Feel better?" she asked, with a mirthless smile.

"Yeah, dude. Things were getting a little intense there." He rubbed a hand across his eyes and shook back his hair, degenerate rock star–style.

Katie didn't want to spend one more minute in his company. But she still had a mission to complete. "Doug, this is how I see it." She put both elbows on the table and fixed him with her best stern-but-fair look. "You've completely screwed up, in so many ways I don't even know where to start. You nearly killed two people. You ruined my father's business and now he probably won't even get the insurance money. And an innocent, non-fire-starting person is about to take the blame for what you did. If you think I would ever get back together with someone who did those things, you're more stupid than I ever imagined. There's only one thing you can do to make up for all this."

Doug squinted at her. He scratched at the edge of his cast.

"You can step up and admit what you did. We still probably won't get the insurance money. But at least Ryan won't be charged."

"But . . ." He scratched his chin. "Then they'd charge me."

"For what you did."

"I never said that. You're trying to confuse me."

Katie slammed her hands on the table and stood up. "Man up, Doug. Whatever you did, tell the truth. That's all I ask."

"Way, way, way, wait a second." He shot her

a blurry smile. "Got an idea. If I say I did it, will you get rid of Ryan? That's all I want. He can . . ." He flicked the fingers of his good hand. "Go away. Somewhere else."

White rage flashed through her. "You. Are. *Pathetic.* I'm sick of you trying to control me. I'm not falling for your crap anymore. I can't believe I fell for it this long. We're done. Forever. I thought we could be friends, but I was so, so wrong. Never talk to me again. Ever."

"But Katie . . ." he whined, the reality of the situation apparently penetrating his marijuana haze.

"Ever."

She swung away from him and stalked out of the coffeehouse, barely conscious of the curious looks from behind laptops and coffee cups.

She yanked open the door of her Datsun, sat down in the driver's seat, trembling, and slammed the door shut. Energy still surged through her. It had taken eight plus years to finally tell Doug where he could stick it. Why had it taken her so long to see him for what he was? She grabbed the steering wheel and took deep breaths, trying to get a grip on her emotions. Doug, Ryan, the bar, her family . . . everything swirled around her in a confused mess.

In the middle of it all, one thought surfaced. Yes, she'd finally told Doug off. But now, the chances of his confessing to his crime were zero.

When Katie got back to the hospital, Melissa stood at his bedside, holding Danielle by the hand. Ryan looked as unconscious as ever. Melissa had stopped by a few times, but she hadn't brought Dani until now.

"They stopped the phenobarbital a few hours ago," Melissa told her.

"But he's not awake yet," she said, stating the obvious. She felt silly as soon as she said it.

"Not yet. Should be soon. Danielle wants to be here when he comes out of it. They finally allowed her to come."

Danielle looked up at Katie. Her eyes looked huge in her little face.

"How are you doing, kiddo?" Katie asked her, bending down to her level. As someone who knew how it felt to always be looking up at everyone, she liked to get eye-to-eye with kids.

"We jumped out the window."

"I know. You sure were brave."

"It didn't feel like flying. It felt like, flop. Boom." The little girl mimicked a diving motion with her hand.

"Not fun at all, huh?"

She shook her head solemnly. "Is he going to wake up soon?"

"Well, the doctor said it takes between four and six hours. Maybe if you talk to him a little, he'll wake up even sooner."

Her dark eyes lit up. "I can tell him about my new bunny rabbit."

"Perfect."

Danielle scooted closer to the bed. She leaned her elbows on the edge and stretched confidingly toward Ryan. "It's private," she warned Katie and Melissa over her shoulder.

"We'll be right over here," said Melissa, smiling and backing away.

Katie grabbed her chance and followed Melissa to the foot of the bed. "Can I talk to you for a minute?"

"Sure. I've been wanting to talk to you too."

"Have you heard what they're saying about Ryan?"

"Who hasn't?" Melissa rolled her eyes. "I always say the only places more gossipy than newsrooms and hair salons are firehouses. Everyone's talking about what happened."

"So Captain Brody, your husband . . . he's heard the rumors?"

"Yes."

"He doesn't believe them, does he?" In her anxiety, Katie grabbed Melissa's arm.

"It's not up to him. He's not an arson investigator. He'll have to abide by whatever the investigation turns up."

Katie stared at the older woman, biting her lip. She liked Melissa, how calm and cool under pressure she seemed, how unique in her own particular beauty, with her deep green eyes and hair like bittersweet chocolate. "The thing is, I know Ryan didn't do it, and I think I know who did, but I don't have any proof. I don't want Ryan to get blamed. You still do investigations, don't you? For the news?"

Melissa shook her head gently. "I'm sorry, Katie. I understand how you feel, but I can't touch this one. It's a little too close to home. Ryan's like a brother to me. And Danielle was nearly—" She broke off.

Katie took her hand. "I'm so sorry. It must have been so awful for you."

Melissa took a moment to pull herself together. "Do you know what she did after they landed on the lawn outside the bar?"

"No, what?"

"She wouldn't leave Ryan's side. She just kept yelling and calling for help. She'd had an asthma attack inside. But Ryan had talked her through it. She wouldn't leave him. Fortunately, she has an earsplitting scream. Someone heard her right away and came running. But, God, when I think about it . . ."

Sympathetic tears welled into Katie's eyes, somewhat to her surprise. She thought she'd cried all her tears already. The two women clasped each other's hands, picturing the frightful moment.

A weak, scratchy voice interrupted them. "So that's what that god-awful racket was."

Katie spun around. Where Ryan's eyes had been closed a few minutes ago, she now saw the merest hint, the narrowest slit of blue. A tiny smile tugged at one corner of his mouth.

Danielle jumped up and down. "I woke him up! Mama, I woke him up!"

Melissa yanked open the curtain and called into the corridor. "Nurses! Doctors! Come quick!"

Katie couldn't move. She wanted to fling herself on top of him, kiss him all over his swollen face. But would he want her to, especially once he knew about all the craziness going on?

Besides, Danielle was way ahead of her. Her first shock gone, she climbed up on the bed next to him. "I woke you up!"

"Yeah you did. How are you, kiddo? Breathing okay?"

She nodded and put her little arms all the way around his chest and hugged him tight.

A wince tightened Ryan's face.

"Sweetie, his ribs," warned Katie, coming forward. Danielle loosened her grip but stayed right where she was.

"Ribs?" Ryan's eyes opened a crack wider, wide enough to meet Katie's.

"Yep. And your tibia."

"Oh, that old thing." He attempted a smile that

wound up looking ghoulish. "Never broken one of those before." He lifted a hand off the bed, beckoning to Katie. "You're so far away."

She hesitated, a second too long. In the next moment, a swirl of white coats and blue scrubs surrounded Ryan and swept him away into very serious and important medical chatter.

Chapter Twenty-Six

Ryan followed the doctors' instructions, taking a deep breath when he was told to, following a penlight from left to right. The tiniest movement seemed to take an enormous effort. Even his thoughts felt like thick pea soup. But not green. More like heavy gray sludge. The doctors seemed very concerned about his eyesight, which seemed fine except for some weird dancing spots.

The medical people sent Katie, Melissa, and Danielle away while they did their testing. Ryan didn't mind. He was too exhausted to talk to anyone. And besides, hurt nagged at him. Why hadn't Katie looked happier to see him? Her eyebrows had been drawn together, her face had gone pale. Something was wrong, but figuring it out felt impossible. Only one thing felt doable right now.

He closed his eyes and sledded back into sleep.

The next time he woke up, he felt a hundred times

better. A different batch of people gathered at his bedside. Vader and Joe the Toe gazed down at him like two buff bodyguards. At first they were a little blurry, but with some concentration he was able to focus on them. The spots didn't seem as bad as before.

"Why'd they let you guys in? Did you beat up the security guards?"

He must be feeling better, if he could rag on them. He sat up, then leaned against the pillows as a wave of dizziness passed over him.

"We offered your home phone number to some nurses," said Vader.

Joe the Toe glared at Vader. "Nurses are professionals and certainly don't deserve your sexist drivel."

"My what? All I heard was 'sex.'"

Joe the Toe ignored Vader and focused on Ryan. "All your tests show you're recovering like the magnificent specimen you appear to be. Are you feeling better?"

"Yeah, actually." He blinked and shook his head, testing the effects of movement. No pain. No more dizziness after that initial rush. "I can think now. When I first woke up I was seeing stars and my head felt like a puddle of molasses."

"Do you remember what happened?"

Chaotic images flashed through his mind. Danielle's nostrils turning sooty. His cell phone disappearing across the floor. Breathing in the bitter, acrid smoke. The determined roar of the fire. The long drop from the window. The all-encompassing pain.

"I think I do. I dove out the window with Danielle. She's okay, I saw her when I woke up. No injuries. Gutsy little thing."

"What do you expect? She's the captain's daughter," said Vader.

"True, that." Ryan smiled, remembering how brave she'd been.

Joe dragged over an armchair and settled his bulk into it. He steepled his fingers and gave Ryan a serious, professorlike look. "We finagled our way in here because we felt you ought to know what's being said."

"Said?" Ryan looked from Joe to Vader, who suddenly seemed extremely worried about his own feet.

"The fire was deliberately set."

"I know. They set fires, in front and behind. Maybe on the other side too. Don't know. They used some kind of accelerant."

"They're saying—" Joe broke off.

Vader, still analyzing his own feet, continued the thought. "They're saying it must have been a pro. Someone on the force. And since you worked there, well . . . They're fucked in the head if they think you could do that. Fucked. But no one's asking us."

Ryan's jaw fell open. The room tilted around him like a ship hitting a reef. He grabbed onto the bedsheets to steady himself. "You mean . . . they think . . ." He couldn't finish.

"Doug, that friend of Katie's, is saying he saw you there," said Vader, as if every word was a sharp razor blade he had to spit out.

"Yeah, I was there. Nearly getting burned to death." He fought back the panic. *Accused of arson.* "Why would I . . ." He realized he was yelling, and brought down his voice. "Why would I set a fire with myself inside? Not to mention Danielle?"

"Calm yourself," said Joe, putting a giant hand

on his shoulder. Ryan shook it off angrily. "If they think we're upsetting you, they'll eject us."

It took every ounce of willpower Ryan possessed to settle down. He dredged up a breathing exercise he'd learned at the monastery. In, out, in, out. "Okay, I'm okay. Go on. Explain to me why I'd nearly incinerate myself and a little girl."

"You're angry at the wrong people. We don't believe any of this blasted rubbish, or we wouldn't be here."

"You're right, you're right. Thank you. Go on."

Joe picked up a large cup with a straw and handed it to Ryan. "Sippy cup. Drink."

Obediently Ryan took a long swig of cool water. It helped. He nodded to Joe. "Let me have it."

"All right. I'm going to tell you everything so you can be prepared. Vader and I thought it best. But don't believe for a second that simply because you're in a hospital bed, I won't defend myself if you forget and try to take your anger out on me. I outweigh you and I haven't been unconscious for three days."

"I'm not going to whup your ass. Though I could," muttered Ryan. "Even from a hospital bed."

Joe the Toe ignored that. "Two things. Point one. They're speculating that you wanted to play the hero to get back on the force. Your past record of impulsive, life-threatening actions is considered to support that theory."

"I *saved* lives with those actions! And I saved Danielle."

"But risked your own life. Why? Because you're hooked on the rush. You're not so much a fireman as a junkie, according to this scenario. And as a junkie deprived of his fix for a year and a half, you couldn't resist the opportunity for a blaze of glory, so to speak."

"Bullshit."

"Point two," continued Joe, ruthlessly. "You'd conceived a liking, a tendre, for Miss Katie Dane. You knew the bar was in financial trouble, so you decided a fire would be the ultimate form of courtship, one that would make sense given your training."

"What?"

"As I understand it, that one's been discarded in favor of the theory that you and Katie colluded to set the fire once she learned you're an expert in the field. The insurance company is particularly fond of that scenario."

"That's crazy. I tried to make her—" He bit his words back before he could let the wrong thing slip out. Dizziness threatened again. He sank against his pillows.

"Sippy cup." Joe the Toe thrust out his hand, and Vader slapped the cup into it. Ryan took another deep, long sip.

"What else?"

"You want more? The arson squad is investigating."

"Did they check out—" Ryan stopped himself again. John Springer, aka Carson Smith, ought to be the prime suspect, not him. But turning in Springer would implicate Katie, and he couldn't do that, not until he'd talked to her.

"What about Katie? What's she saying?"

Joe the Toe shrugged his massive shoulders and glanced up at Vader, who shook his head. "We haven't seen her. The Hair of the Dog was completely destroyed. I think she's been busy dealing with the mess."

Ryan gave that information a moment to sink in. Not a surprise, from what he remembered. He braced himself before asking the next question.

"The captain? What does he think?"

"He's got your back. But it's not up to him."

Ryan shut his eyes. He wanted them gone. He wanted everyone gone. He wanted to reverse time to the day before he walked into the Hair of the Dog. No, to the days when he'd still been part of San Gabriel Fire Station 1. Before everything had gone to shit.

He looked at Joe and Vader, who suddenly seemed like ghosts to him. "I'm a little tired," he managed to say. "Thanks for coming by."

"We did good, right?" Vader asked anxiously.

"Yeah. I needed to know all this."

After they'd left, he rested his forearm across his eyes. What a fucking mess. Three people, that he knew of, had already tried to set fire to the bar. Doug, Katie, and John Springer. Either Katie had lied to him and hadn't called Springer off, or she'd set the fire herself, even though she'd promised not to. But he couldn't believe that.

Or Doug had done it and she was, as always, trying to protect him.

Melissa had told Katie that Captain Brody had meetings all morning, but would be at the station in the afternoon. Time seemed to be passing at about the speed of her high school chemistry class, which she'd always figured had bent the time-space continuum with its tedium. This was worse. For one thing, she was stuck with her family, and she couldn't say a word to them about what had really happened . . . or what she planned to do.

She didn't want them to talk her out of it.

Now that the Hair of the Dog had been picked over by investigators, the Dane family was allowed to remove whatever valuables—using the term loosely—they wanted to salvage. All six of them gathered in their grungiest clothes. Even Bridget wore an old pair of sweatpants that had become loose in the crotch. Jake and Todd, in the last hours of their visit, delved into the mess with relish, but everyone else moved with a kind of solemn sadness.

"There's gotta be some liquor in here somewhere," said Jake.

"All the bottles exploded from the heat, doofus," Katie explained in her nicest voice, given the circumstances.

"Man, I wish I could've seen that. Course, my eyeballs probably would have exploded too."

She gave him a scathing look. "Daddy, what about the sign?" She lifted up the only remaining fragment, still warm to the touch.

"'Og'? That's it?"

"Good name for a gnome," said Todd.

"We could hold a garage sale with all this stuff." Bridget held up a blackened frying pan, touching it with only thumb and forefinger. "Or donate it to a homeless shelter."

"Why would a homeless person need a frying pan? They don't even have a home," pointed out Nina, whose immaculate sleeves were rolled up above her elbows.

"Fine. Salvation Army. Whatever. It's the thought that counts," Bridget grumbled.

It occurred to Katie that the family hadn't worked together like this in a while. "I appreciate everyone coming to help."

Bridget straightened up. "Well, why wouldn't we? It's our bar too. It's our million dollars down the drain too."

Katie hung her head. The lost insurance money ate at her conscience. She'd lain awake last night thinking of new cars, vacations, new washing machines, all the things her family could have done with a million dollars.

"Anyway, it's not like it's your fault," continued Bridget. "It's Ryan's fault. I don't believe you were in on it no matter what they say."

"He didn't do it!" Katie said for the hundredth time since the fire.

"I knew he looked too good to be true. Anyone that gorgeous has to have a flaw. Turns out his is that he's a criminal." She dropped the frying pan into the pile of kitchenware.

Katie launched herself across the pile of rubble and tackled Bridget. Bridget spun around just in time. She stepped aside so Katie went soaring past her. She hit the ground, rolled into a somersault, then sprang to her feet to go after Bridget again.

Bridget braced herself in a martial arts stance, hands held before her like claws. "I've studied Tae Bo, Gidget. Don't mess with me."

Katie ignored the horrified protests from her parents and the hoots of laughter from her brothers, and barreled toward Bridget again. This time Bridget grabbed her by the shoulders, stopping her in her tracks.

"Are you psycho? I'm twice your size."

"Stop saying that about Ryan."

"I'm only saying what everyone else is. You don't even really know the guy. Are you so sure he didn't do it?"

"*Yes.* Why won't you listen to me? You never listen to me!" She swung futilely at Bridget.

"Katie girl, if you're in need of any assistance, we're right over here." Archie's booming voice cut through her haze of fury.

Katie looked over her shoulder. Archie, Sid, and the rest of the Drinking Crew stood in a tight knot at the edge of the sidewalk. Even with their canes and Dr. Burwell's oxygen tank, they looked feisty and ready to rumble. Mr. Jamieson was polishing his glasses, Archie rolling up his sleeves.

"That's . . . uh . . . okay." She dropped her fists and took a long, shaky breath. "You know Bridget, right? We're having a sister bonding moment. Right, Bridget?"

The expression on Bridget's face at the sight of the old men would have made Katie laugh, if things weren't so all-around awful.

"Right. Like a pillow fight without the pillows," said Bridget gamely.

Archie didn't look convinced. "She's our girl. We can't allow her to get beaten up. She'll always have a place of honor with us after the way she poured her heart and soul into this place."

"Hope you appreciate her," piped up Sid. "Even if the Hair of the Dog's no better than a burnt sausage now."

Katie winced.

Her father strode over to the Crew and shook their hands. "Thanks for stopping by, gentlemen. Came to say good-bye to the old place, eh?"

"We're tying up loose ends," said Mr. Jamieson. "*Veni, vidi, solvit.*"

"Eh?"

"Translation, we came, we saw, we paid our tab."

Archie whipped out a worn leather wallet and extracted a check. "We realized, upon reflection and calculation, that we were in arrears with our bar tabs. We hope this helps."

Tears sprang to Katie's eyes.

Frank looked down at the check. "Well thank you, fellows, but this is made out to Katie."

"She worked her fingers to the bone," said Archie dramatically. "She deserves it."

"As the French say, *Bon sang ne saurait mentir*, right, Katie?" Mr. Jamieson winked at her. *Blood will out*. She tried to speak but couldn't.

"You got yourself a fine daughter," said Sid. "A real peach."

"Don't I know it. Come here, Katie girl. Come take this kind gift. You earned it, my dear, putting up with this crew." Her father beckoned to her, holding out the check. His loving eyes, surrounded by new worry lines, twinkled at her. The Drinking Crew leaned on their canes and smiled at her expectantly. Jake and Todd ran to join them, no doubt to see how big the check was. Her mother looked unexpectedly thrilled. Even Bridget seemed excited. She nudged Katie in the back.

"Go on, Katie. It's for you. Go get it."

Katie couldn't take it. She didn't deserve all this niceness. She deserved to be raked over the coals, read the riot act, locked in a dungeon for a hundred years. If not for her, the Hair of the Dog would still be standing, and still insured.

She ran, stumbling past the blackened wreck of the bar, past her shocked family.

Driving the few blocks to the firehouse, she realized that before she talked to Brody, she had to talk to Ryan.

If he had seen anything before the fire broke out, she had to know. She veered in the other direction, toward the Good Samaritan.

She used the short drive to collect her thoughts. She had no idea if Ryan had been told about the investigation. Maybe the insurance people or the arson investigator had already visited. Hopefully the overprotective nurses had kept them out. This whole thing would be such a shock to him.

By the time she reached the hospital, she felt more composed. She dashed up the steps and through the glass revolving doors. Reaching the intensive care unit, she waved at French Twist behind the desk and hurried toward the locked door.

But the usual click that opened it didn't come. Instead she nearly slammed her face into the door.

The nurse stood. "Ryan has requested no visitors."

"But it's really, really important. I have to talk to him."

"There's nothing I can do. He was very specific. He doesn't want to be disturbed."

Katie pinned a pleading gaze on her. "This isn't personal. It's about him. His career. Could you just go in there and ask him? Tell him it's me, and that it's extremely important. I won't stay long, I promise."

"You mean, tell him his sister's here?" The nurse smirked.

"I apologize for that. Really. But please don't hold it against me. This is about Ryan. If you want to help Ryan, tell him he's got to talk to me. Please."

Clearly reluctant, the nurse moved from behind the desk. "Fine. I'm not going to tell him anything, but I'll ask him if he'd like to talk to you."

"Thank you. Thank you."

The nurse took her sweet time unlocking the door, moving through it, then relocking it behind her. Katie couldn't blame her for her attitude. She probably didn't appreciate being lied to.

Katie paced around in a tight little circle, going over exactly what she'd say to Ryan. First she'd find out if he'd seen anyone at the bar. If he'd seen Doug, that would count as proof and she could tell Brody everything. She'd tell him he didn't need to worry, that she was going to clear everything up. And then she'd kiss him and nuzzle her head into his neck and tell him she loved him. She wouldn't let the fact that he was conscious stop her. She'd had enough practice with the unconscious Ryan. Maybe he remembered hearing the words, maybe he'd say them right back to her . . .

The nurse reappeared, locking the door behind her once again. She stood before it, arms folded. "I'm sorry, Ms. Dane. Ryan doesn't want to see you."

"What?" Katie felt color flood her cheeks. "You told him it was me?"

"Obviously. If you're going to make a scene, I'll have to call security."

"I'm not going to make a scene. I just . . ." She swallowed hard. Ryan didn't want to see her. The shattering truth settled into her bones.

"You should go now."

"Yes." She turned blindly toward the entrance. "Tell him . . ." *I love him* . . . But that would probably be the last thing he wanted to hear. "I'm sorry."

Chapter Twenty-Seven

Ryan had always moved swiftly when circumstances required. During fistfights and fires in particular, he'd been able to shift into another mode, one in which everything around him seemed to slow down and he could see perfectly what needed to be done.

To be trapped in a bed, in a hospital, in the midst of events that seemed entirely out of his control, had to be the worst experience of his life. Much worse than tumbling out of a burning building. That was movement, that was action.

This was hell.

The painkillers in his IV didn't help matters. They dulled the sensation of pain, but they didn't stop his thoughts. Nothing did.

The nurse brought in a tray of food. "Banana pudding today," she told him. "Your favorite."

"Thanks, darlin'." He said the words automatically, although he couldn't care less about banana pudding. Food had lost all flavor since Joe the Toe had dropped his bombshell.

"Anything else I can get you?"

"No thanks, I'm good. Think I'll take another nap."

"Excellent idea. Rest is very important."

He forced a smile as she left him alone. *Rest*. He might try to sleep, but he knew he'd get no rest. How had things come to this? How had a man like him, who lived to put out fires, come to be accused of starting one?

And how could he clear his name, without telling Katie's secrets?

Katie.

Her name brought such a flood of emotion that he shoved the tray of food off his bed in a tangle of shrink-wrapped containers. From the first moment he'd seen her, Katie had upended his life. Without even trying. From the very beginning, he'd wanted to protect her—and impress her. He should have let those guys beat up Doug. He should have let Katie burn down the Hair of the Dog. He should never have gone to the Dog with some crazy romantic notion of declaring his love.

If he'd never met Katie, he'd probably have his job back by now. He certainly wouldn't be lying in a hospital bed accused of arson.

When the day shift nurse had told him Katie wanted to see him, he'd felt a surge of adrenaline. *Yes,* he'd wanted to say. *Show her in so I can tell her how she's ruined my life. By the time I'm done with her, she'll wish I'd never walked into her bar. Which is exactly how I feel.*

Instead he'd shaken his head. He couldn't bear to

see her. And didn't want to lose his temper with her. After all this, he still wanted to protect her.

Damn her.

Katie pushed open the gray steel front door of the San Gabriel firehouse. She felt like she was entering some kind of sacred male haven, even though she knew some of the firefighters were female. But the atmosphere reeked of masculinity, of tools and gear and equipment and testosterone. The planters of red geraniums out front provided the only feminine touch, if it could be called that. With a kind of military order, the blooms stood up straight. Not a single browning petal to be seen.

Clearly, firefighters liked order. She remembered all the times Ryan had cleaned the bar. He liked things to be clean down to the ground, from the inside out, without any pockets of hidden grime. He relaxed his standards a little at home. She recalled a mussed bed and a pile of dirty shirts without a hamper . . .

Enough. No more mooning over Ryan. She had a career to save.

She moved through the foyer, which featured a few framed photos of groups of firemen and some firefighting paraphernalia mounted on the walls—an old-fashioned helmet, a fire axe in a glass case. Firefighters valued their history, apparently. She walked through a narrow hallway, thinking, despite herself, of all the time Ryan had spent in this place. She pictured him ambling down the hall, hands in his pockets, a sparkle in his blue eyes, a teasing smile on his lips.

By the time she reached the lounge, she half expected him to be there, rising up from the couch, opening his arms to her. Her heart raced when someone stood and turned to face her. False alarm, of course. Fred the Stud smiled at her.

"Hi, Katie," he said cheerfully. "I hear Ryan's a lot better. Got his thinker back."

"So I hear. Is Captain Brody in?"

"Right over there." He pointed to an office with a closed door. "Just knock. He won't bite. Unless you overfilled the generator and spilled diesel on the patio." He pulled a rueful face.

"Nothing like that," she said. No, only a thousand times worse.

"Come in." Brody's deep voice responded to her knock. She took a deep breath, reminded herself why this was so important, and opened the door.

Captain Brody sat at his desk in his fireman's uniform. He looked grim and preoccupied. He took her in with intense gray eyes that seemed to see right through her. "Katie Dane. What brings you here?"

"I have to talk to you. Is this a bad time?" She eyed the piles of paper on his desk.

"No more than any other," came his not very encouraging answer. "Sit down."

He beckoned to a chair in the corner. Katie eyed it dubiously. Did he want her to sit in the corner like a schoolgirl getting punished?

"You can bring it over here," said Brody, with a hint of amusement warming his voice.

"Right." She dragged the chair in front of the desk and sat down. The chair, of the folding metal variety, put her about a foot below Brody's eye level. Never had she felt so small.

Too bad. What did her height matter, when she held the key to Ryan's future? "I want to talk to you about Ryan Blake," she said in a clear voice.

He sat back and steepled his fingers.

"Okay," he said.

"Ryan didn't set that fire. I'm responsible for it."

"Responsible for it? You mean you set the fire?"

She hesitated. She didn't want to lie. But what if that was the best way to clear Ryan? Brody narrowed his eyes. Under that serious charcoal gaze, she realized that lying was not an option. "No, I didn't set it. But I might as well have. I am ultimately responsible, although I can't name the person who did it. I don't have any proof."

Brody frowned. "Why are you coming to me? I'm not involved in this case, except for providing background information." He pushed at the papers on his desk with a disgusted air.

So that was Ryan's file, Katie thought with a chill.

"I'm coming to you because Ryan trusts you. And you know Ryan. And once I tell you the whole story, I'm hoping you'll know what's the best way to clear him. And what I should do so that *I* face the consequences. Not Ryan."

"I'm sensing there's quite a story to be told here." He flipped open a yellow legal pad and picked up a pen. "Mind if I take notes?"

Katie swallowed. Notes made it seem so official. "Of course, that's fine. Notes. Okay, well, it started with the insurance payment coming due. No, it started when my father had his heart attack. Or maybe when he put me in charge of the bar. No—" She stopped to collect her thoughts. "The idea of burning down the Hair of the Dog was entirely mine. It seemed like the only way out, for me and for my father. See, he was under too much stress, so my mother asked me to take over. I was desperate and went a little crazy . . ." And from there, the story flowed. The enormous pile of bills, her hopeless sense of being alone and in over her head. The appearance of Ryan. Her insane idea of burning down the bar and collecting the insurance. How Doug had offered to help. The fires that Ryan kept putting out.

"See? Why would he start a fire after putting out so many of them? It doesn't make sense."

Brody nodded gravely. She couldn't read his expression at all. She barreled ahead.

"And then he did the bachelorette party strip show, and—"

"The *what*?" Brody braced both hands on his desk and leaned forward. "Did you say, 'strip show'?"

Oops. How was she to know Brody hadn't heard about that?

"Not full frontal, or anything. Just full back-tal. Backside. The front was turned away. And covered by a helmet."

"A fireman's helmet?" His voice was low and dangerous. If she got Ryan into any more trouble, she'd really never forgive herself.

"All the guests really enjoyed themselves, and no harm came to any San Gabriel firefighters. I'd say the department's reputation was enhanced by the firemen's willingness to . . . um . . . pitch in and help out a friend."

Brody shook his head. "Never should have gone along with that one," he muttered. "Go on. What happened after the striptease?"

She decided to skip ahead to Carson Smith and Doug's role in locating him. "Ryan thought he looked suspicious, and that his father might know him. So we went to his dad's trailer."

Brody looked genuinely surprised by that. "Ryan saw his father? And he took you along?"

"Yes, but his father didn't remember Carson Smith. Until later, when it was too late. Carson Smith set the fire that you put out."

"So you paid him to set the fire that burned down the bar."

"Well, not exactly. I mean, I was going to, but instead I paid him to go away and not set any more fires. I felt so terrible after you and Ryan put out that fire. I wanted to call it off. But he wouldn't stop unless I paid him. So I did."

"In other words, you paid him *not* to commit arson."

"Yes, but . . ." This was getting off track. "Only after I hired him to commit it."

Brody rubbed the dented lines between his eyebrows.

"I know it's confusing. The point is, why would Ryan go to the trouble of finding out the truth about Carson Smith if he intended to start another fire himself? That isn't his real name, by the way, in case you're writing things down."

Brody had stopped writing notes a while ago, so Katie thought he might need a reminder. He picked up his pen, shook his head, and put it down again. "Just keep talking. Might be better if I don't have all this on paper."

"Oh, right." That certainly made sense.

"Go back to the part where Ryan visited his father. How did that go?"

What did that have to do with anything? "Well, fine, I suppose. He didn't shoot either of us. Apparently he does that sometimes."

"And how was Ryan afterward?"

Katie's face heated. Afterward they'd steamed up the interior of his truck while parked under a grove of orange trees. She didn't think that needed to go in the report. "You saw him soon after. On the way back I told him that I'd hired Mr. Smith, and that's when he called you."

"Hm." Brody delivered another of his long, probing looks. "Something tells me you're a good influence on Hoagie."

"Hoagie?"

"That's our nickname for him."

"Geez, that's the best you could do?" Katie sniffed. She could think of many nicknames better than that one. Hottie McHotstuff. Mr. Sexy. Ultimate Dream Man. *Focus, Katie.* "I'm not a good influence on him at all. In fact, I've pretty much ruined his life, especially if he loses out on getting his job back. I can't let that happen."

"It's not really up to you, is it?"

She flushed again. "No, of course not. It's up to you."

"Mostly, it's up to Ryan."

"If you knew how much he studied for that exam." She scooted the chair forward, forgetting how nervous Brody made her. "He worked so hard. He had piles of books at his house. Sometimes he brought the manual to work. And I've seen him put out fires. Twice. He's amazing. How can you not want him back?"

Brody stood up from his chair and clasped his hands behind his back. He walked in a small circle, as if moving helped him think. "Ryan Blake is the best fireman I've ever had on my crew. No one else has ever come close. Here's something you may not know about Ryan."

"What?"

"Deep down, he's a family man. To him, this firehouse is a family. He'd do anything to protect his family. Something tells me that now applies to you."

Katie stared at him, appalled. "That doesn't mean . . . you don't think . . ."

"Do I think he started that fire? No. It would go against all his training, all his instincts. But some will interpret his history and profile that way."

Katie squeezed her eyes shut. *It couldn't be, it couldn't happen.* "Charge me."

"Excuse me?"

"Take my confession. Isn't that what cops do?"

"And priests," Brody murmured.

She stood up to face him. "I hereby confess to the intention and committing of resources to willfully and foolishly burning down the Hair of the Dog."

Brody walked around the corner of the desk and loomed over her. "Do you know what happens to people convicted of arson?"

But she held her head high, straightened her spine, and held his gaze. "I don't care. They can put me in jail, fine me, whatever the law requires. I assume they don't burn arsonists at the stake."

His grim face lightened a bit. "Some would like to, it's true. In your case, I'm not sure what the punishment would be. No one was hurt, except Ryan. He could probably sue you for damages."

She gulped. If he did, she'd deserve it.

"And then there's the false confession issue. The law doesn't like that sort of thing."

"False confession? But I just told you the story. I started the whole thing."

"And you stopped it. Several times. Using your own money. Someone didn't get the message. Who actually started the fire, Katie?"

Staring back at him, she saw why Ryan looked up

to him so much, why he had such a legendary reputation. The man was a commander, through and through. She'd seen the same steel in Ryan, though masked by his playfulness. "Captain Brody," she said, clearing her throat. "I can't say any more than I've already said. I suspect someone, but I have no proof. And I can't accuse someone without proof. Anyway, it doesn't matter. I'm the one who's to blame."

She saw a glint of respect in his charcoal gaze. "Are you so sure it wasn't someone with a deep-seated grudge against the Hair of the Dog? Someone with nothing to do with you?"

She'd never thought of that. "I'm not sure of anything, to be honest. Except that it wasn't Ryan, and that I did, at a certain point, have the intention to commit arson. Which is more than Ryan ever had."

She withstood more scorching scrutiny from Captain Brody, until he made a brisk turn back to his desk. "I'm glad you came in today, Katie. It was very illuminating."

"But . . . what will you do now?"

"Get back to work."

"You're going to write up my confession? Take it to the arson squad or whatever? I don't want to confess to the insurance guy." She shuddered.

"I'm sure one confession will do," he said as he sat down. "Maybe you should go tend to Ryan."

Right. She'd stood up to Captain Brody, but the reminder of being turned away at the hospital punched the courage right out of her. "He won't see me."

She turned to go, shoulders drooping. Brody murmured something. She turned back. Brody, seated behind his desk again, no longer looked like the fearsome leader of men she'd stared down. Now he looked like a kind older cousin. The type you might have a crush on, if you weren't already hopelessly in love with someone else.

"Give him a chance," Brody repeated, louder this time. "He's going through a lot right now. He probably feels like a failure."

"A *failure*?" How could a hero feel like a failure?

"Firefighters are supposed to fight fires, not get caught in them without a cell phone and no way to escape."

"You're saying he should have put it out?"

"I'm saying he probably feels like he should have. The bar had fire extinguishers, right?"

"Yes, thanks to Ryan. I never bothered to check them until he came."

"And yet none of them had been discharged."

"So?"

"And why didn't he call 911? He's probably lying in that hospital bed second-guessing every move he made."

Katie's vision blurred. She no longer saw a kind older cousin when she looked at Brody. She saw a traitor. How could he say such things about Ryan?

She strode to the desk. "If he didn't use the fire extinguishers, he had a good reason. If he didn't call 911, there's a good reason. Maybe he didn't have time. Maybe he was more concerned with rescuing your daughter than putting out the fire. I don't know. You're the expert, not me. All I know is"—she poked him in the shoulder for emphasis—"if you doubt Ryan Blake, you're not the captain he thinks you are. And you don't deserve to have him back."

She'd never forget the look of shock on his stern face. Or the snort that followed her out the door.

Chapter Twenty-Eight

Ryan had heard it said that your life flashes before your eyes in the moment before you die. He wondered if he was experiencing a very long, extended death scene interrupted by doctors and nurses at regular intervals. In between medical visits, he kept reliving every fire he'd fought, every rescue he'd performed.

Dr. Kinder interrupted the Fillmore wildfire, in which he and Double D had worked forty-nine hours straight without sleeping. Ryan knew Dr. Kinder from past hospital stays. He'd endured several lectures about his daredevil ways. The nurses didn't like Dr. K much. He had a bad habit of talking down to them, when he wasn't making awkward advances. Logan Marquez had dated him a few times. The night Ryan and Logan hadn't had sex, she'd fielded a few stalker-ish calls from the doc. Ryan had a feeling she'd used him as a convenient excuse to dump the man, which might explain the nasty expression on his face as he sat down next to Ryan's bed.

"Well, Mr. Blake, it appears you've sustained some damage to your lungs, which is hardly surprising since you've never listened to any of my advice." With a smugly triumphant expression, the doctor held up an X-ray that showed an array of white blobs. "Patchy infiltrates. High carboxihemoglobin."

Ryan knew the lingo well enough. "Smoke inhalation?"

"No doubt. We see this often with fire victims."

Fire victim. Was he, Ryan Blake, a fire victim? That didn't sit right. He was a fire conqueror, not a victim. "Well, how bad is it?"

"Hard to say. Bad enough so you should stay away from fires for a good long time."

"So I'll cut down on the camping trips. Sauté instead of grill."

The doctor rattled the stiff paper of the X-ray for emphasis. "I would advise you to take some time off from your firefighting career."

Ryan stared at Dr. Kinder, who was small and round as a potato bug. "I am taking time off."

"More time. A lot more." The man looked almost gleeful. "Things might be different without that uniform."

"Well, that's perfect," Ryan drawled.

The potato bug cocked his little head. "Oh?"

"Yep. It'll give me more time to concentrate on my boxing career." With more energy than he'd had since the fire, Ryan sat up and hauled back his fist. The doctor scuttled his chair backward.

Ryan sank back against the pillow. Not that he

would have actually hit the man, but he'd made his point.

"That's not civilized behavior." The doctor pointed the X-ray at him, the paper shaking in his pudgy hand. "You're an animal."

"And you're a bug."

"What?"

"Why don't you treat the nurses like professionals?"

The man jumped to his feet. "You've . . . you've bewitched them."

Ryan snorted at the absurdity of this conversation, in which they'd swung from the potential end of his firefighting career to accusations of witchcraft. The act of laughing drained him. Fatigue tugged at his eyelids.

"Want my secret?"

"What?" Frowning, the doctor fiddled with the pen in the pocket of his white coat, as if he might take notes.

"It's a magic spell known as not being an ass."

"You—"

Ryan longed to close his eyes, but he had to make sure the potato bug didn't attack him first. For a doctor, he didn't seem to have much concern for human life. Then again, Ryan wasn't sure he had much concern for his own life at the moment.

"Leave my son the fuck alone." A caustic voice interrupted whatever violence was about to occur.

Ryan dragged his eyes open to see, of all people, his father standing in the doorway. He leaned on his cane, his white hair practically flying off his head from fury.

"Lucky for you, I had to hand over my firearms to get into this place. But that don't mean I can't kill with my bare hands if anyone messes with me. Or him," he added, almost as an afterthought.

The doctor looked like he might jump out the window. Instead he ignored Zeke and addressed Ryan. "If you have any sense, you'll listen to what I'm saying. Do you want to have children? Do you want to see them grow up?" He rattled the X-ray again. "Patchy infiltrates don't lie."

He brushed past Zeke, who snarled at him but stepped aside to let him pass.

Then Zeke stumped to Ryan's bedside.

"What are you doing here?" Ryan asked him. "It's not your type of place. They have doctors and pharmaceuticals and insurance forms here. It's like the heart of darkness of the health care system."

"Don't I know it. I can smell the evil." One of Zeke's nostrils curled.

"I think that's antiseptic." Ryan couldn't help it. His eyes closed, and he might have fallen asleep for a microsecond. When he snapped himself awake, his father was settling into the armchair in the corner.

"You sleep."

"You're . . . thtaying?" His tongue seemed to already be asleep.

"Yepper. If you don't mind. Someone's got to stand guard in case that quack comes back."

As sleep dragged him under, Ryan wondered if he minded or not. When had his father ever watched over him?

He didn't mind that much, he realized, right before unconsciousness claimed him. In fact, he slept deeply for the first time in days.

Zeke explained his presence when Ryan woke up. "Katie drove out to see me. Gave me a real lecture. Told me that you might be getting down on yourself, thinking you're a failure, and if that was so, it would be my doing since I'd never given you the proper emotional support as a child. She's got a tongue on her, that girl."

"I've noticed." But amazingly, his father didn't seem put out.

"First I nearly tossed her ass out of the trailer."

Ryan struggled into a sitting position, ready to let his father have it. But Zeke held up his hand.

"Don't worry, I didn't do her any harm. I like that girl. Straight talker. Cute as a button too."

"Hope you didn't tell her that," muttered Ryan, wondering if maybe he was having a bizarre dream that just *felt* like waking up.

"She gave me something to bring you, too. Said you didn't want to see her, but you might like this." He reached into a brown paper bag under his arm and drew out a copy of *The Little Prince*. He laid it on the bed next to Ryan. "I remember how much you liked that book when you were a kid."

The delicate, familiar drawing of the little prince on his surreal planet sparked such a flood of emotion that Ryan couldn't speak. At all.

"So." Zeke cleared his throat. "I'm here to give you some of that support she kept blabbing about. What do you need, boy?" He folded both hands on the head of his cane and looked at Ryan expectantly.

Ryan dragged his eyes away from the book. What the hell was Katie talking about? He didn't need anything from his father. He never had. Except an exit door. Silence stretched between them. His father didn't seem to mind. Zeke kept looking back at him, blue eyes peering from under crazy overgrown eyebrows.

It occurred to Ryan that he had his father's eyes. Odd that he'd never thought about that before.

Zeke cleared his throat. "I knew this was stupid from the git-go. Waste of your time and mine. I told Katie—"

"Why'd my mother leave?" The words popped out before Ryan realized it. He hadn't thought about his missing mother in years. Had he? Except . . . the question had come out. Just like that.

Zeke shook his head wryly. "Oh hell. You tryin' to put me in a hospital bed too?"

"Forget it," Ryan muttered, already regretting the question. Zeke had it right. This was stupid. What had Katie been thinking?

"Well, pick a reason. Top of the list, I drove her crazy."

Good God, his father was actually answering a question, in a reasonable if rusty tone of voice. Once again, Ryan wondered if his coma was playing tricks on him.

"She was too young to be a mother. Only eighteen, you know. Very pretty. You get your looks from her. Some guy showed up claiming he could make her a model, and *whoosh,* she was gone. She came back to see you a few times."

"She did?" Ryan had no memory of such a thing.

"Every time she'd have a breakdown and leave a nervous wreck. Sensitive girl. I guess she decided she couldn't handle it anymore. She stopped coming."

Ryan turned this over in his mind. "Did she become a model?"

"She did. Even had a bit part in some movies. Her pretty face pops up now and then. You could probably track her down if you go to Hollywood."

"Wouldn't want to cause a breakdown," Ryan answered bitterly.

Zeke shrugged. Sugarcoating was not his style. "Anything else?"

"I guess it must have been hard for you, getting stuck with a baby."

"Well." Zeke gazed off into the far corner of the room. "You sure got in the way of my overthrowing of the United States government. Fact is, I might be in prison today if I hadn't had a kid to take care of."

Ryan gestured for his water cup. Zeke used his cane to push the swinging tray table closer. "Guess you owe me. Not to mention the entire U.S. government."

Zeke chuckled. "Joke's on me. I spit out a hard-headed kid and then got surprised when he wouldn't do what I said."

"Was I that bad?"

"Never knew how to handle you. Wild kid. Smarter than anyone knows. Yelling didn't work. Whipping didn't work. Finally I let you go and hoped you'd find your way."

Well, he'd found it, all right. He'd met Captain Brody and become a firefighter. Fire Station 1 had become his new family. His home. His everything. And now he'd lost it all. Ryan turned his head away from his father, toward the beige wall, blank as his future.

Zeke used his cane to prod Ryan in the side.

"Jesus, Zeke. My ribs."

"I never worried about you after you left."

"That would explain why I never heard from you."

"I never worried," repeated Zeke, "because people always loved you. Before you were good-looking.

Before you were a fireman. Before you were a hotshot. Before all of that—and I bet I'm the only one who can tell you this—you were the sweetest child anyone ever saw. Always hugging on me. A little love bug, that's what you were. I don't know where you got it, 'cause I'm a mean old son of a bitch. But that's how you were. Until you started hating me. Didn't surprise me when you became a firefighter. Saving lives. Perfect fit."

"That's not . . ." Ryan's throat worked. Why was his father saying these things? Nice things. He wasn't going to cry. No fucking way. "That's not why I became a fireman. I liked the rush. The adrenaline. Being the hero. Besides, I was good at it. Don't make me out like a saint or something, that's crap."

Zeke got up and stomped to the door. "Hell no, you're no saint. You do stupid shit. Take dumb risks. I've heard some stories. But you're still my little boy with the heart as big as California."

"Where are you going?"

"This place is giving me the heebies. 'Fraid if I stay much longer the chemicals they pump into the air will brainwash me."

"Well, thanks for coming, Zeke."

"If there's thanks to be said, it's to Katie. Talk about a love bug. Two of a kind, you are." And he was gone, the crooked rhythm of his footsteps and cane echoing down the hall.

Ryan lay flat on his back, staring at the acoustic ceiling tiles until the little black dots did a tarantella across his vision. It was a lot to process. *His mother . . . Hollywood . . . overthrowing government . . . love bug* . . . And then there were Dr. Kinder's words. *Do you want to have children? Do you want to watch them grow up?* In all the swirling thoughts, one stood out. *Before you were good-looking, before you were a fireman, before you were a hotshot.* He'd forgotten about "before." He'd forgotten there had ever existed a Ryan who didn't fight fires.

And yet, the last year and a half, he hadn't gone near a fire. Well, until they started reappearing in his life, thanks to Katie. And those fires didn't have anything to do with a "rush." All he'd wanted was to protect Katie.

He fingered the book she'd sent. When he flipped the cover, it fell open to chapter ten. The part with the king. He read the words under his breath.

> "*. . . It is much more difficult to judge oneself than to judge others.*"

He groaned and pulled a pillow over his head. Too much thinking.

Or maybe not enough thinking.

The hell if he could decide which.

Bridget wore her step class teaching outfit, black and sapphire spandex, for the occasion of her confrontation with Doug. It brought out her dominatrix side—never too far from the surface in any case. She only wished she had a whip.

"I gave you lots of chances, you worm." She added the mental *whoosh* of a whiplash. Doug cowered on the bar stool where she'd found him, at T.G.I. Friday's, of all places. Guys up and down the bar kept checking her out, as well they should. "I kept inviting you to our family gatherings. I let you hang out with my friends. I took your side when Katie dumped you."

"I-I never had any problem with you," Doug ventured, hopefully.

"Well, now you do. Katie's covering for you, like she always has. Do you want Katie to go to jail for something you did?"

Doug turned white. "Jail?" Bridget would have felt sorry for him if she hadn't known he was more worried about his own future behind bars.

"I knew Katie was acting funny. Even for her. Now she's planning to take the blame for burning down the bar."

It had taken quite a while to pry that information out of Katie. Bridget had vowed not to tell their parents yet, but she hadn't promised anything about not killing Doug.

"I'm sorry, Doug, but I cannot allow my sister to take the blame for your asshole-ness."

"But . . . you don't even like Katie." With a smirk, Doug leaned an elbow back on the bar, nearly knocking over his basket of potato skins.

"Wrong. I love Katie. It's annoying when she doesn't do what I say, that's all. She doesn't want to be my mini-me, and that's a crushing disappointment. But she doesn't deserve to go to jail." Bridget sighed deeply. Every second she spent with Doug made her more aware of the apology she owed Katie for not supporting the breakup. Maybe this would make them even.

"Here's the bottom line, Doug the Slug. If you don't come forward and confess, no hot girl in San Gabriel will ever look at you again."

Doug pushed his unruly black hair off his forehead. "Who do you think you are, the Queen of Hot Girls?"

Bridget quite liked the sound of that. She flicked Doug on the shoulder. "Close enough. Not only that, I'll kick your ass. You know it wouldn't take much, Doug the Slug."

"Stop calling me that."

"Oh, that's just the beginning. I'll go all mean girl on you. You know I can do it. It'll be fun." She rubbed her hands together. "Rumors to spread, YouTube videos to upload, high school secrets to reveal . . ."

Doug shrank back as if she were stabbing a knife into his gut, over and over again. If only. "You're so full of crap. I'm Douglas Atwell the Third. My dad'll sue YouTube if you do that. He'll own YouTube."

Bridget tucked a strand of hair behind her ear to hide her annoyance. Doug had been a lot easier to manipulate in junior high. "Oh Doug. Always hiding behind your daddy. That's why you get no respect, why—" Then it came to her. "Dougie, you're a genius."

"Huh?"

"You're the Hair of the Dog arsonist. You could be famous. An outlaw. A rebel." She lowered her voice to a purr. "If you had any brains at all, you'd milk this for all it's worth. It could make you a rock star. Breaking the rules. Living on the edge." Leaning close, she whispered the coup de grâce into his ear. "Of course, not too far on the edge since your dad can always get you off."

She wheeled around and catwalked out the bar. Ah, the sensation of thirty sets of male eyes staring at her ass. The only flaw in the moment was that she wished Katie could have been there. But her stubborn little sister never wanted her help with anything. And she was too damn loyal to someone who didn't deserve her. *Katie, I got your back. Like it or not.*

When Ryan's next visitors arrived, he felt like a new man. "Captain Brody! Dani, come give me a hug."

As the little girl ran into his arms, he thought of Zeke's description of him as a love bug. Could be worse. Could be a potato bug. He looked up at the tight little family beaming down at him. His heart swelled. Yeah, he loved these guys. If that made him a love bug, he'd live with it. Danielle burrowed her head against his ribs, which didn't hurt nearly as much as it had the last time she'd hugged him.

"How are you feeling?" Brody asked.

"Better every minute. At first it was hell being here, then it reminded me of the monastery—but with cute nurses. I worked a lot of stuff out in the past few hours."

Brody raised a black eyebrow. "I'd like to hear about that. Maybe when you get back to the station. You aced the test."

Ryan nodded. He wasn't surprised. He was a damn good fireman. Always had been, always would be. If he chose and if his body permitted. "I studied my ass off."

"I know."

"How do you know?"

Ryan guessed the answer, saying it at the same time as Brody.

"Katie told me."

"Katie told you."

So, Katie'd been out there fighting his battles

while he'd been lazing around being tended to by gorgeous nurses and psychotic doctors.

"What else did she tell you?"

"That I don't deserve to have you come back." A smile quivered at the corner of Brody's mouth.

"She's what they call a straight talker."

"Yes, she is." Brody looked no more put out by Katie's bluntness than Zeke had.

"Katie's my friend," announced Danielle from Ryan's armpit.

Ryan was trying not to give in to the tickles when he caught the serious look that crossed Brody's face. The captain scratched at his chin as if debating something.

"What's going on?" Ryan demanded. "Something's up. More bad news? Don't dance around it. If it's the investigation, let me have it."

"It's Katie."

Ryan's stomach tightened. Danielle wormed her way from his embrace and ran to her father. Ryan felt suddenly cold in her absence. "What about Katie?"

"She's called a press conference to announce that she's the arsonist behind the Hair of the Dog fires," said Brody. "I thought you'd want to know."

"That's crazy! She didn't do it. Well, she—" He bit back the rest of his sentence, which had to do with the other times Katie had tried to commit arson and failed.

"I know the whole story, Ryan."

"Katie told you."

Brody nodded. "She wanted me to know you didn't do it. I imagine she wants the rest of the world to know too."

Ryan threw aside his blanket and swung his legs

over the side of the bed, the left one bundled in a white cast. He sucked in a breath as his broken ribs adjusted to the new arrangement.

"What are you doing?" Brody moved to his side and put a hand on his shoulder.

"I need to get out of here."

"Right this second?"

He pushed himself to his feet, balancing on one leg. If not for Brody's steadying hand, he would have fallen.

"Yes. When's this damn press conference? Excuse me. You didn't hear that, Danielle."

But Danielle had discovered *The Little Prince* and was tracing the prince's spiky hair with her forefinger.

"An hour from now."

"Is Melissa there? Can you call her and get her to stop Katie?"

"No, Melissa's on something else. A hot tip from an anonymous source."

"Then help me up, for Pete's sake. Brody, can you get me some crutches? There's a blonde nurse out there who can get some. Tell her they're for me. And Captain . . ." Ryan barely noticed the amused look in Brody's eyes as he issued orders to his boss. "Stay close. I have an idea you're going to love. I worked it all out in my head while I've been lying here with my sippy cup."

Danielle giggled at "sippy cup," and skipped alongside as Ryan thumped out of the room, ready to take on any medical professional who might try to stop him, with airborne chemicals or otherwise.

Chapter Twenty-Nine

The Hair of the Dog, or more accurately, the charred wasteland where it had formerly stood, was being invaded. A jumble of grumpy newspeople hauled equipment from vans, staked out their spots, and set up cameras.

If you asked Katie, they might as well be setting up a guillotine. Ella Joy stood near her, patting powder over her perfect foundation. She barely needed a mirror.

"Wow, you're good," Katie told her admiringly.

"Thanks." Ella winked at her. "It's part of the job, that's all. I once applied false eyelashes during the E.T. ride at Universal Studios. The part where you fly through the forest? I missed the whole thing because my glue was still drying."

"Wow."

"I'm a professional. It's all part of the presentation. Do you think I wore the right outfit for this press conference?"

Katie surveyed her olive-green pantsuit with emerald-studded lapels. Emerald-ish, that was. "You look good to me."

"Good isn't the point. This is a serious story. I can't look too flashy." She lowered her voice. "The Hair of the Phoenix has finally run out of second chances. Never again will the Hair of the Dog rise up from the ashes to serve another cocktail."

From the way Ella Joy held her arm, as if clutching a phantom microphone, Katie knew she was trying out lines for her report.

"What tragic behind-the-scenes drama led to this sad day for San Gabriel, the day a beloved landmark went up in greasy smoke?"

"If it was that beloved," corrected Katie, "it might still be standing. And it wasn't greasy."

"Fine. I'll cut greasy." Ella made a note on her reporter's pad. "When is Ryan getting here?"

"He's not."

"What? I thought the Hair of the Dog arsonist was coming forward. If we don't have an arsonist, we don't have a story." She pulled out her cell phone and punched some numbers. Katie snatched the phone out of her hand.

"He is! I mean, it is! The arsonist is coming forward. But it's not Ryan."

"Not Ryan." Ella gave her a long, speculative look. Katie saw an unexpected intelligence at work behind those china-blue eyes. "I always thought it was absurd. I even interviewed that loser who claimed he saw Ryan. Doug something."

"It wasn't him either." Katie almost choked on the lie. *You are responsible,* she reminded herself. *It was your bonehead idea from the beginning.*

"Hm." Ella looked like she wanted to say more,

but her cameraman beckoned her over. "Hold that thought. We have to line up our shot. But I have to say, Doug looked like a weaselly little liar to me."

Katie worried at her bottom lip as she handed Ella her phone back. She couldn't argue, really. It hurt to think that the boy she'd loved had grown into a weaselly liar, but he had. And it had taken her a long time to see it.

"You about ready?" The cameraman gestured to Katie. "You're representing the Hair of the Dog, right?"

"Yes. I'm ready." She took a deep breath and walked toward the cluster of microphones that had been set up.

"Hang on a minute." Ella Joy stopped the proceedings with an imperious gesture. The newspeople erupted in grumbles. Katie saw a reporter from another station throw up a hand in disgust.

"We've got deadlines, Ella. This isn't all about you."

"Oh, put your vibrator on low, would you? This won't take a second." Ella spun Katie around and marched her a few feet away from the crowd. Then she plunged her hands into Katie's hair.

"What the hell are you doing?"

"Shhh. You can't go on TV looking like that. It offends every bone in my perfect body."

Katie snapped her mouth shut. Quite frankly, she hadn't even looked in the mirror this morning. She'd been preoccupied with the false confession she was about to deliver on live television. With the whirlwind precision of Edward Scissorhands, Ella jabbed and teased at her hair. A whiff of hairspray followed. It must have magically appeared from a secret pocket somewhere on her body, because Ella wasn't even carrying a purse.

"Open your mouth," the anchor commanded.

Katie opened her mouth to tell her where she could put her orders, but before she could say anything, lipstick was being smoothed across her lips.

"I never wear lipstick," she hissed.

"This is your big moment, missy."

"My *what*?" How did falsely confessing to arson qualify as a "big moment"?

"People are going to be looking at you, lots of people. And then this might turn up on YouTube. You have no idea how many times this one little news clip will get played, over and over again. I don't care what you say, you're wearing lipstick."

Katie wondered how Bridget and Ella Joy would fare in a cage match. Bridget had been trying to get her to wear lipstick for years. But Ella was making some valid points, she supposed. She might as well look her best while destroying her reputation. And no one else had bothered to think of it.

"As far as outfits go, we'll have to go with a head and shoulders shot. Where did you get this blouse, a thrift shop?"

"Yes." Katie got all her clothes at thrift shops, and the black blouse she was wearing happened to be designed by Calvin Klein.

"Well, it's not bad. Tailored. And I suppose black is appropriate for the sad farewell to a local legend."

"Thank you," Katie muttered. "So glad you approve."

"Just part of the service at the Sunny Side of the News." One final tweak, then Ella spun her back around and propelled her to the microphones.

Had Marie Antoinette worn lipstick to the guillotine?

Katie marched grimly to the knot of microphones. About ten people waited for her. Three were on-air talent she vaguely recognized. Three others were sheltered behind their cameras. The rest must be random onlookers and passersby. She leaned into the mics.

"Isn't there anything else going on in San Gabriel today?" She jumped at the whine of feedback.

"It's July," said the public access station's reporter, who looked about twenty. "Ancient Chinese proverb. Nothing ever happens in the news in July."

A murmur of assent rippled through the crowd.

"Well, thank you all for coming out to hear about the fires that have plagued the Hair of the Dog." Good God, she sounded like Ella Joy. She shook her head in disgust. "That is to say, I'm here today to set the record straight about the tragic demise of the Hair of the Dog." She made a face. "Blech. Can I start over?"

"Until the little red lights go on, you can say whatever you want," said a cameraman.

Ella Joy waved her notebook. "How about this? I'll ask you questions. All you have to do is answer them."

A storm of protests rose from the other reporters, but Katie nodded. "That sounds good. I'll answer your questions." Who cared about the other reporters? Only Ella Joy had fixed her hair and offered her lipstick. She touched her tongue to her lips, tasting the unfamiliar flavor of expensive makeup. It added to the surreal quality of the whole scene.

This was it. The end of . . . something. The beginning of something else. Her big moment.

She tugged the hem of her blouse down so she didn't flash any skin on TV. Her heart raced at twice its normal speed. Sweat dripped down her sides.

Maybe black wasn't the best color for standing outside on a scorching summer day in front of a ravenous horde of reporters.

All of a sudden a cameraman put his hand to his ear then lifted one finger. "We're live in ten . . . nine . . ."

The atmosphere switched from loose to utterly alert. The reporters stood at attention, the camera operators bent to their viewfinders, and Katie felt suddenly very, very alone in her spot in front of the microphones.

And then the little red lights went on. Three of them, leering at her like tiny demons.

"Three . . . two . . ." A pause, then he swept his arm down in a gesture that looked disturbingly like the fall of a guillotine. Katie stood, paralyzed. Ella Joy smoothly stepped into the breach. Her cameraman swung his camera toward her.

"This is Ella Joy here outside what used to be one of San Gabriel's most-loved watering holes. The Hair of the Dog survived a series of fires over the past couple weeks, only to finally succumb to an arsonist's torch this past Thursday. With speculation flying over the identity of the firebug, the manager of the Hair of the Dog, Ms. Katie Dane, has decided to come forward with new information that she hopes will put the rumors to rest. Katie, do you know who set the fire that burned down your family's business?"

The camera swung toward Katie. At least that question was easy. "Yes. I do know."

"What can you tell the viewers of San Gabriel about this heartbreaking fire?"

Katie took a deep breath and straightened her spine. "First of all, I'd like to say that Ryan Blake had nothing to do with it. He's been a loyal employee and I'm so, so sorry about everything that's happened since he started working for us. He is a hero who saved a little girl's life, and anyone who says otherwise should be ashamed of themselves."

There. That felt good. Very good. Ryan might still never forgive her, but at least she'd given it her all.

"If Mr. Blake didn't do it, who did?"

Katie took one frantic look around the crowd. What if Doug finally came through? What if he strode to the microphones, leaned down, and fessed up? She closed her eyes, waited a breath—giving him one last chance—then opened her mouth.

"I have something to say," someone interrupted from behind her.

Her eyes sprang open. He'd done it! Doug had finally come to his senses! Except the new arrival sounded like Ryan, and when she turned toward him, she saw he looked like Ryan too. All the way down to the white cast on his leg.

Her jaw dropped. "What are you doing here?"

He ignored her and aimed his summery, charming, teasing, devastating smile at the newspeople. "I'm Ryan Blake, and I have an important announcement to make to the city of San Gabriel, something that's going to make all of you pretty happy, I think."

A volley of questions bombarded him.

"Ryan, did you set the fire?"

"Are you here to confess?"

"How's your leg doing?"

"Is your career as a fireman in jeopardy over the recent accusations?"

"How does it feel to be suspected of arson?"

Katie grabbed his hand. She wanted to throw rotten tomatoes at those newspeople. Couldn't they see Ryan was hurting? Balanced on crutches that seemed to be too short for him, he had to hunch over to speak into the mics. His breathing sounded harsh and she caught a whiff of sweat mixed with hospital disinfectant.

But even so, God, he looked good. A little paler than usual, his cheekbones more prominent, his hair a little shaggier, some stubble showing on his jawbone. It all made him look even more masculine and . . . seductive. She wanted to sigh and rub her cheek against his arm.

But he was probably still angry at her. He'd probably shown up to yell at her on live TV. He was probably only holding her hand to keep from falling over. She squeezed her eyes half shut and braced herself as Ryan spoke into the microphones. He didn't bother to answer any of the questions the reporters had flung at him. He spoke in an easy, conversational tone that held everyone spellbound.

"As you might know by now, I'm one of the firemen of San Gabriel. I nearly got fired for bein' kinda reckless, which didn't do much for my pride. Worst of all, I let down my captain, Captain Brody over there. He trained me, and he trained a bunch of us crazy young kids. San Gabriel is known around California as the place to go if you want to learn things the right way. We have to turn away applicants right and left. Seems like a loss, to us and to anyone who doesn't want their house to burn down."

A murmur of laughter sounded among the reporters, as well as the growing throng gathered on the sidewalk.

"So I proposed something to the captain, and he thinks it's a good idea, if we can get the funding. For that, we need to put up a bond in the next election."

Breathless silence punctuated his announcement. Ryan took a ragged breath before continuing. Katie gripped his hand tightly and felt his answering squeeze.

"We're planning to purchase this land from the Dane family. We're going to build a training center for new recruits. We believe this will become the finest firefighter academy in the country. It's close to Station 1, which makes the location ideal. Captain Brody will oversee the school and work with as many trainees as possible. And he'll train other people to help him out."

"What about you, Ryan?"

He held up his hand. "I'm not done yet. The centerpiece of the academy will be a mentoring program for troubled kids. Young people having a hard time at school or at home, we'll pair them up with a fireman or a trainee. It doesn't matter how good you are, if you don't share what you know. I'll be in charge of that program."

Katie drew in a breath of sheer delight. "Ryan, that's great."

"Does that mean you won't be fighting fires anymore?"

Captain Brody, holding Danielle by the hand, strolled to Ryan's side. Katie felt pathetically grateful to him. He must have seen how tired Ryan was getting. Ryan shifted closer to Katie so she felt the warmth of his body. She put an arm around his waist to help him step away from the mics. His crooked smile shone down on her like sunshine.

"I see some benefits to this whole cripple deal," whispered Ryan.

"You're not a cripple," she hissed fiercely. "Don't even think that."

He gave a blue-eyed wink. "I will only if it gets attention from a certain hardheaded bar manager."

"*Former* bar manager. There's not much left to manage." A smile quivered on her lips. It felt so good to be next to him again, to be looking into his summer-sky eyes and sparring with those quick comebacks of his.

"Ryan Blake has returned from his leave of absence," Captain Brody was saying to the reporters. "I'm delighted he's chosen to come back, even though we'll miss him in the field. His main responsibility will lie with the new school."

"What will it be called?"

"Don't know yet."

The public access kid raised his hand. "Do you anticipate any trouble with the bond?"

"No."

"Will the Dane family sell the land or try to rebuild?"

Everyone looked at Katie. "I . . . I suppose that'll be up to my father."

"What will you recommend to him?" Ella Joy asked. "Surely as the manager, he'll listen to you."

Katie didn't hesitate. "I'd recommend he sell the land to the fire department. And yes, I do believe he'll listen to me."

"But what about the arsonist?" The question didn't come from any of the reporters. It came from someone at the edge of the crowd, which had now spilled onto the street. Which just went to show how easily distracted the media was compared to regular people, thought Katie.

Katie stepped in front of Ryan to reach the microphones. "About the arsonist . . ."

"Yes, about the arsonist." A hand waved wildly

from the middle of the crowd. Melissa elbowed her way through the crowd until she reached the little ring of news professionals. "Do you have any comment on a reported confession from a Douglas Alan Atwell the Third?"

"What?" Katie gasped. "No. I . . . uh . . . hadn't heard about that."

"My informant says he left town earlier today in a Saab stolen from his father. But before he left he wrote a full confession in the form of a song and uploaded it to YouTube under the name Atwell the Outlaw. Any comment?"

"Well, he's a pretty decent songwriter." Katie couldn't come up with anything else to say.

"Apparently it's already been downloaded several hundred times," continued Melissa, who seemed to be working very hard not to laugh. "The chorus goes like this. *My my, sparks they fly, flames they burn and so do I.* Apparently the song's going viral."

Doug, an Internet video star. Worked for her, as long as a YouTube confession satisfied the investigators. "I have no comment on Doug Atwell. All I can say is the Hair of the Dog was a wonderful place and will be missed."

Ella Joy shouldered Melissa aside, which reminded Katie that they'd worked together in the past. "One more question, Katie and Ryan. I see you two are holding hands. Do you have any comment on that?"

Heat flooded Katie's face. She dropped his hand as if it were a burning coal.

Ryan leaned into the mic. "Just one." He handed one crutch to Brody, then turned to Katie and swept her into his free arm.

"Ryan, your ribs!"

"Shut up and kiss me, Katie," he whispered. "Unless you stopped loving me." Crystal clear, as if seeing right into his heart, she saw his nagging doubt, the fear that a kid like him, with a father like his, would never be good enough for . . .

She wrapped her arms around him as gently as possible while still making her point. "I couldn't stop if I tried." She stood on tiptoe and tilted her face to his. Their lips met tenderly, deeply, their kiss a private communion, a public promise, and the most satisfying moment of her life.

Chapter Thirty

The reporters' shouted questions pulled them from their kiss. "Does this mean another bachelor fireman is off the market?"

"Has the curse been broken for good?"

Katie peered from the shelter of Ryan's arms. "Have we been live this whole time? The little red lights are off."

Ella Joy sauntered up to them, pouting. "No, they cut away for the mayor's budget hearing. Talk about a snoozer. They missed all the good stuff, as usual."

"So why are they all still here? Just being nosy?" Ryan cast a glare around the ring of reporters. Katie noticed white lines around his mouth and a droopiness around his eyelids.

"You should get back to the hospital."

"Hell no. But I wouldn't mind some private nursing back at my place." He winked. She let herself relax a little. He couldn't be too bad off if he could still joke around. But still, she intended to keep an eye on him. Not that she could keep her eyes off him anyway.

Captain Brody tapped on the microphones for attention. "I believe that concludes the absurd news media nonevent of the day. Thanks for coming out. You'll be hearing more about the bond very soon."

"Hey," protested Melissa, as she joined him and Danielle at Ryan and Katie's side. "We nailed the Hair of the Dog arsonist, got you well on your way to getting your bond passed, and broke the Bachelor Curse *again*. I believe you owe the news media an apology."

"You're so right. I always forget how much I owe the news media." He handed Ryan's crutch back to him. "Excuse me for a second, Danielle. I have something to say to the news media." He swept his wife into his arms and kissed her full on the lips.

Katie felt Ryan's weight press more heavily against her. It could have been due to exhaustion, or affection inspired by Brody and Melissa.

Ella Joy stuck her perfect nose in the air. "It's a good thing someone hasn't forgotten about work around here. That someone being me. And if someone—I mean someone else—doesn't give me an exclusive on this whole story, I'm doing another Bachelor Fireman of San Gabriel piece."

Captain Brody broke free. "No."

"Don't you dare," said Ryan, simultaneously. "Besides, I'm exempt from the curse. I was on a leave of absence."

Ryan and Brody looked at each other, revelation dawning on their faces, one so stern and handsome, the other so golden and playful. Melissa caught Katie's eye and winked. *We got ourselves some gorgeous men.*

"I didn't meet Katie until I left," Ryan said slowly.

"Ten thousand broken hearts, then you temporarily leave the force and meet The One."

"I never really thought much about the curse, but now—"

"Wait. Ten *thousand*?" Katie interrupted with an appalled squeak.

"Captain Brody, permission to tell you to shut up. The curse won't be broken until we get married and I can't have you scaring my girl."

"Married?" Katie was having trouble catching her breath.

"Let's get out of here before Ella Joy gets any more dirt for her story."

Ella looked up from her BlackBerry. "What? Did someone say Ella Joy?"

"I was just saying how much I like that suit on you." Ryan blinded her with a smile, then nudged Katie away from the Hair of the Dog toward her waiting Datsun.

He stretched out on the backseat, his cast taking up most of the room. She drove carefully, watching out for every little bump and pothole. She angled her rearview mirror to keep an eye on him. Every time she looked at his reflection, her heart ached with love and worry. Whether from pain or exhaustion or something else, he looked older. Lines etched his face where she didn't remember any. They didn't detract from his good looks one bit, at least to her they didn't. They probably wouldn't for any other woman with a heartbeat either.

The thought cast a shadow over her joy at being

in Ryan's presence again. She loved him, through and through, but wouldn't he always have women trailing after him? Could she handle that? She knew ten thousand broken hearts was an exaggeration. It had to be. But who wouldn't fall in love with Ryan, once they really knew him?

"What's the matter?" His head rested against the window, his eyes closed. She'd thought he was sleeping.

"What do you mean?"

"You got sad all of a sudden. I felt it."

"I was just thinking . . . nothing."

"Come on. Where's that famous Katie Dane bluntness?"

Apparently it had gone for a long walk around the block. Anyway, bluntness was one thing, exposing all her worst fears and insecurities was another. "I don't want to upset you. You're exhausted."

"Seeing you sad upsets me. Is it because of the bar? I thought I fixed it so your family would come out okay. We can't pay a million dollars, but we'll pay fair market value. A lot in the middle of town like that must be worth quite a bit."

"Yes. A hundred thousand dollars. I saw an appraisal."

"Will your family be happy with that?"

"I think they will." So Bridget wouldn't get her own studio and Dad might have to cut back on his gnome acquisitions. And maybe they wouldn't move to Baja. She didn't want them to move, anyway. She wanted them to stick around, as long as she didn't have to run any more bars.

"That's good." He cranked open the window and turned his face to the breeze. "I missed this smoggy air in the hospital."

"You could have anyone," Katie blurted out, then instantly turned red. "Lots of anyones."

Ryan's eyes flew open and met hers in the mirror. "What are you talking about?"

"Girls are always chasing after you. They always will."

"No, they won't."

She didn't answer. If he couldn't see that he would always be a magnet for women, that the female gender would always be drawn to his smile, his fun-loving spirit, his unfairly, ridiculously extravagant good looks, then what was the point?

She pulled into his driveway and opened the back door to help him out of the car.

He was still glowering at her from his supine position on the backseat. "We're not done with this discussion."

"Maybe we should continue it over some pain-killers."

"No painkillers. Just help me get inside."

She held his crutches while he maneuvered him-self out of the car, head first, then grabbed the roof to swing his legs out. Her heart ached for him. The skin around his eyes looked bruised from fatigue.

"I should have taken you back to the hospital," she scolded as they headed up the tidy walkway to his door.

"I don't want to be there. I want to be with you." He faced his front door blankly. "Hell if I know where my keys are. Spare's somewhere in the shrubs."

She found the key, opened the door, and watched him swing himself inside. She hovered outside, wondering if she should let him rest. Maybe run to a pharmacy and pick up some supplies. He turned and looked at her impatiently.

"Well? If you're expecting me to carry you over the threshold, you're going to have to wait until after the wedding. Or at least until I get rid of these crutches."

Her face burned as hot as the fire that had ended the Dog. "The *what*?"

But he'd already turned away and headed for his bedroom. He couldn't keep dropping these hints about marriage, like little bombshells, and get away with it. She found him flat on his back in bed.

"Don't you dare go to sleep yet."

"I thought you said I needed my rest." One eye opened in a slit of lazy blue.

"I think I hate you right now."

"That's not a nice thing to say to your future bridegroom."

"There!" She pointed at him triumphantly. "You did it again."

"Come here."

She took a step toward him. He crooked his finger. Really, she ought to protest at the nerve of him, expecting her to come when he beckoned, but he looked so pale and tired that she didn't have the heart. She stepped closer, then closer still until she stood at his side. Then, so quickly she barely knew it was happening, he flipped her onto the bed next to him.

Now she was the one flat on her back. He leaned over her, braced on one elbow, surrounding her with the blue heat of his gaze.

"I only want one woman. I don't go chasing after girls, never have. I liked to flirt as much as the next guy. But ever since you came along, everything's been turned upside down. I felt things I'd never felt before. I didn't know what it was at first, all I knew was I wanted to be with you and keep you out of trouble and make you believe in me."

"I believe in you—"

"Shhh. Don't interrupt. I love you, Katie. And that's for good. If other girls pay attention to me, I can't do anything about that, except maybe wave a big wedding ring in their faces and go on and on about the wonderful girl I'm married to, the one I love with all my heart, the one I plan on spending all the rest of my life with."

Katie's heart seemed to have turned into a manic bunny rabbit, hippity-hopping around her rib cage. And something strange was happening to her face. It was melting into a smile she had no control over. That goofy grin spread and spread, until it felt like her face would crack open. "I love you so much."

"Good." He nodded as if to say, *That's settled.* He rolled off her, onto his back, with a long groan of satisfaction. "And what about you? Are you going to be happy with a dyslexic guy who doesn't read thousand-page novels in French for fun?"

"As long as that guy is you." She curved a hand under his jawbone. He snuggled his cheek against her palm. The pleasure of it made her blood sing.

"Am I going to have to fight a bunch of textbooks to get my Katie time?"

"Yes. Big ones. How does sociology sound?"

"Sounds like it has nothing to do with literature, and something to do with people." He adjusted the pillow under his head.

"I think people are growing on me. Especially the older ones. I want to switch fields and study ways to help the aging population. The Drinking Crew gave me a check, did you know? I love those guys. They were the best thing about the Hair of the Dog besides you."

Ryan pulled the covers up to his chin with a long, ragged sigh. "The Drinking Crew rocks. It all sounds great. I gotta sleep now." He sounded drunk with oncoming slumber.

"About time." She traced his forehead with loving fingers. "I hope you do what I say more when we're . . . married." The word "married" danced along her skin like a fairy wand spreading shimmers in its wake. She was going to be married. To Ryan. Her heart nearly cracked with joy.

"One more question." Ryan sounded already half asleep.

She snuggled her face into the warm curve where his shoulder met his neck. "What?"

"Are you wearing lipstick?"

From her intimate nest, she giggled. "Ella Joy gave it to me. For my big moment."

"Your big moment?"

"Yeah. Apparently one must look one's best when one is going on TV to confess to an act of arson one didn't commit. It's probably in Emily Post somewhere."

He laughed softly and ran his fingers through her hair. It felt divine. "That was not your big moment. This is. The beginning of us."

An exquisitely tender meeting of lips ended that discussion. As big moments went, Katie thought it hard to beat.

When Ryan woke up, Katie was still cuddled in a curlicue under his arm. He touched her silky hair with a sense of reverence. This girl, this fierce-hearted, loyal, smart, honest, wonderful girl, had agreed to become his wife. No moment in his life, not even the day he became a fireman of San Gabriel, could compare with this.

Funny, though, about the curse. He hadn't even considered it a curse back then. He'd seen it as a convenient excuse for not getting serious. And now—he couldn't wait to get serious, if it meant being with Katie and starting a family and all that stuff he'd always assumed wasn't for him, not the way he'd grown up, not with a father like Zeke.

But now, with Katie by his side, everything felt different. So what if he'd had to leave the force, leave San Gabriel, leave his buddies in order to come back and find her? It was all worth it. As for the rest of the guys—the other Bachelor Firemen of San Gabriel—well, they'd have to find their own way to break the curse.

He couldn't wait to laugh his head off the entire time.

Next month, don't miss these exciting new love stories only from Avon Books

Scandal Wears Satin by Loretta Chase
Struggling to keep her shop afloat in the wake of a recent family scandal, dressmaker Sophy Noirot has no time for men, especially the Earl of Longmore. But when Longmore's sister—and Sophy's best customer—runs away, everything changes as Sophy finds that desire has never slipped on so smoothly . . .

Willow Springs by Toni Blake
Amy Bright is the ultimate matchmaker . . . when it comes to everyone's love life but her own. Writing anonymous steamy love letters to handsome firefighter Logan, Amy strives to make the perfect match: for herself. Will Amy overcome her shyness and turn friendship into something more? Or will the return of a woman from Logan's past ruin everything?

How to Be a Proper Lady by Katharine Ashe
Viola Carlyle doesn't care about being proper. Suffocated by English society, Viola longs to be free. Captain Jin Seton is the object of Viola's desire. Though Jin vowed not to let Viola steal his heart, that won't stop this improper lady from trying . . .

Tarnished by Karina Cooper
Cherry St. Croix knows as much about genteel London society as she does its dark underground of vagrants and thieves. Hunting murderers by night, blending in by day, Cherry is caught between two worlds…and many men. Will she be exposed and cast out from polite London society, or will she take one risk too many and wind up dead?

Give in to your Impulses!

These unforgettable stories only take a second to buy and give you hours of reading pleasure!

Go to ***www.AvonImpulse.com*** and see what we have to offer.

Available wherever e-books are sold.

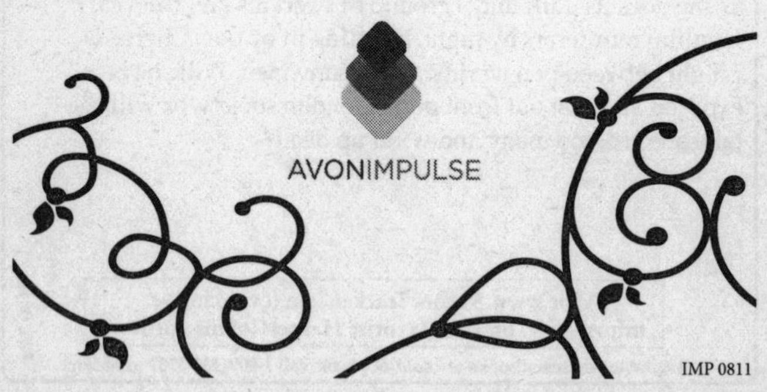

IMP 0811